AUTHO

The Horns has been written from my knowledge of being born into what was Southern Rhodesia, then Rhodesia - and of being someone whose best playmates for my first five years were three African children. The paths our lives eventually took could not have been more divergent.

I have been presumptuous enough to try to write from my acquired knowledge of the amaNdebele people. In the next book this moves on to the maShona as well. Inevitably, this has been difficult, and I am constantly aware of big gaps in my knowledge. All I can say is that I have had sound mentors, whose comments and contributions I have enjoyed, rejected, considered and absorbed! As a result, I hope I have managed to portray with some measure of authenticity, the lives and stories of each actual/fictional character and their part in our history

The Horns is presented as storytelling – oral storytelling, as practised in the passing on of oral history in African culture, sometimes indulging in the nostalgic prose of cherished memories, sometimes in the practical narration of the observations of young children making mud cattle, the terror of a teenager in acute distress, or the wise words of experience and learning from an older generation.

Particularly in the early stages, the use of language and speech patterns has been adapted to maintain the authenticity of those for whom English was a second or third language.

The Horns covers the period from August 1939 to May 1966. The terminology and place names used are those that were current then. Working within a precise date frame of this nature is complicated by the insistent intrusion of today's prevailing wisdoms. I have had to draw deeply on my own memories of the various and perceived intentions of that time in all their frailties and strengths.

These are stated, then debated, using growing changes in perspective from the four main characters to arrive somewhere near a potential truth - in the welter of extravagant deceptions and vested interest portrayals of what really might have happened.

Within its fictional base and to ensure a degree of historical accuracy I have drawn upon much valued, but only occasionally available oral history, as well as the writings of early missionaries, pioneers, hunters, traders, and concession seekers, with rare access to the records of the British South Africa Company and British and Southern Rhodesian government and parliamentary archives.

The story itself unwraps the history of the country through the questions of the four characters - from the *mfecane* and the growth of the Matebele nation under King Mzilikazi in the early 1800s, through colonial settlement in 1890 to the day-to-day lives of the country's mix of cultures in the mid-1900s.

By the inclusion of verifiable landmarks in our history, bound together by some fact and some fiction, the early lives of those four key players form the first book of the trilogy.

That precious land between the Zambezi and Limpopo Rivers has left a compelling and indelible mark on the lives of everyone who has ever lived in it. We have wept over it; we have shed blood for it; we have despaired at its failures and rejoiced in its successes. Too many have left and, in doing so, have grown apart. None forget and most long to return, at least for a reliving and refreshing of what was once so much a part of us.

Wherever we are, we continue to dream dreams alive with imaginings of a country where men and women co-exist peacefully, making endless plans together for the good of God's own country.

ACKNOWLEDGEMENTS

I would like to thank my dedicated early readers who persisted, helped and encouraged while this was shaped into a workable manuscript Celia Burnett Smith, Joy Elford, Richard Hammond, Kennedy Mavunganidze and Dr Dumiso Dabengwa; Marina Cano for her inspired 'HORNS' photograph; Paul Richards for crafting this into an arresting book cover and my editor Aaron who inspired and persuaded me never to worry about word counts or to hold back on description! Most of all, my husband Ray who has suffered in supportive silence as I became ever more wrapped up in this fascinating, but isolating process of authorship.

THE ZAMBEZI TRILOGY: BOOK ONE

THE HORNS

JILL BAKER

ISBN: 978 1 98295 440 6
Copyright © Jill Baker 2018
Edition 3

Cover photo: Marino Cano
Cover design: Paul Richards

MAPS

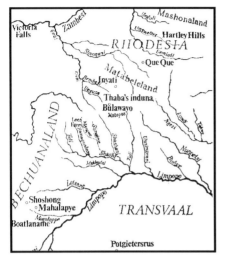

An early colonial map showing what became disputed territory as King Mzilikazi made his way north across the Transvaal during the 'mfecane, skirting around the Protectorate of Bechuanaland and on to Matebeleland.

With the discovery of gold, the land between the Tati, Shashi and Ramokwebane rivers was claimed by the amaNdebele, the baMangwato, the Boers and the British. To enable mining to commence the rights were given under a private concession, and allocated to Bechuanaland (Botswana).

In 1838, Mzilikazi with three regiments, made his way north to cross the Zambezi, but sent his uncle Godwane Ndiweni to Bulawayo with the rest of the tribe to form the Matebele nation.

Southern Rhodesia as it was during the period covered by this first book in the trilogy; the thumbnail of Africa in the corner shows the position of the country in the context of the continent.

The south-western boundary is largely defined by the Limpopo River and its tributaries, the northern boundary by the Zambezi River.

At Independence in 1980 the country was re-named Zimbabwe.

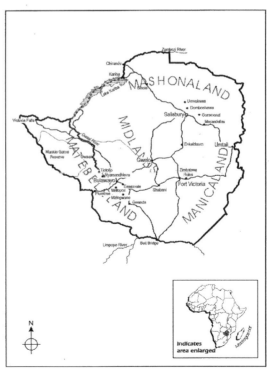

CONTENTS

PROLOGUE

It had been a relentless struggle; the lifeless scrap on her chest was the fruitless result of months of anguish. Months of a haunted and terrified existence since she fled from the father she loved.

"You are not my daughter." His face had contorted with outrage and disbelief. "Go from here, *mahure*[1]. Find another place to have your *mubhoni*[2]. We do not share your disgrace."

Now, as she remembered her father's words, exhausted tears welled up beneath her eyelids, creeping down her face and tracing the dark crevices of her nose and mouth. She wondered again, as she had so many times, about her determination not to give herself to anyone before she married. It was a decision that had made her a challenge and a target.

She remembered the increasingly suggestive demands for "a taste of her honey" – the touching, the pinching . . .

Then on one drenching storm of an afternoon, still in her school uniform from the mission – she remembered the ambush. She struggled, she screamed. They fought, they laughed. They tore her . . . then left her to her pain and bleeding. She would never forget their hateful, triumphant cries of "*Ndachitsika*"[3].

She had bled from their beating, bled from their brutal possession of her body. The pain had torn through her in sudden, sharp, gasping shards. She had bled for weeks afterwards.

It had left her, first with the guilt, the anxiety, then the realisation . . . and a raging anger, as movement within her increased to become a hated reminder of every second of what she had been through. It survived and it grew, until her swelling belly was noticed and her degradation was complete.

So she fled.

South – to a place she didn't know, a place where nobody knew her.

South – to spin stories and try to start again. But in the end, they had known there too.

She was alone and she was with child. She was wicked and a whore.

---

[1] *mahure*: whore
[2] *mubhoni*: illegitimate child; bastard
[3] *"Ndachitsika"*: "I have crushed her" (Shona)

The heat of Matebeleland just before the rainy season suffocated and dried her out. She begged for food, and like an animal she foraged in dust-dry riverbeds for water.

Then one night – and too soon – her anguish became all too physical. She pulled thorn tree branches across the crevice of a deep cave in the maze of granite rocks of the Matopos *kopjes*[4]. Thorns to protect her. Thorns to greet the bastard child. She bled. She muffled the cries of her agony. She sobbed silently in fear and shame.

But the child would not be born. She could hear the cough of leopard – and she knew he could smell blood and climb the trees around the cleft in the rock. So she left and scrabbled higher, fingers torn and bleeding from the sharpness of granite – all the time trailing the tell-tale blood. She found another cave, piled up more thorns, searched for wood, and lit fires to keep leopard away. But still the child would not be born.

She was too tired and too weak.

The need to survive drove her out to some nearby huts, and she found the strength to ask . . .

"There is a clinic . . ."

She stumbled into the night and stopped, doubled up, to howl out her pain as the strength inside tore her flesh again and again.

She reached shallow red polished steps and knew no more.

As the child broke free of her body, she was shocked into consciousness – to a hospital bed and the worried face of a nurse, a *murungu*[5].

"*Hlalane pasi ntombi*[6]. . . your baby has come." The nurse gently laid the child on her chest. "But I am sorry . . . he has not breathed."

The girl was glad. She sighed in acceptance . . . a sigh that did not stop – on and on, weaker and weaker, she slipped down into the blessed relief of nothing.

Sister McLeod, immaculate in her starched triangular headpiece, allowed herself a few precious seconds to wonder about this young black girl. Who was she? How far had she come in the baking October heat to lie gasping in pain on the blood-red cement steps of the school clinic - so

---

[4] *kopjes*: small hills topped with granite, balancing, rocks
[5] *murungu*: white person (Sindebele from here on unless identified otherwise)
[6] "*Hlalane pansi ntombi*: 'lie down young girl"

far from any large population centre? Where was her family – her husband? Or, as she was so young, perhaps more realistically, her boyfriend?

Sister McLeod looked at her matted hair. There had been no time for vanities for this girl. As she turned her over to wash her down, she saw there was no *icholo*[7]– the knob of hair that signified she was a married woman.

There was nothing more the Scottish nurse could have done to stem the angry haemorrhage betraying savage mutilations – some angry, previous scarring, some present rips and tears from a precipitate birth. She had felt the pulse weaken and fade. Watched the traumatised face smooth into stillness.

She prayed briefly. "Lord who knows the reason for all things, look after this young girl and give her peace."

She busied herself with the after-death procedures until something caught her attention. She turned to see, in growing astonishment, a feeble movement from the impossibly tiny and wrinkled grey infant.

"Quick Naison!" She turned to the Orderly next to her. "Bring me something to put this baby in – he's alive."

She clasped and snipped the umbilical cord and went through the motions of weighing and cleaning up the wrinkled folds of the very premature.

"I could only find this, Sister." Naison rushed back, proffering a worn but clean shoebox lined with a laundered tea towel from the kitchen.

They caught the baby's flailing arms, wrapped him tightly and put him in the shoebox.

"The puir wee thing – only one and a half pounds – he has little chance."

"You can take first milk from the breast," Naison said, "like this . . ."

The Sister didn't believe it would be possible – and yet the girl could have been in labour for some days, allowing colostrum to come down. Between them, they were able to extract a tablespoon from the still-warm young mother.

"He will probably die, but . . . good Naison, that will bring him some

---

[7] *icholo:* a distinctive sign of marriage in pre to early colonial days. No longer practised

comfort." She dripped the milk between the baby's lips.

Two days later, the child was still alive. A week later, he was stronger and beginning to lose his just-born greyness to turn a deep, healthy brown.

Nobody knew who the girl was. She was not from the area, and she had nothing on her that would tell them anything. The only clue to her identity was a cheap bracelet with "Rosie" inscribed on it.

They were not allowed to bury her until there was some identification so that all the correct amaNdebele ceremonials could take place. She was ritually washed with water containing crushed *umsuzwane*[8] herbs then placed in a bath of ice. More water was prepared with ritual herbs for mourners to wash themselves.

Nobody came.

Sister McLeod took photographs with her box Brownie and sent them off to Bulawayo on the school lorry to be developed. A week later, she drove for ten hours there and back to collect them. She drove carefully, nursing the unpredictable antiquity of the clinic's bull-nosed Morris back to the government office in Tjolotjo to see if they could throw any light on who the girl might have been. Having heard the story, Native Commissioner Angus Davidson promised to come up to the clinic the next day.

She was always glad to see his jovial presence in the clinic – his handlebar moustache and ready laugh made him a popular figure. His understanding of the history and culture of the amaNdebele people and his ability to speak their language fluently gained him great respect.

"What do you think Naison?" Angus asked.

"I think the child is *igola*[9]– living in a home where he does not belong, or without a father - without a chief."

"Yes, I think you're right. The girl's so young. I think her father has not yet been paid his *amalobola*[10]. I will circulate the photograph to all the other Native Commission offices in Matebeleland – and Mashonaland too."

He turned to Sister McLeod. "Can I see the child?"

---

[8] *umsuzwane:* special herbs used for burials: gives off a lemon-like fragrance
[9] *igola:* illegitimate, a bastard child
[10] *amalobola:* the price paid for a bride, usually in cattle

They walked to the storeroom, which had now become a makeshift nursery. To his amazement, the baby was still in the shoebox, tightly wrapped in a clean tea towel.

"Babies like to feel secure. And he is so small, we had nothing better to put him in."

Angus peered at the gnarled little face, surprised by the baby's lusty cries.

"Poor little fellow – so dark and wrinkled. He looks just like a prune."

They smiled, for it was true. He should not yet have been born.

"I estimate he was at about 26 weeks gestation," Sister McLeod volunteered.

"Well, he has problems. If we cannot find the father, he will not have a totem. That will disadvantage him all his life."

"Could I adopt him?" asked Sister McLeod. "I have grown fond of the little chap. He's so determined to survive despite everything."

"I don't see why not," replied Angus. "But to be fair to him, he must be brought up as an amaNdebele boy."

"Naison," said Sister McLeod, "if I adopt him, I will make sure he gets cared for, his clothes - education . . . and anything else he needs. Could you take over his training as an amaNdebele boy?"

"Yes I could Sister. But we don't know if he is amaNdebele or maShona. If we do it wrong that could bring trouble in the future. But . . ." he paused and reflected, "if he will be my son too, I would like him to be called after my father, Vusimuzi."

Angus nodded. "As far as finding out about him is concerned, let me take care of that part and see if we can identify the mother and, hopefully, this little chap's father. If you two look after him in the meantime and we still have no identification in three months' time, I'll draw up formal papers for adoption for you, Sister. And to give you a legitimate place in his life, a guardianship deed for you, Naison."

As he walked back to the NC's office, Angus pondered the life ahead for this premature baby with so little going for it.

The chances of finding out who his mother was were pretty slim. She'd been wearing ordinary Bata tackies that most people in the area wore and a homemade maternity dress with a slightly unusual pattern and style. It was likely that she had bought it second hand or perhaps even been given the dress. A photograph in the Bulawayo Chronicle might help – if only the newspaper was in colour.

And so Prune got his names. And he got his home. And he "adopted" his guardian's totem as an amaNdebele boy. Most important, in the establishment days of this the youngest of Britain's colonies, he got a certificate: date of birth August 12, 1939. Mother: unknown. Father: unknown.

He grew up in the half lands of white and black, but in their wildest imaginings, nobody present that day could have foreseen the convoluted twists and turns that would take this little boy into his country's history

1

MAKING MUD AND THE ANCESTORS' OWL

When they were going to make mud oxen, Prune got up *kuseniseni*[11] before the sun shone. He would sit in his best sandy place on the much-trampled path from the clinic to Carol's house, waiting for antlions to make traps in the sand. He was looking for tiny squirts spitting up and out of a pointy downward cone. A small insect with fierce claws was in there, throwing out dry sand and small stones he didn't want. When the squirts stopped, the trap was ready.

Everything would go still.

Prune lay on his stomach. Still, like a chameleon, only eyes moving. Watching. Waiting. He heard crickets screech in the bush. They stopped the screech and waited to see ants caught too.

Prune's eyes were itchy from watching, watching.

A fast ant came running, not looking. And *zoop* – into the hole. It tried and tried to get out but the antlion, with its long claws, shot up wet sand to hit the ant. The ant fell – and fell again. It struggled and struggled to escape. Then it fell too deep. It was caught and pulled under the sand.

Prune knew the antlion would suck the ant's juices dry. He also knew, because the ant could not escape, that the red ant heap sand was just right for the antlion. That meant the sand was just right for him to make good mud.

He stood up.

But he couldn't quite leave the antlion. Not yet!

He broke a twig from the flat-topped thorn tree beside him. Squatting on his heels, he waited and waited – still as a stone – for the sand to stop

---

[11] *kuseniseni: kuseni* means early; *kuseniseni* – very early

moving. Then he plunged his twig into the side of the hole, and his hours of practice paid off as the antlion was flicked out of its trap. He yelled in triumph, jumping with delight to see the little insect flying through the air. He watched it land and immediately start to burrow again.

This was a hungry antlion!

Prune had waited too long. Now he had to move fast. He broke off pieces of anthill to fill his tin bucket, watching the sun as it climbed up through the thorn bush. He filled another bucket with water so he could half-walk half-run to the big fig in Carol's garden before its shade reached the mahobahoba tree, or it would be too hot for good mud to shape the animals.

Breathless, he flopped down cross-legged on the grass in the densest bit of shade, pouring water from one tin basin onto the dry and broken bits of ant heap in the other – moving, kneading and mixing it to make it just right. He rubbed and stretched, rubbed and stretched, then cupped his hand to pick up more water. He stretched it again till it was soft. Then he smoothed it out on a flat stone to about one inch thick. He stretched out straight fingers and thumb, tight together, and put his hand on the mud. A careful cut-out of his hand with a bit of tin from the bucket, up the sides and round the fingers, would make one 'nkomo[12].

Prune picked up the mud and held it right at the bottom so it stood up in the air. When the top flopped down before you could say "zinkomo" three times, it was just right. Then quickly, quickly he wrapped it in pawpaw leaves, piling mudpacks in two heaps – one for Jabu, one for Carol. No pile for Themba today, because he was in Bechuanaland.

Jabu and Carol made many, many cattle, so they were quick. He had to work fast to make enough mud.

"Salibonani[13] Prune!" Jabu had arrived from the School. His father was a teacher and had a real teacher's house made of bricks - like Prune's house with Sister McLeod, but bigger.

"Yebo[14]. Linjani?[15]" It was important to greet each other in the traditional way. Prune stood up and cupped his hands in greeting.

---

[12] 'nkomo: cow/cattle (singular)
[13] Salibonani: greeting. (lit) "we see you". equiv. Good morning
[14] Yebo: I/we see you
[15] Linjani: (equiv.) "how are you?"

Carol came running out of her house. It was brick too, but even bigger. A verandah ran right round the house, with a garden of flowers at the front and vegetables at the back. *One day*, thought Prune, *I will have flowers in my garden. Then I will be rich.*

"Hi guys – oh good, that's lots of mud you have made."

Prune was pleased.

As he watched the making of bulls and cows, he started thinking. Some days he did things right. Mostly, he did things wrong. When the shade moved, he had to move the mud, or it would get too dry. Sometimes he was too slow and would forget to move because he thought of other things all the time – like having flowers in your garden. Then when he was too long in the shade, the mud was too wet. When the mud was too wet, it would make a hard and very cross day's work.

"Prune! *Woza!*"

Prune shuffled up on his four-year-old knees, and offered Jabu more mud, as a boy, he clapped his hands together with straight fingers and thumbs touching. Girls clapped greetings with hands crossed. Then he looked Jabu in the eye, showing he had nothing to hide. It was tradition, because Jabu was the first grandson of an important Chief. So he was important too, even when he was just his friend.

"Can I make bulls today Jabu?" Carol asked.

"*Hayi[16]!* No!" Jabulani replied, disgust contorting his four-year-old face. "I, only, make the oxen and the bulls. They are my *mali* so I can look after my tribe. Girls don't need *mali*."

"But I am your tribe."

"*Hayi*. You are white. You have no tribe."

"But I do!" she pouted, "mum, dad and Tim. And my cousins . . ."

"*Hayikhona*[17]– not tribe. Cousins like *izinkomo*[18]– part of family." Jabu stood up, chin in the air, a miniature of his straight-backed father.

"Tribe is *zonke*[19]." He gestured. "We make many *izinkomo* for my tribe and for my Chief. For *amalobola* – paying for a bride. Boys work for the tribe to feed *mombies*[20] and to grow more fat."

---

[16] *Hayi:* shortened version of hayikona – no

[17] *Hayikhona :* emphatic no

[18] *izinkomo:* cattle (plural)

[19] *zonke:* all/everything

[20] *mombies:* generic term for cattle

"Don't speak Sindebele Jabu, I don't understand!"

"You must learn." Jabu turned away. "Prune – *woza*[21]."

"Jabu, you are shouting at Prune all the time today," Carol said. "Why can't he make cows with us?"

"He is *bandlulula*[22]" Jabu muttered. Carol didn't understand, but she knew it was not a good thing to be. "We need thorns for the kraal."

Prune sighed, looked at Carol, then backed away to the edge of the shade. He jumped up and ran to fetch thorns.

Carol hated thorns. The long jabbing needles scratched and stabbed and made her bleed. It was funny though, how Jabu's blood was the same colour as hers, but his skin was dark, shiny brown. Hers was pale white and went red in the sun – it would make her cry sometimes with soreness and blisters. Mum made her wear her hated hat, but she took it off quickly in the shade of the fig tree. Jabu and Prune didn't wear hats and didn't get sunburnt even when they sat in the sun for ages.

Carol and Jabu were twins, born the same day, but they weren't the same. She thought twins were always the same. That was funny too.

They built kraals with the thorns Prune brought back – fierce white thorns with a sharp black tip, long as a middle finger.

They carefully drew the size of the kraal, making a line with a stick, then scuffed up the ground inside the line. They were careful not to rough the path where the cattle came in and out, or the gate would stick. To make them extra strong, they pushed thorns into the ground with the points up and leaning a bit outwards. When one thorn crossed two other thorns, then leopard couldn't get in to kill the calves.

They kept many cows and calves in one kraal to keep them safe from lion and leopard. Another kraal was for oxen with long, bent horns and another one for humpy bulls with big heads.

Carol took a parcel of mud and unwrapped the pawpaw leaves. She rubbed it till it was all one piece and shaped it into a fat, red sausage. Then quick, quick – pinch it in for the throat and cheekbone and smooth it back for a long neck. Front legs, back legs, long tail . . . up to the head to make two long horns – and then, very carefully, the teats because they always broke off first. Last of all, fat noses – little fingernails made beautiful nose

---

[21] "*woza*": "come here"
[22] *bandlulula:* rejected (illegitimate)

holes and a dent for the eyes.

If you did it carefully, every cow was different. Some had sweet faces, some were very bossy.

"My cows need eyes."

Carol ran into the house to ask Mum for beads.

"The yellow and brown ones, Mum! Only the yellow and brown!"

Mum laughed. "How many cows today?"

"Seven," she pouted, "and I still can't make a bull. Now Jabu is making a boy to ride on his bull. So I will make a girl to ride on my cow."

Mum carried in a tray with a plate piled high with tender young mealie cobs. "I've cooked mealies for you. But where's the hated hat?"

"Yumm . . . Aw Mum! It's just a little way from the shade to the house!"

Mum made a face and shook her head.

They started separating the yellow and brown beads from the rest, putting them first into a little dish, then onto the tray. Mum carried the plate of mealies over, and Carol breathed in the sweet buttery smell before she carefully picked up the tray to carry the precious load back to the big fig. There were eight mealies: two each, plus two. Mum must have thought Themba was with them. Themba was allowed to make oxen, because his father was DA (District Assistant) Motlane like Jabu's father, Teacher Ncube. Mum told her it was very important to always say DA and Teacher, because then everybody knew they were important and would treat them with respect.

But Themba wasn't here today because his grandfather *baba 'mkulu* [23] had died. Themba had told them he was excited because he was going on the bus to Plumtree, then to Francistown in Bechuanaland. There would be two days of long, hot walking on winding dusty paths through the bush to his family's village near Shoshong. He wasn't excited about the walking. But then there would be the watching and talking days of the funeral, with much storytelling about his beloved *baba 'mkulu.*

Themba had told them that when the sun fell from the sky, he and the other young boys were supposed to be safely in their huts for the night - but they'd hide in the long grass and with pointing and mouth-covered

---

[23] *baba 'mkulu:* (lit) big father. Grandfather/great-grandfather

5

giggles, watch the feasting and dancing. He had been really excited.

Jabu had one more mealie. Carol and Prune shared the other one. Prune was allowed to sit and eat with them, now that the important cattle business was finished. Little tummies filled quickly.

"Are you having drumming in your village tonight, Jabu?" asked Carol.

"There is always drumming in Jabu's village," Prune teased. "I think *tokoloshe* [24] is coming to get you tonight."

"Don't joke about *tokoloshe*!"

"Look!" Carol whispered, "there's one just there."

She'd seen a hare hopping into the bush behind them. When she suddenly stood up, it leapt out, splashing wildly through Prune's poured-out water.

So did Prune and Jabu. They fled in different directions, yelling. The mealie cobs went flying, and cattle scattered. Carol was frightened because the boys were scared. So she ran away too.

"Just joking," she tried to laugh as she walked, uncertainly, back again.

Jabu was very cross.

"Don't ever do that again. Never, never, never lie about *tokoloshe*."

"Sorry Jabu. Sorry Prune."

"The cattle are broken! Look! There are too many broken for my bull fight." Jabu was downcast. As he picked them up, he started saying the names of each animal that had broken: "amaThambo, Uwomile, isiBunumkulu . . ."

He collected the pieces and gently put them in a calabash.

Carol started to name some of her broken cows too. "Sibongile, Nomvula, Thandiwe . . ."

"Those are girls' names, not names for cattle!" Jabu said scornfully. "Names must tell the story. Like this. AmaThambo. He has big bones. Uwomile is thirsty, because his mud was too dry and he cracked. And this one" – he picked up a very fat bull – "isiBunumkulu, has a big bottom."

Sadly and carefully, they put the unbroken cows, calves and bulls that still needed to dry, into their kraals for the night - trying not to get jabbed by the thorns. Then they made a stick roof and softly laid pretend mealie

---

[24] *tokoloshe:* bad spirit

stalks on top of it. In the night, the animals would pull down stalks to eat them. Then the cattle would make manure, and the next day, the manure would have to be cleaned out and put on the fields to grow more mealies to feed the family.

Even though these were just pretend cattle and pretend mealie stalks, Jabu would not leave till the new cattle were safely in the kraal, the thorn gate was shut, and mealie stalks were on the roof. He said it was an important lesson he had learned from his father, and the others must learn it too.

All the broken pieces were now in the calabash so Jabu could take them to the *umkhokho*[25]. He gently covered them with dry grass so he could carry them safely, the long run to the *umkhokho* village.

He couldn't mend the broken ones . . . but he would ask the *umkhokho* to release their spirits, so they could be put back in the ground. In time, their mud would make more cattle.

Carol had heard stories about *umkhokho* and *amadlozi*[26] and *tokoloshe*. They were scary stories. Mum said she must shut her ears if the *piccanins*[27] talked about these things. She thought about how she had been frightened when she scared Jabu and Prune about the *tokoloshe*.

Then she wondered what the ancestors did to the cows and calves and bulls, because they came back strong and shining. When they had been to the ancestors, the cows' teats didn't break any more.

But the ancestors sometimes didn't want to see the cows, so Jabu had to take special presents. Today, he would tell the story of the broken cattle, and the *tokoloshe* and the ancestors would be very angry. Today, they would have to collect many *marulas*[28] as payment for the ancestors.

Prune helped them pick *marulas*.

Carol wondered a lot about Prune. How sometimes he was helping, like *marula*-picking helping and making-mud helping, and sometimes not helping – like not helping making *izinkomo*, but then, eating-mealies helping. She wondered if it would make a difference if Prune was called by his real name, Vusimuzi. But Prune had stuck. She wondered about these

---

[25] *umkhokho:* ancestors' spirits

[26] *amadlozi:* different ancestors' spirits

[27] *piccanins:* a word derived from Portuguese: pequenino, originally meaning small (boy) but assumed later to include small girls as well

[28] *marulas:* delicious native stone fruit

things all the time, but she did learn to speak Sindebele and the boys learned to speak English.

When it got too hot, she went home to do painting with Mum, and Prune went to fetch more thorns for the next day and to help sweep the clinic for Naison. Jabu had to make a ceremony to the *umkhokho* in a village many miles away. It would give him time for some important thinking as he ran all the way.

Jabu liked important thinking, but he knew he had to be quick today, so he could get back to his home for his favourite part of the day. He pushed more grass into the calabash to hold the broken bits tight and started a slow run down the road behind the Native Department.

His father, Nkanyiso, waved at him and called out, "Hey Jabulani!" But Jabu saw only the road to the *umkhokho*.

Nkanyiso watched and wondered.

As he left the small town of Tjolotjo, Jabu moved off the tar strips onto the dirt path, because the tar was too hot for his bare feet. He did the slow run all the way to the other village to make sure he would not be too tired to get there. He slow-ran till the sun blinded his eyes, and he knew time was very short.

The *umkhokho* village was not as big as Tjolotjo, but it was more important to the Matebele people. All the houses were made of sticks, mud, and thatch which the white people called "pole" and "dagga". There were twenty-three houses built in a circle with a big space in the middle for dancing, for cooking and for eating. Right next to the big space was the grass hut, with two smoke holes, because it was very long.

Jabu fast-ran into the village to find the *umkhokho*. Because it was the custom he sat on his haunches just outside the big grass hut with two smoke holes and stared at the entrance for the first sign of movement. But many minutes later, nobody came to see why he was still sitting waiting. The *umkhokho* were not there today.

He stood up, then bent double to walk through the low door very quietly, holding out his calabash towards the *umkhokho's* owl, *khova*[29]. Even though the owl's back was turned, *khova* could turn his head right round to look at Jabu from the corner, with no-blinking eyes. Because it was

---

[29] *khova:* a type of owl associated with spirit mediums

tradition, Jabu knew he had to tell *khova* everything, and *khova* would know if he left anything out. Sometimes it was worse talking to *khova* because of the no-blinking eyes than it was talking to the *umkhokho*.

So Jabu talked. He told the whole story from Prune bringing the right mud, to the fright of the tokoloshe and the breaking of the cattle. He kept forgetting, then remembering, then worrying it was taking too long, then saying something . . .

Khova blinked. Jabu turned, ready to go. *Khova* screamed his two notes, and Jabu felt wings smack the back of his head as the owl flashed past into the still-bright sun.

Jabu's heart was in his mouth. The *umkhoko* were very angry. He ducked out of the door and started to run fast, because he was frightened. And fast because he had to be back before the sun dropped from the sky.

The growls of hunters and the snorts and squeals of the hunted were already making terrifying pictures in his head as the tropical night closed in so quickly.

He ran even faster.

Exhausted, he flopped panting at his father's feet and dipped his *isitshwala*[30] into the boiling pot of meat and gravy. This was the best time of the day – eating and hearing stories he loved. Every time he listened, he learned. And he remembered new stories – of King Mzilikazi and his son King Lobengula.

And most important, of Mtjaan, his own *baba'mkulu*, the most revered *Induna*[31] in the whole Matebele kingdom.

---

[30] *isitshwala:* firmly cooked mealie meal porridge formed into a ball, and dipped into relish or stew
[31] *Induna:* (equiv.) Officer in a Matebele regiment

2

THE BLOODING OF THE SPEAR

And now he was a man at last. The first spill of semen had signalled the start of a long journey. He left the comfort of his father's brick house at the Government School in Nyamandhlovu, with its comfortable bed, an inside *piccanini kia*[32] and a kitchen warm with the lingering smell of last night's stew and mealie meal. Then, shivering with a thrill of apprehension at what lay ahead, he walked into the bush to heap up mounds of long grass, beating and dropping each armful twice to make sure there were no poisonous snakes lurking inside. Satisfied, he curled up, spreading the grass round his naked body for warmth.

Although initiation and circumcision had now almost stopped since the Zulu nation had grown by so many people, so fast, Jabu had specially asked to participate in the traditional circumcision for a Zulu and amaNdebele warrior as soon as he became a man.

He had watched and waited till the time of early dawn before waking his father to quietly tell him of his manhood.

"You are the grandson of an important Chief, Jabulani, and you have decided. We now walk to the village of our clan."

So father and son walked in the chill of morning before the sun chased the night away and until it was too hot to walk without shade. They walked for two days through the granite hills to their ancestral village near the sacred mountain 'nThaba zikaMambo[33]. They walked fast, with no talking to take up too much breathing, then they walked slow, and then fast again for there were many miles to cover.

On the third day, when the sun stood over their heads, making only

---

[32] *piccanini kia*: small house; toilet
[33] 'nThaba zikaMambo: a range of hills along the forest – Mountain of the Chiefs

small black shadows, they saw the shape of their village against the hills. "Go well my son. You carry the blood of the Matebele nation. You are the grandson of great Mtjaan, the clan of *Khumalo*[34] and the Bull Elephant."

Jabu walked up and then stood in his nakedness at the entrance to the village of his forefathers to declare his manhood as custom demanded. He was still a young boy, but now he stood straight and tall before the cousins and friends of his early childhood. He was strong from fights, from hunting and herding. The sons of the village came to greet and beat him lightly with sticks. Some beatings were hard – to show revenge for angry things in the past. He did not flinch from the pain. Now all would be forgiven.

As tradition demanded, he asked for the *'sangoma*[35] to come, for he would need to prove his courage and strength. He would have to stand still, no leaning, no moving until the *'sangoma* arrived.

The initiation

He waited. Standing. Naked. Not moving.

The *'sangoma* lived in the caves of the 'nThaba zikaMambo. He would talk of the booming voice of Mkwati, the powerful spiritual leader of the Matebele people, in years past. But that voice of prophecy, of warnings and anger was quiet now. The *'sangoma* still looked after the caves, and he sometimes spoke out warnings for the village and made the rain fall. But he was not the Mkwati. No longer did the Chiefs and Headmen pay their regular visit every year to give thanks for the harvest, or to tell of great triumphs and bad disasters - and to ask for good rains for the next year.

Jabu knew he would stand still for many hours before the *'sangoma* came to him. He had practiced for many moons, standing without movement and needing no water.

He heard sounds in the distance – the ululating of village women who were escorting the *'sangoma*. He watched the bent old man walking so, so slowly through the village of grass and mud huts, to the thump-thump foot stamping of men and the louder and louder ululating and dancing of women and children. The *'sangoma's* headdress of feathers made him as tall

---

[34] *Khumalo*: the clan name of the royal family of the Matebele
[35] *sangoma*: spirit guide; traditional healer; rainmaker

as ostrich. His head and neckbands told important stories, decorated with the teeth of lion, the tusk of warthog, and the skin of snake.

As he got close, he locked his eyes on this son of Khumalo and slowly, slowly straightened up, getting taller and bigger, until he stood high over Jabu with narrowed eyes that dimmed, sparkled, shone, dimmed again – and saw everything. They blazed as he screamed at Jabu, shouting out ancestral imprecations.

Jabu's worth as a Matebele warrior was being tested.

The 'sangoma was no longer old. The light in his eye became bright and hard, he danced and jumped and screamed again. His necklaces of seeds and beads rattled and flew, and the ochre face paint and leopard skin around his body moved and moulded together until he became as one with the animal of his ancestral spirit.

The 'sangoma brought his face close to Jabu and stared hard for a long time. He moved around to each side – eyes wide, looking – then he walked behind him and shrieked. Jabu did not jump, did not look away, did not shut his eyes as the 'sangoma prepared the sharp stone for the ritual cutting.

Jabu made no noise or movement as the 'sangoma bled his childhood away. The people pressed closer and closer to watch the cutting. To watch Jabu's face. Some came even closer to catch the blood and make them a good future. He knew that to show any pain was weakness and unworthy of a son of Khumalo.

The 'sangoma women gave him *insangu*[36] to help with pain. He inhaled the smoke gladly, but allowed no relief to show.

Herbs were mixed, and the chanting grew as *muti*[37] was smeared on the bleeding, while the gleaming dark skin of young sable antelope was fitted round his shoulders. The 'sangoma lunged at him with the sharp stabbing spear of the Matebele, the tip closer to Jabu's eyes than a hair of his chest.

Jabulani[38] did not move.

He was strong. He was brave. His name would be changed to mark this day and show his courage.

"Jabulisani," his father now used his childhood name, "you have

---

[36] *insangu*: dagga or marijuana

[37] *muti*: medicine. Taken from the word for tree, from which most medicines came

[38] *Jabulani*: boys' name meaning "happiness" or "rejoicing"

indeed brought us the rejoicing of the name we gave you when you were born. But now you can take your place in the regiments of your great-grandfather. Now you have the strength and the courage to look after and restore our people." His father placed the palm of his hand on his son's forehead. "You are *Bhekisizwe*[39]. The restorer of your people."

Jabu was bursting inside. He had been given a powerful name: Bhekisizwe. It was more than he had hoped. He had purpose now – to look after his nation, to lead them, to restore their former kingdom with wisdom and firm rule.

His father had been to the Chiefs and Headmen of all surrounding villages to tell of the initiation. They had listened and nodded and agreed he was indeed the right young man to be called Bhekisizwe. They wished for this young man that he should have good going before him and good following behind him. They made him his own shield and stabbing spear. His shield was strong cowhide of the black and red of his clan, denoting his chiefly family, but with parts in pure white to show his leadership.

The *kraal* Headman brought forward the new *amabetchu*, the traditional loincloth of skins and wildcat tails. Jabu knelt on one knee and offered the traditional straight finger clap of acceptance, as he took the *'mbetju*[40] and tied the thong round his waist. His father stepped forward to place a single strand of pale pink beads round his neck to signify his membership of the royal family.

"Go, son of Khumalo. For six days, you stay on the 'nThaba zikaMambo to learn and remember. Do not return until the white of your shield is marked with the blood of your bravery."

And so Jabu walked. But not alone – for the *umfana*[41], a young boy, was there to watch and keep him safe from snakes and wild animals. They walked barefoot, along winding dust paths down to the flat land and up into the hill. He drove himself to keep walking as pain and exhaustion threatened to overpower him. Slipping in and out of consciousness, with the *umfana* prodding his buttocks with a stick if he threatened to fall, he only just managed the walk up to the cave where he would stay and heal, eat no food, and drink only one small sip of water at the four quarters of

---

[39] *Bhekisizwe:* boys' name meaning "restorer of the people"
[40] *'mbetju:* as for amabetchu: a traditional loincloth of tails and skins
[41] *umfana:* young boy

the day.

He stayed for five sunsets, and he remembered nothing.

No pain. No heat. No cold. Five sunsets with dreams raw with the jabbering hysteria of hyena, the choking roar of a hunting lion, the sliding menace of snakes, and the *umfana* lighting fires.

Then the dreams stopped.

When he woke late in the night, he sat in quietness for a time. His brain was alive. His body was strong. He woke . . . and he thought of his early childhood.

He remembered sitting at his father's feet with the mesmerising flicker of a wood fire shining yellow and orange on his face.

He remembered his long journey to see the *umkhokho* and their anger at the broken cattle. He remembered his twin – she was his friend. They had bled fingers to mix the blood and swear they were family. But he hadn't seen her for many months, and he wondered what she looked like now. He still saw Themba, because they were both at the same school. Themba was clever – always going to school and trying to be the best at everything. Jabu didn't like him anymore, because he thought too much of himself. Yet he was nothing. Nothing. Themba wasn't brave for the bleedings of circumcision.

"Ptaa!" Jabu spat in disgust at the thought.

The thrill of the Zhiiii . . .

Then he remembered the stories told and re-told by his father every night, as he watched, and heard, the gargling squeak of nightjars swooping for insects in the moonlight – their extended wing feather, one on each wing, floating and waving like flags.

Mostly, he remembered the stories. How he loved and learned those stories, specially those stories of the great Zulu King Shaka.

His eyes were fixed on the lightening of the day as his imagination pictured the oil-shined bodies of warriors, sweating with the excitement of preparation for battle. The King needed more cattle, and he had thrown the spear at the *Inxwala*[42] so that warriors could blood their spears against

---

[42] *Inxwala*: the Great Dance and the first fruits ceremony

15

a troublesome tribe. He imagined the brave shouts of the *amabutho* [43] as they told each other "never fear pain"; "die with courage"; "the enemy will fall as water to our feet".

He imagined the battle itself – the silence of the 'creeping' as the *amabutho* moved imperceptibly closer to the enemy in the blackness of night, their backs to the mark where the scouts told that the sun would rise. They would creep and stop . . . and creep and stop . . . but not too close – never too close.

The first creeping was the new *maShoja* [44] – once they were enemy who were hated, then they became slaves. When they were loyal and proved they were brave enough, they became *maShoja* or *aMatcha amaZulu* – fighters of the Zulu people.

While the enemy kept sleeping, it was time for the second creeping – this time, the trusted warriors, the *impi* [45]. Even in the dark, their oiled bodies gleamed against the featureless bush.

Then the 'kneeling' – with no sound – no moving until the sky behind them washed with early morning red. As they knelt, the strong runners circled, up and round behind the enemy to form *'iphondo zinkomo* – the horns of the bull – running on noiseless feet.

Then – the silence.

Last of all, the backward legs. The *a'madoda* [46] *impi* – looking back and to the sides, keeping eyes wide for enemy attacking from behind. The *umfanas* were hidden with them, ready to take long shields and *iklwa* [47] to the warriors when they needed them.

As the red streaked across the sky just before the sun leapt up bright behind them, he imagined the slow half-standing of the first creeping, with shields turned sideways. Still silence – silence for as long as a big pot took to boil on a wood fire.

Then – the *Zhii* [48]. Tchzhee . . . zhee. The hissing.

Jabu's body ached and thrilled to the fear of the *zhii*. The enemy, hearing and understanding, running, running all over like frightened ants

---

[43] *amabutho:* Matebele warriors
[44] *maShoja or aMatcha:* warrior, fighter (single)
[45] *impi:* once meaning a group of armed men; Shaka changed this to mean a regiment
[46] *a'madoda:* the old men
[47] *iklwa:* the short stabbing spear of the Zulus, the name derives from the sound made as the spear was pulled from a body
[48] *Zhii:* The closed teeth hissing of the regiments just before they attacked.

when their nest is disturbed by a big foot. The Zulu would hear shouts of "AmaZulu! AmaZulu!"

The awful, inescapable *zhii* until the horns were in place. The frightened ants – running this way – then that way. Looking. Running again. The *zhii*, the *zhii* – louder and louder.

Then – the King shouts.

The first creeping, crack their shields flat in front of them with a loud noise – their *iklwa* in the other hand – moving slow, steady, strong. Now bending so the enemy can see the second creeping behind as they stand up tall and roar and leap and gyrate and scream, their ostrich feathers making them giants in the early morning.

Jabu's imagination was filled with the sights and sounds of the battle. The ants flee – into *impi* horns on the one side . . . then on the other side. The spears grow red. Above the screams and roars, he hears the squelch of *iklwa* as the warriors pull them from the weak and the dying.

Jabu's head sank between his knees – he felt exhausted by the intensity of the imagined battle. After a few moments, and as the images faded from his mind, he remembered the Zulu rules.

Strong fighters were tied together, and a chosen clan herded to the Zulu place for punishment. All young children were killed. Women were chosen for strength and beauty – those still suckling were allowed to take their babies with them. Old men and women went too – it was tradition – to bring blessing to them for wisdom and kindness.

Nobody was ever left alive to fight the Zulu in vengeance.

Then the victory songs would start – as the *umfanas* herded the captured cattle back to the Zulu capital of Mhlanhlandhlela. The sharpest ears of their women would hear them coming from many miles away. There would be shouts of triumph, joyful preparations and excitement for the feasting.

The cattle were paraded in front of King Shaka. He was in the Goat *Kraal*[49], waiting impatiently and seated on the big rock under the indaba tree. He greeted his leading warriors as they bent in obedience, loudly shouting their stories of courage and bravery as they came near. The King stamped his stick to signify his pleasure. He would take time choosing the best cattle for the Royal Herd. He knew his cattle well, and the Royal Herd

---

[49] *Kraal:* village

always produced the strongest calves. The rest of the cattle were divided among the families of those warriors who had told of their bravery and had the loudest and longest stamping of the King's stick.

And so the Zulu people grew, from 1,000 warriors when Shaka became King, to 2,000 warriors the next year and 20,000 warriors in the time a young child grew to lose his first tooth. Then came the greatest of them all, Mzilikazi Khumalo, the founder of the Matebele nation.

A vow to the King

Jabu felt his hunger grow and knew it was time to find food, for him and the *umfana*, before the daylight came. He wished he had dogs. But he knew he must eat – a little at first. He called for *umfana*, who came clapping and running, happy that Jabu had stopped sleeping. They climbed the granite rocks as sure-footed as goats, bare feet and toes fitting into tiny fissures and spaces. Stopping – when Jabu saw movement.

Ah! fat *imbila*[50]!

He knew by doing the swaying which he had been taught from a young boy, they would become very interested. He could then get close to stab with his spear. He knew too that if he missed, he would get no *imbila* that day.

He moved slowly so *imbila* felt safe. Moving head - to side and to side – small moving only – one toe and one toe. One stab, one squeal, and break the neck. The *umfana* jumped and laughed. He took *imbila* back to roast on the fire and remove the skin to help make a warm *kaross*[51].

Jabu climbed higher, for this was a sacred hill – sacred as far as back as the Rosvi people until the Zwangendaba Regiment of the Matebele defeated the Changamira and the people dispersed. It was still sacred when Mkwati tried to bind the maKalanga and the Matebele together to fight the white man. He remembered how Mkwati's instructions were not followed as the *amabutho* were impatient and did not wait for the full moon.

And the white man won.

He took a deep breath and looked down to the shining width of the sleepy Gwaai River in front of him and the land of the ancestors farther

---

[50] *imbila:* dassie, rock rabbit
[51] *kaross:* a mat made of rabbit or dassie skins

away below him – Tjolotjo, Nyamandhlovu, the gusu – the thick forests where, the stories told, the body of King Lobengula rested. He could see many elephant down there in the forest, following a big old matriarch and pulling down trees and branches. He heard the fussy trumpeting of worried mothers punishing their calves.

He smiled with contentment, because he knew that the soul of the great amaNdebele King, the Bull Elephant, was still being well looked after.

He drank in the fall of steep crags below him and the hills and flat valleys of the country he loved so much stretching into the smoky distance. Almost in slow motion, the acrid dust below swirled like sluggishly curling eddies of smoke round a group of young boys herding cattle down to the river. The shimmer of early morning heat was already causing false lines of water to shine on the parched dry lands of the plains. The massive rocky hills beside and above him were rich with trees, and the air burst with twittering song as the birds' chorus gave praise for another dawn.

"One day, my Chief and my King," he said, looking down and pointing at the gusu forest below him, "one day I will follow your command and avenge your death by chasing the white man from our land. One day . . ."

Exultant, he stretched up to the rising sun with a great shout. He was glad he had passed through the tradition of the cutting. He knew the time was right to bring that back to his people. He was deeply, deeply happy that his people had confidence in him and that he had been chosen to be Bhekisizwe.

And now he had made his vow to King Lobengula.

As he held the mopani branches to steady him, dropping his feet into cracks between great slabs of granite rock, he thought of his father and mother and he was split in two. He knew his father wanted him to go to the white man's school, but it was not right – for him. He had too many other things to learn.

"Jabu, things have changed. If you are to be a great leader, you have to speak and understand the things of the white man, "his father had told him when he had asked him to conduct the initiation ceremony. "You must learn everything he knows, so you can be cleverer than he is."

And so he agreed, a little, and he learned, a little – just as much as he thought he needed.

"Could do better," his teacher always said. "This boy could achieve anything he wanted to. He is bright and intelligent but lacks application."

"Your teacher says you are very lazy," his father told him.

"Jabulisani," his mother cried. "Why? Why are you so lazy – your brothers and sister are not so clever, but they work hard. And they are beating you." His mother cried all the time about Jabu and his laziness.

"One day *umama*[52], you will be proud of me," he'd say. But she cried and cried. He knew in his heart that one day he would use what he learned. One day his *umama* would be proud of him. He thought of her face, so gentle and beautiful, and he wanted to please her.

Hunting leopard with no dogs

But now he could smell roasting flesh and called out to the *umfana* that he was ready for his meat.

It was the last night of the initiation before the weeks of feasting and teaching would start. Although he was still young, Jabu wanted to blood his spear with more than just *imbila*.

He climbed to the top of a flat rock to see if there was any animal hunting in the bush below. He was looking for the young leopard that had been taking dogs. The people in the village were very careful because of their small children, but they were now frightened. This was a cunning leopard and he took the dogs with no sound, even when they were tied to the house. Leopard left the bloodied end of the *riempi*[53] rope to say, "I have your dog."

I will get leopard before the sun comes, Jabu vowed. He knew it would be brave to hunt leopard without dogs to fight for him, but Jabu knew the blood of Mzilikazi and Mtjaan flowed in his veins. He was of the clan of Khumalo – fruit of the Bull Elephant – and he would blood his spear with leopard to prove it.

He slept with no dreaming until there was enough time before the sun

---

[52] *umama:* mother
[53] *riempi:* dried leather thongs sometimes twisted into a rope

shone to start tracking, to prove his manhood and affirm his bravery. Time to meet that leopard. The most cunning of cats hunted at night, but with a full stomach he slept in the daytime. Jabu watched as the dark fell, for he needed shadows, showing dark and light because of the clear sky and a small moon.

When the moon was right, he grunted approval and *umfana* rose with him, walking this way and that way, with that small moon to show him, until he picked up spoor. It was good spoor – with the grass lying on one side, showing which way to go. But it was hard with no dogs and only that small moon, and he went the wrong way, many times.

There was better light as the sky grew brighter. Jabu found fresh spoor and smelt droppings. Leopard was close to the big farm with sheep and cattle. He would watch the sheep when they ran to see which way they went. Then he would see leopard. After leopard had killed, he would wait until the stomach was full. Then he would be easier to kill.

The sheep were already frightened, scattering and crying, stopping, looking back with startled eyes. He saw the flash of leopard as he streaked past, jumping on the back of a too-slow young sheep and biting down hard behind the head. This sheep was dead. The others ran away, happy it was not their turn this time.

Leopard dragged the sheep away, so Jabu and the *umfana* ran silently through tall trees. Following, watching. They saw his great strength as he clawed and pulled the dead weight of the sheep up a tree, leaping with front legs and paws stretched wide on either side of the tree trunk to dig in to the wood and hold him. He was so strong that he pulled that big sheep onto a wide flat branch easily.

Umfana stood with mouth open and whispered, "*maaiwe!*"[54]

Jabu's throat tightened to see the power of this splendid animal. He knelt quietly, feeling tingles of fear in his chest. He watched every move. His eyes never left the shape and size of leopard. Between the leaves, the skin gleamed gold in the first colour of the morning. Yes – a fine leopard – worthy of the name Bhekisizwe.

Leopard licked the dead sheep clean. He was comfortable and not worried. He ate bit by bit, unhurried, delicately separating and eating his favourite organs and fat pieces, leaving the back legs for later.

---

[54] "*maaiwe!*": expression of amazement, disbelief

Jabu knew he must wait, still as a statue. He sat on his heels in grass higher than his head. The sky grew lighter. He waited, knowing that if he struck too soon, leopard would not be sleepy. Then he could not win. He watched as leopard licked and cleaned itself after the feed. Long lazy sweeps of his tongue along his front legs. Then shorter licks deep between the claws of his front feet, with half-closed eyes.

Sometimes leopard would stop and stare into the bush – checking. When there was nothing, licking again. Then checking. Gradually, and lazily he stretched out along the branch. He would not hunt again, but it would soon be too light to stay in this place, and he would move into thicker bush so he could hide in the light and shadow of leaf and bark.

Jabu made every muscle in his legs move independently to stand half way up, always in full control, before lowering his body down to a crouching position to move forward. No quick movement, no noise. Eyes fixed, backing away, toes feeling for a leaf or twig that might crack. Slowly . . . slowly . . . turn round, till he felt a gentle early morning breeze on his face and smelt the fresh blood of the kill. *Umfana* copied every movement. Leopard had not seen him. He had not smelt him. He did not know they were there. Jabu waited, crouched, to be sure.

He was frightened. He took a deep breath. He needed dogs. It was chilly cold, but he was sweating. He looked for the unprotected places on leopard's body where the spear must strike, but leopard had his back to him. The spear would only work with a quick throw through the underbelly to the heart. He watched and planned. The throw must be deadly – wounded leopard is a dangerous leopard.

He signalled *umfana* to stay close behind. If he did not kill, leopard would attack, and he would kill *umfana* first. That would bring disgrace.

The position was not right. They would have to track a long way, so they could come from behind and beneath, with the breeze still in their faces. He marked the place, where it would now be nearly sleeping.

They moved off in a wide circle across the edge of the field, creeping silently. Hunter and *umfana*, crouching. Using the fleshy side ridge of their feet, before rolling each foot onto the toe pads to make sure there was nothing to crack and break.

No noise to startle leopard.

They walked a long way, and now it was close to the edge of the thick bush, and they could start to move back in to where they had seen leopard.

"Hey boy!" There was a shout behind him. "Where do you think you're going?"

Jabu stopped in alarm. *No shouting! Please no shouting!*

"That is my farm. If you want work, take off all that Matebele warrior stuff and I will pay you two shillings to herd my cattle."

Jabu stood tall and turned to face the farmer behind him. He knew him, but the farmer did not recognise him now he was a man.

Quietly, but standing proud, he said, "Today, I do not herd cattle."

"Well then, you bloody well don't walk on my land! I don't want you stirring up trouble."

Jabu boiled with humiliation. *You wait, Tertius Engelbrecht. One day you will not speak to me like that.* But it was not yet time.

"Excuse me Nkosi," he fawned, "leopard is taking your young sheep. I am here to catch him."

"You! Catch him with your *ikhwa* and no dogs? You're joking man. You need to think about getting some proper work to pay your hut tax. Don't mess about hunting leopard. Go on, *voetsak*⁵⁵."

That hated word – *voetsak*. The Dutchmen in South Africa used it with a snarl. It said, "Get out, you useless person!"

Jabu stood tall and looked straight at Tertius Engelbrecht. Their eyes locked. Then he deliberately turned and moved away.

But he did not leave – he had to blood his spear with this leopard.

He walked along the edge of the thick bush as though he was leaving, but he circled back so he could find a good place to see and wait for leopard to settle again and sleep with his stomach full of young sheep.

He waited and waited. He couldn't see him. The sun was high now. At the sound of voices, leopard had moved into deeper bush. He waited. Watched.

A tiny flick of tail, and Jabu saw leopard again, hidden in the dark leaves of a bigger tree, lying with a full belly.

Suddenly leopard lifted his head, golden eyes wide and staring. He wasn't moving. His eyes were fixed. This was not good – he should be

---

⁵⁵ *voetsak* : (literally) go away. But used more forcefully

23

sleeping with so much sheep in his stomach.

Jabu had crept closer, but now he stopped. He dared not breathe. He had to get closer but keep the wind right. The time was near. But the eyes were too bright. He felt his heart shake inside him and bit his teeth to get strength. Leopard was still watching something over there.

Then thunder cracked.

Umfana screamed, "*Duma*[56]! *Duma*!"

Jabu saw leopard jerk and the brightness of eye fade. Gradually, it slipped out of the tree like a falling sheet of cloth. Jabu watched, transfixed.

Then he heard a laugh. "So much for killing your leopard, boy. This leopard has been killing my sheep for many months. Your spear would never have killed that young animal. It was too big and strong. It would have killed you easily. I saw you come here, so I followed with my gun."

Jabu dropped his head. "Thank you baas."

But inside he burned. He was close to bloodying his spear and marking his shield. This Engelbrecht had stolen his honour.

His anger wanted to choke him.

---

[56] *Duma:* thunder

3

ST DOMINIC'S MEDICINE

Carol ran as fast as she could . . . wracking sobs tearing through her chest as though her heart would break. She ducked round the toilet block and squeezed behind the rough brick bath fire. She heard them dash past, shouting and egging each other on.

"She can't escape, come on! Down here!"

Please God help me, Carol nearly screamed. *Please help. Please help me.*

Her pursuers raced off down another path, away from the toilet block. Carol put her head on her knees, pulled herself tight into her hiding place and wept soundlessly, her chest aching with suppressed sobs.

Weeping by the Matsheumhlope

When she was sure there was nobody around, she moved cautiously towards her hostel, taking the back way. The path meandered down along the Matsheumhlope River. Even though the schoolgirls weren't supposed to go there, Carol loved it. She'd sit in her special little space, chosen to make sure nobody could easily see her - and she'd find her peace, in the smell of the bush and the croaks and warbles of frogs and birds.

It wasn't much of a river, more a trickle of muddy water, but it just reminded her of home. The leafy canopy of *mukwa* trees gave her dappled shade while the tall elephant grass growing on both sides of the ripples, made plenty of places to hide. She knew the girls who were chasing her were townies. They didn't like long grass because of snakes and scorpions, but she was used to it and looked for tell-tale signs before she sat down.

Today, she knew her Mum and Dad would collect her for half-term exeat at half-past five, and her eyes brimmed with a sudden rush of hot tears at the thought of seeing them again.

She found her special hiding place safely and sat with her head on her knees. She hated school so much. Why did they have to live in Tjolotjo, so far away from this horrible school in Bulawayo? She did know she had to be at boarding school because there were no schools for her in Tjolotjo, but knowing, didn't help how much she hated being here.

She still had an hour to wait and didn't want to chance running into the bully girls again. She sat with her head on her knees, thinking how things had changed - of how much she hated school now . . . and how much she had loved school before.

Mum used to teach her through correspondence school. It was so exciting ripping open the brown parcels, which came all the way from Australia. They were full of reading and picture books with beautiful photographs of the sea and beaches and a red desert they called the Outback. She once tried to be clever and asked where the 'In-front' was. Mum didn't even laugh at that! There was no sea or beach in Southern Rhodesia. And the books from Australia were so different – lined exercise books to write in and arithmetic books with tiny squares to put your numbers in. And precious plain thick paper for drawing.

Carol couldn't wait to do her lessons with Mum. Afterwards, she'd take her books down to the big fig tree to teach Prune. He was very slow, and she would have to be fierce with him, because he'd rather go hunting antlions than do sums and spelling. He couldn't go to school at the Native Department because his father was not employed there. He couldn't go to the Government School any more either, because now the waiting lists were too long.

So he did listen sometimes, and he did learn his spelling and his sums. Then one day Prune was better than Carol at sums, and she was not happy about that.

Her life was filled with music – playing the piano and singing songs. Mum taught her until she was ten and finished standard three. She learned piano to grade IV, but Prune didn't learn piano because he only wanted to play *mbira*[57] – little pieces of strong tin were stuck into a gourd and they made sounds when you flicked them with your thumbs. Carol and Prune would play the piano and tinkly tunes together for hours.

In the afternoons, she'd go to Mum's dressing-up box and make up stories so she and Prune could act the stories for Dad when he came home. Sometimes Themba dressed up and acted too. He could sing really well.

"Themba has a beautiful voice," Mum told Mrs Motlane. "And he has perfect pitch. That's a rare thing. I would like to teach him more." So Themba came for singing lessons with Mum. Then they would all act and sing stories for Dad.

Jabu didn't act. In fact, Jabu didn't like school at all, so they didn't play with him much anymore. Carol was sad about that. It wasn't the same fun making cattle with only Prune and Themba. So they stopped.

Before she was ten, the sun was always shining, and every day was a play day. The very best day was riding. She couldn't wait to put on her jodhpurs and white pith helmet. She'd run to the old truck, hooting for Mum to come and take her to Mrs Booth. Mrs Booth had three horses. Carol rode a filly called Flicka, because when the filly was born, she'd been allowed to name her. She chose the name Flicka after the horse in one of the best books that came from Australia called *My Friend Flicka*.

Carol didn't have a horse at home, but she and her brother had two donkeys, Mputu and Sadza. If you sat right back on their tails, you could get them to trot and sometimes even to canter - but you had to hold on to the hair along the ridge of their necks, because it was a very bumpy canter without a saddle.

Then correspondence school stopped.

Mum and Dad said she would have to go to boarding school. Her brother Timothy would have to go to boarding school too, and he was only six. He was frightened. He sat quietly with his eyes very wide, and his bottom lip shook when Mum and Dad had told them.

Afterwards, Carol and Tim went to their favourite place in the old rondavel beside the fig tree. They promised each other that they would

---

[57] *mbira:* traditional musical instrument fashioned out of a variety of gourds to provide a sound box, with seven strong metal 'keys' inserted in different lengths, so they play a tune. Modern mbira are considerably more sophisticated.

27

read their Bible every day and be good children so they didn't get dooks (the cane). And they would write to each other every week. When the holidays came, they would go riding again and have more donkey derbies with Mputu and Sadza.

And everything would be all right. Really.

The day came. Carol dressed in her new pale blue-and-white striped uniform with a grey hat and grey blazer, while Tim wore his white shirt, grey shorts, purple-and-white striped tie, purple blazer, and purple cap.

And so they went to boarding school.

Mum wore dark glasses, because she was crying all the way to Bulawayo. Carol wanted to put her head on her lap and hold on to her forever. But she couldn't, because Mum was in the front seat and she was in the back. So she and Tim just huddled together and felt miserable.

Dad knew the headmistress of the boarding school, Miss Finlayson, and said she was a good headmistress and that school would be the making of her and she would learn better at school than with Mum.

Carol wasn't sure about that.

She was even less sure when they drove up to a huge red brick building. It was the biggest she had ever seen – two storeys high, with a huge staircase going up to the dormitories. There was nothing like that in Tjolotjo. Dad took out her trunk and was told where to put it so that it could be carried up the stairs later.

They then went to see Miss Finlayson. She was small and thin and strict. Her glasses rested on her nose, and her hair was drawn back tight in a bun. She was pleased to see Dad, and they talked for a long time. Carol sat quiet as a mouse, wishing she could go home.

"Cat got your tongue, girl?"

Carol jumped in fright. She couldn't speak and looked desperately at Mum.

"She's very shy," said Mum. *Oh thank you Mum!*

The time came to say goodbye. Tim was being brave and wouldn't kiss her goodbye. He tucked in his chin, making his fair hair droop over his eyes. He couldn't look at her.

Carol was left sitting on her bed. It was hard with bits of coir sticking out of it. The matron came bustling in to show her what was what and said, "Make up the bed girl! Start as you mean to carry on!"

Carol nodded mutely. She was so frightened she couldn't think.

There were clean sheets and a blanket for her to make the bed, but she wasn't sure what to do with the spiky bits of coir. A locker stood at the end for her clothes. When the matron left, she turned the mattress over to find worse bits of coir sticking out on that side. She turned it back again and made the bed, then sat on the locker. She counted 40 beds in a long room – 19 on one side of the door and 21 on the other.

Girls came rushing in, in sports uniforms. They all knew each other and shouted and laughed. Nobody said hello, but one girl with straight black hair said, "Are you the new girl?" Carol nodded numbly. "Well you'd better come down to supper." She went off with her friends.

Carol followed, but she couldn't eat. She couldn't sleep that night either. She heard 39 girls go to sleep. She was still awake. Her heart felt frozen. She did go to sleep when it was nearly time to get up, but she was too tired next day.

It had been six weeks since that first day to this first half-term exeat, and she still couldn't sleep at night. Or eat her supper.

There were many South African girls in the hostel and they teased her because she spoke "proper" English. Miss Hoity-Toity they called her.

Then they had the initiation ceremonies. There were only six new girls, so they were all initiated at the same time. They had to push a peanut round the Common Room floor with their noses while the other girls beat them with long balloons. But some of them had sticks and they hurt.

Then they had to drink St Dominic's medicine.

It was given to them in a dirty glass, and it had floating things in it – from the toilet. They were told they had to drink every bit, or they would be sent to Coventry. Carol decided she would rather be sent to Coventry. The other new girls drank some of it, but she couldn't. Her turn came last. Everyone was watching. Two big tough girls held her on the floor as the disgusting liquid was poured into her mouth. She vomited all over them.

Then everything went quiet, and the girls ran out of the Common Room. Carol got up, retching from the taste with vomit running down the front of her uniform. She looked at the mess round her, numb with despair - just as a teacher walked in. She was reported and sent to the Headmistress.

"I thought you might be a troublemaker," the Headmistress said. "Your father will be very disappointed." Words wouldn't come out of Carol's mouth. She just cried inside. "Two order marks, and no supper until you've cleaned up that mess."

She cleaned it up. She wasn't in time for supper, but she couldn't have eaten anyway.

She went up to the dorm. The other girls were watching a film downstairs, so it was quiet. Her heart was beating so fast that it started fluttering. She was just so tired. She felt as if she had been broken in two. How could she write a good letter to Mum and Dad this week? But she did. How could she even go to school? But she did. Then the worst thing happened – but she didn't want to think about that.

She heard a bell ringing. It was half-past five! She had been thinking so much that she had forgotten the time.

Wait, Mum and Dad! I'm coming, I'm coming. She raced into the hostel driveway, frantic with apprehension - and, relief, to see them still there.

Crossing the Gwaai and avoiding fist fights

She burst into tears. Mum burst into tears. Even Dad looked teary while Tim sat in the back seat, pink in the face.

"Come on my girl, I've got your suitcase. Where have you been?"

She was crying too much to say anything. She climbed into the back of the car, and they set off onto the Victoria Falls Road. She kept saying out loud, but very quietly, as they passed the signposts, all the words that were so much a part of her life and home. Nyamandhlovu – meat of the elephant. Tjolotjo – skull of the elephant. They were going home. At last.

As they drove further out of Bulawayo, the rain came lashing down. *The earth is crying with me* she thought as she stared past ribbons of water streaming down the window.

The car bumped and swerved over the narrow tarmac strips, with Dad struggling to pull it back after they passed another car or lorry, always making sure there was a strip for the wheels at least on one side, as the rain was making everything slippery. They drove carefully – it was dark, and Dad didn't want to hit a big buck or, worse, an elephant. But Carol and Tim just wanted to get home.

The rain poured and poured. Dad said he thought it was wise to pull into the Gwaai River Hotel, as the bridge might be under water. Soon, there it was, a place where they'd always had fun.

"Come in, come in," the voice of Mrs Baron echoed into the darkness. "You'll be soaking wet. Have you had supper?"

"We've just picked the kids up from school. Can we stay?"

"Yes, we'd love supper."

"Is the Gwaai over the bridge?"

Many questions, much laughter, countless hugs. Beers went around, Fantas for the kids, followed by huge family-sized omelettes. "Ostrich eggs," Mrs Baron boomed.

Yummy, Carol thought. But she couldn't eat more than two spoons. "Feeling carsick Mum." More hugs, then off to bed.

She was sharing a room with Timothy.

"Hey Tim! You OK at boarding school?" she asked with concern.

"Ja. Fine."

"You got some friends?

"Ja. Lots."

But Carol knew he was not telling the truth, because his eyes were sad. And he didn't look at her. She was sad and tired. So tired. But she still couldn't sleep, even though Tim went to sleep straight away.

So she lay and thought about the wonderful times they'd had in the swimming pool of this hotel. How sometimes they would be swimming, and the zebras would stand there, looking and waiting. When they got out, they would come and drink. And she remembered the playground, and Mr and Mrs Baron. And how much she loved them.

But the faces of the bully girls pushed out the loving memories. She still could not sleep.

The door opened and Mum peeped in carrying a *phhht phhht*[58] lamp. Carol shut her eyes tight and pretended to be asleep. Mum stroked her face and kissed her goodnight, then stroked Tim's face and kissed him goodnight too. Carol heard her quiet crying as she shut the door.

They stayed at the hotel, waiting for the Gwaai to go down - sharing a breakfast of bacon and eggs and sausages and tomatoes and all agreed

---

[58] *phhht phhht*: there was no electricity at that stage and this was the children's description of the lamps which required pumping up with a phhht phhht noise.

nothing had never tasted so good. Then the sun came out, and Mum and Dad played tennis while Carol and Tim played putt-putt and swam before going back in to stare at the animal heads and stuffed fish in the big sitting room. Tim showed off by telling her all the names of the animals and fish.

At last they were told that the Gwaai had gone down and it was safe to cross the bridge. Carol hated crossing the bridge while the water was still speeding over it in a hump. She always imagined the truck being swept down and gobbled up by the roaring and swirling of the water. But Dad was cautious and went walking into the water with a stick to make sure it was shallow enough. *Oh Dad, please be careful!*

Half-term was five days. Five wonderful days. But still Carol couldn't eat or sleep. Mum and Dad were worried.

"Darling, you're so thin. You look so tired. I don't think you've slept at all since you've been home. What's wrong?" asked Mum.

Carol couldn't answer.

"You'll be sick if you go on like this. I will have to speak to Miss Finlayson."

"Oh no! No, no please!"

"Well then. You must tell us."

And it all came pouring out. She cried and sobbed and told them about the initiation ceremony and St Dominic's medicine. Mum and Dad were so shocked. Tim just looked embarrassed.

"Is that everything, darling?"

"No."

"What else?"

Oh no. She couldn't tell the worst thing. Not that.

But she did.

"They call me a kaffir lover because my best friends are Prune and Jabu and Themba and because you work in the Native Department, Dad.

And they come up to me after breakfast and say, 'After school we'll be waiting for you by the tanks, and we're gonna have a fist fight'" – Carol was sobbing uncontrollably – "and . . . and I don't want to fist fight."

She couldn't stop crying. She didn't know that it could hurt your chest so much. "So they wait until they see me coming, and they shout 'Kaffir lover! Kaffir lover!' and they chase me" – she sobbed – "and they catch me and I have to fight and they really hurt me. But you can't tell Miss Finlayson. Please, you can't tell Miss Finlayson!"

But they did.

When Carol went back to the hostel after the exeat, everyone knew she had told about St Dominic's medicine and about the fist fights. And she was sent to Coventry anyway. Nobody spoke to her. She still couldn't eat, and she still couldn't sleep.

Making Situpas and riding donkeys

When the holidays came, she was sick in bed for a week.

But she and Tim had some donkey derbies, and Prune was still funny and lazy, and they caught antlions and had more fun at the Gwaai River Hotel. And she got better. She listened to Mum playing the piano – wonderful Chopin waltzes and that difficult Liszt piece that she played so well, but sometimes with cross words and lots of stops for mistakes.

She loved the evenings when Dad would pump up the lamps – phhht, phhht, phhht, phhht, phhht, and the light would grow brighter and hiss gently then dim again and need another phhht. She only didn't like going out to the PK[59] at night in case there were *skellems* [60] out there, so she was allowed to use a potty as long as she emptied it and washed it herself. At school, there was electricity and PKs inside the building, so she supposed at least that was a better thing.

Dad came home one day and said he'd bumped into Mr Engelbrecht.

"Your friend Jabu nearly got himself into serious trouble," Dad told her. "He was all dressed up in a '*mbetju* like a Matebele warrior, trying to hunt a leopard with only a small spear and no dogs! What does that boy think he is doing!

"Anyway, Tertius thought he'd better follow him, and just as well he did, as Jabu was very close to a leopard. A big male. There was no possibility he could have killed it. He wouldn't have had the strength and would have been killed himself."

"So what happened Dad?" Carol was anxious.

---

[59] PK: short for piccanini kia – toilet.
[60] *skellems:* covers a variety of 'nasty things', from spiders and snakes to scorpions or ants

33

"Mr Engelbrecht shot the leopard just as Jabu was about to use his spear."

"Oh, thank goodness," Carol breathed.

"He needs to spend more time worrying about how he's doing at school, that boy, and less time playing at being a Matebele warrior."

Carol looked for Jabu but didn't find him those holidays. Then she heard he had gone with his family to Tegwani School, where Teacher Ncube was hoping to get another job.

She and Tim and Prune and Themba had donkey derbies every day and they made dams down by the school next to the Native Department. If you dragged a stick down the path, the water from the irrigation would follow quickly and spill into their dams. Themba knew when the water would run and when it would just stop and stick in the path. He was clever. But you had to mend the path afterwards, or you would be in big trouble from the school. The schoolboys were learning to water oranges by digging canals to the orange trees. They would not be happy to see their water being wasted in dams.

Themba was such a bright boy. His brown skin shone like a polished table, and white teeth filled his face with his bright smiles and laughter. It was good to have Themba around. He could even make sadness happy.

One day, Themba's father, Kuda, called round to Carol's house when they were putting the donkeys away in the paddock. "I need help getting new *situpas*[61] ready. Can you kids come and give me a hand?"

Ooooh yes! They loved helping.

They ran to the office where Kuda had a big old table and some chairs. Many people sat outside waiting. Some were dusty and dirty, because they had walked a long way. They sat and sweated a lot, so the smell was strong. Themba wrinkled his nose and turned to share the wrinkling with Carol.

"Themba – no," Kuda scolded his son firmly.

"Sorry baba."

Kuda brought over a big pile of papers. The children knew it was important work, because there were so many *piccanins* now that sometimes they didn't know who belonged to who. Carol had asked Dad why there

---

[61] *situpas*: an identification card

34

were so many *piccanins*, and he told her that once upon a time *piccanins* died because of diseases and fighting, so the mothers would have sometimes 10, sometimes 12, children. Maybe only 2 would not die and would grow up. But now the clinic was good, and Naison and Sister McLeod made sure all 12 children lived, even when they got measles. So there were many, many *piccanins*, because the mothers had got used to having 12 children.

She also learned that in African custom, you must marry outside your clan. This was important. The Chiefs and Headmen asked the Native Commissioners in the big office in Salisbury to register everybody, so that a man could come and swear that these were his children. They would then be photographed and everyone would know they belonged to that man and his clan.

So now all children got *situpas* when they grew up a bit.

Kuda asked Carol and Prune to stick a photograph onto a special place on the paper and Themba to write a number in the top left-hand corner and pass it on to him. He checked the photo and the number and called the father and his child to come forward.

Then the father said, "Yebo, this is my son" or "Yebo, this is my daughter". And Kuda would ask him to sign the paper. Some people had not yet learned to write, so they put an X instead of signing. Then Kuda passed the papers to Dad. He also signed to say he had seen that person signing or making the mark. Now that person had a *situpa*. That *situpa* said who he was and named his clan and where he came from – and named all his children. It also gave him a number.

If an uncle who was living in Salisbury had twenty pounds to give him, the uncle went to the Native Commissioner's office in Salisbury and gave them the money and the *situpa* number. Then the Salisbury NC would tell the Tjolotjo NC that there was money coming. When it arrived, the NC in Nyamandhlovu would check the *situpa* number. When they knew who it was, Kuda would ride out on his bicycle, sometimes for nearly a whole day, and tell the man he had twenty pounds waiting for him from the uncle. He must come to the office in Tjolotjo to fetch it.

It was important work, and they were not allowed to make mistakes.

Prune wished he had a rich uncle to send him money. But he hadn't.

When Carol went back to school at the end of the first school holidays, St Dominic's medicine was banned, and the bully girls didn't come back. School got better, and she made a friend called Bundi.

Carol learned that God and Mum and Dad did look after you, but you had to stand up for yourself and tell the truth. Or else, things never got better. But it was a hard lesson, and she still didn't understand why she was a kaffir lover. She knew by the way the other girls snarled when they said it that it was a bad thing to be, so she didn't talk about Prune or Themba or Jabu anymore, and she said Dad worked for the government.

Just easier.

4

MOTSHODI AND THE CROCODILE CHILDREN

"You would have been killed by Mzilikazi."

Themba's jaw dropped in astonishment. "What do you mean?"

Kuda laughed gently. "My son, it is good to see things from two sides! If you are going to write your scholarship essay about the Matebeles, I need to tell you something that will change many things.

"We were baKwena, the Crocodile people, and we lived close to what is now Bechuanaland. Once we had big villages with herds of cattle and goats and strong storehouses to keep our mealies in. Our village was the biggest and the best of all of them."

Themba's eyes shone with interest at this revelation.

"Our houses were beautiful," Kuda reminisced. "They had mud walls with holes about three feet wide for light and air. A high, pointed thatch roof with more shallow thatch all round to keep the rain out. The main roof had a hole in the top so the smoke from our cooking fires could go out. Everybody was strong and healthy.

"The walls were covered in brown, orange and white patterns. Every year, when the rains were finished, all the women, except those with very young babies, would go up into the hills. They would spend many days looking and looking and collecting special rocks and stones in the bush. There was much dancing when they came back. Everyone would show off their stones. Then for a few weeks, the village was noisy with talking and singing. The women used rocks to smash those coloured stones to powder and mix them with water. Then there would be the time of great painting."

Kuda smiled, his mind filled with memories of his carefree childhood. Themba waited, impatient to hear more but knowing this was an important memory. Then Kuda laughed. "You should have seen it Themba. Every woman was trying to make the best patterns. As each house finished, all the other women would stop what they were doing to come and dance and sing to greet every new painting. Each house had a low mud wall round it to keep our chickens and geese inside, and even these chicken walls had paintings.

"We grew our own *rapoko*[62] and millet and our people and our cattle grew fat. We were a people of peace, and we had been in our village for many, many years.

"Where was this baba?" Themba asked.

"Now it is part of the Northern Transvaal, near the hills of the Magaliesberg."

"Have you got any photos baba?"

"No, we did not have photos in those days. But when the Governor came down to see the school last term, he gave the headmaster an Encyclopaedia Britannica. There might be some pictures in that one."

Themba had heard about the books in the Encyclopaedia. But you were only allowed to use them if you had a "project". Now he had an excuse. Kuda was speaking again.

"During the *'mfecane*[63] we had a worrying time . . ."

"What was the *'mfecane*?"

Kuda was sad. His eyes were deep and unhappy when he looked up. "You have a lot to learn my son. In Zulu it means, 'the crushing' and describes a terrible time in the history of southern Africa. It was a time of the killing. The Zulus and Matebeles went after tribe after tribe, destroying them and their villages. In fact, they depopulated huge areas of southern Africa in the 1820s and 1830s."

"You mean they killed all the people till there was nobody left?"

"I mean exactly that," Kuda nodded. "They were either killed or they ran away. It was a time of Zulu nation building by Shaka. He fought mainly against other Nguni tribes in the Natal area. The Zulu and Matebele were always warriors, and they would stay in an area for a while until it was tired and used up, or they needed more cattle.

---

[62] *rapoko*: one of the most productive of many varieties of native grains
[63] *mfecane*: the 'crushing' of other tribes resulting in almost complete depopulation of a large area in northern South Africa in the early 1800s

"Mzilikazi was building his new nation of the Matebele when he broke away from Shaka. He was soon inaugurated as the Matebele King. The word '*mfecane* began to mean the fear going ahead of them. They killed anyone or anything that stood in their way. Every few years, at the *Inxwala* that was the celebration of the harvest, Mzilikazi would point his spear. Any tribes in that area would be wiped out.

"At first hundreds, then thousands of Matebele would leave their capital to start a new capital. And every few years, every tribe around would be wiped out. Only the strongest young men were allowed to live and become part of the Matebele.

The Matebele are coming . . .

"Our village was one of the biggest of all the baKwena villages. There was panic one day around 1830 as Mzilikazi's Matebele *impi* were coming. But the King had heard that we were different, an unusual village that had lived in the same place for many generations. He was interested. From a distance, he waited and he watched.

"He came to talk to us and asked if he could move one of his small regiments of *impi* to stay with us. Mzilikazi himself stayed for many months, asking many questions. And we were happy to welcome him." Kuda gave a wry smile. "It was better to welcome him than to fight him.

"He was impressed with our big airy houses and painted walls. He wanted to know why our people were so strong and healthy, why the baKwena didn't fight other tribes to get their cattle, and why they still had big herds. He was asking questions all the time.

"Some of our Headmen were invited to see his new capital. They came back saying that it was bigger than anything they had ever seen. It was made in a great circle, with the Chief and the royal family protected on the inside, near a big meeting area they called the *bok*[64] *kraal*[65].

"But they said their houses were terrible! Their huts were made of grass, with round thatched roofs. They were full of smoke, because there was no way for it to get out except through the thatch. To enter, you had to bend in half to get down and in through the door. So they were not impressed!"

---

[64] *bok:* buck or goat
[65] *bok kraal:* the name of the King's meeting place

39

"Some of the villages are still like that," Themba laughed, "so they didn't learn much."

Kuda agreed.

"One special thing was that our baKwena village had a good way of getting rid of sewage. Everybody had to dig a shallow trench, which was just a bit higher than the main trench. Then waste from people and animals was put in the trench. The young boys collected it and put it out to dry so it could go on the millet crops and make them grow better.

"Pooh." Themba made a face. "Didn't it smell? I wouldn't like to be the one collecting the sewage."

Kuda laughed. "What do you think the floors of the huts in Tjolotjo village are made of Themba?"

"I don't know! They are shiny and polished . . ."

"They are dung! Dried and mixed up then spread over the floors. The Matebele and most of the Nguni people have been doing that for a long time. There's no smell."

"Did you collect the dung from the sewage for your floors too, baba?"

"A bit yes, but not all of it, because we used it to make strong compost to grow our vegetables. One of the missionaries at Kuruman was an engineer. He helped us plan sewage drains. Then they would come and buy cabbages and peas that we grew from the seeds they gave us. The village was kept so clean that there was no sickness.

"Mzilikazi watched the herds of fat cattle and goats and asked questions about why we gave them extra food, how we herded them, how they bred so many fat calves. He was interested in how we ploughed the fields and grew the big crops of millet and *rapoko* as well as vegetables for the missionaries. But perhaps most of all, he was amazed that we had been in one place for 30 years. He was our friend. His people mixed with our people.

"Wow Baba! I have always heard that Mzilikazi killed everybody unless they were amaNdebele!"

"Well one night, they were no longer our friends. The stories we are told say that nobody knew why they changed. I think Mzilikazi was just used to living in grass houses for a short time then moving to get more cattle and raid more tribes. His young men had grown restless and wanted to wash their spears in blood.

"The Matebele attacked us."

Themba was horrified. "What happened, baba?"

"We had no defence because it was so unexpected. They killed everyone they could see. They burnt our homes and stole our cattle, goats and chickens and took away all our food. Our rivers became blood. It was a massacre, the worst in the history of the Matebele killings during the 'mfecane. Nobody was spared.

"Mzilikazi was ruthless. He impaled our leaders on sticks through the anus and jabbed the poles into the ground. He left them to die."

Themba could picture every single thing. He wanted Kuda to stop, yet he was morbidly fascinated by the story. His head slumped between his shoulders.

Kuda spoke quietly, his voice harsh. "He roasted some alive. He even took headmen and stripped their skins off while they were still living . . ."

Themba's horror became a groan of despair.

Kuda stopped talking, remembering the agonising stories of his childhood. The stories that had been so fresh in the minds of the elders of his tribe.

"Very few escaped, but one was your great-grandfather Motshodi, who was a young man of 15 at that time."

"You mean my baba 'mkulu that we used to go and see in Bechuanaland?"

"Hayikona. You did meet him when you were only 6 months old. He was very, very old. I am talking about your baba 'mkulu's father. I remember him well as a young boy. He used to love to see me run to catch him after the long walks. He was pleased that I was a fast runner, because he himself was once the fastest in the village.

"When Mzilikazi struck, Motshodi was lucky to be so quick. He just ran. He was filled with fear, filled with the sounds of slaughter and cries of the people behind him. He ran and ran until he found a cave behind a tree in the Magaliesberg. There he hid and watched what was happening in the distance, crying out in terror at what he saw and heard.

"He sat. He watched. He hated the Matebele for their deception. He hated them for their savage brutality. He vowed he would one day take revenge on them for what they had done. He would never forget.

41

"When the *impi* had finished, all you could hear were the groans of the dying. Motshodi stayed hidden and waited before deciding what to do.

"He wanted to know if his mother and father and brothers and sisters had also escaped. If they were hurt, he must go to them. He had seen movement against the flames of the burning huts, and there was now another noise among the sounds of people dying and children crying. It was the snorting and laughing of hyenas in a feeding frenzy as they fought each other to steal the bodies of the dead and the dying.

"Motshodi knew he couldn't wait. He had heard the triumphant singing of the Matebele as they left the village. There was no reason to leave sentries, as they thought they had killed everyone and nobody would want to miss the victory celebrations.

Motshodi had to help if he could. He crept closer. But the hyenas were aggressive, protecting their territory.

"He put together a bunch of wood and twigs and lit it. He knew this would keep them away." Kuda looked at his son, and very quietly with the images colouring the agony in his voice, said, "Imagine it Themba. Imagine creeping into the fires and seeing the bleeding and torn bodies of your family, your friends. Motshodi must have been crying inside.

"He did find his father stuck on a pole. He was still alive, but close to death. Motshodi brought him down. He couldn't bear to see him in his agony. He cried as he stroked his face. He cried until his father was cold. Then he buried him near their special swimming place beside the river. He looked and looked but couldn't find any brothers or sisters. He couldn't find his mother. There were too many bodies and parts of bodies."

"He sat on his heels and just cried. He heard his voice roar from his stomach. He told me it sounded like a wounded lion."

Themba could almost hear it.

Crying with no sound

"When he was quiet again, he looked up to see small children watching him. Nine boys and girls, the oldest about five. I remember him telling me the oldest one could not *touch his other ear*[66]. The youngest was a girl not yet walking. She was crying, with tears running down her fat little

---

[66] *touch his other ear*: before the issuing of birth certificates, it was decided that a child of about six years old could reach across his/her head and touch the opposite ear.

face, crying with no sound because she was so frightened. The children got braver and moved nearer. He opened his arms, and they huddled together in shaking, sobbing, howling sadness and pain.

"Motshodi could not believe these children had been left to die."

Kuda went on speaking with great sadness.

"But Mzilikazi always left the small babies and children to die in the fires. Those that didn't die he knew would be eaten by hyenas and cheetah. The Matebele would now be moving fast to get back to their capital - they couldn't take children with them. They didn't even care what happened to them. But Motshodi knew there would be spies coming to the village in the next days to see if anyone was still alive. They would be killed as well."

"Your great-grandfather couldn't leave the children, so he helped them to the cave where he had been hiding. He kept looking behind to see if they were being followed, wishing the children could move more quickly. He told them they must be quiet, but they were so hungry and crying. He put them near the cave and found water. He filled a gourd, and every child had a drink. Then taking the two oldest children, he crept back to the village.

They found another six crawling and just walking babies and two older boys. Seventeen altogether.

"They carried them back to the cave ... and the babies just wanted to sleep. But Motshodi could see the sky was black with no moon. He needed to get back to the burning village one more time. He thought perhaps he should leave it to the next night, but then he thought this was the best time to go, as the Matebele would be celebrating and dancing for many hours.

"So Motshodi took the oldest boy back with him, leaving the oldest girl to look after the rest of the children. The boy was from the second group and getting near to nine years old. Motshodi had seen that one of the store huts stood a little way away from the rest of the village. Although it was burned on the outside, it looked safe inside. He knew he could find *rapoko* and millet and perhaps some milk in there.

The boy was so frightened, but Motshodi taught him to be brave. They got back to the village, hiding behind some still-standing huts. They found the store hut and carried back with them as much as they could to feed the children."

"Why haven't you told me this before, baba?"

"I wish Motshodi had been here to tell you himself, but now he has died. I thought for your sake you should feel you were amaNdebele and not be different by knowing you were also baKwena. As you're growing older, your skin is starting to grow lighter. I knew one day the questions would come."

Themba nodded gravely. "That was a wise thing baba. But what happened next? How did he look after the children?"

"Motshodi knew the only way to escape was to take the children high into the Magaliesberg. He did not sleep that night. Before the sky grew light, he woke the children, as they had to move from this small cave before daylight.

"He knew a beautiful valley with clear water, where he and his friend Pinde would come sometimes when they were supposed to be herding cattle or hunting."

Themba relaxed a little – the story was kinder now.

"Pinde was smaller than Motshodi, with light golden skin. He didn't live in a village because he was a one of the San people. Today people call them Bushmen. For most of the year, Pinde stayed on the edge of the desert near the Magaliesberg.

Once when there was a great drought, he had been sent to the baKwena village to ask them to fill some gourds and ostrich eggs with water. Motshodi helped him carry them back to his people. They became friends and had many adventures together. Pinde gave Motshodi's family two goats to say thank you.

"One day when they were climbing in the mountains, they had walked through a tight passage between big rocks, which were closed overhead like a tunnel. They found a beautiful valley with a spring of clean water, which was running all year round. It was their secret place. They would laugh and dive into the rock pools, swim up to the waterfalls and catch some bony and not-good-to-eat fish.

"So Motshodi took the children there. He taught them how to get through the rock passage. He told them to help him build some houses from the good thatch grass growing between the rocks. These houses could not be seen from the water. They could be seen only if you went through more passages.

"Many times over the next days, he crept back to the village, which was still burning, to look for anything he could find to help feed the children. As soon as the Matebele had killed the people they didn't want and taken the people they did want and left the children to die, they left in a hurry – and they sometimes left things behind."

"Motshodi found chickens, four geese, and two lambs. The geese were good sentries, as they made a big noise cackling and attacking people they didn't know. They also laid eggs.

The children wanted to eat the eggs, but Motshodi would not let them. He told them the geese needed to have grandchildren, then there would be many eggs for everyone. They also learned how to cook the bony fish.

"He trained those children to hide, to be as still as death if danger was around. And sometimes, it was. Once some Boers nearly came right down the stone passage but didn't, and one other time, two amaNdebele walked through and sat beside the water in the pool. They left without knowing the children were there.

"He trained even the young children to be like guards for each other. Every child had his duty time when he or she would look after the babies and make sure they didn't go near the water till they could swim.

"Nobody saw them. Nobody knew they were there. But Motshodi told me he felt so sad to see that the baby girl, who was only about six months old when he found her, was still crying without sound. Tears would run down her face and into her mouth and down her chest. But still no noise. She was too frightened. Motshodi would pick her up and rock her. She wanted her mother. He cried inside for that little baby. He wanted to see her laugh and play. Her heart was broken, and one day she did not wake up.

Motshodi told me about her so many times.

"Early one morning, there was a terrible honking from the geese. The children fled to their hiding places.

"Motshodi! Motshodi!' a whisper echoed round his cave. It was Pinde.

Pinde comes to help

"'Pinde! Pinde!' The two friends danced and laughed. The children peeped out to see what was happening. Then clip-clop behind him came Motshodi's two best goats – one called Lololo, because she was always running far away, and the other called Gopo, because he was just a stupid goat and always in trouble.

"'These goats came to find me,' Pinde said.

"When all the excitement calmed down, and the children had stroked the goats and the goats had been fed, Motshodi and Pinde talked.

"'I knew something had happened when I saw the goats,' Pinde told him. 'But I hoped and hoped you were all right, then I thought they would have taken you because you are strong and you can run so fast. I kept going back.

Once I thought I saw someone carrying something from the village. So I wondered, 'Is that Motshodi?' I followed until it was too dark, and I lost that someone. Then last week when I found the goats, I knew, if that someone was Motshodi, he would be here.'

"So Pinde went back to his family to ask if he could stay to help Motshodi.

"They lived about three years in the Magaliesberg valley. But Motshodi knew he could not look after the children much longer. Two little babies had died, and the others were getting noisy and careless. Sometimes they even ran out to the veldt through the rocky entrance, to play near the Matebele village.

"Motshodi and Pinde decided they must move to the desert because there they'd be safer. The Matebele were not good in the desert, so they didn't go there. But their new royal capital, Mhlanhlandhlela, was close to the hidden valley in the Magaliesberg. So they had to make careful plans.

"That day Motshodi came to Pinde and said, 'I can speak good Sindebele and I can cut my hair in the amaNdebele way. I learned when I was a young boy and the Matebele were in our village. Can you help me make an *assegai*[67]? We can kill two monkeys from up on those rocks to make my *'mbetju* and find some feathers for my head.

Then I will wait until they come back from another raid, and I will

---

[67] *assegai:* a hard-tipped spear

46

hide with them, and they will not know I am there. I need to live with them for a short time in Mhlanhlandhlela so I can find out what they are doing and learn how to find those missionaries who used to buy cabbages from us. I don't know where they live, but the Matebele will know. Can you look after the children for me?

"Pinde said he could if he could first go home and get two sisters to help him.

"So it was agreed. When Pinde and his two sisters came back, Motshodi left for Mhlanhlandhlela.

Before he left he dressed as an Ndebele warrior and one of Pinde's sisters shouted 'Aiyeeee!' in fright because she did not recognise him.

"Motshodi lived with the Matebele, pretending to be one of the *mashoja* captured from another tribe. He was there for eight days. He heard about the missionary that Mzilikazi called Moshete and how to find him. He heard they were going on another raid in two days because they were boasting about how many cattle they would bring back. He also heard them talking about children living in the Magaliesberg."

"It was definitely time to move," Themba said.

A long walk to Kuruman

"When he knew most of the *impi* had gone off raiding, Motshodi, Pinde, and his two sisters started to guide those little children through the mountains and the hills. Some were still small, and it was rocky and steep. With all the wild animals and snakes, it was a wonder they got through.

"They made some baskets to hold the chickens and six baby geese and strapped them to the backs of the goats. Gopo, the stupid goat, tried to roll and nearly squashed two chickens. They made such a squawking that he didn't do it again. They left the big geese behind and blocked up the rock entrance, as they knew they would be happy in the valley.

"They walked far on the first day and got beyond Mhlanhlandhlela. They didn't see any Matebele. But early the next morning, there was a great squawking. The four geese they left behind had escaped from the valley and followed them. Pinde was cross.

"'We should not have taken their babies,' he said. 'Now the Matebele can find us.'"   But they didn't.

"It took them four days of walking and resting. The oldest boy, who could help with carrying, was now only 12 years old. Pinde's sisters carried the young ones. Motshodi was happy to see the children smiling and laughing again now that there were girls to hug them and be like mothers.

"They hid in the daytime and walked at night, but the little ones were too tired. Then your great-grandfather was lucky. He found two other baKwena who had escaped from another massacre, so they helped them carry the younger children.

"They all learned to live with the goats for milk. Two days later, six wild goats joined them. So one day, Pinde thanked the biggest new goat for coming to provide food for the children and said he was very sorry he was going to have to kill him. Motshodi swore to me that the goat became quite calm and said that was all right. After the goat had had his throat cut, they roasted him on a fire. The children tasted meat for the first time in many years.

"Pinde also showed them bulging roots that gave them water, but they couldn't grow food because the desert was too dry. So they learned to poison small arrows and darts that the Bushmen used to kill buck. And they all learned to say sorry to the buck they had killed and let him know that he was brave to give his life, and he could now feed the children.

"They had to be careful, because the children were much lighter than most Matebele. Even so, they were darker than the San, but it was hard for baKwena children to 'disappear' into the bush like the San children did.

"Your great-grandfather was worried, because the baKwena people knew learning was important. He would try to teach the children with one of the sisters telling them stories of the ancestors. She would teach them using the sayings of the baKwena people, like the one I say to you sometimes *'It is better to live like a servant now so that one day you can live like a king'*.

"But the children grew tired of living like servants.

"Motshodi knew that the missionaries were training people in farming and woodwork. He had decided they had to get to Kuruman Mission to speak to the one they called Moshete. He knew his name in English was Moffat. Now he also knew where his mission was and how to get there.

"But he would have to be careful, because it meant leaving the desert and going back through country where there were still many Matebele. So again he dressed as a member of the Matebele *impi* and melted into their newest regiment to hear what they were saying. Mzilikazi was moving north across the Shashi River because his warriors were restless again.

"Motshodi waited until they were ready to go before he crossed into Khama country. Pinde had told him that King Khama was very kind to people who had been damaged by the Matebele."

Themba was fascinated. He had heard stories of the wonders of Mzilikazi the fearsome king warrior, but never this side of the story.

"I wish you had told me all this before, baba," he said.

"As I said, we live in Matebeleland, Themba. When Mzilikazi conquered new tribes, the people he conquered trusted him to look after them when they became Matebele. The Matebele Chiefs treat their slaves harshly, but once they have proved themselves, they become part of the tribe and are looked after very well. It is a bit different now because I was appointed from the Bechuanaland police to become the District Assistant here. So I am accepted. As a boy born in Tjolotjo and with an amaNdebele mother, you must become amaNdebele too. It is dangerous for you to know these things when you are too young.

"When I was a child, we lived for many years, never knowing when a stronger tribe would come and kill us again. Since the white people came, Southern Rhodesia has had borders so that other tribes and armies cannot come and just kill people.

"We have now become Matebele, and we know this because we have been well looked after. But at heart we are sometimes still baKwena."

"Is there anything written about this?" Themba needed to know more.

"Robert Moffat wrote diaries and books. Before his time, there is very little, because nobody could read or write. So the stories were told by the elders of the tribe from grandfather to father to grandson, sitting round the fire. You remember those evenings of stories."

Themba nodded with a smile. He did remember them so well. "But you didn't tell us this story baba!"

Kuda smiled. "Now you can write it down for your scholarship. I have something else you would be interested in."

Kuda went off, leaving Themba pondering all he had heard.

Themba was now 12 years old, and he was studying and writing for a scholarship to Goromonzi Secondary School, the leading government school in the country. By learning there for six years, he would be able to go to university. This was his dream.

When he was a small child he loved going with his father to watch him help the Chiefs and Headmen hold their *enkundleni*[68] or tribal court. Everyone was entitled to tell their story, and everyone involved would say their part in the problem and ask questions. If the decision was too difficult, the Chief could ask for help from all the Headmen. And if the person complaining didn't like what the Chief ruled, then Carol's father, Mr Davidson, the Native Commissioner, would speak with the Chiefs and suggest ideas to them to help fix the problem.

Themba loved the *enkundleni* days, especially the feasts and meat and dancing they shared afterwards. The court sessions made him want to learn all he could about law so he could help his people more.

Finding Robert Moffat

"This is what Robert Moffat wrote."

Kuda was back. He handed Themba a piece of paper to read: "*Many an hour I walked pensively among these scenes of desolation, casting my thoughts back to the time when these now desolate habitations teemed with life and revelry, and when the hills and dales echoed with heathen joy. Now nothing remains but dilapidated walls and heaps of stones and rubbish, which form a covert for the game and for the lion.*

"*Oh, that I had a thousand lives and a thousand bodies! All of them should be devoted to no other employment but to preach Christ to these degraded, despised, yet beloved mortals.*

"That was written by Robert Moffat when he was reporting back to the London Missionary Society. He was talking of the baKwena – our people. He was talking about our village. We had been a peaceful, healthy people. Now any baKwena who had survived from other Matebele raids dared not look up, dared not speak the truth. They survived on food nobody else wanted.

"Your great-grandfather wanted to find a different way for his children to live. So Pinde agreed to look after the children, and Motshodi

---

[68] *enkundleni:* (lit.) "in the field". Came to mean the occasion when the Native Commissioners went out to villages to hold local court cases and resolve other tribal issues.

went to find Kuruman Mission. He wanted to see the man Moshete, who was a good friend to Mzilikazi. Moffat could speak Setswana[69] and a bit of Sindebele. His mission had many children learning things that would be helpful for them.

"You remember how your great-grandfather was such a good runner? That was so lucky again, because he didn't want to leave the children and Pinde too long. So he ran and ran and ran for many hundreds of miles.

"When he reached Kuruman at last, he found that Moshete was away. He was so sad and tired. He was sadder and more worried when he heard that Moshete had gone to see Mzilikazi. He was told that Moshete had already been there for one moon – that would be just under one month.

"It was known that Mzilikazi completely trusted Moshete and had commanded him to come.

Motshodi was nervous, because if Moshete was friends with Mzilikazi, he might not welcome baKwena people."

"But speaking a little bit in Setswana, Moshete's wife became excited when your great-grandfather told her his story. She said he must wait and that it was important that he should wait.

"In the meantime, Moshete's wife fed him and looked after him. They sat for many hours as Motshodi told her everything that had happened to them and how important it was now for his children to get education so they could have a better future. Moshete's wife taught him many things about woodwork, heating metals, and beating them to make what you wanted in the forge.

"Motshodi taught me all of that too. That is why I am very useful to Mr Davidson and I can fix anything," Kuda said proudly. "At that time, Motshodi had never seen anything like it! He was amazed and knew his children had much to learn from Kuruman."

"What happened when Moshete got back?"

"Well, it took a long time. Motshodi had to wait another month before he saw the wagons, which meant Moshete was returning. Motshodi had worried so much about Pinde and his sisters and how they were looking after the children that he had nearly decided to say to Moshete's wife that he would have to go.

"Now he had seen the wagons, he felt he could stay one more day. He

---

[69] Setswana: language of the 'Tswana people living primarily in Bechuanaland

watched Moshete's wife go up to the white man who got down from the wagon. The man looked very tired. She helped him back into their house. Motshodi knew he had to wait for many more days before he could see Moshete, so he hung his head and wondered whether he should go now and come back later.

"When he looked up, there was the white man standing, looking at him for a long time. The white man did not move.

"It was Moshete. It was as though he didn't want to talk to Motshodi.

"Motshodi now knew it was polite to stand up when you were with white people. He did so carefully and slowly, clapping his hands in welcome. He didn't want to do anything wrong.

"'I see you Motshodi. I see you as amaNdebele,' said Moshete in a loud voice.

"'I see you Moshete. I am Motshodi. I am baKwena.'

"'From where?'

"'From Magaliesberg kraal that was destroyed.'

"Moshete walked to Motshodi to be nearer to him. He looked him in the eyes and shook him by the shoulders as though he was angry. 'You cannot be,' he said. 'They are all dead!'

"'I am not dead. I ran from the Magaliesberg when the Matebele burnt our village. Then I went back. I have some children . . .'

"'Moshete put his hand on my grandfather's shoulder again and he just cried. Then he knelt at Motshodi's feet, looked to the sky and spoke so softly,

'Thank you Lord, for this remnant of your most persecuted people.'

"He translated what he had said so Motshodi could understand.

"Moshete could not believe that this man had survived. He had been to his village and written that piece I read to you just now, because he was so sad. He wanted to know everything.

"When Motshodi told him he had 15 children living in the desert after the raid in their village, Moshete cried out and held Motshodi's hand for a very long time.

"We must bring them here. Tomorrow!" he said.

"So the next day, Moshete and Motshodi got the wagon ready and inspanned some new oxen to pull it. And they went in the wagon to fetch the children.

When they grew near, Motshodi told Moshete he needed to go ahead of the wagon, or they would all be very frightened and would run into the desert to escape.

"Only Pinde had ever seen a wagon before, so Motshodi told him what was happening. Then he ran back to Moshete and said all was ready.

"When the wagon arrived, the children were so excited that they danced and sang all the way back to Kuruman. Lololo and Gopo, the geese and the chickens came too. They became a little baKwena part of Kuruman. The 15 children and Pinde and his sisters lived in the mission in Kuruman, and they told Moshete of the dreadful things that had been done to the baKwena people.

"'Moshete wrote them all down. That is how we know so much. That is how the London Missionary Society heard about it.

"In the end, Motshodi decided to stay in Khama country, where there was a good king and the people were happy.

Kuda finished up saying, "When your great-grandfather died, there were so many people who loved and thanked him. Many important people from Bechuanaland were there. Also white people from Kuruman Mission and men from the British government in Cape Town. There was even one man who came from London."

Themba couldn't believe he hadn't known all this. But already he felt different – stronger and more determined to be like his great-grandfather.

"There is one interesting thing that I have never been able to find out about," Kuda was talking again. "Your great-grandfather had another name."

"What sort of name?"

"Jan Grootboom."

"That sounds Afrikaans. Big tree. Why would the Voortrekkers give our grandfather another name? They are the ones who must have called him that."

"Perhaps one day you can find out, Themba."

Themba knew he was going to spend a lot of time with that Encyclopaedia Britannica. He also knew that his essay for the scholarship to Goromonzi would no longer be about the military might of Mzilikazi but about the courage of his great-grandfather and the 15 children. And about the killing of the baKwena people and Moshete's diaries.

There was a time to be brave, and this was that time. Goromonzi was in Mashonaland, where they would probably agree about Mzilikazi anyway.

But first he needed to tell Prune and Carol.

Probably not mention it to Jabu.

A painting by William Cornwallis Harris of an unnamed Matebele capital. It was painted in 1836, so it was probably Mhlanhlandhlela, Mzilikazi's capital, near the Magaliesberg hills.

5

ROSIE AND THE JAYCEE[70]

"Why Lalan? Why are you my mother, but you are white and I am black?"

Sister McLeod sighed. She was helping Prune make his bed before school.

He had been coming home with a tight face lately, his eyes not meeting hers. When she asked him about it, he brushed it off with slips of phrases "Ah, the boys are saying things" or "What is illegitimate?" She had smiled, as he loved using big words, sometimes blissfully inappropriately. Five syllables were indeed a big word, but what did that question hide?

The time had obviously come to tell this precious child, the only one she could ever call her own, the story and the anguish of that October night nearly 13 years ago.

"You are my miracle baby, Prune. I am your mother because I signed lawyers' papers for you and adopted you. Naison signed more papers to be your guardian. But we are not your birth parents."

"I did not come out of your tummy because of your copulation?"

Lalan answered thoughtfully and slowly, to give suitable gravity to the question, looking into the anxious face beside her. "You did not come out of my tummy, Prune. You came out of the tummy of the most beautiful young girl who I found lying unconscious on the steps of the clinic. You were born too small and too soon. And she died much too soon."

"Did she die because of me?"

"I don't think so. She was very sick. We don't know what happened. We don't know who she was or where she came from. Mr Davidson put out notices all through Matebeleland, but there was no answer. So he put

---

[70] JAYCEE: J.C. Junior Certificate. This was introduced to provide a level of educational evaluation for children who were unlikely to continue to O or A levels.

out notices all through Mashonaland too. But still there was no answer."

Prune's face puckered. His lip trembled and brown eyes grew large with apprehension as he found the courage to ask in a tight voice, "Did my father never come to find her? Does nobody love me?"

"Two people loved you so much that they fought many battles and overcame many difficulties to look after you."

"You, Lalan . . . and Naison."

"Me and Naison and Mr Davidson and lots of other people who helped us try to find out about her. We all love you Prune. But no, we could never find out who your mother or father were – and we don't know why."

Lalan moved over to the battered old bandage cupboard and pulled out a shoebox. "You were so small that we had to make this your bed."

She had left the much-washed, ironed and faded old tea towel in place – exactly as it had once been.

"Ayee no! I did not fit here Lalan!" Prune laughed. "This would fit only a big rat. Not even a rabbit could live in here." He gently pulled back the tea towel in astonishment. "My head was here," he said solemnly as he looked and thought it through. Then his attention was caught by the rusty links of a tiny chain. He gently pulled it out and looked at the little plate in the middle. But rust had obscured the writing.

"Does it say anything Lalan?"

"Aye it does. It says Rosie."

"Rosie." He breathed. "It is a beautiful name for a beautiful mother."

"I will get it cleaned for you Prune and keep it safe for you."

He wasn't going to let it go. "Lalan I'm a big boy now. Can I keep it?"

"Of course, of course."

Oh, how hard it was going to be to let this little boy go. His quick smile, his cheeky face, his constant optimism, his willingness to help. She loved him achingly – great waves of warmth would sweep over her precise little Scottish nature whenever he breezed into the clinic.

Sister McLeod had acknowledged a generation ago that she would never marry or have her own child, living in this remote part of the world. But this hadn't mattered once Prune came along. When his first word was "Lalan", she had a new identity and that was who she became to everyone.

"But Lalan! Will I succeed without a mother?" the anxious little pucker was back on his face.

"Prune, life is a game, and it depends how you play the game whether you succeed or not. Nobody knows where they will be born, or who their mother or father will be. They don't know if they will be Chinese or Arab, white or black. They don't know if they will be born in a house full of beautiful things with good food to eat, or if they will be born in a tent with only camels to ride on, only dates to eat, and no furniture but rugs on the desert sand."

Prune tried to imagine that tent, but it was too hard. "Or if they would be born in a hut of pole and dagga?"

"Yes indeed . . . or in a hut of pole and *dagga*[71]. But once they have been born, they can learn. They can copy, they can work things out, they can watch those people they love, even those people they don't love very much. I know that you must go to school so that your game of life will give you chances. That is why I was such a *shuper*[72] to the headmaster at the village school till he made you a place. I know you must keep going to church, so you understand that God looks after you no matter what. And I know that you must also learn all about being an amaNdebele boy. That is what you are and that is why Naison is your baba too."

"And one day, if I work hard and play the game right, I will own a big shop and a motor car. Then I'll look after you for ever, Lalan."

They laughed at the thought. "But do you mind . . ." He faltered ". . . but does it matter . . ."

He paused again, running the little chain between his fingers

"Does what matter, my boy?"

"If one day when I am very rich, I can try to find my birth family?"

"One day, when you are very rich, I will help you find your birth family."

His face relaxed into a big toothy grin.

Lalan watched as the boy carefully laid the rusty little bracelet under his pillow.

As quickly as it had come, it was over. He ran to give her a quick hug

---

[71] *dagga*: this word has two meanings: mud, or, in context, marijuana
[72] *shuper*: nuisance

and disappeared through the clinic door. It was time for night time talking with Naison. He was after all an amaNdebele boy.

Prune reckoned he was one lucky guy! Now he knew just what was what and it was time to stop those boys at school saying angry, bad words about his mother. He could now hold his head up and say, "My mother's name is Rosie and she was beautiful. But she died because she was very sick when I was born. I am lucky, because so many people loved me so much that they adopted me. So now I belong to everyone."

He figured a little extension of the truth was allowed after all the years of being told he was nobody at all.

Prune was now clever at sums and writing, and he copied everthing Carol had shared with him. After he had helped with *situpas*, Lalan had caused big trouble until he was allowed to go to school. At first, the headmaster hated him and beat him all the time, but now he was clever, the headmaster liked him. When he finished standard six, he said he was now clever enough to do *Jaycee*.

Only problem was, there was no school in Tjolotjo where he could do *Jaycee*. It needed another two years of learning at junior secondary level, and that was going to be a bit of a "process". Prune really didn't know about the process. He just wanted to do the *Jaycee*.

"Could I go to school in Bulawayo?" he asked the headmaster.

"Well you could, but it would be hard to get you into a school there. The only place where you could write the *Jaycee* would be at Kutama, which is near Salisbury."

Prune's eyes widened apprehensively.

The headmaster of his school wasn't sure how that could be done either, so it all looked pretty hopeless. One day the headmaster knocked at the door of the clinic and said, "Prune, it would make our school very important to have a pupil doing Jaycee. Maybe the government might even listen to us and let us do two more years of teaching after primary school. I will help you study if you are prepared to work so hard, harder than you have ever worked before. And we can do it by correspondence."

So for two years after junior school had finished, he had worked at home, doing all the learning he needed by correspondence. But this time the brown paper parcels did not come all the way from Australia as Carol's had; they just came from the Ministry of Education in Salisbury. He was sad that Carol was no longer in Tjolotjo, but Mr Davidson had been posted as Native Commissioner in the Arcturus area. So they had to write letters to stay friends now.

Sometimes what he was learning and what Carol was learning was the same, so he would write to her about it and work things out until he understood them. He worked and he worked. The letter had at last come, saying he was good enough to do *Jaycee* and that he had special permission to go to Kutama Mission to write his exam with the other pupils there.

"Well!" Lalan was almost as excited as Prune. "Now we've got to get you up to Salisbury. I need to get more supplies for the clinic because I am running very short of *muti* for malaria and it will soon be mosquito season. So I think the government could afford to send me up there. We'll go by train and worry about how to get you out to Kutama once we get there!"

"Wow! By train! That would be so exciting Lalan, thank you, thank you, thank you!"

Everyone wanted to do *Jaycee* now, because you could be a teacher and earn much money. Teacher Prune Msipa. The title made him feel important.

But he knew he didn't really want to be a teacher, but maybe something to do with selling things. There was now a big hurry to learn, so he must work hard. Not everyone was a hard worker, so they were not clever enough to do Jaycee. But now that he could do it, his friends were jealous and didn't like him anymore. He thought there were still many "buts" about doing Jaycee.

Prune really wanted to work in a store. The storekeeper in Tjolotjo had said he could, but he must get his *Jaycee* first before he could pay him. That was why he had done all that hard work and helped in the store on weekends, because working in the store was MUCH better than being a teacher.

Working in the store was more fun than sweeping baba Naison's clinic, and if he passed his *Jaycee* he would get money to save and buy things. Sister McLeod said you must always save half the money you earn. But Naison whispered that she was "amaScottish", which meant she saved all her money and didn't like to spend it. So perhaps Naison would now allow him to spend a little bit.

Sister McLeod spent a lot of money on Prune, so he didn't understand the not-spending amaScottish that Naison had told him about. She paid fees and bought him a new khaki shirt and shorts with a blue-and-yellow striped tie. And he had shiny new shoes too. He didn't like wearing them, so he would polish them, blow on them, polish again till they shone like mirrors, and then wrap them up in their box when he got home.

Here he was now 14 years old, wearing his own striped tie, khaki shirt and shorts, and smartly polished shoes. Sitting at a desk in a big hall at Kutama with other boys doing the *Jaycee* too.

Now, he looked like all the other boys. It was good to be one of them. He looked round the room at all the faces. Then he looked again and then he was sure. That boy near the back was Jabu. He was writing *Jaycee* too! He tried to wave, but Jabu didn't want to look at him.

His eyes took it all in. Lots of striped ties – he had never seen so many. He looked hopefully at Jabu again. But – no luck

While they were waiting, he counted the number of boys writing *Jaycee*. There were 58 boys. But no girls.

He knew African girls had so much work to do in the villages that they did not need education, but he now had a sister, Maura, who was cross that she was not allowed to go to school. Prune gave her all the books he kept from the time he sat under the fig tree with Carol. He rubbed out the answers so Maura couldn't cheat, but he had seen her holding the pages up to the sun and he knew. She cheated! But even so, she was learning and talking to Prune and asking questions.

"Open your folders." A hard voice cracked across the hall. It came from a big loud man with ginger hair who was called "the invigilator". That was a hard word, but it meant the one who watched to see if you were looking at anyone else's work.

Prune opened his folder and read the writing:

Junior Certificate 1953

Southern Rhodesia Department of Native Education,

Causeway. Salisbury.

"Start . . . now!"

He carefully wrote his name, VUSIMUZI MSIPA, took a deep breath, and turned the page.

6

SWOT VAC AND LALAN'S 70th

Carol packed up her books for the last time. Ahead stretched another six glorious weeks of swot vac before she returned to school to write A-levels. The first two weeks had escaped too quickly . . . catching up with friends or lying toasting in the sun beside the sports club pool. They'd been interspersed with piano practice, rules of composition, theory of music and musicians – all enjoyable, easy stuff. Too easy really. There had to be a catch!

Now she had to get down to concentrated study, especially for history. She had heard the stories so often and taken so much for granted, but her chosen essay subject, *"Lobengula and Rhodes, traitors or heroes?"* was proving to be so full of contradictions and anomalies that she'd made several false starts only to crumple up the sheets and target the waste paper basket in sheer frustration. She glared at the pile of scrunched writings from yesterday afternoon, the trash of her muddled thoughts.

Usually Carol was much more productive in the early hours of the morning, but today, after another hour of scrumpled papers she pushed her chair away from the desk. Today was just not going to work.

In the pre-dawn quiet, she went to the fridge to pour a glass of her favourite Grana passionfruit cordial, then walked out to a favourite long legs-up chair under the big fig. This wasn't the same big fig tree of her childhood, as her father had been transferred to Goromonzi, no longer as a Native Commissioner but a full District Commissioner. They'd moved from Matebeleland to Mashonaland as a result.

Her father didn't feel as much at ease up here, not knowing the language or the people as well. It had been a difficult posting, and he was not enjoying it. It seemed far removed from the advances he had been able to make in the Nyamandhlovu area. She was glad they lived a good half hour away from the office, in a village called Ruwa. It was distanced just enough, from the problems he was facing.

From Angus's perspective, there'd been an almost imperceptible but definite increase in what he felt was an undermining of the work they were doing. It was causing agitation in young black Rhodesians. That agitation in itself seemed to have a pattern - quickly showing up as truculence and obduracy.

Carol had listened sadly, as her father described it to her as it as being a 'well organised' affair, but couldn't trace exactly what it was or where it came from. Patterns of discontent seemed to change instantly and unpredictably. - but his instincts were aroused because with that change, the young people in particular, suddenly seemed to be saying the same thing, in exactly the same way - even to using the same words. At the same time, they were showing less and less respect for the Chiefs. His concern was that in some way or other they were being 'programmed' - but whatever it was, was an enormous distraction, delaying urgently needed development of the area.

Getting through year 12 had to be Carol's focus this year, rather than really understanding the ins and outs of her father's concerns. But she did notice his face was often drawn with anxiety and the stress of the office.

She gazed into the distance, following the horizontal dips, troughs and heights of the line of deep blue hills. The sky lightened, anticipating the moment the sun would burst above the horizon as it did so suddenly, at this latitude. Within the first hour in the promised heat of this November day, it would quickly bleach out the vibrancy of that blue horizon.

There was an almost breathless, stillness in these early mornings, anticipating the day ahead. No movement in the leaves – no clouds welling up - just the uninterrupted white-blue of a heating sky, against the still-sleeping land. The paean of welcome from the chirrups and whistles of bird song, complemented the crystal-clear air, thinned at an altitude of almost 5,000 feet above sea level.

She heard a sonorous *hoo hoo-hoo-hoo* followed by the quiet double time answer *hoo-hoo hoo-hoo* and smiled contentedly, trying to spot the distinctive stately walk of a pair of ground hornbills as they boomed their way across the veldt . . . but knowing they could be up to three miles away. Their shining sable black feathers, brilliant scarlet necks and faces and yellow eyes, fringed with absurdly long eyelashes were a thrilling sight, as they made slow progress, searching for frogs or lizards among the tufted grass of the veldt below.

Carol shut her eyes and drank in the sounds, smelt the dung dust of the bush and the warmth of sun on her face as a rush of air brushed her cheek like warm silk. A sudden gust whipped up a whirligig of twigs and leaves. *Oh thank you God*, she breathed, *for allowing me to be born in this unique corner of the world. I feel completely one with you even with all the disruptions of our move to Mashonaland.*

Her thoughts drifted back to life in Tjolotjo and of how much everything had changed since they left.

Jabu. She wondered so often where he was now. Their paths had diverged when his family went to Tegwani. The last she heard of him was a few years ago, when Prune said he had seen him when they had both been writing JC at Kutama Mission.

She'd often find herself staring out of a window, wondering whether Jabu had been able to persist with his education long enough to write year 12 as she was doing. She was doubtful, because he was simply not very interested in school. But he was a natural leader, with his gentle charm and intelligence – a promising young African hope for the future of what was now the Federation of Rhodesia and Nyasaland.

Carol's father and Jabu's father had met again about five years ago, when they had both been made part of a team of people elected to help set up the African Affairs Board for the Federal Government. This Board was designed to look after the interests of Africans, and its formation gave it statutory power to act on any apparent discrimination – which of course there was, although it was an awful lot better than it had been.

They had met regularly since, on their frequent trips to Salisbury for meetings.

Angus always got on well with Nkanyiso Ncube and found him a serious and forward-thinking man. But lately, he had confided that he was concerned about Jabu. They hadn't had enough time after the last meeting to discuss it much further or go into details. "His impatience and temper are short," he had said in passing . . . "it's not like him . . ." was the only indication he had given.

Angus had meant to write and encourage him, but more insistent demands and a raft of pressing problems and priorities pushed back that all important follow up.

Prune's flying colours

Prune? Well Prune! She smiled involuntarily, thinking of smiley Prune. He had passed his JC with flying colours. When Lalan was transferred to a clinic near Balla Balla about 20 miles the other side of Bulawayo, she had insisted Naison came with her as the clinic Orderly. So Prune's parents were still with him. Lalan lived in one house near the clinic, and Naison and his wife and children lived in another. Prune lived in both houses.

He had been offered a job with a big-hearted Italian storeowner, Mr Bellini. From his first menial position, he progressed to making lists; lists of every stock item, how many articles they had bought, how many were left from the last lot. As they sold, Prune was the one who decided when it was time to advise Mr Bellini to get new stock.

He wrote to Carol every month, so she had a pretty good idea of how he was doing. He told her he was making sure he was popular with the customers, black and white, always asking them how they were and trying to remember details about sick children or happy events, just as Mr Bellini had told him. Then he would find out if there was anything they would like the store to get for them. And he always made sure that customers were happy with the help they got from the store.

Carol had smiled as she read the letters. Prune was insatiable. He was always learning, always proving himself by doing little extra, thoughtful deeds. He must have really proved himself, as the good-hearted Mr Bellini trusted him with more and more responsibility.

His only sadness was that Mr Bellini had a son called Marco, who did absolutely nothing but eat chocolates all day and lounge about. Marco resented Prune and was getting more and more angry and belligerent with him for taking "his" job. He constantly accused Prune when things went missing or were misplaced, nearly always covering up his own stupidity.

But, fortunately, Mr Bellini knew his son - very well.

A few months ago, Prune's letter had been bursting with excitement, as Mr Bellini made him "the accountant". So now, along with making sure there was enough stock, he oversaw all the book-keeping and banking as well. His little sister Maura also worked for Mr Bellini, helping behind the counter. Prune and Maura were such good friends, that she was like a real sister, but she wasn't – because she was Naison's blood daughter . . . she wasn't adopted like him. Prune still had an ache in his heart because despite trying everything, nobody had any idea who his real parents were.

Prune's letter last month, said he had been saving up for months so he could afford to give Lalan a party for her 70th birthday. It was to say thank you for everything she had done for him as well as to celebrate her years of hard work in the clinic.

Prune had said that everyone Lalan had helped or worked with, loved her and she deserved the best birthday he could give her.

Although he seemed very excited by what he had described in his planning for the party – he gave a hint that there was going to be another very important event taking place. It was a secret – even to Carol.

Carol studied a recent photograph enclosed in yesterday's letter. She was aware of how much time had passed. She hardly recognised this tall, slim man in jacket and tie, but still with that distinctive wide grin; or the pretty girl standing beside him, with Maura dressed to the nines in a frock with the cinched waist and large, puffy skirt so fashionable in 1957.

Carol thought of how she and her friends at school would spend their pocket money buying lemons to take back to the hostel and squeeze out the juice. Petticoats were soaked in lemon juice then without squeezing and dripping everywhere, they were draped over an umbrella, or anything that would hold the petticoats open. When dry, they were as stiff as paper and made nipped waist skirts stand right out! There were lemons galore in the dorm before any dance with Prince Edward, or PE, their 'brother' school. As the wall of hopeful maroon blazers walked across the room to choose who to dance with, the fullest skirts and tiniest waists were vital to a girl's popularity! BUT beware the rain! When it rained, you ended up with sticky legs as the juice ran out of the petticoat! What memories!

Putting on the party

Prune and Maura were dressed up because they had been practising what they'd wear for Lalan's birthday party. Prune was organising it in the Village Hall, but he was determined that Lalan's 70th birthday party must be a surprise. He was also determined that he wanted all Lalan's friends there.

Carol had been a bit anxious about this, because in a rural area like Balla Balla, black and white were not yet used to attending parties of this kind together.

She laughed to herself, as she saw every spare inch of paper covered in writing - sideways, upside down – wherever he could fit in a forgotten sentence. She started reading and was pleased to see that his detailed descriptions bubbled with enthusiasm.

Prune had decided to ask Mr Bellini what he thought about inviting everyone who should come whether they were black or white. The genial shop owner had looked stern for a bit, then nodded gravely, suggesting Prune should send out the invitations and just see what happened. He concluded that Prune should not be upset if not many people accepted the invitation, because some might not make it. But Prune should know that those who did accept really wanted to be there.

He also decided Mr Bellini was indeed a wise man.

Prune sent out over fifty carefully written invitations, drawing a little flower on the corner of each pink page and emphasising the need to keep the event a surprise, with instructions that they would have to be at the hall at 6:15 on the dot. He was excited, pleased - then bothered, because they had all accepted! Mr Bellini might be a wise man, but he had certainly been wrong about this.

Prune had worked out that he had about enough money to cover the costs if up to 80% of the people had accepted. Now he was going to be short. That was a real problem because he couldn't borrow money from Lalan this time!

Prune wanted everything to honour Lalan, so with Maura, he decided to make it a Scottish party. The two of them went hunting round a funny little shop in Bulawayo, where they had found the X shaped white cross on a blue background that was the flag of St Andrew of Scotland. On the way home, they saw thistles along the main road. After many ouch's and much pain, they picked a basket full of the horrible spiky things, only because they were the national emblem of Scotland. Maura hoped their passionate purple flowers wouldn't clash with the pale blue and white of everything else. Prune just couldn't understand why any country would have a thistle as its national flower, but he had decided it was something to do with how tough – and prickly – the Scots were.

Lalan had always been brisk and determined in her very Scottish way. Nothing ever seemed to get her down. She and Naison had coped with epidemics of typhoid and cholera, as well as ongoing leprosy. And of course a constant and particularly virulent strain of malaria. Things were not quite as bad in Balla Balla, but even so, she worked as midwife, surgeon, specialist all rolled into one nowadays, patching up, or sewing up, the slashes and wounds of fights and the mauling of wild animals. It was a tough job.

She still sported a broad Scottish accent, and the only time she lost her brusque no-nonsense personality was when she spoke to Prune, always so wistfully, about "Aberrdeeen". She had never been able to afford to go back and see it again since she had come out to Southern Rhodesia over twenty years ago. One day, Prune vowed to himself, he would be rich enough to send her back to Aberdeen.

He knew that the only time Lalan's personality changed was if anyone said she was Scotch. "I am not Scotch," she would chastise them. "That is a bottle of whisky, not a person. I am a Scot, or Scottish." Nobody called her Scotch any more.

As the day of the party drew closer, Prune realised to his dismay that he still needed about £35, even though he had saved every penny he could. Now he'd have to decide what he couldn't buy. Mr Bellini saw him looking dejected and asked what the problem was. Prune told him.

"Well you're just going to have to cut down on all those drinks you're supplying, Prune."

So Prune did that, but he felt sad not giving people what he would have liked. It was important to him because he wanted to show not only that he was able to provide a good birthday party for Lalan, but that as a black African he loved and cared for his white European mother.

It was an interesting time in the country because a few years ago, Southern Rhodesia, Northern Rhodesia and Nyasaland had been brought together and called the Federation of Rhodesia and Nyasaland. The Federation had made black and white people think a bit harder about how they got on with each other. Some did better, some did worse.

Prune and Maura had made plates of sausage rolls, tomato sandwiches, cheese straws and chipolatas with tomato sauce in small dipping bowls. They carried them over to the Village Hall to set everything up. This time, people were just going to have to have home-made lemonade or water to drink. Maura had said it wouldn't matter - and he trusted her.

Bob, the manager of the Village Hall, had not charged Prune any fee for the hall. He said the whole community needed to honour Lalan. Prune made him swear he wouldn't let Lalan know about the party because Bob talked to everyone about everything all the time, especially on the party line. And he knew old Mrs van Rensburg listened to their conversations, because she had been caught many times - then when she was challenged, she got flummoxed. But she didn't stop listening and somehow Lalan's party had to be a real secret.

Prune had eighteen packs of crepe paper in blue and white, which the store had ordered specially for someone else's party that had been cancelled. Mr Bellini said he could have it at cost price. So not only could they use them as table cloths, but also as decorations, with big clumps of thistles in jam jars covered in blue or white in front. He and Maura had cut some of the crepe paper into long strips, which they twisted together, blue and white – and Bob helped them string streamers up across the room. It all looked very fine.

He walked over to the big fridge to put the food in until the party started – but it was full of beers and mixers. *Oh no*, he panicked. The day was very hot, and the food had to go into the fridge.

"Bob! Somebody has put their drinks into our fridge. I have to get this food in!"

Bob smiled. "A big Italian man you probably know came in and filled up the fridge, saying it was for Lalan's party. He didn't want any payment, as this was his present to her. Here, I have another fridge you can use."

Prune's eyes prickled with tears, but Ndebele men didn't cry under any circumstance. He turned away quickly so Bob couldn't see, stacked away the food then ran across the road to find Mr Bellini. He was just about to throw his arms round the big Italian to thank him, when he remembered he was his boss and he was white. Young black men didn't do that. But Mr Bellini smiled his big-mouthed smile and put his arm round Prune, hugging him as he stammered out his thanks.

"Well we couldn't have only half a party for Lalan now, could we?"

Marco watched and glowered like an angry, disagreeable, bullfrog from his seat behind the counter.

At breakfast, on *the* day, Prune gave Lalan a pretty card and some flowers. Then he got home from work early and told her to go and take off her white starched uniform and put on her special-occasion blue-and-white dress, because there was an important meeting about a new road that was going to go right past the clinic. This was going to make life difficult for her. That part was true, but the meeting was really the next night. Prune knew that Lalan never remembered days or dates, so he knew he was safe. But he did think it was funny that she would have to wear her blue-and-white dress two days running!

Bagpipes and Laphroig

His friend Neil Thain went to a school in Bulawayo called Northlea, and he learned to play those weird howling and squealing bagpipes, so although Prune thought it was awful noise, he knew Lalan went all soft when she heard it. Neil offered to play "Speed bonnie boat" as they walked up the steps to the front door. Which he did!

"Och now!" exclaimed Lalan. "Listen Prune – someone is playing the bagpipes! Och stop! I must listen." Lalan stood on the steps, her eyes shut, gripping Prune's arm tightly.

"They're playing the Skye Boat Song." She spoke in a quiet little voice, then started to sing "… carry the lad, that's born to be King . . . over the sea . . ."

Her voice cracked, and she couldn't carry on. She dropped her head to listen.

Prune waited. "Come on Lalan," he said quietly. "We'll be late . . ."

As they opened the big double doors to walk into the darkened hall, the lights went on and everyone shouted "Surprise!" Lalan cried, then laughed, then cried again!

It was such a happy party! Everyone loved the sandwiches and sausage rolls that Prune and Maura had made – Maura had been watching carefully in case there was not going to be enough food, and she relaxed when she saw that there was a bit left over on each table.

She signalled to Prune across the room with her thumbs up.

Mr Bellini's powerful voice rang out as he tinkled his glass to get attention. "Ladies and Gentlemen. Would you please charge your glasses as, on this very happy occasion, I would like to tell you a little more about our remarkable Sister McLeod."

There was a buzz of activity as everyone filled up their glasses – then Mr Bellini rose to his feet.

"I was looking round the room just now I felt how extraordinary it is that we have 10 different groups of people here tonight." He stopped then pointed out people from each table. "English, Greek, amaNdebele, Tswana, Makorekore, Afrikaans, German, chiChewa – and of course the most important of all, Italian and Scottish!"

Everyone laughed.

"We all bring our skills and our work to our community which has developed so well in the last fifteen years. We have our new village hall and the memorable morning markets, held here every week by Miss Bell and Mrs Welby - then we have new schools at Mzingwane and St Stephens, our beautiful little stone church built by the Mzingwane schoolboys, new mining up in Bushtick, big farms being developed, and now even I have some competition with a new store being opened next to the Post Office."

"That'll keep you on your toes Mario."

"You'll have to keep your prices down now."

Mr Bellini laughed. "OK! OK! I asked for that. But perhaps we are only now beginning to realise that one of the most precious things that has happened to Balla Balla recently, has been the new clinic. There is not one single person in this room that has not been treated, brought back to life, soothed and loved by our wee Scottish Nurse, Sister MacLeod whose 70th birthday we celebrate today."

"Sister MacLeod was trained at the Royal Infirmary in Aberdeen. She qualified as a Theatre Sister and specialised in European diseases. But then she was bitten by this bug to go out and help in the development of Southern Rhodesia. The one thing she did not know anything about, was tropical diseases!"

There was a murmur of surprise.

"But that did not bother our tireless little Sister MacLeod. She just worked, and read, and gained valuable experience in the difficult conditions round Tjolotjo – and she is now one of the country's tropical diseases experts. Well done Sister MacLeod"

Everybody clapped and shouted, "Well done Lalan!"

Mr Bellini continued: "It doesn't seem to matter whether we have tertian malignant malaria, typhoid, snake bites, rabies or pneumonia in our community – we have Sister MacLeod and Naison to make it better. Lalan, we salute you and we honour you for your hard work, your dedication and your love for all the people in this little town. Thank you for coming to bring us your wonderful medical knowledge and nursing skills. Thank you for bringing us your friendship. Most of all, thank you for leaving your precious home in Aberdeen to help us all."

"A toast, ladies and gentlemen – to Lalan, may she live among us for many more years to come in good health and happiness."

Everyone said, "To Lalan!"

Then old Mr James who never said anything and who sat hiding in the corner because he didn't like people very much, jumped up, held his glass high and sang "For She's a Jolly Good Fellow" – and everyone joined in.

Prune was just sitting thinking how wonderful everything was and how the party had been better than he had ever thought it could be. Mr Bellini turned towards him.

"The whole of Balla Balla has been donating towards something very precious for Lalan, Prune. We would like you to give it to her. But you must read the instructions first."

71

Prune stood up as he took a piece of paper and a big paper cylinder from Mr Bellini.

"Lalan," Prune read, "this comes to you with love on your 70th birthday from everyone in Balla Balla. It is something that you have often talked about, saying how much you would love 'a wee dram'. Well there are many 'wee drams' in this package, and you will know full well that every dram is revered for its medicinal malts."

Everybody laughed. Prune glanced at Lalan's face as he went on reading. "It is to be kept in a dark place and treated with great respect. Wee drams should last you for the rest of your life, and although it is already 10 years old, it will get better as it gets older."

Prune handed over the large cardboard cylinder. It had been beautifully wrapped to match the blue and white theme and look like the flag of Scotland.

She opened it – and gasped.

"Och no! It's Laphroaig – single malt – 10 years old!"

Then she really did cry. Tears of happiness poured down her face. Everyone went quiet as she sipped her first wee dram in twenty years and pronounced it the very best she had ever tasted.

There was no nastiness at all, but black people and white people just stayed in separate groups. Lalan, Mr Bellini, Prune and Maura, Naison and the local DC and the headmaster of the school were quite happy sitting down and talking to everyone. So that was fine.

Then it was Prune's turn to give a speech.

"Lalan – not many people know about the shoebox – or how you saved my life. So on this important day for you, it is important for me to tell everyone what happened."

There was a rustle of interest among the guests.

"In August 1939, a beautiful young girl was found on the steps of Lalan's clinic in Tjolotjo. She was so weak from the loss of blood that she was nearly dead. Lalan and Naison brought her in, and although the clinic was a school clinic where they didn't see many people giving birth, they helped this seriously ill girl and I was born. Nobody expected me to live because I was so little."

He turned to Lalan. "Lalan, how many more weeks should I have spent in her tummy?"

"Well, I estimated that you were about 26 weeks – so you still needed another 14 to go."

Prune laughed – then preened his biceps as he said, ". . . but I was strong!"

There was a ripple of supportive laughter round the room.

"They didn't have any cots, but they made a little crib for me out of some tea towels and a shoe box."

"All we know about my birth mother is from a little bracelet that was on her wrist. Her name was Rosie. We have not been able to find out anything about her, but one day, Lalan has said she will help me to find my birth family."

Everyone clapped and smiled – then they took turns to go and hug Lalan and shake hands with Naison.

Prune waited impatiently because he had an important announcement to make. Finally, he tinkled his glass and as things quietened down, he said: "And I have another announcement to make. I have been very lucky to have four brothers and two sisters from Naison's family. They are not really my blood brothers and sisters, but I love them all very much. And I love one of them particularly very much. So Lalan and Naison, I want to ask for your permission to marry my beautiful Maura."

So everybody clapped and spoke all at once.

"Yes, yes! Wonderful."

"They're a bit young, but yes, that is very good."

"They are just right for each other of course – perfect!"

Lalan and Naison ran over to give them their blessing.

It was decided that Prune and Maura would be married as soon as possible!

7

TIMES OF TRIUMPH AND DISASTER

Carol finished Prune's long and detailed letter, her thoughts underpinned by another favourite "call-and-answer" conversation, this time between two Heuglin's Robins in the tree above her. She managed to find one of them, perched facing the early morning sun, beak open and little breast puffed. She watched and listened, reluctant to break the glorious salutation to the morning. She loved the way their tails seemed to conduct their whistles and sweeps of sound.

It was going to be yet another distinctive Highveld day, deep early morning shadows and that almost breath-taking stillness. There was never much wind, except in August – then it was simply a flurry of dust or a suddenly slamming door.

She could hear a group of African women laughing and chattering away at the tops of their voices as they made their way down towards the village below. In true rural tradition, they were making sure everyone heard what they said so they could not be accused of gossiping or talking about anyone. She envied them their joyful companionship.

Themba spreads his wings.

She returned reluctantly to the house . . . trying to re-focus on her studies, when Themba rode up on his bike. He was also on swot vac, having won that scholarship to the school at Goromonzi six years ago. He was preparing to write his A levels as well.

Carol didn't see him around much anymore, but often, when he couldn't get all the way back to Tjolotjo for holidays or exeats, he would come and stay in their thatched cottage in the garden.

"Carol!" he called joyfully. "Guess what? I had a letter from some lawyers called Dodds and Brown. They said they'd heard I had done well at Goromonzi and would I like to go and talk to them about my future!

"So the headmaster took me in last week, and we had an interview. It was so hot, but I dressed in my uniform and wore my maroon Prefect blazer with all the badges pinned on very straight. They asked if I would like to take it off, and I did."

"What happened then?" Carol asked.

"They wanted to know what I was going to do when I left school. I said that when I was a child, I used to go to the enkundleni, the tribal court cases, with my father, so I thought I might also become a District Assistant or even, one day, a District Commissioner. Then they wanted to know about my father too.

"I told them that now I was older, all I wanted to do was to go to college or university to study natural resource management. But my father couldn't afford that, so I was going to see if I could get some work with National Parks. After I had worked for a bit, I told them I might be able to get a scholarship to the new Chibero Agricultural College in Norton. It is opening in about 18 months' time. They were very interested, but they didn't say anything more except to wish me good luck. So I thought that was the end.

"Oh Themba - after all that! How disappointing." Carol felt very sad.

Themba didn't wait for her to finish:

"Ah – but that's not the end of the story! Just now, I got a call to go to the headmaster's office. Mr Brown was on the phone. Carol, they are going to pay for me to study law at the University of the Witwatersrand! I said I didn't want to be a lawyer any more, but they said that law was a useful basic degree. I could specialise in law governing wildlife and National Parks as well as natural resources. What do you think?"

"I think that's absolutely fantastic Themba! But Wits is going through a troubled time at the moment. It would be awful if you were caught up in it, or worse, if you were detained in a South African jail. They are much more anti-black down there than we are. The rumours are horrible. You might never come out. Most South Africans think we are pinko liberals in Rhodesia. It could be difficult to find someone to get you out. I suppose you do at least have a firm of lawyers behind you – but still – it is South Africa. What does your father think?"

"He has the same reservations as you, so I had better think about it a bit more."

"Why not talk to Dad, Themba? He knows a lot about these things. He'd give you good advice. I don't know what an alternative to Wits would be though, except maybe Fort Hare at the moment."

But Themba didn't want to go to Fort Hare, and the new University College of Rhodesia and Nyasaland didn't have a law faculty yet, although he had been told that was coming.

So their lives were changing. Carol and Themba had only a month or so left at school to write those final exams, Prune was getting married. And Jabu? Nobody seemed very sure.

Researching the Matebele Kings

In the meantime, she had her essay to write. Why did Lobengula seem to trust white men? Did he let the Matebele people down? Some younger Matebele thought he was a traitor and sold his people too cheaply. Was the Rudd concession a con trick as other people thought? Was it Rudd himself who broke the rules, or Jameson or Rhodes? What was Rhodes like? Some researchers showed him as a compassionate humanitarian, while others saw him as a dastardly empire builder who stomped uncaring across the land and its people.

Dad always said, "Compare as many pieces of written research and articles as you can find about a particular action or time. As many as possible. Read them, understand that every one of them will be written with the pretty undisguised bias of the writer, but each will contain some almost identical components. Those will be the truths. Find them, harvest them, use them."

Still finding it hard to concentrate, Carol was staring out of the window when she saw her father approaching.

"Hello my girl! How are you getting on?" Dad was home for breakfast.

"Finding, harvesting and using! But oh Dad, the more I read, the more confused I get. Why didn't we ever go and see these places that have so much history about Lobengula and Rhodes when we lived in Matebeleland? We've been to World's View in the Matopos of course and seen Rhodes' grave and the Allan Wilson memorial, but that's about it. I don't know where anything else these articles talk about is, even on the map, and I just can't imagine how it all worked. How can I write about it with any understanding?"

"Darling you were away at boarding school, and I was busy sorting out constant problems. Ever since this involvement in the African Affairs Board began, I don't seem to have a second to myself."

"Hmm . . . I know." She pursed her lips. "Mum says she hardly ever sees you."

"Well - here's a thought. I have to go down to Matebeleland next week to talk to Chief Khayisa Ndiweni at Ntabazinduna. He was the one who insisted that the African Affairs Board be set up as part of the Federal Government structure in the first place.

"In itself, Ntabazinduna is one of the most historical places in Matebele history. I have plenty of leave due, so why don't we tag on a couple of days and find some of these places? Mum can come with us. She can catch up with her friends, and it'll be a bit of a break for us all. I'd really like to give you my interpretation of what happened when, and if possible, why. How does that sound? While I am in meetings, you can do a bit more research yourself."

"Yes, that sounds fantastic. But will I have time to write it all up once we get back?"

He smiled at her fondly. "Your mind will be so full of a million truths and speculations" he said, "that it'll just fly off your pen."

"I don't suppose we could go and see Prune on the way? He's having a few problems from what he says in his last letter. After describing all the success of Lalan's birthday, he finished it off by saying he is now thinking of going back to Tjolotjo for a while. Something's not right."

"Well that's a thought. It's a bit out of the way, but I would like to go and see Garfield Todd too. He's had a tough time recently with some disturbances in the government. Hard on him. He's been a family friend for many years, but he'll need encouragement to keep the flag flying for black enfranchisement. And you know that's something that worries me."

And so, the plans were made. Carol wrote to Prune, asking if he could take some time off and join them at Ntabazinduna. She knew he probably would – if he could.

Marco's revenge

That night the phone rang – it was Prune. Mr Bellini had just fired him. And it was all because of Marco.

Since Lalan's birthday, Marco had been whispering accusations to his father, about Prune stealing money. Then one day, Mr Bellini asked if he could see the ledgers where Prune carefully wrote details of all the income and expenditure. Prune was happy to give them to Mr Bellini, because he knew they were right. In fact, Mr Bellini used to call him "a pain in the neck", because he was only happy when sums added up backwards and forwards, with extra checks just to make sure.

Three days later, Mr Bellini asked him to come into his office.

"Prune," he began with a sad, serious look on his face "some of these figures in the cash book are not the same as the ones in the ledger, or the bank. And there is about £175 missing."

"No that can't be. I checked everything backwards and forwards! Everything matches the bank accounts."

"They might match the bank accounts, but the amount written in the ledger doesn't match the daily takings receipts. Here, here and here . . ." Mr Bellini prodded each point emphatically. Each prod going through Prune's heart like a knife.

In a small voice he said: "Please can I see?"

Mr Bellini passed over the ledger and pointed out the figures he was worried about. He had the daily takings receipts with him. Prune looked. They didn't match.

But he knew how careful he had been. This didn't make sense. The dates were all around the time of Lalan's birthday. Had he been careless because he had been so busy? He had a hollow feeling in his stomach. How could this be?

He looked again at the ledger. Sometimes, when they were in a rush because of too many customers in the store, he did the cash receipts in pencil because he couldn't find a biro. He'd fill them in later, double-checking against the bank accounts. The figures in the ledger and the bank were definitely less than the cash received slips.

His face was frozen in agony and disbelief as he looked at Maura. She came over, and the two of them looked and looked while Mr Bellini waited for an explanation.

"That is not your writing Prune," Maura whispered.

He held the cash receipt up to the light. Then he looked at the others. In many places, where there should have been a 5, it looked like an 8. Sometimes a 1 looked like a 7. Each time, the cash receipt amount was more than the amount banked. Maura was right – it wasn't his writing. Prune held the slips up to the light again and could see the ones that had been changed even more clearly.

"I didn't change them, Mr Bellini. You know when we are really busy, I sometimes write in pencil until the bank statement comes in. Then I check and write over them in biro. If they don't match, I spend hours going through everything that was sold that day to make sure there are no mistakes. The statement only came yesterday. I haven't had time to check and fill them in yet. And you can see this is not my writing."

But it could have been.

With those changes, there was £174.6.6 missing.

Mr Bellini was very sad and let down. He thought so much of Prune and couldn't believe that this had happened. But he also knew he would have to ask Prune to leave.

Prune pleaded with him. "Mr Bellini, let me do a stock check, and I will quickly tell you which cash receipts are wrong."

Marco came to the door of the office. "I cleaned up the kitchen as you asked Papa, and the lining in the drawers was very dirty, so I've put some new paper in those drawers," he paused for dramatic effect. "Guess what I found hidden at the back of the cutlery drawer."

Mr Bellini counted it out: £174.9.6.

Prune sat, shocked. He couldn't move. He knew with awful certainty what had happened. He also knew that if he had really stolen the money, at least he would have made sure the amount in the drawer was exactly what was missing . . . not 3/- more. Marco's addition was terrible, and he was careless.

"Prune obviously didn't have enough for Lalan's precious party," Marco gloated, "and he was obviously going to quietly pay off what he owed. Then we would never have found it."

Then Prune knew that he couldn't prove Marco wrong, because Mr Bellini wouldn't let him check the stock. In a small tight voice, he swore that he didn't owe any money and he would never do this to Mr Bellini.

"I am not going to go to the police Prune, because you have been a good worker and a good friend. But I am afraid I will not be able to trust you again. So you have to leave."

Prune was stunned. He looked at Marco and saw his triumphant face. He took out his purse and said: "One day I will prove to you that this was not my fault – but because I cant do it now, here is the three shillings difference."

He told Lalan. She went to Mr Bellini and pleaded with him, but nobody could prove who was right and who was wrong. Eventually, it would be better not to have a police record than to make a fuss and perhaps go to jail.

Even Maura couldn't comfort him. Every time she tried, he was reminded again of how kind Mr Bellini had been in giving so many drinks and presents for Lalan's birthday party.

When Prune phoned to give her all the details, Carol immediately asked if he would like to join them at Ntabazinduna.

With even Maura unable to comfort him, the only bright spot in Prune's life right at that moment was the thought of spending a few days with Carol and her father in Tjolotjo.

Yes, he would certainly meet them at Ntabazinduna.

8

MZILIKAZI'S SONS

Going back to Bulawayo was never a pleasant experience for Carol. It stirred up just too many memories of wretched years at junior school.

As the country flattened out past Gwelo, she felt a lump of apprehension in her throat. She'd rather doubted that the trip was going to be of any value anyway particularly as her thoughts were already moving way beyond schooldays, to enticing memories of summer square dancing. A few promising moments between hilarious but exhausting do-si-dos, chains and circles led to a hope that a new guy in the district, Simon Watson, might be back from University by the time they got home. He was divine! Tall, a bit thin, with a flop of fair hair, and the bluest eyes she'd ever seen. She'd felt a stir of excitement every time she thought of him. He had actually said he was looking forward to seeing her at the end of term.

On such snatched phrases, great hopes build! Only a few weeks to go.

Carol had just got her driver's licence, but after a long morning of driving, she was happy to hand over to her father and sink low into the back seat for a little uninterrupted fantasising about Simon. Were his eyes really that blue? Was he really as much fun as he'd seemed? Her eyes closed, letting her imagination conjure up improbably romantic thoughts.

It was a long, hot, journey, broken by the luxury of new bits of road where the car ran smooth and secure on a single strip of tar 8 ft. wide. If a vehicle approached, both vehicles still had to come off the side of the tar, clinging on with the two right side wheels . . . but it was a step up from the old roads with just two narrow tarred strips to navigate. As she drove Carol coped all right passing a car coming from the opposite direction but found it nerve wracking to be stuck behind another car, or worse, a lorry.

As there was so little traffic on the road, drivers forgot to look in their rear-view mirrors. When they realised there was another car behind them, they'd shoot off in fright, in a scattering rush of gravel and dirt.

It was stinking hot, so windows were down to allow for a cooling thread of air. But it meant that when they passed other cars, the dust swirled in, settling everywhere. Because they wore dark glasses, they'd arrive after long journeys with the skin round their eyes startling white against hot, red, sweating faces coated in red-brown dust. It took ages to get the dust off and out of their hair. She'd be so glad when they arrived.

"These old strips have been remarkable in helping to change the country," She heard Dad speaking. "They were expected to last only 10 years, but they are well over 20 years old now. I remember travelling on this bit of road between Gwelo and Selukwe when it was the first bit of strip road in the country. It seemed so luxurious after winding dirt paths meant for slow old ox wagons or even the new Zeederberg coaches. The roads were full of deep ruts and holes. It took a lot of careful maneouvering to get through with an overnight stop in Gwelo . . . but now we sail along in a day."

"Yes Dad, I know!" Carol mumbled, slightly irritated at having her imaginary moments interrupted

"Seriously, it is exciting and interesting, because strips started out as two bits of concrete. But of course that was too expensive, and tarmac replaced them at about a third of the cost. At least it gave us a chance to open the country up more quickly . . . and building the strip roads gave people employment during the depression 25 years ago, when currencies collapsed and there were no jobs at all." Carol was only half-listening.

Ntabazinduna

"Oh look! There's Ntabazinduna," said Dad pointing to their right as they neared Bulawayo. "Hill of the Chiefs."

She roused herself enough to look at the distinctive flat plateau top of Ntabazinduna. It was definitely a hill, not a mountain and it didn't look particularly imposing. Carol had seen it many times but hadn't given it much thought.

"Is that where the Chiefs live Dad?"

"Yes and no. There is a significant village of Ntabazinduna there and there are certainly senior Chiefs and Headmen living there. Chief Khayisa is the most senior of them all. But the hill has great importance in Matebele history. It is reported to have immense spiritual power, and there is talk of a lake that never dries up. I haven't seen it - and I don't know. But what I do know from various written articles and reports is that in 1838, King Mzilikazi moved his Matebele people north from the Transvaal. He then instructed his uncle Godwane Ndiweni to turn right towards to what is now Bulawayo, while he went further north towards the Zambezi."

"Why did he do that?"

"As King, his role was to look after his people. He know the Boers were close behind him - and they were trying to get away from the British, so they didn't want the Matebele in the way. Mzilikazi wasn't often defeated, but he'd just been soundly beaten for the third time by one of the leaders of the Voortrekkers called Potgieter. The thinking is that he was heading north to clear the area north of the river and put the more easily defensible Zambezi between them. The fact that Matebele numbers were at an all-time high was slowing him down. He needed somewhere for the bulk of his people to go in the meantime. We're not quite sure what the numbers were, but it is thought that they were between 15,000 and 20,000 by that stage."

"Wow!" Carol was focussed on his words now. "I had no idea there were so many."

"You can imagine that Mzilikazi didn't want to drag the whole lot along with him, so his uncle Godwane Ndiweni, was entrusted to take the women, children and old people to a secure, easily defensible place, which had already been described to the King in a prophecy . . . and establish a new royal capital in time for his return.

"Godwane took several crack regiments with him to make sure they all made it safely into what remained of the Rosvi kingdom while Mzilikazi took the fittest and fiercest young fighting warriors, to clear out tribes to the north."

"In fact, Godwane established that first capital somewhere near here. For two harvests the people increased in numbers once one of the key regiments, the Zwangendaba had subdued the Rosvi kingdom and got rid of their Chief Changamira.

"BUT . . ." Angus emphasised the word

"Zulu and Matebele tradition held that the most important event of every year was the *Inxwala* – the purification of soldiers for battle. During the *Inxwala*, the king would set the direction for the next raids. Therefore, for the *Inxwala*, the King had to be present.

"They'd already missed one year. The warriors were impatient and restless. Nobody had heard from Mzilikazi and rumours were rife that he was dead anyway.

"Godwane proclaimed Mzilikazi's eldest son Nkulumane as king . . . more than anything, to keep the *impi* happy. But he did make a fatal mistake. If Godwane had really thought Mzilikazi was dead, he should have organised the traditional rituals and ceremonies praising the glorious achievements of a newly dead King. He didn't do that! Inevitably, the bush telegraph went into overdrive."

"What happened then?"

"Mzilikazi had been trying to cross the Zambezi to claim the Batoka headlands, but malaria was killing his men and the wretched maKololo just kept getting in the way. They were tough fighters. Tough enough to defeat his best regiments anyway . . . so it was the first time the King had come up against another tribe like his – but this time, it was a tribe with guns.

Carol interrupted. "Ah - now hang on Dad, you told me that the British didn't want any tribes to have guns.

Angus had to smile to himself. Someone was getting more interested!

You're right - but while the Batoka took their front teeth out to make sure they weren't attractive to the slave traders making their way up the Zambezi, the Makololo, for the same reason, applied for permission from the British Administrator in Bechuanaland, for guns to protect themselves. They were granted just a few. But enough to make the difference.

"So when the rumours of his death reached him, King Mzilikazi gave up on the maKololo, intending to pay them back later , and came storming back through the Gwaai river valley - close to where we lived in Tjolotjo."

Carol sat up. This was becoming real and definitely more interesting.

King Mzilikazi: nation builder

"Mzilikazi marched back to nThaba zi'Nduna, the Hill of the Chiefs, today's Ntabazinduna, brushing aside the sycophantic apologies of Godwane and the ululating welcomes, shouts and whistles of people dancing, bowing and scraping before him as they realised with horror that they had been wrong, Mzilikazi was very much alive and there was going to be BIG trouble.

"Everyone talks of Mzilikazi's quiet way of speaking, his gentle voice – an attribute much respected in a Zulu leader. This time, he was not going to be appeased. With that soft gentle voice, but eyes as hard as a snake, he ordered the men who had been with him to round up everyone who had, or even might have, conspired against him.

"People threw themselves down before him, or crept towards him with their eyes desperately fixed on his. And the King – looked all the time for the slightest hesitation - a twitch or the shift of an eye - then the steely eyes would harden, and his slightest gesture indicated death. You can almost hear the wailing of the women, as the loyal warriors pounced on yet another helpless being, dragging them away to be cast aside. Imagine the courageous but desperate silence of the men as they knew their end was near. To die with courage was vitally important to the amaNdebele."

"How many were killed, Dad?"

"Hundreds. Estimates vary so much that we can't be sure, but several hundred at least were rounded up and thrown off the top of that hill . . . uncles, cousins, close friends, wives and sons. Including, according to some, Nkulumane, the heir to his throne."

Carol gasped. "He didn't care, did he? Why would he kill his sons?"

"I am quite sure he did care," Angus continued. "But that was what was expected of an amaNdebele king."

"That's awful! I didn't know it was quite so bloodthirsty."

"Just a different culture . . . abhorrent to our eyes, but in those times, essential for maintaining discipline. That was the way it was done. As a Matebele King or even a Matebele individual, you were held in great esteem – or otherwise – by your actions and your courage."

Carol was rather relieved to be able to change the topic.

"Oh look! The cooling towers! We're nearly there."

9

SEARCHING FOR A KING

They turned off the Salisbury Road into Borrow Street - and there was the old swimming pool. What memories it held of screaming excitement, water bombs and school galas!

The parks and gardens were laid out with perpendicular pathways and landscaped shrubberies fringing precious, carefully watered lawns which were kept green even in drought. Fountains overflowed with a joyful welcome.

It was reassuring for those from gentler climes to be reminded of their homeland and see a grassed park, splashing fountains and botanical walks - even within the desolation of the harsh thorn and sparsely treed bush country of Matebeleland. They learned, in time, to love the flamboyance of hedges topped with profusions of bougainvillea, their tumbling heads of purple vying with spectacular splashes of colour in lines of flowering street trees – scarlet Flamboyants, lilac Jacarandas, deep red Poinsettias or golden Cassias. It was a semi-tropical palette of glorious colour.

Carol had to admit it was a beautiful city.

"Look Dad! That brings back a few memories."

They laughed as they watched a rag-tag crocodile of boarders in school uniform and wide brimmed hats, chattering away as they walked beside the park, towel rolled swimming costumes under their arms.

Oh boy! Glad I'm not at that stage any more, Carol thought, watching their faces flushed scarlet with the heat of walking - but bright with anticipation of that first plunge into an icy blue swimming pool on a stifling afternoon.

Everyone commented on the width of Bulawayo's streets – a dictate from Cecil Rhodes that they be wide enough to allow a span of oxen and a wagon to turn round easily. Nowadays, that allowed a double row of cars to be parked in the middle as well as along the pavement.

Somehow those gracious tree-lined avenues didn't seem as wide as they had five years ago. A big difference was the number of cars on the roads and many new multi-storey buildings. Bulawayo had certainly grown since they left in 1953.

They turned into Selborne Avenue, driving past the manicured lawns and palms of the City Hall, crisp, white and neat with its tower clock on time as always. How often had she looked at that clock in apprehension, hoping she might squeeze another five minutes away from boarding school – perhaps a cup of tea at Haddon and Sly? But the clock was relentless . . .

So many mixed emotions flooded back at seeing it all again. She was not sure the visit would help with her assignment, but she was very sure it must be the hottest afternoon ever.

The ominous four o'clock build-up of bulbous, black clouds to the south still looked as threatening as it had done every day for the last few weeks. But, as it had done every day for the last few weeks, the clouds would probably dissipate in the cool night air.

They slowed down to drive through yet another enormous dip in the road designed to disperse the deluge of tropical rains and she wondered whether, after all these years of drought, they would ever again roar with water as wild and rushing as she remembered.

"Mzilikazi established his capital Mhlanhlandhlela very close to where we are, in memory of one of Shaka Zulu's capitals near the Magaliesberg," said Dad, interrupting her thoughts.

"But rumours persisted that Nkulumane had escaped."

"If Nkulumane escaped, why didn't he take over from Mzilikazi?"

Dad chuckled. "That's a whole new story!"

They were now in Abercorn Street, pulling into the driveway of an old friend's home where they would spend the night. And there to meet them were Prune – and Lalan!

They sat under the dense shade of enormous fig trees in the garden catching up on the detailed chatter of missed times. Iced lemon juice in long chinking glasses helped with the heat while Carol's mum and Lalan stayed in the cool of the house. They heard shrieks of mirth from them both as they caught up on years of colourful stories.

It was hard at first to get Prune's mind off the store and Mr Bellini – not so much about the job, but about Mr Bellini even thinking he would steal money. He vowed he would one day repay Mr Bellini.

Matebeleland in early November was always horrendous, but Carol had forgotten how enervating it was. Her thoughts were dragged back to the days they had a mandatory afternoon rest – and how perspiration would gather, wet and sticky, then run round her neck as she read her book. She hated it. Airless, oppressive heat: dogs seeking shade, tongues lolling from panting mouths and donkeys across the road with heads hanging low. She longed for that burning ball to drop below the horizon – then they'd all come to life with the speedy onset of sub-tropical darkness.

"If Nkulumane didn't die at Ntabazinduna, why didn't he take over from Mzilikazi?"

Having filled Prune in on their discussion, she was impatient to get back to the story . . . and Prune needed to be distracted.

"Simple – nobody could find him. Even today we don't really know what happened to him. There's a grave in Bafokeng near Rustenburg with a message on a rough stone headpiece. It's not easy to read, but have a look at this photo and see if you can decipher it Prune.

Inkosi xa Madebele Ako Mzelikaze Ukolomane mzelikazi
wafa nao nyaka wo 1883 nsenyane ka August 21.

"That means King of the Matebele, Mzilikazi's son Ukolomane Mzelikazi died August 21st 1883" said Prune. "Seems pretty definite."

"It does - and of course 1883 is another 40 or so years after the killing of the Chiefs, so in time to come, there may be sons of Nkulumane trying to pave their way to the throne of the Matebele – but as he was never inaugurated as king, they would be unlikely to actually have any claim.

A little girl called Sarah

"The twist to this story is that one of Mzilikazi's sons did survive. He would have been 5 or 6 years old at the time of the killing of the Chiefs . . .

"A few years before this took place, Mzilikazi's army had attacked a Voortrekker laager in what is today's Northern Transvaal.

It was a big group of several Boer families, the Potgieter Trek, all trying to get away from the rapidly encroaching British in the Cape. For some unknown reason, one of those families, the Liebenbergs, decided to go on alone. But they made the fatal mistake of not respecting the Matebele people by asking the King for permission first, before they crossed the Vaal River.

"They were easy targets. The Matebele attacked, leaving the main laager untouched, but surrounding the Liebenbergs. They took the family's oxen, horses and anything else they could, killing everyone – except three children – a boy and two girls. For some extraordinary reason, the indunas decided not to kill them - and for some equally extraordinary reason, they gave them as a present to Mzilikazi."

"What on earth would Mzilikazi do with three white kids?"

"I shouldn't think he wanted to be bothered with them. So he gave the oldest girl, Sarah, to the youngest of his wives - a high ranking, but much despised, Swazi Princess. She had a sickly young baby called Jandu and Sarah became her helper, or more realistically, her slave.

"While Godwane was busy preparing for the *Inxwala* ceremony and rumours flew to say Mzilikazi was returning, it is thought that Sarah with another important chief 'Mncumbata took Jandu in the opposite direction and hid him in the Matopos.

"The Swazi Princess was thrown off Ntabazinduna - so Jandu would have been killed as well.

"As it turned out, this little boy was dependent on Sarah Liebenberg to look after him, and he'd grow up knowing her as just one of the tribe.

"History doesn't relate how long they lived in the Matopos. But one thing I've felt happened is that Sarah and Jandu would frequently go to see Mlimo. He was the most important spiritual and traditional healer and the Matebele would seldom make any move without paying their respects and consulting Mlimo for advice, particularly about the next season's rains."

"What happened to Sarah, Dad?"

"The only reports I could find", Angus responded, "suggest she died of snakebite in the Matopos in about 1845. Jandu would have been about

11 or 12 then."

"Whether Jandu ever returned to Mzilikazi is not certain. There is anecdotal evidence that he did and was forgiven. But most stories seem to agree that Jandu was not completely acceptable in the King's presence, nor did he receive training in chieftainship – but he was known to be a spiritual healer."

"Perhaps because of all those visits to Mlimo" Prune interrupted.

"Perhaps indeed." Angus conceded.

"Mzilikazi died 30 years later, without leaving a known heir to the throne and he appears to have been not the slightest bit worried about it."

"What an amazing story."

"It is - but with no succession in place, it was chaos.

Nkulumane - alive or dead?

"There were two violently opposed factions. Mbigo, commander of the powerful Zwangendaba regiment led one. He had come up with Godwane and having overthrown the Rozvi people, he held great sway of course, and was supported by three other powerful regiments: the Induba, Ingubo and Nyamandhlovu regiments.

"The other faction came under the direct blood line of Mzilikazi, the royal house of Khumalo—"

"Khumalo?" Prune jumped in. "Like my friend Matsho Khumalo?"

Angus laughed. "He might well be related, Prune. Anyway, to get back to the story, the hereditary regent of the Khumalo royal house, headed up the other faction. This was the same Mncumbata who went with Sarah and hid Jandu in the Matopos. He'd have watched the leadership qualities of this young man over the years, even though he was a bit of an outsider. He supported Jandu, of course, because he had, most important, Khumalo blood - and he had been born after the inauguration of his father as King.

"It took two years to sort it all out. It was a torrid time for the new nation. Mbigo refused to allow any inauguration to take place while he searched for Nkulumane. He was convinced the heir to the throne was still alive and that he had not been executed but instead was hidden, then sent to Bechuanaland to await his father's death so he could become the next Ndebele King."

Prune jumped in. "What do you think happened to Nkulumane?"

"There are stories that say that he did go to Bechuanaland and spent his time at Kuruman Mission with Moffat and Sykes. They say Nkulumane became a Christian and no longer wished to be King, so he disguised himself and made sure nobody found him. The missionaries, who were always shocked by what they saw as the barbarity of King Mzilikazi, would have been quite happy to give him sanctuary.

"There were pretenders to the throne all over the place. One named Kanda in Zululand for example. He was actually supported by the British Administrator of Natal then found to be a fake.

"But Nkulumane was nowhere to be found.

"Meantime, on hearing about the death of his father, Jandu used his ability as a good horse rider, to flea to one of the few people he did trust, Mr Thomas, the missionary at Inyati. He stayed there till things quietened down.

"When you think about the young Jandu, you have to feel sorry for him. He was even more reluctant to be king. But he wasn't missing, so it was difficult for him to disappear. He tried everything – encouraging the Nkulumane factions to keep looking and reminding other Chiefs that after all, he was the son of a despised Swazi woman!

"I've always felt Mr Thomas must have spent some time in prayer that too, that Nkulumane would be found. Apparently, the only times Jandu left the mission in that two years, was to travel to Njelele in the Matopos, to see Mlimo. The nation would have been waiting for days on end, to hear an answer from the voice that boomed from the depths of a dark, creeper covered, cave.

"But whatever Jandu did to appease the ancestors did not work!

"Eventually Mncumbata came to see him, saying it was time he assumed royal duties. Jandu sent him away, asking with him to reconsider. While there was the slightest hope that Nkulumane was alive, he wanted nothing to do with it. Several months later, when a large number of other indunas came to Jandu with gifts of cattle, he realised he had no more options. It was now time to consent to become King.

"In 1870, when he was about 36 years old, Jandu was presented to the people and proclaimed as King of the Matebele.

"I've always felt Bishop Knight Bruce's description of him, as being *'partly worried, partly good natured and partly cruel'* – was very accurate."

"Wow Dad, that's quite a story! Fancy Jandu being hidden in the Matopos to save him from being executed."

"It's like Moses in the bulrushes," Prune added.

They agreed.

Angus went on. "Have you made the connection yet?"

Prune said tentatively "Jandu was Lobengula in disguise?"

Angus laughed. "That's right. He wasn't in disguise, but he was given the name Lobengula on his accession. There are many versions of what that name actually means, from 'the scatterer' to 'he who was sick'. The second one indicates that he was indeed, very sick at some time."

"Perhaps Sarah being part of the tribe explains why he seemed to like white people," Prune volunteered.

"Yes, I think Lobengula did trust some white people - particularly the missionaries. His father Mzilikazi had a close relationship with Robert Moffat at Kuruman, even naming his son after the mission – Nkulumane. Lobengula in turn had a close relationship with Robert's son, John Moffat, and spent a lot of time with Charles Helm and the Carnegies.

"Now here's another connection for us, Carol. You remember all the great Christmases we had with the Carnegie family at Shiloh farm?"

Carol remembered them well. Full of families and fun, singing carols and patter songs from Gilbert and Sullivan operettas, playing charades and cricket on the lawn. Wonderful times.

"Yes of course. There was an old mission station there."

"That's right. Alastair Carnegie and I became firm friends through our work as Native Commissioners. He's related to Thomas Morgan Thomas, the missionary who helped Jandu stay out of sight while he was at Inyati. After he was made King, Lobengula gave Thomas that beautiful land at Shiloh to establish the mission."

"I've managed to find a description of Lobengula's inauguration which was written by missionary Thomas. He was one of only three whites invited and allowed to attend. I've typed a bit of it for each of you to read tonight before we head out tomorrow."

What a day it had been. Stories that had definitely touched Carol's heart, firing her imagination and understanding about King Lobengula but leaving her with thousands of questions she still had to ask.

As she snuggled into bed, lightning, which had been flickering on the horizon, turned into a dazzling sheet. She ducked involuntarily, counting the seconds before the thunder came to find out how far away it was. Not even two seconds later there was a deafening crack of thunder. Wow! That was close!

The old house they were staying in had a corrugated iron roof, and Carol listened as individual drops fell loud and heavy. Then there was that almost-mandatory pause, pregnant with anticipation, before the deafening clamour as torrents of rain simply poured down, filling gutters and spilling gleefully into dehydrated, spider-webbed drainpipes.

She couldn't resist throwing the window open to capture the first waft of earth infused freshness as the downpour hit the thirsting African veld, coaxing it back to life. Indescribable. Yet understood so well by those who have been there and breathed it in every year with thankful reverence.

The country had grown more parched as they had approached Bulawayo, but at last, it felt as though, drought-breaking rains might have arrived exactly on time.

Carol took out the copy of missionary Thomas' description of Lobengula's inauguration. She started reading.

Extract from *Eleven years in Central South Africa* by Thomas Morgan Thomas

22nd January 1870

"It was about nine o'clock in the morning, when great clouds of dust were observed ascending towards the skies about a mile to the south of Tsholotsho and the approach of the mighty army soon became known to the people of the town. The army rapidly advancing, was soon near the town and passing at a quick march on the east side, and in a short time stood in battle array on the north, about half a mile distant. When thus situated, it presented a figure of a half moon or semi-circular shape and extended about a mile from east to west.

Many long speeches and traditional songs about the one who was hiding but who now was strong enough to eat up all his enemies ensued.

Carol's imagination ran riot as she turned off the light.

10

BHEKISIZWE AND THE BEAUTIFUL BONGANI

Carol needn't have worried about Jabulani – he was achieving exactly what he hoped - with quiet determination and absolute planning to pave the way for his ultimate emergence as a leader of his people.

For that, he needed recognition, status, direction.

He'd promised himself, in the flowering of his youth, that he would learn only as much as he needed from white man's education to give him the skills and tools for leadership.

Bhekisizwe – the name rolled off his tongue, thrilling in its portent. *One day, Bhekisizwe – the world will know your name.*

Despite his impatience, it had been important to step carefully round the puddles!

Nkanyiso - a man of learning

Jabu's father, Mr Nkanyiso Ncube, esteemed *umfundisi*[73], was an outstanding teacher. In the mid-1950s, Southern Rhodesia still had to import most African teachers from South Africa and Botswana. As an amaNdebele and a locally born teacher, he was a respected and important man to both black and white.

Nkanyiso's education had started with his own father and Jabu's *baba 'mkulu* Mehluli. He had watched the changing roles of chief and tribe. An astute and wise man, he kept his eldest son immersed in the traditional practices of hereditary chieftainship. But he sent his bright younger son to the mission school at Inyati.

---

[73] *umfundisi:* a learned man; a teacher

When Nkanyiso finished primary school, missionary Thomasi told him that the boy was very clever and would do great things for his country if he became a teacher. Thomasi wanted to send Nkanyiso, to learn with a good friend of his in Shoshong, in Bechuanaland. Here he would learn to teach other young boys about conservation and agriculture. *Baba 'mkulu*, after many consultations and deliberations with the elders of the tribe as well as with Mlimo and the ancients, had, in time, agreed. Now everyone he talked to said, "Nkanyiso is a clever boy, and it is good that he will look after us in this new world."

Baba 'mkulu was happy, but sad, because now he had to send his most loved son to Shoshong in Bechuanaland. He was fearful for him and needed him nearby. Thomasi said the Tswana people would welcome Nkanyiso, but *baba 'mkulu* had seen many things and knew many things. There was anger and hatred of the Matebele in Bechuanaland. In time, he would perhaps trust Thomasi's friend to look after him, but it was a long, uncomfortable decision.

After four years in Shoshong, Nkanyiso came home alive – and he came home as a teacher! There was great rejoicing. A prize ox was slaughtered for the village to welcome him. Teacher Nkanyiso Ncube. There was pride and recognition in that title.

He was not just any teacher. He had great passion about the correct use of the land, animal husbandry and cropping. After two days at home, he was given the job as teacher of agriculture at the Government School.

The headmaster was pleased. The students did not respect the South African or Tswana teachers, but now he had a local amaNdebele teacher on the staff. What was more, he was not just an amaNdebele, but from the Khumalo royal family.

Many years later, when Nkanyiso became a father, he was determined his own boys would go to school and be the best teachers too.

But he had a great disappointment.

His own brightest son, Jabulani, didn't want to work hard and learn. Nkanyiso looked proudly at the other boys he was teaching, all of them as hungry for learning as for their favourite food. All of them working harder and getting better marks than this brightest son. It was not a time for lazy boys. There was humiliation for Nkanyiso in this lazy boy.

Jabu's mother remained the constant loving protector, as father grew impatient, irritated – and even ashamed – of his son.

"How can he learn at school with all your intimidation?" she cried. So Nkanyiso sent him away after junior school to Dadaya Mission School.

Jabu agreed with his mother of course. Every time he went home, Nkanyiso was coaxing, persuading, getting angry. Sullen and reluctant, Jabu agreed to write Jaycee – but no more!.

Then Jabu saw HIM there. He couldn't believe his eyes! He sniffed in disgust. *If that bandlulula Prune can write Jaycee, then this white education is definitely not what I need.*

He sat with arms folded.

Prune doing Jaycee! Jabu was astonished and knew Prune was saying to himself, "I see you Jabu. And now we are both writing Jaycee together. I am no longer *bandlulula*. I am as good as you."

Jabu had made sure not to look at Prune. How did he get here? It had been hard for Jabu to get to Kutama to write Jaycee from Dadaya, let alone Prune from Tjolotjo.

But seeing Prune writing his JayCee stirred something deep inside him. He could not let him beat him, even in white man's education. Never! *I will learn to write and speak good English. I will learn the ways of the whites, for by knowing them, I will learn to be a better leader of my people.*

Jabu passed Jaycee - just - but now he told his father he would like to continue to "O" levels.

His father was very happy – but still a little unhappy because the JC results should have been better.

Nkanyiso was now a senior teacher at Tegwani High School. So after a great deal of discussion, Jabu was given a place in the school to continue to GCE "O" levels. He worked and worked and worked.

His mother was shocked. His father was amazed!

Jabu had also become a thoughtful and passionate participant in the Debating Society. He'd sit up late in the night with all the other boys in the debating teams, asking questions and making comments about everything. At the end of 1956, Jabu passed "O" levels with matric exemption. A proud Nkanyiso thought he could now become a teacher and trainer in agriculture and follow in his footsteps.

Matric exemption had gained Jabu entrance into a South African university, but this was perhaps not quite the agenda Jabu had in mind.

He had thought of being in agriculture, because of his love of school holidays, when he joined the family on his *baba 'mkulu's* farm.He remembered how he used to love getting up feeling the crisp, chill of an early morning, with fourteen other boy cousins shouting, chasing each other in rowdy clowning about and singing as they went to milk and herd the cattle.

Jabu found he was particularly good at helping labouring cows to drop their calves without complications. And the herd's numbers grew. In the busy time, all the boys worked with the *m'dalas*[2] to plough their fields, while the young girls tidied houses and planted vegetables or went to reap mealies and *badza*[74] the fields. Each boy was given money to thank them for their work. Jabu saved every penny.

Girls didn't get money because they didn't know how to use it, so when they worked, more money was added to their husband.

When they finished their work, the boys tracked and hunted for that night's meal as the sun dipped and shadows grew longer. They learned to become invisible, hiding in dark places, or flattening their bodies to the ground. Still as a stone. They waited sometimes for a long time, ignoring the itch of mosquitos and ants biting at dusk, itching that cried to be scratched. No movement. Just bite the teeth. Just wait.

The outline of a timid impala appeared, suddenly visible because of a twitching ear or the lift of a wet, shining nose. It sniffed the air gently before stepping nervously from its safe place away from the heat of the day. Jabu knew which animals to hunt so there would be good buck left to increase the herds. As leader of the hunting, he decided which animal was right for the next meal. He told the others, signalling with his eyes so he did not disturb the buck.

Almost without movement, he drew his spear right back. Then a cousin broke a twig near him. The buck looked straight at Jabu. He threw, making sure it died quickly with his spear through its heart. If his throw was not good, another boy could rush in to quickly club the head. But Jabu's throw was always good. He practiced every day to make sure.

The younger boys would plead to set traps for rabbits and dassies and even for small buck like duiker, but Jabu hated traps. Young boys would

---

[74] *badza*: hoe

forget to check them, and caught animals would take a long time to die from broken legs or strangled necks. There were no traps when Jabu hunted. There were better ways.

They would sing victory songs all the way back to the farm, carrying the buck, head hanging and feet tied together on a *mopani*[75] pole. Then it was time to cut chunks of meat that the girls would roast. As night fell, stories of the ancients began, and each new generation sat wide-eyed in wonder at the bravery, the strength and the might of their uncles and the battles of the Matebele. The nightly drumming and dancing would last late into the night. Good times.

It was a healthy rural life, full of the traditions of his people. Jabu listened and learned. Then it was his turn to look after the festivals, the story telling and the teaching of the young ones. He often felt the watchful eye of father and grandfather neither of them quite sure where this strong, good-looking young man might go.

Fear and anger: the Land Husbandry Act

The last visit to the farm had been very different. This time, Jabu heard that people were angry because of the Government's Native Land Husbandry Act, which had been introduced five years ago in 1951.

His *baba 'mkulu* was worried about it too.

Jabu's current affairs class had debated, discussed and analysed this Act but now he was here with people who were crying.

The class decided the Act it was trying to put things right because of the degradation of native reserves and another because - too many babies were being born. He had learned about improving farming methods and conservation. But he now he was on the farm, he wondered if this Act spoke in two ways – one good, one bad.

"To regulate conservation measures and ensure good farming practices". Jabu agreed that was a good intention.

"To relate the stocking of each area to its carrying capacity". Of course, every good farmer would do that – in a country like England. But it was difficult in Africa.

When the rinderpest came many years ago, it killed hundreds of cattle

---

[75] *mopani*: native tree

in two ways. First it killed the cattle that became sick with the rinderpest – then it killed more cattle because government men came and shot all cattle from any herd that was sick. They said it was to stop the rinderpest spreading. But the people did not believe it. They were bewildered and angry, thinking they had been punished.

How could they live without cattle?

Now people had been told they must de-stock, which meant they had to get rid of many more cattle. But when cattle were all sold at the same time, the prices were low.

Anyway, people did not want to exchange cattle for money, because when they had money, sons and daughters and cousins and uncles and aunts from the city would come and demand their share of the money. Then they would be left with no cattle and no money for the future.

Wealth for Africa is measured by a man's cattle, particularly for getting married. Jabu knew this was a bad mistake the government was making. He wrote *Land Husbandry Act* in his notebook under a heading "Flashpoints" and added a sharp star symbol so he could pick it out easily.

"To allocate grazing rights to individuals" and *"to distribute arable land into compact and economic units and register each owner".*

It was very good for the individuals who got to own grazing rights, but what about the hundreds and thousands who didn't? And what land did people who lived in the cities have for their families? All land belonged to everyone in African culture.

Jabu had to think about this.

As a chiefly family, his grandparents was given land by Rhodes. Now, because of *Baba 'Mkulu*, Nkanyiso and Jabu himself, that land was farmed well. It was productive, it fed their family and the community. It left enough to sell and make good money in the hubbub of busy Bulawayo markets. Their vegetables looked the best and sold first.

Jabu thought about his *baba 'mkulu*. He was a man of wisdom and he himself wouldn't be hurt by the Act, but he was worried about something. It was not Jabu's place to ask such a question of his *baba 'mkulu*.

So he asked his father.

Nkanyiso explained that one of the most important responsibilities of a Chief was to allocate land to people in his tribe. The Chief would give land for many reasons – to reward, to chastise, to maintain discipline, to give the land time to rest, time to grow, time to decide to move on, all his thinking always, was about the whole tribe. The government wanted to take this most important job away.

This would damage the status of Chiefs and make it harder for them to look after their people. When government gave land to a person who was not a Chief, it was not valued and would not be looked after.

Undermining the Chiefs – Jabu made another star under "Flashpoints".

All the villages had to do exactly what the land inspectors wanted them to do. First, they wanted to gather the scattered villages together. Then they wanted to separate grazing land from ploughing land. Then they wanted them to move the cattle into different paddocks. Then all cattle had to be dipped.

Africans didn't understand – didn't want to understand – because they had been doing things their way for so long. When land grew tired, they moved to the next place.

Now there was no new land, and no next place. Just too many people.

Jabu knew all that.

He knew that moving villages together and separating land usage would mean they could put in contours and grow bigger crops, which would earn foreign currency, which was important. He knew that moving cattle into different paddocks meant the dung would fertilise the grass and improve the soil. He knew that by dipping cattle you could stop the ticks.

But the people didn't know.

The people didn't understand.

These new things frightened them.

Jabu knew that most of what the new Act said was right. He had seen how good his own family's cattle were - how much better their mealies and rapoko were and how many trucks of vegetables were taken into Bulawayo every week. He knew, because he had been taught. There wasn't enough teaching about these things. People were slow to change. They distrusted being moved about and wanted to stay in their villages and do things their own way.

After hours of *indabas* and talking with the Native Commissioners and other Chiefs and Headmen, people were saying that it was another trick of the white people to keep the natives poor. Unhappiness was growing.

There were many "Flashpoints" to be considered and many sharp star symbols to help him find them again.

Climbing kopjes

When he needed to think about difficult things, he would climb *kopjes*. Sometimes, he climbed the *kopjes* behind Ntabazinduna so he could look back at its flat plateau and think of the great King Mzilikazi and the throwing of the Chiefs.

He was sorry the voices of Mlimo at Njelele and Mkwati at 'nThaba zikaMambo no longer spoke. His *baba 'mkulu* used to go to Njelele every August or September to tell of his problems and say sorry if he or his people did not follow the Mlimo's advice. Then he would thank him for good rains last year and ask for good rains this year.

Jabu would have liked to talk to Mlimo in the Matopos – there were many new questions to be asked. Then he thought it was time for a journey to the 'nThaba zikaMamba, where his initiation ceremony had taken place. He knew that only sometimes could Mkwati's voice still be heard.

But sometimes it could - even now.

He sighed. He did love his school holidays on the farm, but not enough to make his life there, or even to become a teacher.

More and more, he wanted to fight for people who couldn't understand the white people and their government – and who wanted their old life back – with a Chief to look after them. In all this thinking, he realised that because his heart was on these bigger things, if he was really going to be able to help, he needed even greater skills. And that probably meant going to University, even if it seemed to be against everything that seemed more important to him.

Time to tell his father and he might be worried.

He walked reluctantly back to the farmhouse to find his father. He saw him looking at some of *baba mkulu's* Tuli cattle. He walked up to him, greeted him, then said: "I have decided that if I am going to be able to help my people well, I need to go to University."

He spoke in a great rush.

His father tried not to look surprised. Instead, he looked thoughtful and said, "An admirable decision. However, there is one problem my son, universities cost a lot of money." He paused.

Jabu waited.

Then Nkanyiso placed his hand on his son's shoulder "You might be able to teach the younger boys at Tegwani perhaps. And help me also by saving up for some of the fees yourself. I'll speak to the principal."

Father and son stood quietly, companionably – their eyes met . . . each recognising the other, for the first time, as a man of stature. They understood that they were leaders in an unspoken future. The tie between them grew stronger.

Jabu's quiet, measured speech reflected a maturity well beyond his just 16 years. This, plus his sports strengthened body, meant most people thought he was at least 18, sometimes even 20. Even to his parents, his slightly serious demeanour and questioning mind had helped to mask his single-minded pursuit of only those things that would achieve his objectives. As a student, he often caused surprise when he proved to be the ringleader in many a daring and mostly forbidden escapade!

It might be time to stop that for a start, he thought ruefully.

The principal at Tegwani agreed it was a good idea for Jabu to take on some teaching. It was still difficult to find enough amaNdebele teachers, so he started by teaching standard II.

The teaching was easy because it was work he had done many years ago. All he had to do was to follow the syllabus and think of clever ways to say things so the students remembered easily. But maintaining discipline and having authority over the class wasn't easy.

Most boys started school much later than he had done, because parents still weren't sure that education was more important than looking after cattle, especially in rural areas.

So children started school later, and at least half the class of Standard II was older than he was. In fact, there was one boy of 23 who had only started school when he was 21! Jabu had been 8 in Standard II. So he had to find a different way to hold the interest of young men, not children, and convince them of how important it was to learn their tables and writing. They were not as co-operative as the younger ones in the class.

If ever there was trouble, it came from the older boys.

The work was discouraging and difficult. He learned not to tell anyone his age and resolved that in future, he'd give information about himself and his activities only to those who absolutely needed to know. It was a decision that might be useful later on.

Most of all, Jabulani learned what it took to be a leader.

Because he had been a pupil at the school and even though he was now a teacher, Jabu still enjoyed the Debating Society, making sure he went to all the political and current affairs debates.

The Head Teacher encouraged all students to discuss current affairs and politics. Jabu became engrossed in these debates, more and more interested.

Unnoticed by school or family, he had also signed up and become one of the youngest members of the Southern Rhodesia Youth League, and he ached with longing to get out and do something. Quite what, he didn't know, because Tegwani was far away from Bulawayo and even further from Salisbury, where there was great excitement at the moment around events involving big names like James Chikerema and George Nyandoro of the City Youth League, the CYL.

Last year, the United Transport Company had said they would increase their fares. When the CYL worked out what that would mean, they found that people using buses would spend 24% of their income just to get to work! So Chikerema and Nyandoro called their members to organise their families and friends to get out and tell everyone, "Nobody must use the buses. Stay away from work. We are fighting for you now."

The students in the Debating Society had listened to the radio in class and heard that there were no buses running in Salisbury that day.

"Hau! Is it true?" they asked.

And it was! After two days, the United Transport Company decided it would not increase its fares after all. So Chikerema and Nyandoro won.

"Hau!"

The Head Teacher put another point of view all the time – arguing that further research had found that 24% of a person's income was not correct, it was only 8%, and that the Land Husbandry Act did talk about important things needed to be done. So they were trained to see things from all sides.

But mostly they still saw things from their own side.

Meeting Joshua Nkomo

Last night and full of excitement, the senior boys and teachers had been allowed to attend a meeting to hear a leading young politician speak. His name was Joshua Nkomo. Jabu had known Joshua in his Tjolotjo days, when he was teaching carpentry at the school there. Now he was the president of the new Southern Rhodesia African National Congress.

Jabu felt his heart pumping with excited anticipation, as Joshua told them first how in 1951, the Prime Minister of Southern Rhodesia, Sir Godfrey Huggins, had asked him to go to London as part of a delegation to talk about the proposed Federation. Joshua Nkomo had insisted that the African majority must be consulted before any Federation took place and he would not sign the report at the end of the conference. The rest of the delegation took no notice, and the Federation was formed, but now with two journalists – Jasper Savanhu and Michael Hove – representing African opinion.

"There is one good thing about Federation," Joshua declared "now that Huggins is the Federal Prime Minister, we have Garfield Todd as Southern Rhodesia's Prime Minister.

"I can talk to him and he listens. He has already increased the minimum wage, made some increases in funding for African education, and is trying to increase the number of Africans who can vote. He is a disciplined man. A strong, but good man."

There was a lot of clapping and chatter all around the hall at this.

"Unfortunately, there are a lot of important people who don't like him," he continued, writing points on the blackboard as he spoke.

"The SRANC is a non-violent reform group. We work to increase universal suffrage, we are against discrimination, we will eradicate racism, expand the education system, improve our standards of living, make sure there are free trials for all, and support the inauguration of democratic systems . . . finally, direct participation in the government."

Then Nkomo went on to talk about the Land Husbandry Act. "You know there have been many riots going on around the country which we have organised."

There were some nods, but not very many, as the riots were far away. Unless you were in Current Affairs, you didn't hear about them in Tegwani.

"The Chiefs understand this Act is undermining their authority, so we are working together with them, because it must stop. The Chiefs are refusing to process permits and we will continue the riots."

Jabu was glad to hear this, because he had wanted to talk to his *baba 'mkulu* about what he could do to help the Chiefs. So it was good to hear this man, Joshua Nkomo, who understood their fear and had made them understand what they could do to fight it.

Joshua took a sheet of paper from his briefcase and began speaking.

"I have just issued a statement to the press. It says

'Any act whose effects undermine the security of our small land rights, dispossess us of our little wealth in the form of cattle, disperse us from our ancestral homes in the reserves and reduce us to the status of vagabonds and as a source of cheap labour for the farmers, miners and industrialists – such an Act will turn the African People against society to the detriment of the peace and progress of this country.'"

There were shouts of applause and clapping as everyone stood to say "thank you" to this brave man.

"So we are making progress – but in slow steps. As you know, I was working for Rhodesia Railways, as a senior Social Welfare Officer, looking after the employees there. A few years ago, I went to Britain. I happened to have a pamphlet from the WFTU – the World Federation of Trade Unions – in my luggage. I was stopped and charged, then told I had to appear in court. I couldn't understand it! I happened to have this pamphlet in my luggage, that's all! So I did not know what to do. To hire a lawyer was too much money, so I decided to defend myself."

Jabu looked round the room. There were jaws dropping all around and excited whispering.

"I was a respectable citizen, gainfully employed. And I did not like the thought that someone could be arrested for bringing in a pamphlet which was of direct relevance to his business. So I went to the courtroom and was shown into the place where criminals stand.

I asked the magistrate for a bigger place to put all my papers, and he was very kind. He brought me down to stand next to the government prosecutor.

"The prosecutor started to talk. He looked at me and called me 'My Learned Colleague . . .'"

Joshua joined in the howls of laughter from the audience.

"I was let off with a caution. So you see, as long as you play it right, you can win.

"I must now finish as I have to catch an aeroplane to go to Cairo tomorrow. And then I will stay in London, because I can speak to many people about the situation here, and they will support us. But before I go, the newly formed SRANC now includes both James Chikerema and George Nyandoro who were with the CYL. This is important for you to know. Although they have been detained because of the UTS riots last year, they will carry on working to find and report cases of discrimination in the workplace while I am away."

He went on to say that although these were exciting times and there should be many opportunities for us, there were only a few jobs open to us because, although we were now well educated, we were still black.

Through the evening there had had been loud arguments and agreement on many points, Arguments mostly seemed to focus in anger on the British "solution for Central Africa" – the Federation. This grouped together the self-governing colony of Southern Rhodesia with the Protectorates of Northern Rhodesia and Nyasaland. It was an unhappy marriage.

Joshua stood quietly listening to what everyone was saying about Federation. He cleared his throat loudly. Everyone stopped talking.

Then, speaking as the President of the SRANC, he told the Tegwani Debating Society about secret discussions he was having with Harry Nkumbula and others in Northern Rhodesia and Nyasaland, as they were all concerned about their future in the Federation. They were told not to tell anyone else.

So everyone left feeling important and serious and part of something exciting. And everyone at the meeting bought copies of *The Drum*, the paper for Africans produced in South Africa so that they could find out more about not only the ANC in South Africa, but also the SRANC.

Jabu had an advantage over his fellow teachers in Tegwani, as Joshua greeted him like an old friend, publicly acknowledging the importance of his family as he did so. Nkomo encouraged him to move to Bulawayo. He gave him contact details of companies employing educated black school leavers on good conditions.

They were able to talk for several hours afterwards, and Jabulani's stature grew. He had learned much as a member of the Southern Rhodesia Youth League, but now they knew he was already a member of the SRANC itself.

After Nkomo's visit, he knew his views would be even more respected and his leadership unquestioned on this campus.

A few days later, he woke knowing that he had grown beyond this particular campus. It was time to find a larger one. Jabu decided to apply for any job that might be available, telling the Head Teacher that he would not be here next term.

He didn't tell his father – yet.

The importance of a large wife

There was one thing tugging at his heart at the thought of leaving Tegwani – saying goodbye to the cheeky girl who was the daughter of the administration clerk.

Bongani was very beautiful, with a bright, always smiling face and a clever brain. She looked smart and dressed neatly. She didn't care how important Jabu was because he knew Joshua Nkomo, and she was always teasing him. Her father, Mandhla Moyo, had taught her himself, as girls found it difficult to get places in school.

She was very precious to Mandhla, as she had been born in his old age. The wife he loved had died at her birth. So he called her "Bongani[76]" as a thank you to his wife. Now that Bongani was grown up, she was as small and lively as his wife had been. Mandhla would look at her and say, "My Bongani, you are the fruit of my loins when they were old, and I loved your mother who left me too soon. Now you look like her and you speak like her, and so I love you two times over."

---

[76] *Bongani*: We are grateful

Bongani would give him a hug and tell him she loved him too but only once as much. And they would laugh.

Mandhla did worry that she was so small, because Africans knew that important men liked to have a large wife to show off. He didn't think a very important man would even see his beloved little Bongani.

However, Jabu had decided he would very much like to see little Bongani. To do so, he would need to get to know Baba Moyo better. He could then be close to Bongani and her teasing. When he wasn't busy, he spent time with him, learning all about good administration. He was taught a lot about managing things, and he learned a lot more about Bongani too before he decided he also loved her – perhaps not quite as much as Mandhla Moyo - but close.

She was clever, she was funny, and she was interested in what he was doing. Jabu didn't see Bongani as a small person, so Mandhla felt reassured – because if a clever boy like Jabu liked her, one day an important man would love Bongani even if she wasn't a very big girl.

Jabu goes to prison

Jabu applied for a position at the Department of Prisons, stating that he was now 21 years old. He was interested in the job, because it meant taking post and other things to prisons and looking after some of the prisoners at Khami High Security Prison. The government was detaining the leaders who were causing problems, and Jabu might meet them, if he had a job in the Prisons Department.

All the following week, he would jump every time he heard the office phone ring, in case it was for him. Then it was! A man called Mr Eddington asked him questions about his education and background and why he wanted to work for prisons. "It's difficult work, you know Mr Ncube, and you can end up being very unpopular." '

Mr Ncube! Jabu liked that.

Another week later, Mr Eddington phoned to congratulate him. Jabu was so excited that he had got the job – but now he had to sort out a few more things.

First of all, leaving his job at Tegwani. Then leaving Bongani. How could he leave that beautiful girl? Perhaps there was going to be no place for Bongani in his new life. He didn't want to think about that.

But the biggest sort out of all was the one he feared most.

Jabu straightened his back, took a deep breath and thought positively about what he was going to say, so that he would be brave enough to phone his father.

At first, Nkanyiso was excited to hear about Jabu's new job. But as his son told him of the wonderful chance he now had to meet all the SRANC people who were in prison, the old man's heart sank. He did believe absolutely in the need to improve education and opportunities for black people, but he knew in his heart that this was not the right job for his son.

Nkanyiso Ncube was a member of the African Affairs Board set up by the Federal Government. He had been working hard for many years now with every available hour he had to monitor and correct any signs of discrimination towards Africans in the Federation. At last, the goodwill being shown to African people and the huge changes that this Board was seeing being made every day, impressed and encouraged him.

During another long phone call to his son this morning, Nkanyiso expressed his two main worries – about giving up his thought about going on to university and about mixing with some of the prisoners. He was also worried about Jabu's membership of the SRANC but thought perhaps he wouldn't mention that and instead he encouraged and praised him – then cautioned him – about his two main worries.

"Jabu," he said. "At university, you will be in a perfect position to study politics. Perhaps you will become one of the new junior ministers in the Federal parliament. I must introduce you to Jasper Savanhu and Godwin Lewanika – they are our men of the future. Jasper is always fighting for higher wages and better conditions. At one time, he worked with Enoch Dumbutshena to try and get some new ideas through the SRANC. But he got frustrated because SRANC was not happy to look at other ways of doing things, and he felt he was getting nowhere. Although he didn't like the idea of the Federation either, Jasper eventually realised he could achieve more for our people by being in Government rather than fighting from outside.

"I am excited by what is happening. There are many new jobs being created. There is increased interest from international investors, like the money for the Kariba dam. This will mean we can soon start to generate our own electricity. It's a wonderful time, and you will be in the right place at the right time. But please choose your path carefully and be very careful who you mix with."

Jabu reassured his father that he would do so, adding, "I will be earning three times what I am at the moment, so I will be able to save up for University three times as fast."

He had already decided that it was indeed an exciting time, and he was quite determined to be a man of the future. But his "right time" and "right place" might not be quite the time and place his father hoped.

He was more concerned about leaving Bongani. In the last few days, she had been looking at him through the sides of her eyes and bringing him treats from her kitchen. Leaving her here with all these other young men around was a big risk, and he needed to be sure that she would remember him and make promises. He wasn't comfortable yet doing things girls wanted to do – they didn't want to hunt, or box.

But he still found he liked spending time with Bongani only because she was clever and cheeky and because she too had become a member of the SRANC.

He plucked up his courage two days before he was due to leave.

"Bongani," he said quietly when they met in the corridor outside the office. "Would you like to go for a walk?"

"Oh – OK," she said. She followed him outside.

"I have to go to the soccer pitch to find one of the balls that was missing when we played on Saturday. Will you come with me?"

"Oh – OK!"

Jabu just didn't know how to start the conversation. "Baba Moyo tells me you are a very clever girl."

"I am" she said haughtily, "but I'm not allowed to write matric because I am not enrolled at the school."

"Have you done the work?"

She looked at him with disdain, because she had thought at least he would be one person who felt that girls should be educated.

"Of course," she said with an irritated flash of her eyes, "and I did Maths and General Science, with English and History for my subjects. I wrote them from old exam papers I got from my father."

Jabu's eyes widened.

"And Mr Hawkins looked at the papers I had completed, and he said I would have got my matriculation exemption easily." Bongani dropped her head.

"But then he spoilt it by asking if I had copied the answers."

Jabu felt ashamed. "Bongani, that is terrible."

His mind was searching for an answer.

"If you were in Bulawayo, you could go to a government school. Then you would be able to write your matric."

"But I have never been to Bulawayo. I cannot leave my father."

Jabu went silent, thoughts chasing through his head. Then he said, quietly, "Well, I have just got a job in Bulawayo and I will start off staying with my grandfather at Ntabazinduna. That is like not really being right in Bulawayo. If I could find a family who would look after you, would you come?"

Her eyes brightened, but then she dropped her head again. "I cannot yet leave my father."

So Jabu understood. And he also understood that he was just going to have to come back to see Bongani whenever he could, or she would find somebody else to look after her.

"Can I write to you when I go to Bulawayo?" he asked.

"OK." She lifted her cheek towards him, but her eyes were different – not cheeky. He touched her cheek with his hand, then gently leant forward and kissed her. Then he felt embarrassed and backed away, saying, "I have to go and get ready. See you just now."

He rushed off, but he felt hot and cold and breathless. He looked back. She was standing with her hands on her hips, laughing in her naughty way. Ooh! It would be hard leaving that cheeky girl.

Jabulani left for Bulawayo aged 16 but pretending to be 21. He was fired up with the excitement and energy of first love and more than ever determined to discover a campus big enough for him. For he was after all Bhekisizwe, the restorer of his people.

That year, Jasper Savanhu became the first African to be Federal Government Secretary to the Ministry of Home Affairs.

11

THE DESECRATED CAVE

They were up early – today was not to be wasted. Carol was first in the car, impatient for her father and Prune to get moving. Despite an already overheated sunrise, a quick look at her watch told her it was only 4:45. It would be another typically sweltering Bulawayo day. But after last night's rain, there would be a rare touch of humidity.

"Come on guys!" she pleaded. There was a flurry of activity, and at last Angus and Prune emerged carrying a large hamper and loading it into the boot

Once they had driven past the outskirts of the city, Angus said: "I'm going to give you a number of phrases. Write them down, because this is what we are going to see and talk about over the next few days." Deliberately but hesitantly, thinking through what he wanted to say but giving them plenty of time to write, he listed,

"The Industrial Revolution

"The abolition of slavery

"Darwin's theory of evolution

"The Berlin Conference

"Britain's last colony

"The tale of two kings—"

"Ah! That's easy!" shouted Prune, "Mzilikazi and Lobengula."

"Right!"

Carol smiled to see Prune enthusiastic at last. He grinned back. Eyes bright, teeth white, he was almost back to his old self and looked excited and smiley enough to be chosen for one of the new Sunlight soap advertisements in the Chronicle!

"Moving on," Angus interrupted her train of thought, "a couple more

"Magnificent naiveté—"

"What does that mean?" Carol asked.

"Hang on, Miss Impatient! We'll get to that. Just jot it down for now.

"Corruption, cruelty, savagery, disaster, ineptitude . . . philanthropy, courage, benevolence . . ."

He stopped, lost in thought. "And finally . . .   a Colossus."

"Wow! That'll keep us quiet. Sounds horribly academic Dad. Prune did you get them all down?" Carol asked, as he had stopped writing.

"I got them all till Mzilikazi and Lobengula." He looked troubled. "Then I started thinking about where I fit in. I looked out of the window and saw the start of all those *kopjes* in the Matopos. I felt uncomfortable, because I love this place so much, but I don't know if I belong here."

"Prune - does it really matter? You have a wonderful family and you're going to marry Maura - it's exciting! By the end of today, you'll have a much better idea of where you fit in anyway. For now, just remind yourself how lucky you are to live in this beautiful part of Africa."

"To remind you both, of how fortunate we all are, we're going to sniff the air of that welcome rain last night, watch the trees as sap in their trunks lifts new life up to fill those drooping leaves. In a couple of days, splashes of colour from healthy shoots of grass and bush plants will cover and soften this burnt out old landscape.

"Most important," he continued, "this will underline the fact that the land keeps going – keeps regenerating after drought, destruction and disaster - keeps producing for us, for the wildlife, for the cattle.

'It is only us human beings who make a massive difference - we can encourage the very best or, sadly, we can jill everything and everyone around." Carol noticed that he suddenly looked down hearted.

They'd been driving out of Bulawayo on the old Gwanda road – some of the original strips in parts, but bone shaking, corrugated red dirt most of the way. They were glad to be still for a moment as they pulled into the shade of a magnificent old mountain acacia and stopped the engine to enjoy that first quiet moment in the African bush, away from the perpetual motion of the town.

They all checked for vicious, biting Matebele ants before sitting on a low granite boulder.

Carol dug into a paper bag filled with food and drink, handing out egg sandwiches and a sausage each. As she poured water into tin mugs from a well-worn old thermos flask, she glanced over at her father's face.

"Dad, before we start, you seem to have been worried about something for a while. Can we talk about it ?"

"Yes I am - worried . . . and yes, we can"

The times, they are a-changin'

He took a deep breath.

"I suppose it's relevant to what we're going to see and talk about, so here goes - and I'll try and be quick!

"You know that Jabulani's father, Nkanyiso and I were elected onto the African Affairs Board when the Federation was formed in 1953?"

"Yes." they chorused.

"Many people are talking about it. I know that voting for Africans is now important - and I want to save money to qualify."

"That's one of the difficult areas Prune. We've been arguing with the British for over a year now, saying the voting qualifications they are suggesting for the B roll are discouraging. They're much too high to get a fair overview of African opinion - allowing only a few hundred eligible people to vote. It's not enough."

"My friends say it doesn't matter to us in Tjolotjo or Balla Balla. I try to tell them it **is** important, because even from Tjolotjo or Balla Balla we can influence the way the country is run. They just laugh – and carry on playing jacks in the sand. They say the Chiefs will look after them and tell them what to do."

Prune stopped. Then looked at Angus

"Voting is important – isn't it?"

Angus sighed. "It's hard for you, Prune. You live in two worlds, with Lalan being white and Naison being black, and you have your J.C. So you've learned things your friends haven't even thought of yet."

"Shouldn't all the native children go to school?" Carol asked.

"In an ideal world, of course. The reason they don't is too simple and too difficult. Unfortunately . . ."

"Southern Rhodesia is a self-governing colony, so we're expected to manage most of our own affairs. We don't get as much financial support from England as protectorates - but at the same time, we can't make big decisions without their approval - and that can be infuriating!

"Right now, we have the highest birth rate in the world, at 3.2% increase every year. By comparison, I've been looking at the population increase in Britain for this year, 1957 . . . it is only 0.61% - not even 1%! Britain is panicking because they can't cope with the demand for infrastructure and housing. They have no idea what we're facing."

Carol mouthed "wow" to Prune, but it didn't seem right to interrupt.

"I'll try to put some figures on that. Our population 10 years ago was about two and a half million - new census results will be out soon, and I guess we'll be over three million – and that's in only 10 years."

"That sounds very high very quickly."

"It is frightening - for any country but particularly for us, in these early stages of building from nothing."

"Why have those numbers gone up so quickly?"

"Lots of reasons Prune. Population growth was controlled by raiding and disease. Tribal killing is almost gone now and preventive medicine has reduced disease. Another thing, is that African men want many wives and far too many children. This was good when many died before, but now 8 or 10 children from each wife survive. "

"There certainly seem to be more *piccanins* around," Prune added.

Angus nodded with a rueful look on his face. "Zhanje, our messenger thinks he has 58 children! I'm stunned!" So were Carol and Prune

"Prune, you are already 17 and Carol will be 17 next month. Over half the black population of this country today, is younger than you are! So not only do we have unmanageable population growth - but it's unbalanced, too many young people, making it impossible to educate everyone, even for a massively wealthy country. And we are not that!"

"How many white people are there here Dad?"

"The latest figure I heard was about 165,000 in Southern Rhodesia.

"The thing I hate most though, though, is that although this Federation of Southern Rhodesia, Northern Rhodesia and Nyasaland – has brought investment in big projects, we don't have, nearly enough black people trained to help us build them. So government decided to bring in skilled artisans from all over the world to fill the gaps.

"They came in mainly from the UK, but they expected their children to have the same education here, and to live in the same standard of housing - or they wouldn't have come. So many flooded in just after World War II that they almost doubled the existing white population.

"But then something we didn't even imagine, started to happen. Now, ten years later, Southern Rhodesia has become their home, so they're beginning to dictate policy, because they pay a big chunk of income tax.

"But - they have a different way of thinking. They trample on native culture and rights far more than we who were born here, ever did. I'm not saying we were perfect – far from it. But we were learning together. This new lot demand their rights and I sense antagonism developing towards advancement of Africans – in case they take their jobs.

"Bottom line – and end of conversation. We don't earn enough from income taxes, mining or farming as it is. So we can't provide enough healthcare or education for the massive growth in the black population - let alone enough to provide good housing, hospitals and schools … or enough skills training to build roads, railways, bridges or dams for reliable electricity and water.

"Oh boy, that sounds absolutely disastrous Dad!"

"Oh look – I'm sorry … just feeling depressed about the impossible task we have ahead of us."

"Has the Federation made things better or worse?" Prune asked.

"It was never a good idea. Northern Rhodesia and Nyasaland are Protectorates of Britain. Whites in Southern Rhodesia get irritated: they believe the others get preferential treatment even though Southern Rhodesia drives the economy.

"Africans in the two northern territories are not as advanced in education or healthcare as we are and British involvement is more of a caretaker roll, providing administration and police. Africans there, are worried about losing those advantages, they have help and security, but they mostly still run things as they've always done - and they're suspicious of us being more hard line."

"Are we getting more hard line?" Carol asked.

"Yes . . . I think so. Some of our policies are more like those in South Africa, particularly this blasted Native Land Husbandry Act. It's right in what it's trying to do but it's been badly put together and poorly explained.

"Mind you, the Africans don't always help.

"It is hard to get them to understand how vital it is to retain their own traditions and culture. These are still reasonably intact in the rural areas, but when they see the white way of life in the towns and cities, they know that if they get the right education, they can earn enough money to live in a big house, drive a car and dress well. They diminish their own culture by preferring ours but when we are find it almost impossible to educate them all, they think we are keeping them down.

"The whole thing is a mess."

He paused and looked away.

Nobody felt like talking. Carol felt a lump of fear in her heart — fear for her father, fear for her, anxiety for Prune and Jabu — she knew Themba was going to be fine — but there seemed to be so many problems that she hadn't even thought about. Frankly, she really didn't want to think about them either.

She wished they had never embarked on this trip. It seemed to be more and more depressing.

Angus gave another big sigh and continued in a soft, sad voice.

"After new voters rolls along the British recommendations were drawn up by the Federal Government, they did argue saying they were differentiating and inappropriate. The Secretary of State for the Colonies told the House of Commons last month, he didn't agree. So in February, they just went over our heads and passed them."

He spoke angrily.

"It is ridiculous — we have people in London passing critical laws that affect our country. They're seven and a half thousand miles away, knowing precious little about the situation! They really couldn't care less."

"One of the reasons I am here. as you know, is to see Chief Khayisa Ndiweni and let him know that I have just heard, that I've been removed from the African Affairs Board. So has Jabu's father."

"Oh no!" they chorused. "No wonder you're depressed."

"I must find time to talk to Nkanyiso and we'll go through Tegwani. You two might catch up with Jabu - he is doing some teaching there."

"That's something" Carol agreed.

"Why have you been removed?"

"They've cut the number of officials by half – making sure those who are left will agree with everything 'they' want."

"You and Mr Ncube didn't agree with what they wanted."

"No we did not! It was mainly the restrictions on the new voters roll but nobody else on that committee seemed to have the guts to stand up to the bigwigs."

"What do you think is going to happen now?"

"I don't know . . . it's not all bad - the hydro-electric dam at Kariba will guarantee power, and we have new inter connecting roads and railways between the three countries – Southern Rhodesia could not have done them by itself. There are also big developments in mining and farming attracting world attention – and there's a big increase in funds for African education in Southern Rhodesia thanks to our Prime Minister, Garfield Todd.

"Despite all this, I cannot see the Federation continuing without an awful lot of trouble ahead."

The Matopos, baboons and wild dogs

Carol and Prune were very quiet. Neither of them had cared what the Federation really meant. That was just what government did, and their lives carried on as before.

Prune began looking for ant-lion holes in the sand while Carol stared out at the stark, painted rocks of the Matopos. They looked as though God had thrown thousands of great, lichened granite marbles of all sizes on top of each other for His children to play with. Huge boulders had landed, balancing precariously on top of others, creating cracks, crevices and dark spooky caves that they'd loved exploring as children – always with a thrill of panicky excitement. They were full of spiders and bats; sometimes they heard the growl of something fierce that might eat them!

Looking over the characteristic Matopos view in front of them, she realised how much she missed it all. The great balancing rocks – weathered, rounded and softened by huge trees and wandering valleys - were rich with tales of ancient kingdoms and conquerors, of gold diggers, hunters – and tragedies. Many were protected by the barking of troupes of swaggering baboons.

Carol noticed that the car windows were wide open to let in the freshness of shaded air in the increasing heat, but at the hint of an approaching and challenging bark, they would pack up, jump in the car and wind those windows up very quickly.

Prune looked up from his antlions putting a finger to his lips in a silent "shush" as he slowly raised his arm and pointed. He had seen something.

Equally slowly, Carol and Angus moved their eyes, then their heads, to look - there, crossing the road in front of them, was a large wild dog.

The variegated patterns of black, brown, fawn and white, camouflaged in the shade, were brilliant in the sun. The big male stepped cautiously onto the road, then looked behind him. Several females emerged from the shadows, fussily herding an assorted band of boisterous pups. They watched, mesmerised. Wild dog sightings were rare and treasured. This was a fine group - in good condition and looking well fed and unworried.

Their beautiful coats gleamed in the slanting rays of early morning sun. They were in no hurry to move on and the pups chased and growled, yelped and tormented patient mothers as they lay down to offer yet another feed. A couple of younger males lounged, panting and apart.

This sighting was just what they needed to free them from those sombre thoughts and appreciate the unchanging stability of nature, the bountiful wildlife and the rugged beauty of the *kopjes*.

No wonder the Africans didn't have the wheel when Europeans arrived in this part of the world, Carol mused, thinking about a comment Prune had made earlier. They had everything they needed – reasonably predictable rainfall, deep, rich topsoil into which a dropped seed would yield a mini harvest, and animals galore for the plate. No need for the invention of such a mundane object as a wheel - or the pressing need for education. It was heaven as it was.

After a joyful few moments watching the wild dog family at play, Carol reluctantly whispered, "Dad, we should get going!"

Angus smiled. Of course they should.

As they packed up and moved towards the car, the wild dogs scrambled up a bank, disappearing as suddenly as they had arrived. He gave a little toot to be sure they had all gone and started the car.

"By the way, what on earth does the Industrial Revolution have to do with Southern Rhodesia?" Carol asked, as they turned down a track, insignificant except for a small signpost.

"That's tomorrow's discussion!" Angus replied.

Mzilikazi's grave

They read the signpost "Mzilikazi's grave" then walked quietly up the hill called Entumbane to the stone walls guarding the king's grave. They could see long slabs of granite standing on end at the entrance to a deep cleft.

Carol was overwhelmed by a sense of presence which increased her disbelief that she had never bothered to make an effort to get here while she was still at school in Bulawayo. She looked across at Prune. He had an expression almost of fear on his face ... and seemed reluctant to come any closer.

"Mzilikazi was buried with plenty of company," Angus said. "According to written missionary reports, three of his wives and a couple of hundred 'willing' slaves were killed to accompany him to the next life. He was surrounded by his favourite spears, *assegais*, shields and various items of jewellery. When all had been completed, the King's wagons were drawn round to enclose the area.

"Sentries took turns to keep the entrance guarded, armed with two of the few Martini Henry rifles Mzilikazi had acquired from Voortrekker laagers.

"The sentries assumed such significance as keepers of the Matebele King's grave, that they formed their own *kraal*, bringing wives and children up to ensure the grave was guarded and could not be looted.

" . . . unpredictably of course, during his son Lobengula's time, a bushfire came through and burnt most of the flammable objects. Lobengula was so furious that he had everyone in the sentry *kraal* killed. After that, there was no need to keep guards at the grave and over the following years, everything else of any value was taken. Somebody even took a bronze bracelet from the wrist of the King's skeleton—"

"Oh no! That's dreadful!"

"Unbelievable!"

"—at least, when that somebody tried to sell it to a member of the

Chartered Company, a Major Fortescue, many years later in 1898, the Major bought it specifically to send to the Victoria and Albert Museum in London."

As Angus turned several pages of a notebook he was carrying, he added: "In my position as first a Native, and now District Commissioner, it has been my business to know all the history and culture of the African people in Southern Rhodesia . . . so I have masses of reports to bring what you are learning to life."

"Here, Carol, why don't you read what Fortescue said."

Carol took the notebook and read: *"I am sending by the bearer who brings this small parcel, a bangle, the history of which is that it was taken off the skeleton of Moselekatze when his grave was opened. The bangle contains a certain percentage of gold and I was told resembled the metal used for ornaments by the Phoenicians. Of this you will be a better judge than I am. I can vouch for the authenticity of the bangle as it was given to me when I was at Bulawayo in 1896, by the man who opened the grave. I shall be very glad to give it to the Museum, if you consider it worthy."*

"I wonder who it was who opened the grave," Prune said sadly.

The area round the grave entrance was tidy, with the grass cut short. But without the signpost, it would have been easy to miss. They spent time pointing out spots where they thought they could still see a mark of the wagons or where the sentries might have stood.

A short walk down the hill from the gravesite was the monument to Mzilikazi, erected in 1941, just after Carol was born.

"Mum and I were invited to the opening of the memorial by Sir Herbert Stanley, who was the Governor of Southern Rhodesia. You were about six months old and I remember mum was anxious about leaving you alone with someone else for the first time while we came to the opening. But it was worth it." Angus laughed. "And you were fine!"

Pointing to the right, he continued, "Do you see that big old tree there behind the monument?"

"The one that looks as though it is dying?" asked Prune.

"That's the one. Unfortunately, people keep pinching little bits of bark, believing it will heal them and it is now almost dead. But use your imagination – this is one of the sites thought to be the original capital of Mhlanhlandhlela. We might be standing in the Bok Kraal. This was the most important place in the King's capital. Anyone wanting to see the

King would come here. Their meetings, or *indabas* as they are still called, would take place under that old tree. Of course, by just a nod of his head or a twitch of his whisk, many people were condemned to death right here. That was the price of the King's displeasure"

He stopped and turned to Prune, who was looking wretched – all bunched up and shivering. "You all right Prune?"

"Yes," he answered in a tight voice. "Yes I am. But my heart is shaking. I didn't know Mzilikazi was so real. I thought it was just a story - like the King who had no clothes . . ."

" . . . but noe to see the cave where he is buried . . . and this goat *kraal* . . . from the great King who broke away from the Zulus, stole King Shaka's cattle and created the Matebele people? I cant believe I am here."

'He shrugged. "I understand Jabu better now and why he is so proud of his grandfather and other Khumalo ancestors. I knew about Lobengula, but somehow, I didn't understand that King Mzilikazi was here as well."

Carol walked over to the iron plate on the monument and read:

"Mzilikazi, son of Shobana, the Matebele hail you. The Mountain fell down on 5 September 1868. All nations acclaim the son of Shobana. Hayete[77]."

---

[77] *Hayete, Bayete:* Traditional Zulu royal salute to a King

12

FATHER OF A NATION

There were more flat rocks in the shade at the back of what could have been the *Bok or Goat Kraal*[78] and imaginations ran riot thinking what might have taken place when this was the King's kraal.

"Where do we start . . . well, we have no written history, so we learn what we can from oral history - the stories that come down through the generations. These are well detailed in reference to family history – who fathered who, for instance, particularly in chiefly families. But it is hard to know which of the stories are accurate in other respects, as there can be colourful differences.

"First of all - what does 'Bantu' mean?" Prune asked.

Angus smiled. "People who speak Bantu languages and that covers tribes that roamed through Central and Southern Africa."

Drawing the map of Africa in the air with his hand, Angus went on: "You can roughly draw a line west to east from just below the bulge of Africa, somewhere between Nigeria and Cameroon . . . to another line from, say, the bottom of Natal, taking in the Transvaal and Orange Free State to the bottom of Angola – but not including the desert areas of South West Africa or the Cape. That's rough but it gives you an idea."

"The reason they are all classed as Bantu is that there is general understanding and similarities in language throughout that region, despite influences like Arabic on the Swahili language of Kenya. It gives us an idea of how widely Bantu speakers roamed over thousands of years.

---

[78] *Bok (Afrikaans) or Goat Kraal*: An amaNdebele Chief's inner meeting place –also used for rewarding and discipline purposes.

"Within the Bantu, the Zulus and the Matebele were Nguni people, ranging down the east coast of South Africa - roughly today's Zululand. There were many small tribes among the Nguni, some peaceful, some militaristic, all fighting for a place for their people. Sometimes this happened by intermarrying but oral history tells us it was mostly by killing to create fewer, larger tribes.

"Within those tribes were family clans. Mzilikazi was from the small Khumalo clan, which had been absorbed into the Ndwandwe people. Do you remember our wonderful holiday at Hluhluwe Game Reserve in Natal a couple of years ago Carol?"

"Oh yes, I'll never forget how much game we saw. Oh, and that big river! Just beautiful."

"That is exactly where they came from – the banks of the Black Umfolozi river. They were sandwiched between two other tribes. Mzilikazi's father, MatShobana, was chief of the northern Khumalo. He married a daughter of King Zwide of the Ndwandwe. But it wasn't long before King Zwide had Matshobana killed."

"That's marrying and killing for you!" Carol interjected.

"Perfect example! Don't worry about all these names, but it gives you context for that plaque, which mentions Shobana being Mzilikazi's father. The prefix 'ama', 'ma' or 'mat' roughly means 'of' or 'from'.

"AmaNdebele is the name Mzilikazi's people gave themselves, and it is still used by the Matebele people today."

"I am so glad you've explained that because I never quite knew why you always spelt Matebele using an e, while most people say Matabele and Matabeleland."

"I know, I am a bit pernickety about these things. I believe it is more correct as that is the way it is pronounced correctly. As they swept down from Mozambique, through the northern Transvaal and Bechuanaland, to Bulawayo, they virtually depopulated that whole area in what we have already mentioned as the 'mfecane or the crushing. Mzilikazi's people known as the 'amaTebele', or people 'of' or from the Tebele, the sea or the coast. This corrupted over time to the way it's written now – Matebele or worse, Matabele!

"You'll just have to indulge your old Dad on this one!"

Carol nodded and smiled at her knowledgeable father – thankful he'd brought her up to be a bit pedantic over such things as well. Although it did go over the top a bit sometimes!

"So Mzilikazi came from a small clan, inheriting the chieftainship upon the murder of his father. The larger grouping, the Ndwandwe, were gentle people – cattle, fishing, small scale cropping . . . certainly not warriors. But—" Angus paused for effect "— the fearsome Shaka and his Zulu warriors were on their doorstep.

"Shaka made several raids on the Ndwandwe, taking their land, their wives and their cattle each time. So Mzilikazi trained up a force of disciplined young men from the Khumalo clan, developing their strength and courage. And he resisted the Zulus each time. Each time, they fought bravely, but they lost many clan members.

Cutting the ostrich feathers

Mzilikazi wasn't prepared to see his people absorbed into the Zulus. So he took a group of his best young men to see Shaka.

"Shaka refused to see him. For many weeks, he stayed close by, keeping his men hard at work showing off their discipline, athleticism and strength for everyone in Shaka's kraal to see. Reports of all this activity filtered back to Shaka of course.

"The Zulu King was a suspicious man. So suspicious, apparently, that he refused to get married because he didn't want anyone to challenge his Kingship."

"So it was left to his brother Dingaan to get rid of him!" Prune said triumphantly.

"Absolutely! Shaka trusted nobody except his mother, Nandi. He regularly went to her for advice. But as these reports on this young son of the king of the Ndwandwe kept coming, his mother saw in Mzilikazi someone like her son Shaka. A disciplined young leader . . . who for the first time, perhaps, might be a man her son could trust. In addition, nobody had ever approached Shaka before and suggested they work together instead of killing each other.

"Her advice to Shaka was "talk to Mzilikazi". That is how Mzilikazi and the Khumalos came to live in Shaka's capital – which was called . . . ?"

Neither of them knew, so Angus continued. "It was called KwaBulawayo!"

Prune clapped his hands in delight.

"Mzilikazi apparently had a great sense of humour. He made Shaka laugh. He was more a close friend than just a trusted *induna*. For several years, Mzilikazi led all the raids on other tribes, absorbing new fighters into the Zulu nation and creating great wealth in cattle. In fact, at that time, the Zulu cattle herd was reckoned to be the biggest in Africa.

"So the Zulus rampaged through the land, absorbing the fighting men and stealing the women and cattle. But . . ." Angus dropped his voice to a conspiratorial whisper, "the Khumalos were waiting their turn . . ."

He glanced at Prune. "You're quite right, Prune. On their next raid in 1823, Mzilikazi neglected to send the required prize cattle back to Shaka. It was time to build the Matebele nation. There was much feasting and roasting of cattle to celebrate that decision!

"Shaka waited a while. He was sure his friend and chief *induna* would return. But nobody came. So Shaka sent messengers to find out what was happening. Mzilikazi rudely and deliberately cut the ostrich feathers off their headbands and sent them back. This was the worst possible insult."

"What a strange thing to do!" Carol exclaimed.

"Probably not. Those ostrich feathers would have been visible signs of great valour, like our military awards, hard-won indicators of bravery and courage. Anyway, as you can imagine, Shaka was furious.

"*'He has emptied his bowels on me'*"

Prune put his hand to his mouth, aghast. "Is that really what he said?"

"Well, it's what the storytellers say. It sounds a bit rude today, but I can't think of a better phrase to describe how upset Shaka would have been. As far as he was concerned, it was war.

"Mzilikazi was ready. Shaka's men returned with many losses. So he sent his best regiments a second and a third time. Mzilikazi's numbers dropped badly - but fortunately, Shaka's *impi* never found the Khumalo women and children hiding in the mountains, so the tribe rebuilt quickly.

"Mzilikazi knew that if he was caught, he would be cruelly executed. So he moved his people away, up north-west into the bottom of today's Mozambique. Once they'd gathered their strength a year later, this marked the start of an incredible journey. Tens of thousands of people in this increasingly powerful tribe moved a total distance of over 500 miles before they settled near our Bulawayo.

"Mzilikazi was now the Bull Elephant. Far more even than Shaka had done, he chose carefully the young men he would train up for his regiments, building an impressive tribe of even more physically strong, intelligent and courageous people."

"You mean, like we are taught to do to improve milk in our dairy cows?" Prune asked.

Angus laughed. "Exactly right! Mzilikazi was doing that with humans to produce the strongest, most athletic warriors and the most beautiful women to make plenty of babies.

"He was powerful and cruel to those who did not submit to his authority. But once they became amaNdebele, they were part of the family. To them, the King was gracious and generous."

"Who was the greater King, Shaka or Mzilikazi?" Prune asked.

"I think it is generally recognised that Shaka was the best military strategist. Mzilikazi learned all he knew about fighting from Shaka. But Mzilikazi was a clever man in his own right. He deliberately built that fine race of people from the very best of the men and women captured during raids. I've always personally favoured Mzilikazi as the greater of the two.

"Having said that, both Kings had much in common. They were keen and quick to learn from everything new that was happening around them. This made them almost unbeatable. Mzilikazi learned from his mentor Shaka and from other tribes, including the white man.

Mzilikazi demands Moffat's presence

"There is a revealing story about Mzilikazi's first meeting with the missionary Robert Moffat. Just listen to the fascinating questions he asked – an intelligent man, intrigued by things he didn't understand.

"He'd heard about this strange person called Moffat who talked about peace and kindness as a way of life. Something he couldn't even imagine. So he sent two Headmen to the mission at Kuruman, telling them to be his eyes, his ears and his mouth. Mrs Moffat welcomed them as she did all travellers and visitors. She fed them generously, offering the naked warriors some clothes, to make sure the missionary eye was not offended!"

They all laughed.

"The *indunas* needed little persuasion, because they were intrigued by white men 'with no knees'. When it was explained why they had no knees, the *indunas* wanted their own long trousers too of course.

"They were amazed by the visit. First of all, the welcome and kindness of the missionaries; they grew really excited when they attended worship in the mission chapel; but they were surprised and disappointed to hear that hymns were not war songs!

"They wanted to know what magic made the forge work, but most of all, they wanted to understand the 'moving houses' – the wagons. They spent hours feeling and poking the walls and decorations and pulling bits off to take away with them.

"Then they were horrified by a mirror on one of the walls, thinking their reflections which of course they had never seen with such clarity before, meant there was someone behind the mirror, ready to do them harm. They were sure there was witchcraft around.

"So, it was time to go extremely quickly and report back to the King! As they got ready to leave, they asked Moffat to go with them for the first part of the journey where, they said, there were hostile Tswana tribes."

"Moffat would have been a bit anxious, wouldn't he?" Carol asked.

"Very, I should think! Should he go? As a missionary, he wanted to meet Mzilikazi. He was not only very aware of, but had actually seen many examples of his savagery. It was not a decision to be made lightly, but it might be the excuse he needed to extend the trip all the way to meet the King. Moffat was dedicated to trying to convert him from savagery like King Khama II who became a Christian and a changed man."

"What do you mean – a changed man, Mr Davidson?"

"Well, having become a Christian and despite furious disapproval from his people, Khama ruled that a man could only have one wife and worst of all, he banned all drinking of native beer!"

"That would not have been popular!" Prune laughed.

"Back to Mzilikazi and the planned trip . . . Moffat would have talked things over long into the night with his wife and children, as they all knew that the chances of him coming back alive were not good.

"After much prayer, they both decided he must go. He refused to take any weapons with him – just his two faithful Bechuana, or Tswana, men to drive the oxen.

Robert Moffat's diaries

"I've copied a couple of relevant pieces from Moffat's diary. This first bit records something of the horrors he saw on the way. You only had a short piece to read last time Prune, here you are:

Prune started reading:

"' . . . *evidences on every hand of the terrible Matebeles – in places where populous towns and villages had been, nothing remained but dilapidated walls and heaps of stones, mingled with human skulls. The country had become the abode of reptiles and beasts of prey, the inhabitants having perished beneath the spears and clubs of their savage enemies.'*"

"Seeing village after village destroyed must have affected Moffat deeply. He hadn't come across problems like that at Kuruman or when dealing with the Tswana people. It confirmed to him - and his two Tswana drivers - the truth of all the rumours of Matebele savagery.

"The *indunas* probably just wanted a ride in the wagon, as they didn't actually come across any potential enemies.

"They'd probably all been killed," Prune declared solemnly.

Angus nodded in agreement . . .

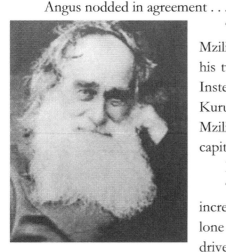

"The bush telegraph preceded them. Mzilikazi found out about the approach of his two *indunas*, with the white missionary. Instead of allowing Moffat to turn back to Kuruman as had been originally planned, Mzilikazi insisted on him coming to his capital.

Exactly what Moffat had hoped for!

"It was a historic meeting and incredibly brave of Moffat, to go there as a lone white man . . . and equally brave of his drivers, who must have been scared stiff, having heard all the hideous stories of the *mfecane* from the wounded and damaged people who arrived constantly at Kuruman.

"What must they have felt as they entered his capital?

"At least we have written descriptions to give us an idea.

"The King apparently watched in astonishment as the wagon approached. Carol, your turn to read what Moffat wrote."

Carol started a little uncertainly, a bit scared that she might have to read some awful descriptions of mayhem and murder.

"'*We proceeded directly to the town, and on riding into the centre of the large fold, we were rather taken by surprise to find it lined by eight hundred warriors, besides two hundred who were concealed on each side of the entrance, as if in ambush. We were beckoned to dismount, which we did, holding our horses' bridles in our hands.*

"'*The warriors at the gate instantly rushed in with hideous yells and leaping from the earth with a kind of kilt round their bodies, hanging like loose tails, and their large shields, frightened our horses.*

"'*They then joined the circle, falling into rank with as much order as if they had been accustomed to European tactics.*

"'*Here we stood, surrounded by warriors, whose kilts were of ape skins, and their legs and arms adorned with the hair and tails of oxen, their shields reaching to their chins and their heads adorned with feathers.*

"Take a break Carol – Prune?"

Prune took the notebook from Carol. He found he could read only barely above a whisper.

"*A profound silence followed for some ten minutes; then all commenced a war-song, stamping their feet in time with the music. No one approached, though every eye was fixed upon us. Then all was silent and Moselekatse marched out from behind the lines with an interpreter and with attendants following, bearing meat, beer, and other food. He gave us a hearty salutation and seemed overjoyed.*"

Angus took the narrative back, aware Prune and Carol were quite stunned by what they were hearing.

"Moffat recorded some of the questions Mzilikazi asked during the time they spent together. Like his Headmen, the wagons amazed him:

'*Is the wagon a living creature? How do the little front wheels keep up with the big back wheels? How does the iron tie around the wheel come in one piece without end or joint?*'

"Apparently Umbate, one of the *indunas* who had visited the mission, couldn't contain himself and explained, pointing at Moffat's hand:

'My eyes saw that very hand cut these bars of iron, take a piece off one end, and then join them as you now see them.'
"'Does he give medicine to the iron?' the King inquired.
"'No,' said Umbate, 'nothing is used but fire and a hammer.'

"I've never thought about anything like their reaction before."

"That's why it's important to actually come down here. Your A-level history will be incomparably better for just having sat here and breathed the atmosphere."

"I understand that now – must admit I was pretty sceptical when you first suggested it!"

She gave him a quick hug. "Thank you."

Angus smiled fondly at his daughter.

He went on: "Moffat received many gifts during his eight-day stay, because he had honoured the two *indunas* who visited Kuruman. Mzilikazi told him in strangely Biblical terms,
'Anything you did for them, you did for King Moselekatse.'

"Moffat, the man, found it hard to reconcile the despot who ruled hundreds of fearsome warriors with a rod of iron and was the terror of the vast territories he had devastated . . . with this man, with a gentle manner of speaking and thoughtful kindness.

"But Robert Moffat, the missionary, was not to be swayed from his primary task. As he contemplated what he termed *'the miseries of the savage state'*, he spoke strongly to the King of man's ruin. But he also spoke about the chance of man's redemption through the truths of the Gospels.

"Mzilikazi listened earnestly, but his reply is reported to have been:
'Why are you so earnest that I abandon all war and not kill men?'"

"You can't believe it didn't seem to worry them at all to kill people."

"Realistically, it was a time of nation building and the men were highly trained warriors. It was the only way tribes survived. As the soil and surroundings of a capital were exhausted and the wildlife died out, they'd move on. To do so, they either had to kill, or absorb, anyone in the way.

"Moffat described his time with them, saying that they would meet every day in the Goat Kraal, surrounded by young warriors. From time to time, these young men would approach in a crouching position, speaking and shouting out praise to the King.

"At other times, they would send up a massive shout *'allow us to go to . .
. x or y . . . and wash our spears in blood.'*

"Moffat's records indicate that Mzilikazi turned and smiled at him.
"'My people want to make war . . .'

"The King stated that Moffat's name would now be Moshete. He urged him to visit him again as soon as he could. Moffat reassured him he would do so, but in his diary note wrote with some despair,
'fighting is their profession, murder their pastime'.

"With his wagon loaded up with presents and massive amounts of food, Moffat prepared to return to Kuruman after two months away. He was keen to finish the translation of the Gospel of Luke into Sechuana.

But Mzilikazi insisted on riding part of the way back in the wagon while his warriors marched beside them to ensure the King's safe passage."

Angus turned to Moffat's diary notes again.
"'Moselekatse found it convenient to lay his well-lubricated body down on my bed to take a nap and on awakening, invited me to lie beside him.'"

"My goodness! What did he do?" Carol asked, astonished!

"He just wrote,

"'I begged to be excused.'"

"When were these reports written Dad?" Carol asked.

"I'm not sure, but it would have been at the beginning of the 1800's."

"There seems to have been a good relationship between the Matebele and the Missionary," Prune said. "I always thought they hated each other."

"You're right and wrong Prune – Mzilikazi had no reason to fear white men because he hadn't come across many of them at that stage … he certainly wouldn't have regarded them as a tribe to be destroyed."

"When did that change Dad?"

"Not until twenty years or so later, when Mzilikazi was threatened by the Voortrekkers crossing the Vaal River in about 1835. They were fierce fighters, well-armed and as fearless as the Matebele.

"But the missionaries didn't want anything – except for the people to listen to their stories about Jesus – and they provided education and clinics which benefitted the people enormously. Mzilikazi and Lobengula trusted them because they spoke truth and didn't steal anything from them."

136

"That is really interesting. I'd never looked at it like that before."

Angus went on with the story. "Having said that, Matebele and missionaries alike were bemused particularly, by the friendship of this great, but savage Matebele King with a gentle, elderly English missionary.

"In fact, it appears to have become a bit worrying as Mzilikazi became almost obsessive about Moffat. He kept sending messengers to bid him come. For various reasons, it was not until 25 years later that Moffat was able to travel up to Matebeleland to see the King in his new capital. This was called Mahlokohloko - somewhere around the Nyamandhlovu /Tjolotjo area.

"That would have been after Mzilikazi threw everyone off Ntabazinduna."

"That's right … you're getting an idea of what happened and when – sometimes it's a bit difficult to follow."

"Mzilikazi must have been an old man by then." Prune was persistent.

"Well yes, he was and Moffat's observations about that reunion are insightful and descriptive. And sad. Come on Prune, you are so interested, you read it."

Prune took the notebook with alacrity.

" *'On turning round, there he sat – how changed! The vigorous, active and nimble chief of the Matebele, now aged, sitting on a skin, lame in his feet, unable to walk or even to stand. I entered – he grasped my hand, gave one earnest look and drew his mantle over his face. It would have been an awful sight for his people to see the hero of a hundred fights wipe from his eyes the falling tears. He spoke not, except to pronounce my name, Moshete, again and again. He looked at me again, his hand still holding mine and he again covered his face. My heart yearned with compassion for his soul.'* "

"I'm nearly in tears listening to the brilliant way he describes it - and the way Prune read it too."

Prune was so pleased that his reading had affected Carol. He tried not to smile too much!

The search for David Livingstone

Angus went on with the story: "The King was suffering from dropsy. Before you ask, Carol, that is known as oedema today – swelling of the tissues probably due to some form of congestive heart failure. Moffat was able to bring him enough relief for him to not only walk about easily, but to want to make a long trip with Moffat.

This trip, entirely by ox wagon, was going to take them back into the Makololo country as they were trying to link up with Moffat's son-in-law, David Livingston. They tried to find out where he was, but were unsuccessful - so after several months of travelling they left supplies for him with the local chief.

"My goodness, this really is coming to life now! I'm in Moffat House at school, and the other houses are Livingstone and Speke! I just need to find out who Mr Speke was now – because I don't suppose it was a Mrs Speke!" Carol added cheekily.

Angus raised his eyebrow in amusement.

"Mzilikazi allocated Moffat some land near his next capital at Inyati for the first London Missionary Society mission in Matebeleland. In 1859, Moffat and his son John put up buildings for the first missionaries, William Sykes and Thomas Morgan Thomas.

"On the same trip, he also secured the release of Macheng, heir to the chieftainship of the Bamangwato people. Macheng had been a captive of Mzilikazi for 16 years.

"Mzilikazi's words to the young man were

'Moffat will take you back to Sechele. That is my wish as well as his . . . when captured you were a child; I have reared you to be a man.

"Well, all I can say is that I am looking at Mzilikazi with new eyes."

"So am I!" said Prune.

"I'm glad to hear it – because by the end of the next couple of days, you will both have a much better picture of our country and the people who were here before us.

"Now we get to the next part of the story . . . Into the car you two – we're off to Inyati mission. On the way, I promise I'll tell you about James Watt and the Industrial Revolution. And throw in the theory of evolution, the abolition of slavery and perhaps even the Berlin Conference."

"Boring," Carol yawned.

Prune laughed.   Angus just smiled.

13

A MAN CALLED JAN GROOTBOOM

They didn't get to Inyati. Angus felt he should ring Jabu's father Nkanyiso to tell him the news he would be shattered to hear – that they were no longer on the African Affairs Board.

They stopped at a roadside store which had a phone they could use - only to find Nkanyiso had gone to see his father at Ntabazinduna. So Angus phoned Chief Khayisa, the man he had wanted to meet there anyway, to make new plans and ask him to try and get hold of Nkanyiso.

Chief Khayisa had made a great name for himself because he refused to be talked down by the British Government or the politicians from the three countries now in the Federation . . . insisting on the formation of the African Affairs Board. So it was highly relevant that all three of them would be at Ntabazinduna together.

They'd packed camp beds in the car before starting out, just in case they decided to spend a bit more time visiting important sites.

Angus, Carol and Prune had chosen mangoes, watermelon, biltong, chips and a little good-for-you food, plus Fantas and lemonades. They made sure the Gourock canvas bag was full of water, tying it onto the front of the truck so the breeze would cool it as they drove.

"With luck, we'll find Jabu has come up to see his grandfather too. If he is there and free and if you're happy with the idea, I'd like to ask him to join us."

"That would be really great." Carol was delighted.

"It would be interesting to see Jabu again" said Prune uncertainly.

He wasn't quite sure if Jabu would be as glad to see him. He'd often wondered about that strange time when they were both writing JayCee. He was sure Jabu didn't want to look at him, but he didn't know why.

It wasn't the sort of question he could ask.

Angus was speaking. "It would be interesting having him along when we head up to Inyati then on to the 'nThaba zikaMambo. That area is almost sacred to him, particularly since he asked for the traditional initiation ceremony. I'd love to talk to him about it a bit more. And I need to tell him how much I admired his determination to uphold amaNdebele culture in this fast-changing world."

"I haven't seen Jabu since I was about 6 or 7."

"I wonder what he looks like now," Prune wondered.

Having stocked up at the store they were now driving back towards Bulawayo, when Angus said, "As we have got away so early, it would be a waste not to stop at the site of the *Indaba* between the Chiefs and Rhodes. I know I keep re-arranging your timeline, but this is important."

He opened his window and pointed out to the right.

"There it is, over there . . . the *Indaba* site. Can you see that tree with the fence round it? And an old ant heap mound leading up to it?"

"There's somebody sitting on the ant heap," Prune whispered. "Look" he pointed out of the window.

"Perhaps we'd better not disturb him. He doesn't look very happy – he's holding his head in his hands."

"We'll park a bit further on," Angus agreed.

They found a shaded spot just beyond the *Indaba* site and wound the windows down to let in some air. They sat, taking it all in - examining the ant heap where Cecil Rhodes had sat to address the chiefs - and looking at that grizzled old indaba tree, then the menace of the *kopjes* around the site.

Angus spoke in hushed tones. "The reason we are going up to Inyati then on to Shiloh is to give you a better picture of what took place from the time the Matebele claimed this part of the world up to the war in 1893 and then the rebellion of 1896.

The man on the ant heap stood up. He looked briefly across at them, then walked down to the bottom. He turned and stared at the ant heap for a moment then glanced up at the surrounding *kopjes* – and shook his head.

He looked over the road again and started walking towards them.

"Themba!" Carol shouted. "It's Themba."

Prune looked up, then the two of them ran across the dusty road, Angus following close behind. They couldn't believe they had all met up at this strange place.

"What on earth are you doing here Themba?" Angus asked.

"I'm doing my history project for A-levels, Mr Davidson. And I remembered something my father told me many years ago. I wanted to check it out and thought I'd come down to the archives in Bulawayo, then walk out here to try and imagine it all. I hadn't realised how far it was to walk! I was going to ask you for a lift back. Not realising it was you of course!"

"Well you can certainly have that! And next time, just check it out to see if we are also heading south! We could have brought you all the way!" Angus laughed. "It's a little cooler in the car, so come and join us and tell us what you've been up to."

Themba's story

Themba sat in the front seat of the old Morris Oxford. Ice-cold Fantas and lemonades were passed around. Then he began his story.

"You remember how I used to go to Botswana to see my *baba 'mkulu*? Everyone nodded.

"Well, when I wrote for my scholarship to Goromonzi, my father told me that I was not actually a full blood Ndebele, but part was from the baKwena people, closer to the Tswana. It was an amazing story. It turns out that my *baba 'mkulu's* father, Motshodi, rescued a lot of young children from a Matebele massacre of his village. He hid them up in the Magaliesberg until they were old enough to take to school at Kuruman. So I used that story for my scholarship - and Motshodi's name is now being included in some history books."

"That's fantastic Themba!"

"Wow, well done."

Themba went on.

"As my father told me the story, I understood a lot – why my skin is a bit paler than yours Prune, and my father is paler even than I am. He told me that Motshodi had another name – Jan Grootboom.

"For years, I couldn't find out anything about this name, until one day

141

I was reading Baden Powell's life story."

"You mean the one who started Boy Scouts?" Prune asked.

"That's the one. He wrote a whole chapter on Jan Grootboom. Here, I've got my notebook." Themba put his satchel down and pulled out a lined exercise book, which was full of writing.

"This is some of what Baden-Powell wrote:

'He had the guts of the best of men. Though I knew Zululand, I was new to Rhodesia and its people and I needed therefore a really reliable guide and Scouting comrade.

"One night we had crept down to near the enemy stronghold and were waiting there to see his morning fires so as to ascertain his position. Presently the first fire was lit and then another and yet another.

"Jan suddenly growled: 'The brutes are laying a trap for us.' He slipped off all his clothing and left it lying in a heap and stole off into the darkness practically naked.

'The worst of spying is that it makes you suspicious, even of your best friends; so as soon as Jan was gone I crept away in another direction, taking the horses with me, and got among some rocks where I would have some chance if he had any intention of betraying me. For an hour or more I lay there while the sun rose until, at last, I saw Jan crawling back through the grass – alone.

"Ashamed of my doubts, I crept to him and found him grinning all over with satisfaction while he was putting on his clothes again. He said that he had found, as he had expected, an ambush laid for us. The thing that made him suspicious was that the fires, instead of flaring up at different points all over the hillside simultaneously, had been lighted in steady succession, one after the other, apparently by one man going around to light them.

'He himself had pressed in towards them by a route from which he was able to perceive a party of them lying out in the grass close to the track which we should probably have used had we gone on."

"And that was your great-grandfather!" Angus was astounded.

"He would have taught Baden-Powell all he needed to know about tracking and bush craft. And I bet B-P used that knowledge to form the

Scout movement!"

"Yes, he did!" Themba's words tumbled over each other in his enthusiasm. "He used to call Baden-Powell Mr Baking Powder."

They all laughed, but were astonished at what they were hearing.

"What else have you found out?"

"He was an amazing man. It all started when Mzilikazi and one of his regiments lived in my great-grandfather's village for about 8 months. During that 8 months, Motshodi learned to speak Sindebele like one of them. As a 14-year-old boy, he wanted to be like them, so he wore an Ndebele style of *'mbetju* made of skins and tails, and cut his hair the same way. He also learned to make shields of cowhide using the right colours and he made the short, stabbing *iklwa* spears. He learned about the ornaments too, the beads and the ostrich feathers and what they all meant.

"The other young Matebele were good to him, so he had decided to become the best amaNdebele warrior there could be. He learned about the hissing before battle, the *zhii,* and all about the horns in their battle formations."

"Then one day, they suddenly turned and killed everyone in his village, Motshodi's anger was terrible against the Matebele. I'll lend you my reports. You can read how he managed to get 17 children out of the burning village and look after them. It is amazing.

"He hid the children in a secret valley in the Magaliesberg. With his bushman friend, Pinde, he looked after them there for three years, until he knew the time had come to take them to see Moshete – the missionary, Robert Moffat – at Kuruman."

Prune couldn't contain himself. "We've just been talking about him."

"We have . . . Moffat must have been lost for words," Angus said almost to himself.

"He was. He couldn't believe Motshodi was from the Magaliesberg baKwena because he had seen the aftermath of the raid on that village and knew nobody could have survived that.

"It is funny, because when Motshodi married the sister of his friend Pinde, he told Moshete that he chose her because her skin was like cream, and she did not look like an Ndebele! Their first child was my *baba 'mkulu.* He and his son, my father Kuda, were both pale skinned like Pinde."

"What happened next?" Carol said "Did Motshodi stay at Kuruman?" Themba nodded.

She went on: "He would have learned English and the ways of the missionaries as well."

"Yes he did. In fact, he became a Christian and learned about forgiveness and love for other people. But although he tried very hard, he could not forgive or love the Matebele. In fact, he hated them with a terrible anger. All he could think about was getting revenge for what they had done. But he didn't tell Moshete!"

"I bet he didn't!" Angus laughed.

"King Khama II heard that Motshodi could dress like a *mashoja* and bring back information on what they were planning, so he asked Moffat if he could 'borrow' Motshodi to do something for him. The revenge against the Matebele began.

"Motshodi found it easy to learn languages. He spoke baKwena of course, as well as Tswana, Sindebele and English. And now he was going to learn to speak Afrikaans!

"One of the Dutch burghers, Andries Hendrik Potgieter, was a leader of the Voortrekkers who wanted to start a new place for themselves, free from the rules of the British in the Cape. He'd seen good country north of the Vaal river that was almost empty of people because of the '*mfecane*.

"We've just been talking about that too," Prune chipped in proudly.

Themba smiled and went on. "Potgieter had had many battles with the Matebele and lost members of his family and many of his trek oxen. He also came to see Moshete to ask if he knew of a Sindebele interpreter.

"Moshete said of course he did, and not only an interpreter, but someone who would be able to bring back information on what the Matebele were planning."

"Your great-grandfather went to help them too?" Prune asked in awe.

"He did!" Themba slapped his thigh in excitement.

"The Voortrekkers asked my great grandfather what he could do - and he said he'd mix with warriors in the regiment, find out what they were saying and what they were doing and bring that information back.

"He introduced himself as John Mthimkulu after his time at Kuruman Mission, but the Afrikaans people couldn't remember that name, so they called him Jan Grootboom. He was happy that people didn't really know

144

who he was, because wanted to be able help many people by working secretly, not openly.

"So my great grandfather Motshodi became a new person called Jan Grootboom. It is interesting, because I tried so hard to find out about him and the descriptions all contradicted each other. Some said he was a Fingo, or perhaps a Swazi, or a Cape Boy . . . others said he was a Xhosa or maybe even a Zulu. So nobody knew. Motshodi got what he wanted. He became a man it was difficult to find out about.

Becoming Matebele

"When he wanted to mix with the Matebele, he cut his hair in amaNdebele style, took off his western clothes and put on all the warrior beads, necklaces and paint, as well as his '*mbetju*. And you couldn't tell he was not amaNdebele!

"He told Mynheer Potgieter he would come back when he was ready and tell them what he had learned. In the meantime, he must advance towards the land where he wanted to settle, but that he must not under any circumstances cross the Vaal River, until he got back.

"So Potgieter moved up and formed a laager with several other Voortrekker families to make a very big trek. Jan went to mix with the Matebele to find out how they were reacting to this."

"When he came back, he told Potgieter he must get permission from the local chief the next day. Once that permission was given, he would be able to move into their land.

"One family thought it was all taking too long and they thought they knew better. So they refused to wait and be part of the Potgieter laager. One night they formed their own small trek and went off right to the edge of the Vaal River. Their name was Liebenberg."

"This is the one you were telling us about yesterday Dad!" Carol exclaimed excitedly.

"It certainly sounds like it. Let's see what Themba's found out."

"When Potgieter heard about the Liebenbergs moving forward, he asked Jan Grootboom to go and talk sense into them and make sure none of them crossed without permission. So Jan went off to talk to them, because he knew they would be killed if they tried it. But they were stiff

145

necked and wouldn't listen to him.

"My great-grandfather looked across the river from his hiding place and he saw that the Matebele were very angry. They were all dressed for battle and parading up and down the river bank with a lot of shouting, fist pumping and dancing.

"Two young girls and their brother were kind to Jan and brought him cake that their mother had made. My great-grandfather liked those children very much and was fearful for them. Perhaps he remembered his own little ones that he hid in the Magaliesberg. He told them that if they were attacked, they must all hide under the wheels of the food wagon.

"The Liebenberg family *inspanned*[79] their oxen at 2 in the morning and crossed the Vaal in the dark. But, before they had a chance even to form a laager or to let their oxen loose to feed, the Matebele attacked.

"The family were at their most vulnerable. As soon as Motshodi saw the Matebele preparations for a raid, he managed to get a message back to the Potgieters, then he ran back very quickly to cross the river, downstream and well out of sight. He watched from nearby hoping the Potgieters might be able to come and help. But they had a very big laager and were slow in getting organised.

"The warriors were furious at this insult to their Chief and started to kill everyone, driving away horses and trek oxen and burning the wagons.

"My great-grandfather ran a bit closer, then hid. Then he ran some more and hid again, quickly getting up to the food wagon, which he knew would be the last one to be attacked because it had no people in it. The children were there."

Angus, Carol and Prune were spellbound by Themba's story and the detail he had found out about what had actually happened.

"My great-grandfather got them out of their hiding place, telling them not to be afraid and to come with him. There were maShoja everywhere, so he had to think quickly how to save these children.

"The only thing he could do was to pretend he had captured them by holding them with their arms behind their backs. He took them to the Chief *Induna* and said the *'sangoma* had told him they were to be given as a present to Mzilikazi. The Chief *Induna* asked the other *indunas*. They

---

[79] *inspanned:* Yolked their oxen to the wagons in preparation for a move

146

weren't sure, but they'd always respect what the 'sangoma told them. So they took the children with them and didn't kill them."

"So that's how that happened!"

Angus couldn't believe he didn't know these stories.

"Themba, did you know that the older girl, Sarah, is thought to have become a nursemaid to Lobengula when he was a baby?"

Themba's mouth fell open.

"No! I certainly didn't know that!"

Angus took up his side of the story.

"Mzilikazi was starting to move north as he had decided Potgieter had become too dangerous for the Matebele. He had taken three of his regiments with him to cross the Zambezi. The white children went with his uncle Godwane Ndiweni as they moved further north and he took the rest of the Matebele across the Limpopo to form his new capital.

"You know about the Chiefs being thrown off Ntabazinduna?"

Themba nodded.

"Well, Mzilikazi's youngest son, Jandu, would have been only 5 or 6 at the time. It is likely that Sarah, with one of the most senior Chiefs, Mncumbata, hid him. There's a bit of a gap there. No written records. But oral history confirms bits of this.

"It is likely he was hidden in the cave of Mlimo in the Matopos. Once Mzilikazi died, apparently having left no heir, Chief Mncumbata was the one who insisted he was the next King.

"After his inauguration, Jandu was renamed Lobengula. One thing that is known, is that as a young boy, Lobengula knew all about traditional medicines, having spent such a lot of time with Mlimo in the Matopos."

"That's incredible," Themba shook his head in amazement, "an extraordinary story."

"Time for a break everyone! But let's be quick, because the fact that Themba is here must mean that Jan Grootboom was somehow involved in the *Indaba*."

A man of mysteries

As Angus stacked up twigs and paper to make a fire, Carol filled the kettle from the Gourock bag. Prune and Themba cleared a space, put down a rug in the shade and took out mugs and sandwiches. Once the tea was poured, they all sat cross-legged in a circle on the rug. It was hot – stiflingly, breathlessly hot, laced with heavy humidity from last night's rain.

As the sun moved towards midday, the usual swirling build-up of massive puffball grey and white cumulo-nimbus clouds again looked promising. Their dusty road lay hidden in the shine of shimmering mirage.

On the rare occasions they stopped talking, the bush ticked like a broken watch in the great stillness. Nothing moved. Even the birds went quiet, their energy spent saluting the rain at dawn.

"Before we get back to Themba's story, you know this was the site where the Matebele Chiefs sat and talked to Cecil Rhodes?" Angus asked.

They all nodded.

"Just look at the *kopjes* around us. Think of them, bristling with thousands of hidden, absolutely silent, but fully armed and very restless young Matebele warriors. They didn't want to waste time talking -they wanted one thing – to wash their spears in the blood of the white man.

"Pretty intimidating from down here."

"Very intimidating," Themba agreed. "I've felt scared just sitting here imagining it all. It makes me admire that great-grandfather of mine even more. And Rhodes, because he too was very brave."

Themba was itching to keep on telling the story. Everyone seemed to be taking so long finishing their tea and sandwiches and talking about other things. He looked at Angus.

At last, Angus smiled.

"Right Themba – let's hear the rest.

Themba was ready and it all poured out.

"Going back a little bit first," he said, falling over his words.

"I found out something else that was interesting. King Khama of Bechuanaland was just as nervous of the Matebele as everyone else. So when the Administrator of the British South Africa Company, Dr Leander Starr Jameson was negotiating with Lobengula for the road through to Mashonaland, King Khama decided to help, by sending several hundred Tswana soldiers and Bechuanaland Police to keep them safe. He asked Jan Grootboom to go with them, look after them and help with interpretation.

Angus couldn't resist saying: "He was a man determined to get his revenge on the Matebele ... but I wonder if he ever knew that the little girl he saved, Sarah Liebenberg, was the one who in turn saved ..."

Angus couldn't get it out fast enough before Prune stood up shouting " . . . the amaNdebele King Lobengula!"

"That is amazing! And yet, somehow absolutely right," Themba said. "I don't believe Jan Grootboom would have wanted to kill anyone. As a young man called Motshodi, perhaps . . . but not as Jan Grootboom."

Angus tried to wrap things up this far.

"By the time the *Indaba* came, Jan Grootboom had become a bit of an enigma to everyone, except to Moshete and perhaps the missionary Charles Helm . . . because as his driver many years before, he had brought him and his family up to Matebeleland. Helm taught him Sindebele and his work after that was mainly with the Helms at Hope Fountain. But they knew he had unique skills and encouraged him to help where he could.

"He also set a pretty good model for modern intelligence gathering,"

"So we know he rescued the baKwena children, then he saved the lives of the three Liebenberg children, he worked with the Chartered Company on initial trek into Mashonaland, with Baden Powell, and King Khama. He must have been pretty old by the time of the *Indaba*."

Themba agreed. "He must have been. I don't know how old he was, but he didn't seem to dress as a warrior anymore."

"He was well respected, Themba." Angus was fascinated.

"He must have been," Themba agreed. "He must have been . . . a giant, I think. I have a picture of him that I was given by the archives. Look at that strong face."

He passed the photo round for them all to understand the man a bit better.

"Before you go on, Themba" Carol turned to Angus and said "I get a bit confused by the Matebele war and the Matebele rebellion. Where did the *Indaba* fit in?"

Angus agreed it was confusing.

"The Matebele war was in 1893. A few horrible battles after an stupid incident in Fort Victoria, led to something you do know about Carol, the wipe-out of the Allan Wilson patrol at the Shangani River. This was followed shortly afterwards by King Lobengula's death.

"The rebellion started in 1896. So we're talking about how the Indaba ended what was called the rebellion - not the war.

14

THE RAISING OF . . . WHICH FLAG ?

"I've found some interesting archive documents showing that Rhodes was getting anxious, because the nature of the fighting during the rebellion had changed. Instead of the traditional Matebele way of fighting with the formation of the horns they were now melting into the bush, using the Martini Henry rifles promised as a result of the concession with King Lobengula, with quick skirmishes and spontaneous killing.

"As Rhodes seemed to have to pay for everything the Chartered Company did, he was rather keen that the fighting should stop. But it was hard to convince rigid British army officers!

"They wanted to fight the rebellion their way, but they also wanted to raise the Union Jack over a defeated Matebele nation, rather than a flag of the BSAC!

"You can imagine that didn't go down very well with Rhodes! He felt strongly that the only way to get peace was to go and talk to the people who could make a difference . . . the Chiefs . . . and hold an *indaba* with the. People thought he was mad and would be killed.

"But he didn't seem to know fear - Rhodes' courage is mentioned many times. Perhaps he felt he had nothing to lose because he lived his life with a weak heart, knowing he might die at any moment.

"At this stage, protocol demanded that Rhodes get permission from the British General, Sir Frederick Carrington, in order to talk to the Chiefs about any negotiations for a peace treaty. Sir Frederick was in charge of the Imperial fighting forces. It doesn't sound as though they liked each other very much. Carrington was suspicious and reluctant. Rhodes was powerful and persuasive. Time slipped past. Costs kept rising. Eventually Carrington grudgingly gave permission.

"The question, then, was how on earth would they arrange an *indaba*? None of the amaNdebele people working with the whites would go near the Chiefs or *impi* – they were scared stiff.

"They cautioned Rhodes, saying any white man approaching the Matebele would be shot.

"So nothing happened, until several weeks later, when a Native Commissioner named Mr Richardson asked to see Rhodes. He was a much-loved man and was given the name *'amehlu KwaZulu'*, which means 'the eyes of the people'."

Jan Grootboom meets Nyamabezana

Angus's smile grew broader as he finished, slowing his speech as he said very deliberately:

"Mr Richardson knew someone 'as brave as a lion' who would talk to the Matebele."

He looked at Themba.

"I've been wondering as you talked, where I had heard that name before. Of course, it was—"

"Not Jan Grootboom?" interrupted Carol.

"Yes!" Themba pumped his fist in the air. "Jan Grootboom himself!"

"You carry on Themba - I'm sure you'll have detail I don't have."

Themba's patience rewarded, he started off again with a great rush. "He met Rhodes, who told him exactly what he wanted to try and do. when he heard this, Jan Grootboom said he needed two other men to help him go among the Matebele. They would move only at night, so during the day, they'd find places to hide close enough to watch and hear what was happening.

"When he was asked if he was afraid, he told Rhodes no, he was not afraid.

"The Matebele knew he had had his revenge on them, and they respected a brave enemy. Now he was an old man, they would respect his age - and when they heard he had a message from Rhodes, they would want to know about it anyway!

"But before he did would do anything, Jan Grootboom asked why Rhodes had been away so long? The Ndebele people regarded him as

152

their Chief. Because he was never there, they didn't know who they could trust, because the Company men in Bulawayo kept changing places.

"Rhodes realised this was a major issue and told Jan he had been stupid and hadn't thought about what was important to the people. So Rhodes respected Jan for challenging him and Jan respected Rhodes because he agreed he was stupid not to understand what was important to the people.

"Jan agreed to work with him.

"Rhodes said, 'I will reward you, Grootboom, and the men you take with you. But just in case you don't come back, you must tell me where your people live so I can reward them instead.'

"Jan didn't want a reward. He just asked for a pair of field glasses.

"It took over a week to get the information back. When he did, he had a big smile on his face and was shouting and doing traditional slow dancing.

"'So what is the answer?' Rhodes asked.

"My great-grandfather refused to be rushed. The dancing was important - but so were two bits of information. So when everyone there knew there was important information, they clapped and were very excited. The first important understanding was that the Matebele were beginning to distrust Mlimo. In 1893, before Lobengula died, Mlimo told them that the white man's bullets would be turned to water and they would all be killed. It didn't happen then, and it didn't happen when they were told the same thing three years later.

"They were even more suspicious now, because Mlimo had only two weeks ago told them that if the white men crossed the Umguza River, they would all die. The week after that, they did cross. They did not die. Instead, they fought a mighty battle, killing hundreds of Matebele with very few losses.

"The second bit of information was that Jan and his helpers had heard two old women talking as they went down to the river to fetch water. They were wailing that they were all starving because there had been no rain. They would now die.

"Jan decided to speak to the old women on their way back from the river. He shared his food with them. They were very hungry. He found the very, very old woman was one of Mzilikazi's wives, Nyamabezana. She was a mighty warrior for the Rosvi people in her time and Jan knew of her.

"This was fortunate, because Jan knew to respect her and he knew that the Chiefs would listen to everything she said.

"There was only one problem! Jan said she was cheeky *sterek*[80], shouting and swearing curses at him.

"He told her Rhodes wanted to have an *indaba* with the Chiefs.

"She must have calmed down then. Jan sent one of his helpers, John Makhunga, to run and fetch something while he kept talking. John came back with two pieces of cloth – one red and one white. Jan tore off a piece of white cloth and gave it to the old lady, then he tore a piece of red cloth and gave that to her as well.

"He asked her to talk to the Chiefs. And in no more than four days, she was to put the cloth on a stick and hold it up in the air so he could see it. The red cloth to say 'war' and the white cloth to say 'we will talk'.

"Jan and John waited for four days and were thinking nothing had worked, when there it was! The white cloth! It was stuck on a long pole and waving! So Jan shouted loudly from the hilltop where he was hiding that he wanted to come and talk to the Chiefs.

"After a long time, a voice shouted back to say that he was happy for Jan to come and talk. So Jan climbed a third of the way down and shouted again that he wanted to come and talk to the Chiefs. He got the same reply. So he moved closer and shouted again, then closer and shouted again. Each time, the reply was the same: 'come and talk'.

"Eventually, Jan reached the Chiefs. They sat on the ground and Jan spoke of what Rhodes had told him and how the *indaba* would work.

"They asked if they could tell Rhodes about their anger and their problems. Jan said they could.

"They insisted: *'No more than four white men, and they must not be armed.'* Jan had agreed and said he must now go to tell Rhodes.

"They agreed to meet again in four days' time. Jan told the Chiefs that one of his men would stay with them as a sign, then hopefully, holding the white cloth up high, he would lead them to Rhodes and the *indaba* site."

---

[80] *sterek*: strong / very much

Themba stopped for breath. "You know, one of the strange things I have found out about looking at archives is that you get the same story, but never quite the same story."

Carol laughed and looked knowingly at her father. Themba explained. "Some people writing history say that Rhodes and his soldiers found the old lady and organised the flag-waving themselves. Then they asked Jan to talk to the Chiefs. But Rhodes' own words in his own book said it was Jan Grootboom who organised it all, so I will believe Rhodes!"

Carol had never seen Themba quite so animated before. His face was alight with the excitement of the tale.

"My great-grandfather told Rhodes some of the lesser Chiefs were not there, but the important ones would meet him and three other white men – no more than that – at Umlugulu, in two days' time. They would only meet if there were no guns.

"There was a lot of talk about who should go to this important meeting, and many more than four wanted to go.

"Jan Grootboom was immovable - if they sent more than four, nobody would be there to meet them - and he would not be there either!"

The Great Indaba

Angus took up the story from there.

"Rhodes took a man called Colenbrander to interpret his words as well as a Dr Sauer, whom he trusted and man called Vere Stent who was a journalist - to take notes and write an article for the Cape Times.

"It was a wise choice," Angus said, "because from Vere Stent's articles we have a far better understanding of what took place.

"I know now of course, that Jan Grootboom was also there, so that the Chiefs had someone they trusted, and with the past antagonism forgotten, they'd feel comfortable if he could speak and explain for them."

Themba turned to them, then spoke in awe, "That is why I have been sitting on this ant heap – trying to imagine what it must have been like. Admiring the strength of my great-grandfather and of Rhodes, with all those Matebele *impi* in the *kopjes*, just waiting for a signal to rush down and kill them."

They looked again at the *kopjes* surrounding them. Great boulders created an unruly landscape against the rising swirl of storm clouds, the granite wedged from ancient times against clumps of thick, flat-topped trees, completely hiding the clefts and caves and deep, dark passages where once a huge army of warriors lay concealed. It was all so close to where they were sitting below the famous ant heap itself.

Rhodes and the other three men, let alone Jan Grootboom wouldn't have had a chance if things had gone wrong.

"Themba, thank you." Angus broke the silence. "I have learned so much. I'll give you a rest now and take up the story from there."

A promising swirl of wind had made it a little cooler, so he stood up and went to sit on top of the ant heap, beckoning them to join him. "We'll get a better feel for what happened if we sit up here.

"Rhodes and the three other men rode their horses to a place near here, out in the open. Over there somewhere. That way, the Matebele could clearly see everything they did. They knew they were being watched.

"Rhodes prepared to dismount. Colenbrander panicked and urged him not to do so.

" '*Dismount,*' Rhodes urged '*dismount – it will give them confidence as they are nervous too.*'

"He tied up his horse and walked about 500 yards to sit exactly where we are now, his hands visible all the time so everyone present would know he was unarmed. He ordered the others to do the same. They followed and sat or stood nearby.

"Nobody came. But in the silence, they could hear the sudden rise of animal and owl noises in the *kopjes*, and they knew probably with a feeling of dread, that hundreds, if not thousands, were ready and watching."

Angus pulled a newspaper clipping out of his briefcase. "This is how the journalist, Vere Stent, described it for the Cape Times.

"It was a lovely winter's day, the sun just beginning to western; comfortably hot; the grasses, bronze and golden, swaying in the slight wind; the hills ahead of us blurred in the quiver of early afternoon. We talked very little.   Must I confess it? We were all a little nervous.
We had entered the hills and were nearing a narrow canyon, where a rough

156

track, commanded by a towering bluff upon one side, was bordered by a deep wooded valley on the other. The track debouched into a tiny basin, rimmed by kopjes and floored by fallow. In the centre of the fallow, lay some tree stumps and the remnants of a big ant heap."

While they couldn't quite understand the old-fashioned words, Prune, Carol and Themba found their eyes following the description – up the towering bluff - the deep wooded valley - the *kopjes* round the remnants of the big ant heap.

Carol felt a chill run down her spine. She could almost hear the blood curdling yells of triumph as the warriors closed in on them. It would have taken no more than a minute or two to kill them all.

"After what seemed a long time, they saw the white cloth tied to a long stick coming towards them with a group of people led by Jan Grootboom's helper, John Makhunga. The procession wound down from one of the *kopjes* and stopped before the ant heap to raise their palms towards Rhodes.

"Rhodes did the same and said, '*amehlo amhlophe*' – the eyes are white. There was a loud response '*amehlo amhlophe, nkosi yenyamazana*[81]'."

"Everyone sat down in a big circle. Headmen. Indunas. Impi. Among the most influential were Chiefs Babayane, Dliso, Gunu, Malevu, Mlugulu, Nyanda, Sikhombo and Somabhulana.

"Rhodes asked the senior chief, Somabhulana to speak.

"In their time-honoured way, the old man recited the proud history of the amaNdebele people right back to Mzilikazi, factually. Unemotionally. But in the telling, he became distressed and agitated telling the stories of the theft of Lobengula's message with the gold, the hunting of the King, the stealing of cattle and the taking of their land. Stent described it in his article for the Cape Times:

"The moment was inflammable. The least indiscretion might precipitate a massacre - to my right, about two yards away was a gentleman with a useful-looking battle-axe. As the excitement waned, I made up my mind that if a rush took place, I would try and settle with the owner of the battle-axe first."

---

[81] *Nkosi yenyamazana*: Lord of all creatures / all animals (loose translation)

"'We are not dogs,' shouted the old Chief. There was restlessness among the crowd – murmurings of approval and anger.

"Rhodes turned to Colenbrander. 'Ask who named them dogs?' Colenbrander did so. Chief Somabhulana spoke out: the unfairness of some native commissioners, the abuse they endured at the hands of the native police, and one particularly hated officer, Colonel D.

"Colenbrander translated this for Rhodes, who gave him a message back for the Chiefs. There was a roar of approval when they were told Rhodes had said there would no longer be any native police and that he would remove the native commissioners the Chief had named."

"At the end of the first *Indaba* – which lasted about three hours – Rhodes told them he would camp on his own in the Matopos for three weeks."

"And Jan Grootboom stayed with him?" Prune cried out in delight.

"Well, he certainly stayed nearby. And probably spent most of his time listening to what the Matebele were saying," Themba confirmed.

"It makes it all so much more real," Angus commented.

Themba interrupted to say: "I have a another photograph of a sketch done by Baden Powell which the archives gave me. He passed it round and they could all identify key points relative to where they were sitting.

A sketch of the 1896 Indaba between Cecil Rhodes and the Matebele Chiefs, drawn by Lord Robert Baden-Powell who was camped nearby.

158

Angus continued.

"Now the really difficult issues were being discussed and debated and progress was being made.

"But behind the scenes, there was trouble with the Commanders of the British Force, General Carrington and Colonel Plumer. Historians tell of their growing resentment at Rhodes' success in his meeting with the Chiefs and of how desperate they were to take the initiative back under the Imperialist Force military wing.

"Unfortunately – and as humans do wherever there is the slightest sniff of success – they now all wanted to be part of it!"

They all laughed and agreed.

Themba interrupted, "In fact, my great-grandfather told Rhodes that he didn't approve of the British soldiers because he told him 'the lines of soldiers march into the Matopos, have a little fight, then go back to camp for supper. Nobody fights the Matebele *impi* like that. They don't like to be beaten, so they gain courage, and form up more confident than ever.'"

Angus smiled. "Rhodes must have made sure he tucked that away in his memory!

"He camped in the Matopos, as he had said he would, and held four more separate *indabas*. He took to heart the fact that the Matebele people had been left leaderless and blamed himself for not recognising that a culture used to strong, although in his eyes, savage, leadership would find it impossible to understand Western democracy.

"The situation was made worse by constant changes of Chartered Company leadership. Dr Jameson was a man King Lobengula liked and respected. He had in fact made him an *Induna* of his Imbezu regiment. But the Matebele people had been bewildered that a man, respected in his role as administrator of the Chartered Company, was now in prison in England. This was inexplicable to them."

"Why?" gasped Prune, "Why was he in prison?"

"All to do with an infamous undertaking known as the Jameson Raid. I'll give you some information, but it will side track us now"

"At one *indaba*," Angus went on "they arrived to find over 500 heavily armed *impi* waiting. There were panicky warnings from Colenbrander about 'treachery ahead'. But Rhodes took absolutely no notice.

"He walked into the middle of the *impi* and said something like – and as you said Themba, every historian quotes it slightly differently –

> *'How can I trust you when you ask me to come unarmed, then you come here ready for war? Put down your weapons now, or I will not talk with you.'*

"Regardless of what he actually said, Rhodes took charge. He asked the Chiefs why they allowed their young men to overrun them. They complained that they no longer had authority. In response, Rhodes said responsibilities and status would be granted back to them immediately.

"It certainly worked because by the end of all the *Indabas*, the Chiefs had ordered their sullen young *impi* to behave and respect Rhodes as leader. They said he was, in the eyes of the Ndebele people, the leader they had sought, the one who would deliver what he had promised.

"They showed their approval, according to Stent's article, shouting

> '*U-Rhodes, Inkoski n'kulu, Baba yami'.*
> "'Roughly: "Rhodes, great Chief, our father"

"What did Rhodes actually promise?" Prune asked.

"He restored the responsibilities and status of Chiefs immediately and assured them that he now knew of their grievances. But he asked why they had not come to him to tell him to put it right, instead of rebelling and causing so many deaths. He lectured them – probably as King Lobengula would have done. And knowing what we know now, he probably took a great deal of advice from Jan Grootboom.

"'You are no better than jackals – you kill women and children who are not fighting you. Anyone here who did such a thing, tell him to go. I will not deal with him.' It was tough stuff, but it gained their respect. The Chiefs agreed unanimously.

"Killing in fighting was accepted. That was now past, but murderers must be tried in the same way they would have been tried under King Lobengula. The Chiefs agreed again.

"Over the next meetings, the Chiefs set out all their troubles. Rhodes listened carefully. They accused Rhodes over and over again of being away so long saying that they did not know who to speak to.

"Rhodes told them again and again that he was on his own in the

Matopos. Anyone could come and talk to him. Every day, he rode alone on his horse to speak to anyone and everyone he could.

"At the final *indaba*, Rhodes asked if all the Chiefs were present. There was some unease at this question. After more discussion, they named four Chiefs who would not come, as they were still seeking blood. Rhodes said, 'Tell these Chiefs I go to their kraals and stay there until they talk to me.'

"One of the four, called amaHoli was the most senior and married to Lobengula's daughter. Eventually, and only because Rhodes and two others went and camped at his kraal saying they would not leave until he came to talk, this last Chief approached Rhodes. Rhodes asked, 'Is it peace?' The answer was 'It is peace. Our eyes are no longer red.'

"When this was finally reported to all the other Chiefs, Headmen, the regiments and their warriors, a great shout arose: *Lamuhla n'Kunzi*, which means 'Hail, now you are the separator of the fighting Bulls'.

'Lamuhla n'Kunzi. Lamuhla n'Kunzi.'
"Now we come to you when we are in trouble."

"The return to the BSA Company headquarters apparently became a joyful and noisy procession of joyfully ululating women, singing and dancing as the Matebele Chiefs and regiments accompanied Rhodes and his men. Grain that had been confiscated by the Imperial Forces to try and bring the rebellion to an end was now distributed freely, along with salt and tobacco. And there was at last peace.

"In fact, Matebeleland was soon deemed to be 'as safe as anywhere for travellers!'"

"Yes, that's all sounds wonderful, but what did Rhodes actually promise?" Prune asked again.

"The major issues were over and land and cattle," Angus replied. "So Rhodes bought two huge acreages of land to be used in perpetuity by the people of the country as National Parks – the Rhodes Estate in the Matopos, where we are now, which spans 424 square kilometres. The other was the Rhodes Inyanga Estate, and that is 472 square kilometres. Any Chiefs he felt had been particularly hard done by, or who had lost land or cattle, he compensated from that, or other unassigned, land.

"'He bought land for African re-settlement as well, promising more land would be made available for Africans. Sad reality dawned on him a few years later, when he realised how much of the land he had promised, had already been given away far too freely, to volunteers who came up with the Pioneer Column. All against Rhodes' express wishes. Of course, those volunteers were not going to give it up lightly now. The blame for most of this irresponsibility and bad administration was laid squarely at the feet of the impetuous administrators.

"It is recorded that Rhodes was extremely angry when he realised how much of that undistributed land was no longer available. Even more shattering to him, had he known, would have been that the two Rhodes estates, meant to look after the Chiefs, were largely divided up and distributed elsewhere on the gaining of responsible government in 1923.

"Another interesting insight on Rhodes - many reports say how depressed he was by what he had found out, particularly about of how wrong some of the BSAC, or better known as the Chartered Company decisions had been. By spending time with the people on one-to-one basis; getting to know the Matebele as a disciplined and forgiving people, this giant among men of that time, had been truly humbled.

"As we've mentioned, the Matebele were used to having a Chief to talk to about their complaints. Rhodes became their Chief . . . but he still wasn't physically there – so they still never knew who to talk to. Each new company administrator was different. Some would sit, listen and help; some were irascible and impatient and wouldn't.

"Rhodes died far too young, at only 49. Otherwise, I believe he could have become a moderating force, changing the whole perspective of those early years to one of greater understanding and acceptance."

A view of the world

"How did he die?" Themba asked.

"He was sent to South Africa as a young man, to try and improve his health as he was not expected to live very long. Although he improved in the Cape climate, he constantly battled with illness. While he was here meeting the Matebele, he must have felt the end was drawing in, because it was in the Matopos that he found what he termed World's View. It was one of the larger kopjes in the Matopos with a smooth, flat rock on top - and Rhodes said that was where he would like to be buried.

"He died less than six years later on March 26th, 1902, in his small tin roofed cottage on the sea front at St James in Cape Town.

"His body was moved to the Prime Minister's residence, Groot Schuur then placed in a coffin of Rhodesian teak. Tens of thousands of people went to Groot Schuur to pay their respects, with wreaths and cables of condolence flooding in from all over the world.

"Then came the move to Parliament House in Cape Town, so Rhodes could lie in state covered with a Union Jack, with a member of the Cape Police, his weapons reversed, standing at attention on each corner."

"Wow! Almost like a State funeral for a member of the Royal family," Carol said in amazement.

"It certainly was! But that was nothing compared to the thousands who lined the streets as the coffin was taken, with a mounted escort, to the railway station, ready for its trip to Rhodesia.

"Here in the Matopos the big granite rock was being excavated so it could take his coffin and a road was specifically constructed to allow it to be taken up to World's View by ox cart.

"The train was draped in black and purple, and his coffin was placed in De Beers carriage. That carriage he used for work when he travelled. At all the bigger stations, the train stopped.

"There was a guard of honour on each platform and the band played the Dead March. At smaller villages, buglers played the Last Post, and troops stood to attention as the train sped through. Mourners packed every platform and path beside the railway line – black, white, mixed, English, Afrikaans, Griqua. A vast mix of masses.

"The funeral service was to be held after his body reached Bulawayo for a second lying in state. That completed, the coffin moved to the huts on Rhodes Estate farm overnight ready for the measured march next day.

"Now here is something for you to imagine. Sixteen oxen had been practising pulling a cart loaded to simulate the weight of the coffin, up that hill two or three times a day. The oxen were led by the man who knew the name and nature of each animal – and who told them what to do, and how important it was, while stroking and encouraging them to do it perfectly. The oxen listened to their handlers and the practices went without a hitch.

Angus mused: "When the day came, my grandfather was one of those who followed that ox wagon with the coffin aboard. He walked all the way from those huts up to World's View - with such a mass of people that you couldn't count them.

"At the top, dressed in their most traditional finery, several thousand Matebele warriors were waiting. My grandfather said it was the most incredible and moving sight he had ever seen.

"As the ox wagon reached the top, and led by their chief *Induna* Mtjaan Khumalo, the Matebele gave a great shout, the Royal Zulu salute of '*Bayete*', then once again '*Bayete*'. And they raised their spears in salute."

"Wow! Incredible." Themba's eyes were shut, suddenly stinging with tears as he imagined it all.

Angus continued

"As the crowd fell silent, that memorable poem, written especially to honour Rhodes by Rudyard Kipling was read out."

"Is that the one written into the stone work beneath the memorial beside Cape Town University?" Carol asked quietly.

"*The immense and brooding Spirit still shall quicken and control.*
Living he was the land, and dead, His soul shall be her soul!'
They had all read the poem.

They were also beginning to understand.

Rhodes would always be controversial, but the grief of the people in Cape Town and along the train line, the magnificent salute by the Matebele warriors at the graveside, and the Kipling poem told them something more.

"After the committal service, everyone left, with the warriors chanting and singing about Rhodes all the way down the steep sides of the *kopje*.

"And we should all be moving on too."

"Just before we go," Themba said, hardly able to contain his excitement.

"I found out something else really important in the Archives."

Rhodes' promise

Rhodes thanked my great-grandfather for everything he had done – apparently he then turned to one of his men and said,

'Give Grootboom at any time he asks for it, a hundred acres of land, a wagon, a span of oxen, twelve cows, a horse and a hundred pounds.'

Then he turned back to my great-grandfather and said, *'You hear that Grootboom?'"*

"My great-grandfather apparently said something like, 'I will ask if I need it. But my score with the Matebele is settled. I go now to be with the missionaries.'"

Themba pulled out a piece of paper stuck between the pages of his notebook.

"I have something else to show you. This note, written in pencil, was from Rhodes. The people at the archives gave me a copy."

Angus, Prune and Carol crowded round to read what was written:

'Don't forget about Grootboom. He did a fine bit of work for me. See he gets his reward. C. J. Rhodes.'

"I wonder if that still stands, because there is no record to say Jan Grootboom ever came back or ever claimed his farm."

Themba grinned. "I wonder if the administrators of Rhodes Estate could tell me if I was entitled to his legacy as his great-grandson . . . But then, how would we prove he was my great-grandfather!"

165

15

THE SRANC AND KHAMI PRISON

Jabulani worked at the Prisons Department for nearly a year. He always tried to make sure he did everything right. *Discipline,* he told himself, *discipline and good manners get you far.* He could almost hear his father talking!

He worked in the same office as a strange guy called Aidan McBride. Aidan was so Irish that at first Jabu couldn't understand either his accent or what he was talking about. They'd take turns to take the mail out or supervise the daily routines for looking after the prisoners in Khami Maximum Security Prison. Aidan was a couple of years older than Jabu and a well-organised administrator. Jabu watched and learned, picking up valuable skills every day. *Don't keep pushing; don't seem too keen, Jabu – everyone must have a fair chance.*

It was hard though, because he was the first African to be employed in the Prisons Department who was not a messenger or a cleaner.

At first, the other Africans regarded him with great respect, clapping their hands in greeting and calling him Mr Ncube. But then some resented him when he instructed them to do something. Others expected him to share his pay with them. Aidan was cross about that. So Jabu explained how things worked in Matebeleland – and that those who had money were expected to share it with those who didn't.

It was sometimes hard when he and Aidan went to the Post Office too, because there, black and white people treated him like a messenger. And some didn't like him queueing with white people.

When the two of them stopped to have a cup of tea in Lobengula Street, other white people would glare at them with hard eyes. Jabu tried to take no notice. He dressed well and was polite but never deferential.

Being obsequious is not good, Jabu, he told himself. *Stand tall.*

Most of all, he made sure that if Aidan did something well, he did it even better.

He loved going down to Khami Prison. At first, he had been allowed only to drop mail at the desk and wait for messages from prisoners to be taken back to the office. After a while, he told his manager that he felt he was being treated like a messenger and that he knew he could do more to look after prisoner welfare if he was allowed to sit and talk with prisoners directly.

Nothing had happened, until last month, when his new boss Mr Eddington asked to see him.

"Jabulani, you have surpassed all our expectations of you. Well done. You've been here nearly year now, and I believe you'd be the right person to talk to the prisoners for us. We need to find out more about them – how they are feeling and behaving. We might get reduced sentences for them if things go well, as we can recommend review if we think it is warranted. We'd also like you to find out about their wives and children and make sure the prisoners have time to see them and look after them."

Worms in the sadza

Jabu started to meet the prisoners – only the low security prisoners at first – but it was a start. He made sure he gave them the right messages and good advice so this would get fed back to the Prisons Department. People on the staff at the prison were used to seeing him and found he was always willing to do more than he had to. It was helpful for them too to know when a prisoner was ill, was being troublesome or was worried about something.

Jabu's aim was to be given access to high security prisoners. In the last year, the nationalists had begun to speak out boldly against injustices. More and more were going to court. More and more, they were sentenced to gaol terms.

He'd been frantic to get finished today, because someone he admired, James Chikerema, had been accused of libel and was in court this afternoon.

Jabu had listened almost in disbelief when he found out what he had done. During a rally of hundreds of people at Stanley Square, Chik had accused the Minister of Native Affairs of theft! The police were waiting for him when he finished speaking.

Jabu had a long session at Khami that day, because four of the prisoners had refused to eat their sadza, saying it had worms in it. The problem required careful thought, as it was a big test in leadership for him.

Jabu started by asking if he could walk through the kitchens and storage areas. He asked the cook how this could have happened. The cook denied it completely, frightened he might lose his job. "Please help me Mr Ncube," he pleaded with Jabu. "I have five children and my wife in Gokwe and I must have this job, because now they have no land and no cattle."

So Jabu asked him to show exactly how he kept records of grain and meal deliveries, where he kept the mealie meal and how he kept mice and cockroaches away. Everything was in good order – clean, well swept, with grain on wooden pallets allowing a free flow of air underneath, with a rotation system to make sure older grain was used first.

Jabu couldn't fault or understand what had happened. Then he looked behind a stacked pile of old empty bags. A fat rat run out of a dark corner.

"What are you doing about those rats?" he asked the cook.

"The prison does not give me money to kill rats."

"You cannot run a kitchen for this number of people unless you can keep the rats out! You have to store the mealie meal and rapoko and other things that rats like to eat so they cannot get inside. Let's find where they have eaten a hole in the bags and something has got into the mealie meal."

They found two bags with holes in them. Big white moths came flying out of them when they lifted them up to check.

So, the prisoners were right – there were worms in the sadza.

It was time to report back to the four prisoners concerned on how this had happened. Jabu felt irritated with himself at not having any answers or ideas to fix the problem. Naturally enough, they were angry with the cook for not checking the mealie meal before it was cooked. They were going to create problems until that cook was fired.

So Jabu told them: "This cook works very hard to make sure you get food to eat. He has a wife and five children in Gokwe, where there is no land and no cattle. He cannot lose his job. The prison doesn't give him *muti* to kill the rats. So I want you to find an answer to his problem. Now go and think about it."

He was pleased that he had thought to ask them to solve the problem! They were pleased too and went away to talk. When they came back, they said the prison should now keep two cats in the grain store to kill rats and that all the mealie meal must be inspected. Any bags with holes must be thrown out. If this was accepted, they would withdraw their complaint.

"Oh and by the way, the cats must be spayed, or there will be too many cats."

"Oh and by the way, there must be a place where the cats can get out, or they might piss on the grain bags."

"Oh! And they must have water, and sometimes some milk and a little tasty food so they know that this is their home."

"Oh and by the way, Cephas will look after the cats!"

So Jabu and the prisoners solved the problem. The cook was happy. The guards and staff at the gaol were happy. The four offered to help sweep out the meal store as long as they had double food rations that night. Which they did - with twice the relish too! So they were very happy.

Whenever he visited the gaol, Jabu made sure he wrote down the names and pass numbers of everyone he met. Today it was the cook, the four and the grateful guard at the door to their cell. One day, he would use those names. He wasn't sure yet when or how, but he knew that one day they would be useful.

Jabu was the only one who was not quite happy. He missed the end of the trial for James Chikerema. He walked past the magistrate's court, just in case. There were people whistling, cheering and shouting. He watched as Chik was carried out of the courtroom on the shoulders of his friends. It was amazing! He had been found guilty of libel and had been fined, but allowed to go with a caution. The Southern Rhodesia African National Council (SRANC) paid his fine.

Jabu was happy for James Chikerema, but still not quite happy for himself! He had hoped Chik might go to Khami Prison, just for a while perhaps, then he could talk to him! Ah well.

Discipline; good behaviour; not too keen; take plenty of notes; give sensible advice - Jabu remembered his father's words, and added one more: *allow others to make their own decisions.*

Not being too puffed up

Getting in to work the next day, he saw Mr Eddington on the steps of the office building. As Jabu approached, he walked over.

"Jabulani, we have had a request from Khami Prison for you to accompany prisoners to the courts. It would mean going to Khami in the police van, collecting the prisoner, taking him to court, listening to the court proceedings, making sure the prisoner understands that what the court says must be done is done, then taking the prisoner back to Khami Prison afterwards."

"What happens if the prisoner is released?" Jabu asked.

"He would still have to go back to Khami to be discharged. He would then come under our Department so that he can get back to work or go home to his family. So once everything has been checked at that end, bring him back here."

It was difficult not to look too puffed up. He was only 17, nearly 18, and it was as though he was at least 25.

Now that he had worked one year at the Prisons Department, most of the other people who worked with him in Bulawayo and at the prison were really pleased for Jabu. He made himself popular with both black and white people with his gentle, quiet personality, his thoughtfulness and his sound and practical advice.

They all said: "Of course you should be the one who takes prisoners to the Magistrate's Court."

But for Jabu there was still a little problem which made him think. Here he was, one year in the job and with many new things to take on. But nobody had said anything about even a small pay rise for the extra work.

He mentioned it to Aidan and asked him what he thought he should do. Aidan got all fired up. He had been a member of his union in Ireland, and he was horrified to hear that there was no increase. He offered to go and talk to Mr Eddington as it was a harder thing for Jabu to do.

Later that day, Jabu received a letter from Mr Eddington saying that "in light of his extra duties", his pay would be exactly double what he was now earning! He was so excited. He took the letter to Aidan to show him and to thank him.

Aidan slapped Jabu on the back, said well done and that it was well deserved.

But then, he sat for a long time looking out of the window.

Jabu asked if he was all right.

He said he was.

But he wasn't . . . because later that afternoon he went to see Mr Eddington again. He raged at Mr Eddington and Mr Eddington shouted back. It was terrible. The whole office could hear the fight. A few moments later, Aidan came out, slamming the door behind him. He started packing up his things.

He had been fired.

Jabu was shocked. What happened? Aidan wasn't talking.

So Jabu shut up.

He went to the SRANC meeting that night, because James Chikerema was talking about his afternoon at court. Everyone was laughing and cheering. There was great excitement, and many fists punched the air. Jabu turned to see Michael Mawema, a leading nationalist, at his elbow.

"Jabulani, we have heard that you are doing very well at the prisons as a rat catcher!"

Jabu was overcome at meeting one of the nationalist legends. He stumbled out a greeting and wondered how the story had got out.

Mawema went on: "We are looking for a membership officer for the SRANC. I have insisted on bringing younger members into the central committee. If you are interested, we will talk some more. It will not come about until next year. We'd expect you to give out brochures and talk to people about joining SRANC. But we still have to print the brochures! Meantime, there are some small tasks we would like you to do for us."

Jabu's face lit up. He felt his future racing towards him. "I would like that very much," he said.

For the next half hour, Mr Mawema asked Jabu all about the work he was doing in the prisons. At the end of their discussion, he said gravely:

"It will be useful for us to have you there, but it would not help if your employers knew you were holding a position in the SRANC. So, this is a good reason to keep you out of the formal structure for a bit longer."

Jabu went home with his head in a whirl.

First the offer from Mr Eddington yesterday and the doubling of his pay; then the four prisoners in Khami and the wormy sadza; seeing James Chikerema being carried out of the courthouse on the shoulders of important nationalists to the whistles and shouts of hundreds of people; and now this talk with Michael Mawema.

The only sad part of the day was that Aidan had been fired.

Jabu wondered if Aidan had been jealous that he had been given a rise and more responsibility . . . while he was still in his old job.

But there was little time for wondering. The very next day, he was to start escorting prisoners to trial in the daytime. And at night, he would carry out some of Mr Mawema's small tasks – talking to young people in particular and convincing them to join the SRANC and take part in the campaign of non-violent resistance.

When he got home that evening, he found a letter from his father waiting for him. It said that there was to be a big sale of the family's Tuli cattle the next weekend. Jabulani was needed. Would he fulfil his obligation to his family and help prepare for this important event by taking Friday off?

He knew he had to go. But he was agitated about letting down his work and – even more important – the SRANC and Mr Mawema.

But it was fine, because when he asked Mr Eddington, his boss was happy to let him go.

On Thursday afternoon after work, he waited at the station for the bus to take him back to Ntabazinduna. He was thinking ahead to what he would have to do once he arrived, and he was excited to see his beautiful Bongani again.

The bus was late, so as he waited he thought about Bongani. He remembered his last visit to his *baba 'mkulu*. It had been a special visit, because Bongani had spoken to her father, Mandhla, about the need to go to school and the offer to stay at Ntabazinduna. There had been tears and unhappiness as the old man's shoulders sagged. Bongani understood the unspoken words. She had written a melancholy letter to Jabu, saying she did indeed love him, but she could not leave her father. Tears had dropped onto the paper, smudging the bright blue Quink ink.

Jabu remembered that his own tears had been close as he read it.

Then he had the idea!

Len Harvey and the Sanda cattle

He had made a special visit to Ntabazinduna a couple of months ago. He spoke for many hours with his grandfather about the pride he had in his Tuli herd. Jabu had never really thought about them. They were just their cattle, even though they were very strong, their coats shone black and dark red, and pale gold and he knew they produced good meat.

"About ten years ago, the Native Commissioner asked me to start a project where we crossed our African cattle with those big red Herefords that you see on the white farms," his grandfather told him. "It was a new thing for me, but the NC made me think about how strong our cattle are in the heat, and how they don't seem to need much water, even in drought."

Jabu had listened with interest, adding that they were of course, more resistant to ticks and disease too.

"Quite right," his grandfather said. "The NC said that mixing the breeds was producing beautiful calves. They've taken all the prizes in the Bulawayo and Salisbury shows and are giving resistance to heat and disease to the Herefords. The Herefords gave our calves more weight and better beef when they went for sale at the same age."

"I can't see any Hereford faces here, Baba," Jabu said, looking out for the distinctive white face and flat forehead of the Hereford.

"I decided against it" the old man continued. "The same week a young man from near Gwanda, Mr Len Harvey, came to see me. He was interesting. He worked for the Department of Agriculture in the 1920s, when they were drawing up these plans and advising African farmers to crossbreed with European cattle.

"Mr Harvey thought it was more important to keep the strain of the original Sanda cattle strong, because they were designed for our climate.

So after some time, the government agreed and allocated 3,000 acres in the Reserve to help him get a breeding programme started. This was to improve the quality of the Tuli so that European farmers would appreciate them as a worthwhile pure breed of beef cattle for our climate."

"After twenty years of breeding up the best Tuli cattle, he came here to Ntabazinduna, to encourage me to take some of them and develop and improve our herd.

"So . . ." he said with a proud flourish "today I have a herd of nearly 200 pure Tuli cattle. Just look at them, Jabulisani. Magnificent!"

Jabu couldn't help but be impressed. The cattle were strong and well fed. The hot sun had deepened the colour and shine of their coats.

He was just a bit sad that they were changing character though, because his grandfather had taught him many years ago how to burn the little horn buds of the calves to prevent them growing. He'd always loved the Tuli with the great horns he remembered as a young boy.

Beautiful horns – wild with the savagery they could inflict – but framing delicately soft native-cattle noses and huge gentle brown eyes.

Grandfather was still talking

"It has not been easy . . . because the bulls from the Angoni next door kept jumping over the fence onto the Tuli cows Mr Harvey gave me. So every time that happened, I had to send those calves away cheaply. Many times, I thought it was too hard to keep up. But all the time I knew Len Harvey was right in what he believed.

His face grew anxious. "Now my big problem is making sure I know from the ear tags, which cow has been made pregnant by which bull. I don't like keeping records because I want to be with my cattle, not with writing records."

Perfect! Jabu thought.

"Baba, I know a man who is an excellent record keeper. He would do that for you. His name is Mandhla Moyo. Do you have a job for him?"

So Mandhla Moyo received an invitation to be head of administration on *baba 'mkulu*'s farm at Ntabazinduna.

The beautiful Bongani went with him, of course, and she went to school. Right now, she was writing her O level exams, because she had

had so much practice on the old exam papers Mr Hawkins had given her, that she was at the top of her class.

"I will get these O Levels with Matriculation Exemption," She had written in her last letter, "so nobody can say I copied anything – even you, Jabulani Ncube!"

Oh! He was aching to see that beautiful girl again but sad that his Bulawayo life had been too busy to see her for a whole year.

Except once, when she had come with her father and they met in a café in Lobengula Street. But, it just wasn't the same as walking together on the soccer pitch.

I'm not a bloody Englishman . . .

The bus was still nowhere in sight, so Jabu thought he would cross the road to the milk bar to get a drink for the journey. As he reached the other side, he saw someone he thought he recognised - and called out, "Aidan! Aidan – it's Jabu!"

The man in front turned round. It was Aidan! Jabu had worried that it might be someone else because a black man shouting at a white man was not a sensible thig to do.

"Aidan! What happened when you had that fight with Mr Eddington? Why did you leave? I hate working there without you to talk to."

Aidan looked sad. "I didn't want to leave Jabu, but where I come from, you don't find out about injustice and just put up with it. So when Mr Eddington refused to raise your pay a bit more, I shouted at him. And he fired me."

"Oh Aidan, that's terrible!"

Jabu saw the bus approaching, but it was too late to run back across the road and catch it. This was more important. "I was just going to get a milkshake. We need to talk."

Aidan had lost his job and Jabu had got a rise. So Jabu bought Aidan a milkshake. But even buying Aidan a milkshake didn't make him happier. "What happened?"

Aidan went quiet. Then he said, "I don't think I should tell you. It will make you sad."

Jabu pressed on.

"Were you upset that I was asked to do those more important tasks at the Prisons?"

Aidan shook his head.

"Was it because I got a rise? But that was thanks to you, Aidan. I would never have tried to ask for more, because I don't think I would have got it. It was because you asked, as a white person, that I got the rise. I do know that."

Aidan looked away.

"Aidan – you are my friend. I want to know what's wrong so I can help."

"You can't help me Jabu. But perhaps if I tell you, you can help yourself and others."

He took a long drink of his milkshake.

"I went to see Mr Eddington because you showed me your letter saying your pay was now double what you started with last year."

Jabu nodded . . . then waited for Aidan to continue, because something was difficult for him to say.

"I told him you had showed me the letter. He got furious and said nobody was allowed to discuss what they earned with anyone else, and that we knew that was a rule. I told him it was only because you were so happy and wanted to thank me for helping you get it that you showed me the letter.

"Mr Eddington wasn't listening. He was still angry and shouting. So I shouted back and said it was disgusting that my salary was still higher than yours, even with the rise. I shouted at him and told him this was unfair, because your responsibilities were now much greater. And it was discrimination, just because you were black."

Jabu was uncomfortable.

Others in the milk bar were looking at them, because Aidan was now shouting. He didn't quite understand what Aidan was saying. Discrimination? Because he was black?

Jabu put his fingers to his lips, cautioning Aidan to speak softer.

"Mr Eddington kept shouting, saying that was exactly why employees were not allowed to talk about what they earned. I told him that he had better look at your salary again or I would not keep quiet. This made him really mad. He shouted, 'You bloody Englishmen come out here. You don't understand the situation. What right do you have to interfere?'"

Aidan stopped and a big grin came over his face.

"He called me a bloody Englishman! So I shouted back, 'I'm not a bloody Englishman, I'm a bloody Irishman.'

"I thought he was going to burst, because he was so angry. And he said, 'Get out of my office, pack up your things and don't come back tomorrow. Your employment has been terminated.'"

Jabu stared at him in shock as the implications of all Aidan had said sank in.

"I'm so sorry . . ."

"Well I'm not Jabu. I might be a bloody Irishman, but that's unfair. The thing that did worry me a bit—" he paused "—was that as I left, Mr Eddington shouted that I couldn't expect a reference from Prisons and that he would make sure all government departments knew I was a troublemaker."

"So what are you going to do?"

"I don't know. I don't have enough money to go back to Ireland."

"Aidan, I am on my way to Ntabazinduna to help my grandfather with his cattle sale. Why don't you come too?"

"I haven't any clothes."

"Well, you don't live far away, if you get back before the next bus . . ."

And so they both went to the cattle sale, talking all the way to Ntabazinduna. Aidan had never been there before. He never stopped talking or asking questions. The bus dropped them off about a mile from *baba 'mkulu's* home.

It was harvest time, so the road was bustling with bulging Scotch carts and chattering women balancing huge, carefully cut bundles of wood or baskets of mealies on their heads, most with babies on their backs as well.

Aidan went up and shook hands with them – with all of them – even with people Jabu didn't know who just happened to be walking along. Aidan wanted to shake hands with everyone, so it took a long time to walk home.

"Aidan, is that what you would do if you walked down the streets in Belfast?"

"What do you mean?" Aidan asked.

"Shake hands and talk to everyone."

"Oh, well – probably not everyone, just the people I knew. But this is Africa, and I want them to know that I like them."

"You are trying too hard my friend," Jabu laughed. "Just be normal. They are feeling awkward. The women are laughing, but they are also embarrassed. Shaking hands is your custom, not ours."

"Oh sorry – I thought I was doing the right thing and being friendly."

"It was friendly, but it wasn't quite right. Don't worry, I will teach you the right way to do things – particularly the traditional greeting of the Chief. You will need that when you meet my *baba 'mkulu*. Don't forget, we are people just like you, even if not everyone has the same level of education. There is a code of respect and understanding that is important in our culture too."

Aidan looked so ashamed that Jabu pushed his shoulder hard, and he nearly fell over. They ended up laughing as they turned into the gate of Grandfather's house. Nkanyiso was waiting for them, relieved that Jabu had at last arrived.

"And who is this?" Nkanyiso asked as father and son exchanged greetings.

"This is my friend Aidan, Baba. He's an Irishman."

Aidan looked at Jabu anxiously. "Do I shake hands with your father?"

Everybody laughed. Nkanyiso extended his hand to welcome the boy to his home.

He did have a lot to learn!

16

BABA 'NKULU'S CATTLE SALE

They had not had much time for learning anything else the next day, as they were busy talking business – how many of the best weaners they could afford to sell and how many heifers they should keep for breeding.

There were three classes of buyer. Most would be white commercial farmers from Gwanda, Nyamandhlovu and Lupane. Then there would be some who wanted to fatten weaners for sale to the Cold Storage Commission. They'd probably pay the best prices because the CSC was only looking at the beef which had been produced, whereas the farmers were still not too sure about buying African cattle. Then there were those who wanted to crossbreed with their European cattle, and one or two who wanted to actually do the same as his grandfather and develop the Tuli brand. The first three would be keen on the prime stock now coming off this farm, but it was this fourth group that Jabu's grandfather was most interested in.

It was an important sale, because only two years ago the government had stopped price controls on different types of beef and opened up free cattle sales. It was hoped that with price discrimination between Native and European cattle removed, more Africans would breed up their stock and sell on the open markets for better prices, as long as they still had enough cattle to work on their farms.

As the local Chief, it was important for *baba 'mkulu* not only to get good prices, but also to show that African farming was as good as European farming. There was a lot of pride at stake.

Baba 'mkulu had not sold at these free markets before of course, so everything had to be just right.

At last, 98 animals were chosen for sale, which still left *baba 'mkulu* with 80 breeding cows, plus small calves and weaners and 4 good bulls.

Jabu, many cousins and Aidan spent the day making new holding pens, using wooden poles which had been collected over several months. They lashed them together with riempie and strong string painted with tar to fix and strengthen it. They also made passages with ramps so the cattle could be driven down and then loaded onto trucks without escaping.

The animals had been dipped a week ago and had certificates to say so. Now the grooming could start. The cousins laughed at the idea of brushing *mombies*! But by the end of the day, they were very interested in washing them, cleaning their hoofs and legs to keep them free of dung and dirt, wiping their eyes and then brushing them all over. The cattle were not used to this either! Some were skittish and jumping, while others stood with eyes half closed, enjoying the brushing.

They started work before 5 that morning, so when Jabu's mother came out to the cattle yards, bringing tin cups of tea and fat slices of bread with dripping, it simply vanished into ravenous young stomachs. By 3 in the afternoon, huge cattle trucks started arriving, and there was great shouting and noise as each animal was bundled in. Some cousins went with the trucks to help unload the cattle again into the big collecting area at the showground.

As night started to fall, the smell of roasting meat and mealies drifted from the kraals – a great incentive to get the last animal into the right pen.

Next morning, before the sun was up, the old farm truck groaned away, objecting to its load of 15 people sitting on the sides of the tray, on the tray itself and on the cab roof - while another three squeezed in next to the driver in front. It needed a lot of gear changing and double de-clutching before it could be persuaded to move up some of the hills leading to the cattle market.

Jabu and Aidan had jumped up to get a good place on the back of the truck, so they could be first off once they arrived. They all sang their way to the sale pens, telling stories about the excellence and character of each of the cattle they had chosen.

When they arrived, they had to take turns driving one animal at a time into a locked pen, where they were examined by vets. The animals were then weighed and graded, a minimum price allocated and called out. This would be written down against the description or number of the animal. They would then be ready for farmers to begin the bidding.

Jabu loved it! Hundreds of people, busy, everyone knowing what they were doing. Whips cracking to the guiding whistles and shouts of the *umfanas* as they led their great beasts through dust filled air. The cattle showed the white of their eyes at all the pandemonium and people . . . until, at last, they moved gratefully into the cool of roofed cattle pens.

Before *baba 'mkulu's* herd was led out into the open area for auction, Nkanyiso was given a loud hailer and invited to tell the story of the breeding of the Tuli herd and the links to Mr Harvey. He said that his father, Chief Mehluli, hoped that most of these beautiful animals would go to farmers who also wanted to work to retain the integrity of the Tuli breed.

The cousins then started to lead the cattle into the auction area. The farmers got excited by the quality of the animals. Most of them had been given a minimum price that surprised *baba 'mkulu,* as it was already so high. He was worried that this would mean nobody would buy at that price.

But when the auctions started, the bids went higher and higher and on and on.

Jabu watched as his *baba 'mkulu* stood, looking bewildered by it all. The old man couldn't speak. He kept shaking his head when he finally understood that, on average, the price paid was 28% higher even than the high minimum price that had been recommended. Usually, most farmers tried to pay the minimum price if they could, so this was unimaginable.

Jabulani felt his heart bursting with pride and happiness for this stately old Chief.

After the sales, *baba 'mkulu* and Nkanyiso were thronged by black and white farmers who wanted to come out to Ntabazinduna another time and see the farm.

They were interested to know how they could work together and wanted to talk about how they were implementing their breeding programmes. They wanted to make sure they were notified about any other sales of Ntabazinduna Tuli.

"Hell man! Look at that bull – not even a year old!"

"Just bought 40 weaners . . ."

"So you were the one who was bidding against me!"

"Never seen Tuli with such great hindquarters . . ."

On and on the comments went. They loved how good the cattle looked and many commented about how calm they were, even in the cacophony of whistles and shouts as they were herded in by the *umfanas*. Jabu stood nearby, in case they needed help and listened to everything that was said.

He watched as his *baba 'mkulu* turned to a tall thin man trying to get his attention. They shook hands. Then the man's eyes misted up, and he put his arm round *baba 'mkulu's* shoulders.

"Jabulani," his grandfather called to him. "I want you to remember this man. This is Len Harvey – the one who has worked with me on these Tuli cattle. Come and shake his hand."

Jabu was quite certain he would remember this man.

"Your grandfather is quite exceptional, Jabulani," Len Harvey said. "So ready to look critically at what I proposed, then to come back to me and say OK, let's go. It's been really tough for him. So many have said he was doing the wrong thing. But look at today. I am so pleased for him."

Jabu found himself absorbing everything – the excitement, the interest, the interaction between everyone there; even the pride of the *umfanas*.

Like old times again

He looked at the rows of people watching and leaning over the rails.

Then he couldn't believe his eyes!

It was Mr Davidson with Carol and, he was pretty sure, with Prune and Themba as well. He rushed over to them – with much shaking of hands and shouts of laughter.

Mr Davidson was so pleased to see Jabu. He called out to Nkanyiso. "Now I know why I haven't been able to get hold of you."

They shook hands and clapped each other on the shoulders. "What a magnificent herd, Nkanyiso, you must please congratulate your father for me. It is so encouraging to see his determination to keep this Tuli strain intact. Just look at the results! I hope these prices will spur him on to greater heights."

The two men went off, deep in conversation. Angus knew he would have to eventually get round to telling Nkanyiso about the bitter developments with the African Affairs Board.

But not just yet.

As they left the group, Nkanyiso shouted back to the four friends, "There's a braai at our place tonight. See you there."

The four decided that would be a great place to catch up as well.

When the sales were over and the cattle had been put into other trucks to go to their new owners, Jabu felt a strange sense of loss.

He knew his *baba 'mkulu* would be feeling the same – he loved his cattle so much. Jabu watched him moving among them, talking to them and stroking their heads. He knew the character of each one. He had brought them into this world, and he was sad to see them leave it.

Jabu went to stand with his *baba 'mkulu*. They didn't need to talk. The old man put his hand on his grandson's shoulder, and they stood wrapped in each other's sadness, satisfaction, enjoyment, loss and gain . . . and a hundred other emotions that surfaced from nowhere.

Jabu suddenly remembered Aidan. He took his leave, assuring his *baba 'mkulu* that he would be at the evening festivities, and found Aidan talking to a blond young farmer. They seemed to have a lot in common.

He shouted: "Hope you've been OK Aidan - sorry I've neglected you."

Aidan laughed and said he'd had a great day. Jabu understood why when he was introduced to a young farmer who was 'another bloody Irishman'. He told Aidan about the braai tonight and asked the farmer if he would like to join them . . . but he had to get home to Nyamandhlovu.

Jabu allowed himself to think at last, of Bongani. They'd be meeting up tonight. He really wanted to introduce her to Carol.

As he and Aidan walked back to the truck, Jabu suggested Aidan left Bulawayo for Salisbury, where he would most likely find a job away from the poisoned pen of Mr Eddington - if he avoided government.

Aidan was fired up now to "do something to help the Africans". Jabu laughed and reminded him that he had a lot to learn, but that someone who might help was a man he had met a couple of nights ago, called Guy Clutton-Brock.

"He is a 'bloody Englishman'" Jabu laughed.

He went on to tell him that he thought Aidan might find him interesting. Anyway, there could be some sort of job for him at the new farm co-op he was planning to open near St Faith's Mission in Rusape.

As they talked, what Aidan had told him yesterday suddenly hit him. He began to understand about the unfairness of it all. He was being paid so much less than a white man who was now doing a lesser job. That hurt. A slow burning anger settled deep inside him.

Why, when things could work so well with *baba 'mkulu's* cattle sales, did the Prisons Department pay him less just because he was black?

It was time for thought.

Time to take life seriously.

Time to get back to Michael Mawema's little tasks.

Despite the fun of all the singing and joking as they rode home in the back of the truck, Jabu was far away. He found himself unconsciously drawing more very sharp pointed stars which he must remember to add to his SRANC notebook as reminders for the future.

17

LOOKING FORWARD LOOKING BACK

"That one is going to keep you under her little finger," Carol teased Jabu, "she's a packet of dynamite, but . . ."

"Cheeky *sterek*," Jabu added with a wry smile. "I know . . ."

They all laughed, the envious teasing laugh of shared adolescent hope that they might also find such a love one day. Bongani had to write two exams, so they hadn't seen much of her. But what they had seen was memorable. *Perfect for Jabu,* Carol thought. Bongani added spice and zest to his rather driven and serious character.

Angus and Nkanyiso were meeting Chief Khayisa Ndiweni – a man respected equally throughout the country and internationally for his wise and measured dealings with Britain. He was a man of great courtesy and humour, and Angus was pleased to find an excuse to see him. While their meeting took place, the four old friends and Aidan sat cross-legged under a flat-topped acacia, catching up on their lives since Tjolotjo days.

Prune was flicking ant lions out of a sandy path, still enjoying the triumph of watching the little creatures fly out of their conical lair and just as intrigued by their speed as they burrowed away.

"Wow! Look at him go! Pity I can't see a big ant heap round here, or I'd make you all some first-class mud and you could show Aidan how to start up a farm."

"You were pretty expert Prune, but I bet you've forgotten how to make the mud just right." Themba slapped him on the back.

"Carol and I haven't much to tell - we're just doing A levels. That's why we're back in Matebeleland. We chose almost identical subjects."

Prune butted in. "How can you say you haven't much to tell!"

He looked at Jabu. "Did you know that a big firm of lawyers in Salisbury is going to pay for Themba to do law at varsity?"

Jabu was stunned. "Where will you go Themba?"

"That depends on my results. They'd like me to go to Wits, but I'm not mad about the idea. Nor is my father. The law faculty is starting at the University College of Rhodesia in the middle of next year. That would be a much better degree because of its affiliation to London. But that is only if I can get really good marks. I don't want to do law particularly, and it does mean I would have to do two years articles with the company afterwards, but it'll put me in a good position for the future."

"What would you do with a law degree anyway? Go into the courts as a barrister or something?" Jabu asked.

"No, that would absolutely not interest me. I want to specialise in agricultural law. That's why I was fascinated by the cattle sale yesterday. Our people seem to be getting the right idea about animal husbandry, but the difficulty is trying to resolve competing interests for the land. So many misunderstandings - which constantly cause trouble. I suppose, that as a member of a chiefly family Jabu, with your land intact and untouchable, you wouldn't see the problems affecting others at the moment."

"Probably not . . ." Jabu agreed, "but then I've actually just been promoted to looking after prisoners at Khami when they have to go to court. Land issues come up all the time. I've been to one court session so far, and it certainly made me think about a lot of things. The prisoners I've worked with are mostly political prisoners, who are beginning to speak out about things they feel are wrong. It's exciting to see it happening, and I feel there are important changes coming."

"If there's anything you think I might be able to help you with Jabu, just get in touch. I'd love to be involved."

Aidan stepped in. "This friend of yours is quite somethin', you know Themba," he said. "He has been there like a little magician, sortin' out huge problems at the prison. And he is so good at it. Prisoners who've done nothin' at all but complain have started to think about findin' answers rather than just sittin' mutterin' away. Prison management is impressed."

" . . . and Aidan has just lost his job, looking after me." Jabu finished.

"What happened?" Carol was shocked.

Jabu told the story. They were silent. Sympathetic. Sad. Angry.

"Now, time to tell everyone what happened to you at Mr Bellini's store in Balla Balla, Prune," Carol insisted.

"Oh, it's not important."

"It is important. It's very important. And you too lost your job."

So . . . stumbling and uncertain, because everyone else seemed to be doing such exciting things, Prune described the store and said how his first job was just being the messenger, then how he started re-stocking shelves, until one day he was promoted to serving at the counter, and then on to becoming the accountant.

He gained in courage as the others were so positive and clapping him on the back.

He went on to tell his friends all the details of Lalan's birthday . . . and as the awful trickery of Marco's plan took shape, there were exclamations of disbelief and incredulity. They all agreed Prune had been 'framed'.

Jabu listened carefully to the details. He must remember to add another flashpoint.

"I am positive again now." Prune finished rather unconvincingly . . . then his face brightened.

"By the way, if anyone is in Balla Balla on January 10th, Maura and I are getting married. You're all invited. I have had some really astonishing and exciting news from Lalan. Her wedding present to us is enough money from her Scottish savings to put down as a deposit on our own business. I know the perfect store too, in Balla Balla —" Prune choked up.

"Wow! That's fantastic Prune!"

"I'm so pleased for you."

"Mr Bellini is going to get a little competition."

"He certainly is!" Carol agreed.

Jabu turned to her. "What about you? What are you going to do?"

"Oh, I don't know," Carol said heavily. "You guys know I've always wanted to be a doctor . . . well, Mum and Dad asked Dr Olive Robertson to afternoon tea last month so we could get some ideas. She's the only woman doctor in Southern Rhodesia right now.

"She wasn't encouraging. She said there's still real antagonism towards women doctors – even from women! And, men wouldn't be seen dead going to a woman doctor.

"Anyway, the cost of six years at varsity are enormous. As a Native Commissioner, Dad can't afford to send me to UCT in Cape Town, which is where I'd really like to go." She paused.

Then smiled half-heartedly.

"Rather grandly, and thinking I was being so generous giving up my dream, I said to Dad, 'That's fine, I'll be a vet instead!'"

They smiled in hope, but Carol's face fell again. "That turned out to be a five-year degree done entirely in Afrikaans at Onderstepoort. I don't speak Afrikaans. They'd find me very different, just as I would find them very different. And, it's still too expensive. So I must admit I'm feeling pretty flat. Particularly listening to you lot and the exciting futures opening up ahead of you."

"What other options might be open to you?" Themba asked.

"Teaching, nursing . . . or shorthand and typing. I don't want to do any of those . . . and of course, as soon as I got married, I'd have to give up work anyway. It stinks.

"Nobody in this backward country realises that women do have brains and do want to use them. I can't even get a job to help Dad with varsity fees. If I was in England, I could work in a coffee bar or something. But here I'm not even allowed to apply for those jobs!

She looked apologetically at Jabu and Themba before saying: "Oh, I know it's right to encourage Africans, and African women in particular, it's absolutely right. And I don't want to detract from that.

"But everyone wants a job and everyone wants and needs to earn money" She paused.

"To top it off, it seems as though scholarships for tertiary education only go to Africans. Even though I was born here and so was my father, I have had to realise that as a European, no matter how good my marks might be, I probably won't be considered."

There were surprised looks.

"Sorry guys, I know that that is also right . . . but it feels pretty unfair from my perspective.

"I was delighted when Sarah Chavunduka was the first African woman admitted to the University in Salisbury last year – she really deserves it, and I know she's found it tough going. I was looking forward

190

to being at varsity with her once, as we've known each other for a long time. I do feel pretty resentful that I won't be able to join her even there. Another problem is that there don't seem to be businesses lurking in the background prepared to put me through varsity either, like you Themba!"

Carole smiled ruefully and shrugged her shoulders.

She stood up, brushing leaves and dust off her skirt.

"Sorry guys - whinge over! Here's Dad."

"Right team — we must push on," Angus said. "Jabulani, are you free to join us? I'd like to trace Lobengula's footsteps to help these two A-levellers. I know that Mtjaan was your great-grandfather and we'd love to know more about him. We might try to get up to 'nThaba zikaMambo."

"Would you have room for Aidan as well?"

"If we borrow the truck, no problem."

It was no problem. Sandwiches made and cold drinks at the ready, braai meat and buns bought on the run, stretchers and sleeping bags loaded, they piled into the truck, Angus and Jabu in the front.

They drove away from Ntabazinduna.

"As I have caught up on what the other three are doing, bring me up to date, Jabu, on where you are at - then I'll fill you in on my discussion with your father."

Mhlanhlandhlela or not?

After 15 minute drive south, they stopped the truck on the other side of Bulawayo. Ahead was a large flat, stony plateau - dry bush dotted with insignificant water-stressed trees, cracked earth and the desolate twists of a sand bed river.

The only sign of life was a hovering black shouldered kite - its blood red eye focussed on something in the grass . . . suddenly it stooped, dropping like a stone, to wing away heavily with a beak full of breakfast.

"Does anyone know where we are?" Angus asked.

Jabu responded.

"Another of Mzilikazi's capitals."

"It would have covered three or four acres, with strong fences round the edge and small pens for cattle and other animals, dotted between groups of *amaQhugwana*[82], thatched houses six or seven rows deep round the southern half. They'd have looked more like a beehive than villages today, with doors opening only about waist high. But the area housed a huge population."

"Any idea why it appears as derelict as it is?" Angus asked.

"This is all that what would have been left after Lobengula's inauguration as King, which took place right here. Once he was King he burnt everything and went to build his own capital."

Angus picked up the story, as they walked together.

"So somewhere here might have been another *boma*[83] separating the animals, with fences round the Royal Queens and their children." Jabu nodded.

"This raised, circular, area could have been the King's enclosure . . . with a strong wall built around it, leading to what became known as the bok or goat kraal."

Jabu agreed. "Yes, this was the 'crunch point' where meetings with the King took place. Bravery was applauded, but stiff sentences were passed on anyone who did not do the right thing.

"By the time anyone reached about this point, he or she would either be acclaimed as they walked through the entrance with great promises of rewards and festivities, or they'd be dragged through to await humiliation and frequently, death sentences.

"The King would sit in a prominent position under the *indaba* tree with his most important *indunas* beside him, and rows of those involved in whatever was happening sitting in a semi-circle in front of him.

"Punishment was immediate and very public."

"You can almost feel it," Carol said quietly, having heard details of these trials before.

Angus agreed. Then turning away to a larger, open area, he said:

"This held tens of thousands of massed regiments of warriors plus several thousand onlookers for King Lobengula's inauguration. So let's find some shade and imagine what went on, as I have some great descriptions for you written by people who were actually there at the time.

---

[82] *amaQhugwana*: typical beehive construction homes with low entry doors
[83] *boma*: closely tied stick fence largely for keeping animals safe

A single row of pale pink beads

They walked back to a shady spot near the truck to sit on rocks and old ant heaps. Their curiosity fired with new questions.

"A very tall man. I heard he was something like 6 foot."

"He was large, but not fat . . ."

"I agree, he looked pretty athletic from those old drawings—"

"Wearing a sort of leather ring on his head . . ."

"With the traditional Ndebele tribal dress of monkey skins round his waist and necklace of significant things like a lion's tooth . . ."

Jabu added: "He would also wear a single row of pale pink beads denoting his membership of the Royal Khumalo clan and therefore his legitimate kingship.

"OK – that's interesting Jabu, I wasn't aware of that detail.

Angus picked up a book with many scraps of paper in it. "I hadn't much of a picture, until I came across an great description by the British Administrator to Bechuanaland Sir Sidney Shippard after his first meeting with the King in about 1888, which was before any settlement took place.

In person he is rather tall, though considerably shorter than Khama and very stout, though by no means unwieldy. His colour is a fine bronze and he evidently takes great care of his person, and is scrupulously clean.

He wears the leathern ring over his forehead as a matter of course. Altogether he is a very fine-looking man, and has a most majestic carriage.

"Like all the Matebele warriors who despise a stooping gait in a man, Lo Bengula walks quite erect with his head thrown somewhat back and his broad chest expanded, and as he marches along at a slow pace with his long staff in his right hand, while all the men around shout out his praises, he looks his part to perfection."

'That's a great description! May I have it please Mr Davidson?"

Jabu carefully folded the piece of paper into his notebook, Angus continued: "Lobengula would never allow a photograph to be taken of him – but this is a very good sketch done by a man called Maund, and I think it absolutely confirms Sir Sidney Sheppard's written description.

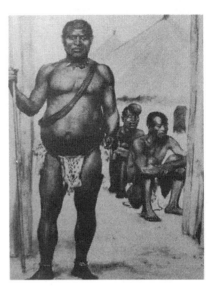

King Lobengula - an original sketch by E.A. Maund, completed by the portrait painter Ralph Peacock

What do we know about Lobengula as a young man?"

Everyone looked blank.

"OK! This does get interesting. When I was looking for information and a bit more detail for you two, Carol and Themba, I found something I actually had to read twice before I gave it any significance.

"Lobengula was dressed in European clothes when he arrived for the start of the inauguration. I didn't give it any importance to start with – then I wondered why on earth he would do that. He even asked several white men to escort him to the inauguration all galloping there on horseback."

"I didn't know he rode a horse!" exclaimed Jabu rather defensively.

"Nor did I! What do you think that indicates?"

"That he must have . . . I don't know . . ." Jabu floundered.

"He must have been comfortable with white people."

"Maybe he was. And of course he knew Sarah Liebenberg who was his nanny until he was about 7. But I was puzzled about it, then found that when he wasn't learning about traditional medicines from the Mlimo, he spent most of his time with a couple of white hunters. Sam Phillips, who became known as Induna Sam, who might have been Sarah Liebenberg's brother . . . and depending on which reports you read, there were others – somebody referred to as Westbeech and someone we have heard more of - Frederick Courteney Selous."

"We had a Selous House at school."

"There's Selous Avenue too. He must have been important."

"He was a scout, a hunter, a good horseman and military strategist. More about him later but there are enough records to indicate that Lobengula – known as Jandu at that stage, Aidan – and these two or three white hunters, spent a lot of time hunting on horseback. Apparently Jandu fell off and broke his arm at some stage and Induna Sam set it for him. They were carefree – good hunters, good trackers, good friends.

"In fact, they were hunting together in what is now Mazoe when Jandu was told that King Mzilikazi had died.

"Do you think that was a shock to him?" asked Themba.

Jabu suggested: "It might well have been, particularly when he realised he was the next in line of course. I've heard the odd story about the King's white nanny. I'm interested that you have found it too."

Aidan burst in: "That's interestin' about the huntin' and the horses too, but how did Lobengula get his trainin' to take over as King?"

"That's a very good question." Angus continued. "In Zulu and Matebele culture, kings' sons were often sent away because the King wanted to be sure they didn't try any tricks, like plotting to take the throne. There's no plausible history, oral or written about the relationship between Mzilikazi and Lobengula or even if he was allowed in the royal enclosure.

"Can you add anything to that Jabu?"

"Actually it's interesting, I don't remember any mention of Lobengula in our nightly talks with my father as a young child – until he was going to be the next King. So there could be something in that."

"He certainly didn't seem to think he would be King. In fact, it looks as though he really didn't want to be! We mentioned yesterday that when he was told Mzilikazi had died, he immediately galloped away to stay with the missionary Thomas Thomas for protection.

"Fortunately, like all the missionaries, Thomas was required to keep a regular diary to report back to the LMS. I found a description of that moment.

"Here Prune, you read what Thomas had to say."

"As for Ulopengule[84], when first informed by Umcumbata that he was the real heir to the throne, he became so alarmed and convinced of the existence of a plot against his life, that he escaped from his own town and riding about fifty miles, took refuge at our house. Three days after, I prevailed upon him to return home. He would do so, only on condition that I would accompany him, and ascertain from the ruling chief what was the real state of affairs in respect to him."

"Why did he think his life was in danger?" Aidan asked.

"After throwing relatives and friends off Ntabazinduna mountain, which was our discussion yesterday, King Mzilikazi left no known heir. It was in the interests of some Chiefs who backed others to get rid of Jandu. So it took 18 months after the King's death to determine that Jandu was the rightful King.

Jabu added: "An elder brother of Jandu, Nkulumane, had disappeared after Ntabazinduna and nobody knew where he was."

"Indeed Jabu and I our chat yesterday, it was clear he had made sure he was well hidden! Jandu kept a very low profile. But one day the major Chiefs presented Jandu with many ceremonial oxen as gifts, and he realised the time had come to accept the kingship.

"What happened next?" Prune asked.

"As you can imagine after that long period of time without a King, the excitement grew and people started pouring in to this site from all over the country, all trying to find a place with a good view to watch this momentous event."

He looked round and gestured up towards the rising land at the back. "They'd have looked for any elevated spot in any space they could find."

They looked around at the countryside – small hills, low ridges - not much to distinguish it, but now filled with a strong sense of presence in the telling and descriptions.

"A lot happened before they got here! Jabu would you read this?"

Jabu was delighted to do so, wondering what it was.

"The custom of the Amandebele upon the occasion of the inauguration of their king is to fetch him from his own town and lead him in triumph into the capital.

---

[84] *Ulopengule*: there were many variations on the name in written records. Nobody was quite sure how these early amaNdebele should be spelt.

On the 22nd of January 1870, the warriors appeared at Utjotjo, Ulopengule's town. It was about nine o'clock in the morning, when great clouds of dust were observed ascending towards the skies about a mile to the south of Utjotjo, and the approach of the mighty army soon became known to the people of the town. A very great lamentation was set up by the prince's wives, children, and other relatives who were present, which continued to a degree until the evening."

"I've haven't heard that detail before Mr Davidson. Fascinating!"

"Glad we can teach you something Jabu!

"That was another report from the missionary Thomas Morgan Thomas, who was one of only three white people allowed to attend the event.."

Prune sat in awe. Jabu was delighted that the story of his King was being told, and had a huge smile lighting up his face.

Themba and Carol – and Aidan – were simply absorbed by it all.

18

KING LOBENGULA'S INAUGURATION

"Utjotjo of course - today's Tjolotjo - is where things started.

"This is roughly what happened.

"Between six and seven thousand men in leopard skins, ostrich feathers, coloured beads and brass ornaments, all with their shields and *assegais*, made up great waves of disciplined warriors a mile wide, stamping and marching their way to the Tjolotjo we know so well!"

He paused again, watching the faces of the youngsters as they imagined the excitement of disciplined regiments of warriors arriving with increasing shouts from the onlookers as they approached.

"They formed up to the east and north of Tjolotjo. For many hours, they staged military manoeuvres, giving portrayals of great bravery and a rhythmic stamping, mixed with a continuous shouted conversation.

"On one side, Utjwabalala shouted out what the Royal Prince wished for the country and the people. He guaranteed raids and subjugation of tribes to the north would continue - to roars of approval from the crowd . . . he gave promises about the royal cattle, but demanded the people's absolute obedience and loyalty to Lobengula as King.

"The other speaker, Uputaza, repeated and acclaimed every detail to the new King's subjects with great theatrics, pomp and ceremony.

The warriors in turn, roared their approval and agreement to each point made.

"Then, at a poignant moment, silence fell.

"Uputaza turned round slowly, to make a direct, formal request to the assembled family members and people of the village of Tjolotjo to deliver the new King so they could take him 'home' to this great capital before us.

"With a shouted salute, they agreed.

"At that point, Prince Jandu came galloping out on horseback straight towards the massed lines of regiments. At the last moment, he wheeled round to look back and raise his hand in a dramatic farewell to his family as the mounted escort fell in beside him.

"With a flourish, they galloped off at great speed. You can imagine the shouts and excitement that followed."

Carol was ready for a turn.

"*Led now by their prince, the soldiers, in high glee, covered the country for a mile in every direction, dancing and singing the whole way from Utjotjo to Umhlahlanhlela. Before entering the town, a consultation was held during which time Ulopengule, with his life guard, stood under a tree nearly surrounded by the dancing and singing crowds.*

"Carol, I'm going to interrupt for a moment to show you this photo of a sketch done by the very famous artist Thomas Baines -

it shows the start of the inauguration with Jandu sitting outside this big space where he had been given a huge welcome but was still waiting to be asked inside. Now to finish off . . .

"*An ox was presented to him, and he was invited to enter the city, which he did by the north gate.*"

Looking round to find North, Themba commented: "That would've been pretty close to where we are now."

"That's about right. Thomas goes on to tell of an old blind man, Umtamtjana, who acted as a priest of the tribe."

"The *sangoma*," Jabu suggested. "He'd prepare the charms and purifications for the ceremony in huge earthen pots and wooden bowls."

"Thanks Jabu. And while they were doing that, the regiments stood in a semicircle round the edge of the kraal, about twenty deep. It must have been an awe-inspiring sight, with their phalanx of black and white, red and white, or speckled regimental shields.

"This is Thomas's description of a warrior for you, Themba."

"With a couple of spears, a centre supporting-rod clothed at the point with the tail of a jackal in his left hand; a long staff in his right, an ample cape of black ostrich feathers, or a bandeau of yellow otter skin, and a blue crane feather fixed in front of it on his head. His arms and legs were ornamented with brass bangles, threaded beads or tufts of white ox-tails; a tippet of the fine umpila skin coverd his shoulders and chest. Bulky kilts of strips of various wild animals skins were fastened round his waist and hung loosely round his hips. To a looker-on from the adjacent hillock, the view was a fine one."

Jabu couldn't resist reading a bit more. He asked Themba if he could take over. Then spontaneously, he stood up, drawing himself up to his full height, and described:

"The motley, moving, mighty mass of people . . . swelling their songs of praise to their illustrious ancestors and former kings, like the chanting of a great cathedral, while with their feet, as they lifted them in turns from the ground, the time was kept. Whilst thus formed, dressed, and engaged, the whole multitude moved from one side to the other, like the trees of a forest in a strong breeze. One veteran soldier after the other leaped out of the ranks, holding his shield in readiness to defend himself against an imagined foe, by rattling it in his face; at the same time vaunting his expertness in battle, evading armed assailants, leaping over fallen ones, struggling to stand as if hard pushed, plunging his spear into one after the other, until the whole number of those imagined as killed by him were counted.'

"You should be on the stage Jabu – that really brought it to life!" Carol laughed. They all clapped and agreed. Jabu sat down, embarrassed by his sudden rush of emotion.

"Try to read and absorb the whole of Thomas's description – it goes on much longer," Angus said. "The dated use of words and colourful phrases bring it all to life – but there's too much to cover here."

A sketch of King Lobengula's inauguration

"Was that the end of the celebrations?" Prune asked.

"Oh no, not by a long way. A couple of days later, Lobengula assumed his duties in a priestly role first, then ceremonially inspected a few prime black oxen, telling each animal why he was an exceptional ox and why he would be sacrificed to his father Mzilikazi, or his grandfather Matshobana, or his great-grandfather etc. Then with a quick stab behind the shoulder, one of the *indunas* killed the ox instantly."

Prune picked it up: "*Then followed and fell a number of oxen of various colours, until the whole of the goat kraal, large though it seemed, was actually filled with dead cattle. The slaughtering of sixty oxen, wild, as they were, the skinning, cutting them up, and carrying the meat into the appointed royal huts in the isikohlo[85] was an exciting scene of hard work. The meat was arranged in the different huts for the night, in order that during the hours of darkness, the spirits of those men to whom it had been offered might come and sanctify it.*"

"What a sight," Jabu sighed. "I wish it still happened. Just imagine the huge fires cooking the meat, then dishing it out to thousands of people. Incredible!"

"Just imagine watching all those thousands of people ripping it apart and gulping it down," Carol's grimaced at the thought.

"With the blood drippin' down their arms . . ."

---

[85] *isikohlo*: loose translation of what we would probably now call a bond store.

202

"No Aidan, no more!" she cried. "You're such a girly girl," he teased.

"Enough you two – a bit more to learn, then we must move on. There was an interesting finale to all this. The King went home hungry. He didn't take part in any of the feasting."

"That's right, because all the meat was for the people," Jabu added.

"Oh wow! That's impressive"

"Over the next three months, Lobengula was separated from his wives and children and left with only his sister Ncengengce or Nina for company. The site was chosen, and a new capital built around him, while he learned and took part in rites and ceremonies for the purification of a King. Every garment that had ever touched him was burnt, and he never wore Western clothes again."

"On successive days he came out of the goat kraal, in a state of almost entire nudity, with his whole body painted like the wolf, wild dog, or spotted leopard, or, dressed with the skins of some such animals. On the 17th March, 1870, in the presence of about six thousand people Umcumbata delivered up the cattle, people, and land of his father to him, saying, There is the country of your father, his cattle and his people – take them, and be careful of them: those who sin, punish; but those who obey, reward."

Carol had been reading. But she stopped and said: "There's that name again Mncumbata – the same Chief who hid Jandu in the Matopos when he was a child. Sometimes all these names are really hard to remember – but when you see them again you can suddenly tie it all together."

"Mncumbata was a very important chief – particularly to Lobengula. So it was quite right that he was the one who, once all the ceremonies were complete, would hand everything over to Lobengula. From that point on, Lobengula owned everything, and he ruled with absolute power over everyone," Jabu concluded speaking with quiet authority.

"He did indeed," Angus agreed. "As soon as the inauguration was over and the new capital established, Mzilikazi's old capital was set alight. That is where we are sitting now – and that's why there is nothing left."

"For someone who sounds as though he never wanted to be King anyway, you can't help feeling sorry for the guy," Aidan added. "Particularly as he was going to be the one who had to deal with all those conniving Englishmen!"

19

KOBULAWAYO

They were now heading out along the Hillside Road. It was comfortable, familiar territory to Themba and Carol, even though both now lived in Mashonaland. They kept pointing out familiar landmarks and telling stories of adventures past.

"I didn't realise Lobengula's koBulawayo was so close," Prune said. "It must be almost straight down that range of hills to Skoveni – that huge round rock made of ironstone, that attracts the lightning."

"Oh! I had forgotten the lightning! It was terrifying!" Carol exclaimed. "You remember Dad, how you, Tim and I drove to fetch Mum from her sister's house just near Skoveni in that horrendous lightning storm."

Angus laughed. "I've never forgotten it . . . poor Mum. We teased her for months afterwards."

"What did she do?" Aidan asked.

"Well, we found her in bed with her tackies on, clutching a rubber tenniquoit ring! Someone had told her to get her feet off the ground as that would help to make sure she wasn't struck. So she put her rubber-soled tennis shoes on, got into bed and held the tenniquoit ring for sort of treble insurance!"

"It must have been very close."

"Oh it was – and not only that, but the electric plugs had been spitting fire at her, and she was absolutely scared stiff. She'd never come across anything like that in England!"

"She might have done if she'd been Irish of course!" They chuckled. Aidan could be relied upon to make a pithy comment.

"As a matter of interest" he went on "how did Europeans behave when they came to see King Lobengula? Did they respect his authority?"

"Oh yes!" Angus reassured him. "There was a very strong code of ethics on what could or should be done – particularly in the manner in which a Chief and particularly the King should be approached—"

"Which was not always followed."

"That's probably right Jabu, but funnily enough, most people did abide by a clause in the Berlin agreement, that nobody should access anything without permission of the local Chief."

"At last! The Berlin agreement! I wondered when that was going to come up!" Angus smiled, knowing she had been longing to tick this one off her list. "And we'll cover that shortly, Carol."

"Once John Moffat, the missionary Robert Moffat's son, was British Resident here, he insisted any abuse of protocol or disrespect was severely punished."

"Until Lobengula was killed."

"There's no evidence he was killed."

Angus frowned, watching Jabu's face and averted eyes after his sudden defiant words. He measured his words more carefully.

"These protocols went on then – as they do now. You and I would never barge into a Chief's area and start farming or mining without getting his permission."

Jabu shrugged his shoulders but nodded, reluctantly, in agreement.

The wealth of King Solomon.

"The unfortunate thing for Lobengula was that only a few months after his inauguration, the pressures on him would increase to a point his father Mzilikazi would never have imagined.

"First of all, a German archaeologist – Karl Mauch – sent reports and articles, describing his excitement at uncovering the Zimbabwe Ruins from beneath generations of soil, trees and creepers. In passing, he made a casual comment about 'reefs of gold'.

"Since biblical times, there had been rumours of the mysterious land of Ophir – rich with gold and diamonds - the biblical source of the wealth of King Solomon.

"Then just after Lobengula was inaugurated, this was stirred up a bit more, by the publication of a new book by Rider Haggard, called *King Solomon's Mines*. It captured everyone's imagination. According to Haggard, this land lay, within a vastly wealthy inland kingdom in central Africa.

"Well, you can imagine the reaction! The excitement of Mauch's archaeological find took second place to the greed of another potential gold rush. This new one looked as though it would be not only the next big thing, but the biggest of all."

"The country was not easy to get to in those days of course. Having no coastline, being so far inland and with no roads or bridges meant fortune hunters had to make their way inland, then cut wagon routes through endless miles of dense bush. This also meant driving their teams of oxen into seemingly tranquil rivers, where currents, crocodiles and the deceptively benign hippopotamus lurked."

Aidan made a face, nodding his head in agreement.

"Let alone all those other fierce biting animals you have here – it seems that everything wants to get you in this country – lions, leopards, spiders, snakes – they're all deadly!"

He leaped up to adopt a boxing stance aimed at Jabu. "And let's not forget the most deadly of all – the Matebeles!"

"Sit down you idiot!"

Even Jabu had to laugh at this irreverent Irish friend of his. Carol took the opportunity of a lighter moment, to head off to the truck to get some more Fantas.

Angus smiled. Aidan was worth his weight in King Solomon's mythical gold with his ability to defuse a potentially tricky situation. He seemed to have a very easy relationship with Jabu. Angus was grateful for that, bearing in mind the anxieties Nkanyiso had expressed to him, yet again last night, about his son mixing with the wrong crowd.

"I should think many of them gave up the task didn't they?" Carol asked as she handed out the ice-cold drinks.

"On the contrary, Lobengula was flooded with prospectors, traders and hunters, all hungry for wealth, and making a hazardous trip up from the Cape. By the end of a long and risky journey, they were desperate for a concession to dig for gold and prepared to stake anything to get one.

"Lobengula, wisely, refused to see anyone.

"Instead, one of his first actions as King was to ask for what he termed 'a paper' – what we'd know as a notice, or perhaps a legal letter.

Lobengula - man among men

"Lobengula wanted it to be known that John Lee was the only man who would handle concession seekers. Lee was a man the King trusted, and he was based at Mangwe, which was close to the only really accessible wagon route into the country.

"So the well-known painter, Thomas Baines, drew up his letter for him." Angus handed his notes to Themba.

"*To my Trusted friend John Lee of Mangwe River, Matabili land.*

"*'I, LoBengula, Hereditary and elected king of the Matabili nation, knowing the esteem and friendship with which you were regarded by my late father Umselegasi, do hereby . . . appoint you to be my lawful officer and agent on the southern boundary of my kingdom to receive all applications from travellers, hunters, traders or other persons desirous of entering my country, and to grant or withhold permission according to my instructions now given or hereafter to be given to you from time to time.*

"Who was Thomas Baines?" Another question from Carol.

"Baines is recognised internationally for his exceptional paintings of Africa – particularly a series on the Victoria Falls and the Zambezi.

"He was probably the man who designed the King's elephant seal. At that stage, every document from the King had to bear a clear sealing wax stamp of the elephant seal, the King's X mark as well as a missionary's signature as proof he had seen the King had sign it.

"John Lee was a man of great integrity and determination, turning away everyone he felt was unsuitable. But gold-hungry men sneaked back across the Limpopo, crossing into the country further up the border from Bechuanaland or, to the King's fury, climbing through the mountainous eastern districts to negotiate with itinerant maShona Chiefs, whom the King of course, regarded as his subjects.

"Despite every effort to keep them out, the King's capital was soon surrounded by a restless, spreading camp of villains and adventurers. A few were honest traders, and even fewer were genuine adventurers! But unfortunately as in any gold rush situation, there were criminals and an overwhelming number of profiteers and carpetbaggers among them.

"As time went on, the number of disgruntled, disappointed and drunk concession seekers grew. Most sat month after month under the burning Matebeleland sun, hoping King Lobengula might agree to see them. Most did not get concessions, but returned to try again. The devil found plenty of work for idle and sweaty hands to do. They swapped increasingly lurid stories and lies about anyone and everyone granted a concession unless they were part of the deal. In fact, lying and manipulation became almost mandatory for survival."

"How did Lobengula know who to believe?"

"He should have sent the lot away."

"I'm sure he would have done exactly that - if he could have done so.

"But it wasn't that easy.

"He was being harassed on another front, as huge numbers of Voortrekkers, Boers escaping from the British, tried to cross the Limpopo.

"And - in their own way, the missionaries were another persistent pressure. This is pretty critical to what happened later."

Angus emphasised his words as he spoke again, very slowly.

"Until now, the Matebele had always occupied conquered territory. The maShona had weak tribal structures and their constant in-fighting meant the well trained and disciplined *impi* raided from the south as and when they pleased, returning with great herds of cattle and beautiful women. The Missionaries, naturally enough, told them they must stop that.

"Oh boy!" Themba's face was a sombre picture of understanding.

"And, naturally enough, the *impi* bitterly resented being told no more raiding. They itched to kill these interfering white men.

"But somehow, Lobengula kept the peace."

"Why?" Prune asked. "It must have been such a temptation to wipe them all out when numbers were small."

"The difference was, that Lobengula had seen what his *impi* had not yet properly understood." Angus explained. "He knew that if he interfered with the white people, their armies and guns would follow. Armies and guns the Matebele could not beat.

"He had another reason for anxiety – his father had been defeated by tribes with guns 30 years ago. Mzilikazi came up against guns, not from Voortrekkers or the British, but from other tribes who used them to fend off Arab slave traders coming up the Zambezi River.

"The Matebele still used traditional short *iklwa* spears and shields in horn and chest formation, effective - but not against guns.

"At this stage, Lobengula's Matebele owned a total of two old rifles, captured from Voortrekkers in Mzilikazi's day. Neither of them worked.

"Then, following a request to Britain from King Khama, a decision was made that no more African tribes anywhere were to be issued with guns in large numbers. Lobengula wanted and needed guns. He knew that if the Makololo could beat them with the few guns they had, the white people could wipe them. He felt - and was - defenceless.

"Things were closing in. Voortrekkers wanting to cross the Limpopo, swarms of concession seekers, other tribes with guns and to top it off, his own highly trained *impi* frustrated and angry as, despite his promise at the inauguration about continued raids, thanks to the missionaries, they were no longer able to raid even those pathetic cattle stealers, the maShona. Tough.

Managing the Matebele

"Lobengula was a wise man. He knew he had to somehow keep those restless warriors disciplined, content – and above all, loyal.

"An example of how he did it is documented in a book of reminiscences called *First Steps in Civilising Rhodesia* by Jeannie Boggie. It shows that Lobengula knew exactly what had to be done to rule his people. It was described and recorded by a member of Rudd's party, a Mr Thompson. I'll give you an overview, because the description is horrifying to read in full.

"One man dared to taste the King's beer. Not done. Ever. Lobengula ordered his nose cut off, because it had smelt the King's beer. Next, his lips, because they had tasted the King's beer . . ."

Angus paused, watching increasing revulsion on his listeners' faces.

"It goes on. Then his ears, because he had heard no one must taste the King's beer; then his eyes, because they had seen the King's beer."

"They didn't poke his eyes out?" Carol half whispered, hand over her mouth.

"No, they didn't poke his eyes out. They skinned his forehead, allowing the skin to hang down, so he couldn't see.

"Then they thrashed him."

Even Jabu and Themba looked uncomfortable, although they had heard similar stories many times before.

"Thompson wrote:

The poor wretch dragged himself to the river, coming right past my wagon and you never saw such a ghastly sight."

"Horrible," Themba murmured.

Aidan looked sick.

Angus carried on with his tale.

"But despite all the imprecations of the missionaries, at the second *Inxwala*, Lobengula threw his spear north – indicating the direction of the next raid. This was greeted by enthusiastic cheers.

"Lobengula was a realist and he intended to follow up on what King Mzilikazi had started . . . to make sure of an area beyond the Zambezi River for the Matebele people. To make it ready, first of all, it had to be cleared of rival tribes - fortunately, he was a clear-headed strategist and an intelligent leader."

Themba pulled out his notebook. "That certainly fits with this comment made by a German called Henry Stabb. He said Lobengula was

'*at least a Century ahead of his people, a far seeing clever man and like most Zulus a clever disputant.*'"

He added: "I did a bit more research while I was in the museum. The missionaries told Lobengula about God and salvation and how bringing the Matebele people to faith was important. Lobengula listened intently.

"Then he said he was sure God had designed each nation exactly as he wished and intended it to remain. The white men skilled in work, the black with plenty of good cattle and accustomed to making raids and war. Then he said if the black man was meant to do the same things as the white, it was unfair that they had not been told how to do it."

This time, it was Jabu's head that hung beneath his shoulders. He was stunned that King Lobengula could admit such a thing. His thoughts whirled. Themba was still talking.

"Mr Lee, who wrote the report and was translating for the King, was disturbed that Lobengula spoke with 'bitterness in his heart'."

"That is so sad. I did a bit of work on that same topic too Themba" Carol added. "Lobengula told the missionaries he couldn't become a Christian, otherwise how could he discipline his people!"

"And that's a critical point" Angus nodded in agreement.

"He was the man born to be King, whether he liked it or not! He had a huge population to control but he also had to honour his father's dictates about the missionaries, one of which was very strong:

'These vessels are not to be broken.'

"Those vessels must have irritated him immensely at times, as they didn't hold back, admonishing him about anything they saw as cruelty.

"Once he cried out,
'What am I to do? When a man will not listen to orders, cut ears off – whatever their punishment, they repeat . . . now I warn them . . . and then a knobkerried man never repeats his offence.'"

"Because he is dead!" Prune said pursing his lips.

The last little bit of unclaimed land

"Just imagine what this poor King was facing. Remember this was the last little bit of unclaimed, unsettled, uncolonized land in Africa – suddenly it was the focus of Europe.

"Growing pressure from the Belgians in the north; Germans advancing from south-west Africa; the French trying to get their slice of Southern Africa; the Portuguese simply walking through the east of the country, persuading Chief Mutasa to part with the King's favourite hunting grounds of Mazoe; the Voortrekkers from the Transvaal . . . then, to cap it all, the British issuing orders from the Cape!

"He must have looked back on those carefree days of hunting with his friends with longing. They would have talked about many things outside his experience as he does appear to have been intrigued by what Europeans could teach him . . . although he spoke out vehemently when he didn't agree with something.

"One of the missionaries, David Carnegie, tackled King Lobengula yet again about what he saw as unnecessary cruelty. So Lobengula asked him, yet again, what he should do. Carnegie suggested he build a gaol and put those to be punished in there.

"He just laughed.

"*Your gaol gives them a house to sleep in, a blanket to lie on, and food to eat! If I build a gaol I'd have the whole Matebele nation in there in a week!*'

"We have an expression for exactly that. 'May the cat eat you, and may the divil eat the cat'," Aidan said thoughtfully, in his best Irish accent. Again there was a ripple of laughter at this irrepressible Irishman.

"But to complicate that simplistic statement" Aidan was serious for a moment. "You do have an exceptional clash of cultures. I had no idea what a massive difference there was between the British and the Matebele cultures … only 70 years ago. I've only ever met sophisticated characters like Jabu here. It is not surprisin' things get a bit misinterpreted and over exaggerated."

"Add a whisper of gold, and believe me, temperatures rise too." Angus concluded sadly.

Trusting the missionaries

"In the end, like his father - and despite all the scolding they gave him - it does seem as we have already mentioned, that the only people Lobengula really trusted were the missionaries. They were the only ones who didn't want anything from him, except to listen when they talked to him about God. And they really cared about him and his people.

"He trusted two missionaries particularly, John Moffat who was the British Resident, as well as being a missionary – and Charles Helm, the missionary sent to open up Hope Fountain, which is not very far away from the King's capital.

"Well, he was the worst of the lot," Jabu exploded. "He sold us out, telling Lobengula lies about what was in the Rudd Concession!"

Angus let him speak, then said quietly, "We'll certainly talk about that tomorrow Jabu. It's a pivotal point in the whole settlement of this country.

There are more exaggerations, distortions, untruths and lies about that one episode than almost anything else.

"However, after many years of my own research, I believe the missionaries were victims of their own rather naïve goodwill and they eventually became 'fall guys' – easy targets for venomous people whose own greedy agendas were thwarted when they didn't get what they wanted. Accusations were accepted as fact. Few bothered to check the details.

"Before we leave this desolate place, I want to share an interesting insight from one of the daily reports to the London Missionary Society by Charles Helm.

We have talked about the necessity to move from Capital to Capital as the soil grew tired and the game was scarce.

" Just look around you and imagine as I read this."

"I have just been present at a most moving spectacle! Five days ago, on Thursday the 15th September, Gubuluwayo was officially destroyed. On the seventh day after the full moon, Makwekwe, the former induna or governor of the capital, received from the king the order to go to the old town and to set all the dwellings on fire. Makwekwe therefore set about burning the king's palace, the queens' huts, all the buildings in the royal kraal, sheds, stables, coaches, and even the chariot of the old king Mosilikatsi. At first I accompanied Makwekwe in his work of destruction, then I retired to a little hill in order the better to view this spectacle.
When his task was finished, Makwekwe came to me, shook me by the hand and said: 'Lambile', that is to say, 'I am Hungry'.

"I'm pretty *lambile* too . . . into the truck you lot – we're heading for Umhlabathini, Lobengula's final capital near the Vic Falls Road.

20

COURAGE AND DEATH

They were sitting enjoying their sandwiches on a low tumbledown stone wall that might once have been the outer edge of King Lobengula's last capital, Umhlabathini. From here, the land sloped gently down to a dry riverbed, with a range of sizeable hills to the north. As they walked up the slope, they passed the area where concession seekers had once camped for months on end, trying to gain access to the King.

In the distance was the dejected ruin of what had once been a solidly constructed building. They'd been studying photographs of early etchings showing the capital in its heyday, so they located the high places in the landscape against the position of the old building to identify the point where it had been drawn.

Then they walked towards what would have been the centre of the capital looking at another etching of King Lobengula holding court outside what remained of that very building.

"I hadn't realised how close this was to the modern city of Bulawayo."

"Look, there's Government House just over there."

"Before we get too involved, Prune, you're closest to the truck – there is a thermos flask of tea and some biscuits in the basket.

As Prune sorted out the tea, they wandered over, falling into the easy companionable chatter of good friends.

Carol walked slowly past the ruin imagining this last, great Matebele King holding court in front of it. She felt drawn to it, intrigued by the thought that her grandfather knew Lobengula as the King. That Jabu and Themba's grandfathers might have lived right here under his leadership.

If only her grandfather had lived long enough for her to ask him all the questions that were now flying around in her head.

Prune wandered up bringing her a mug of tea.

"This trip has made me wish I knew who I was more than ever." He spoke quietly, sadly. "There is so much history and heritage. It's hard to feel sure of yourself when you don't have any background."

"But Prune!" Carol protested. "Look how well you are doing now. Look how much Lalan and Naison love you. And now you've got Maura – you're building your own history for your children."

"I know. Sorry. I am lucky, but somehow, I can't describe this empty hole in the middle of me. And I get so angry with myself for even thinking about it. I'm probably just feeling a bit down because I lost my job."

Carol put her arm round him. "Hey - you have a wedding to look forward to! And a new life in Balla Balla. One day you'll find out about your precious Rosie – I feel sure of it. But you might have to look further than Matebeleland."

He nodded. "Themba's story of Motshodi and Jan Grootboom has made me decide to go to Mashonaland and see if I can find out anything. I'm too dark skinned to have come from Bechuanaland . . ."

Angus was signalling them over to the shade of a large tree. As they walked towards him, Carol and Prune heard him say, "Let's get back to Helm, because he leads us to the Rudd Concession. While I understand what you feel, Jabu, I'd like to give you an idea of why I trust this man."

"OK – I'll give you my perspective when you have finished!"

216

Charles Helm, missionary: hero or villain

"Charles Helm was born in the Cape. He was 'of Africa'. And this was unusual. Most missionaries, prospectors, hunters or soldiers who arrived at that time came fresh from Europe. Like so many others, they'd never seen a black man, let alone talked to one."

"Helm, and his friend, John Moffat, grew up in a group of black and white *piccanins* together. Just as you all did. He was fluent in Zulu, and on the months of travel from Zuurbraak to Hope Fountain, he listened and talked to his wagon drivers to make sure he'd speak fluent Sindebele once they arrived. As we found out yesterday Themba, your great-grandfather Motshodi was one of those drivers.

"Helm arrived in 1875, about six years after Lobengula became King – and at the height of that rush for gold concessions. He was bothered to find Lobengula was giving away far too much to concession seekers with no benefit to the Matebele."

Angus handed out some sheets of paper. "Another notice had been written by Thomas Baines, but over the last five years, it had fallen into disuse. This is what Helm rewrote, distributed it to all entry points – not just Mangwe - but the roads up to Fort Vic, in from Plumtree, and further north on the Bechuanaland border as well as a couple of points on the eastern border with Mozambique."

Prune read out the notice he was holding.

"All travellers, hunters or traders wishing to enter Matabili land are requested to come to Manyami's where they are to report themselves as usual and obtain permission to come to the king's residence and receive their respective licences. The hunter's fee for the districts south and west of the Shashani River will be one gun of the value of £15 British Sterling, one 5-lb. Bag of powder, two 6 lb. Bars of lead and one bag of 500 caps. No occupation of the country is allowed nor any houses to be built except by the king's special permission.
Given at the town of Gibbeklaik. (Gibexhegu) *11th April 1870*
LoBengula his X mark: and elephant seal   King of the Matabili nation

"Time you did a little detective work. What does that notice tell you?"

"It was written quite soon after he was inaugurated as King."

"You can see the use of the elephant seal and the X mark – perhaps Helm was the missionary who signed it. But it doesn't show that."

"That he was somewhere called Gibbeklaik or Gibexhegu!"

"That was the first name for koBulawayo."

Jabu jumped in. "Yesterday you said Lobengula realised he needed guns – well here it is. He was asking for a fee not only in money but also in guns!"

"Yes you're right Jabu . . . and yes, this was only a few months after he became King. The ban on guns was being re-thought as many tribes had got guns, and this was a great way for Lobengula to get some quickly."

"It probably does show that Helm was concerned for the Matebele people.

"Yes, it does. These regular missionary reports back to the London Missionary Society have become one of the most important sources of information for us. They contain objective and accurate historical detail, often making sense of wildcat stories from the hundreds of other reports written by those with vested interests in their material, rather than spiritual, welfare!

"They also give vibrant details of family life. For example, Helm talked of the King's frequent demands for his presence and that of his wife and children. He described how the children would dress in their best clothes and take presents for the King. One would bring an egg, or perhaps a newly hatched chicken, another some beans from their garden. They learned from a young age that they must enter bent at the waist and look the King in the eye all the time, praising him and saying pleasant things—"

"Which he wouldn't have understood!"

"Oh yes, he'd have understood quite a bit of English from hunting with Phillips and friends, probably a bit of Afrikaans too from Sarah Liebenberg."

"Perhaps he didn't want people to know how much he understood. Then he could listen to what they were saying," Prune suggested.

"That's a very good point He also liked to hear the children's voices. They in turn would have learned Sindebele. Once they had approached, they'd have to sit down, making sure their heads were always lower than the King's, as they weren't allowed to stand up unless the King stood up. When he gave the signal, he'd receive their presents.

"Letters written by family members once the children were older, tell of their fear at these visits. The King would roar with laughter the more they shook with fright, so they kept giving him more presents. Then he'd give them a big smile and they were allowed to go.

"The Helms had many children, and each new baby was presented as a courtesy to Lobengula to be inspected. This he did with great solemnity and would declare the new addition to be healthy and strong."

Jabu folded his arms and looked away.

Angus watched him closely - he was obviously still uneasy.

"Here's another report that gives insight into the interaction between Helm and Lobengula. Helm informed the King that he was going to attend a missionary meeting at Inyati, but it meant going past a large kraal. He asked the King's permission to do so.

"The King gave his permission, but something went wrong. As his drivers approached, they were chased away and beaten up. The family was threatened by a furious and screaming mob. Helm stood on the front of the wagon and shouted his opinion of them very forcefully in his immaculate Sindebele, telling their *indunas* the King had granted him passage and the King would be informed of their behaviour.

"At the mention of Lobengula, they melted away. But first, they helped to get the wagons going again and later that evening, they caught up with the Helm wagon, bringing half an ox as a peace offering. Helm thanked them but in fact, he refused it, as he would not accept anything that could be taken to be a bribe.

"When Lobengula was told about this, he ordered the *indunas* to be put to death - but at Helm's request, this sentence was not carried out.

"Helm wrote frequently about his anxiety for the Matebele. He felt saddened by the fact that they believed their only relevance or existence as a people lay in maintaining a constant state of war – and ensuring subservience from other tribes."

"When the King moved from the site we were at this morning, he asked Helm to also leave Hope Fountain mission (which was close to the capital he had had burned) . . . and move to Bulawayo as his adviser.

Helm wasn't at all sure about this. It meant losing his stipend from the LMS and moving away from his first love of missionary work. After an exchange of letters with the LMS, they thought it was important enough to warrant the move and to continue his work in the town. They would find other missionaries for Hope Fountain. So this was a direct request from the King, to someone he trusted completely.

"To supplement the extra cost of living, Helm opened the first postal system to Tati, using post boy runners, for traders, hunters and missionaries. Once there, mail was handed on to other runners to take south. In turn, mail was received for Bulawayo. A 'post' fee was enough to employ the post boys and keep food on the table for the Helms.

"How did those post boys avoid getting eaten by wild animals?" Carol asked, ever the anxious one.

Angus laughed. "They were brought up with wild animals, my girl. There are no reports of any post boys being eaten. It would have been a headline in Helm's reports if they had!"

"Do you have any idea of what the man himself was like?" asked Aidan.

"He's described as brusque, outspoken, down to earth. He was married to an equally brusque and outspoken titled lady, the Baroness von Puttkamer. They were known for their hospitality and kindness. The King liked and respected their no-nonsense honesty and relied increasingly on Helm's advice. Helm saw the Matebele as fine people – disciplined and courageous. But at the same time, he was appalled by their savagery. As a dedicated man of God, he knew it was his life's work to keep encouraging them to adopt a more Christian outlook.

"A lesser known but interesting fact was that Helm loved dogs. From various indigenous species and some imported breeds, he was responsible for the breeding of the modern Rhodesian Ridgeback."

"The lion dogs!" Jabu exclaimed despite his antipathy to Helm. "We've got a couple on the farm. They are fantastic animals I must admit."

He continued with a wry smile " . . . and I am listening to what you are saying about Charles Helm, Mr Davidson!"

"That's all we need. Listen to all points of view and make up your own mind." Angus smiled with relief.

He took a moment to breathe – looking at the group before him, thankful that this young country of Southern Rhodesia, would have a bright future in the hands of youngsters like these.

Prune's face lit up and broke the reverie.

"I want to know what really happened to King Lobengula."

Angus nodded. "Nobody really knows."

Turning to Jabu he said: You must have insights few others do Jabu because your great-grandfather Mtjaan was Lobengula's Chief *Induna* and friend. And I believe he was with him at the end."

Jabu nodded. "He was. He was a loyal friend of the King."

The changing of Blighty's mind

As there was nothing more forthcoming, Angus said: "OK, let's go back a bit and look at what led to the Matebele war in 1893. First of all, and as demanded by the King's old hunting friend Selous, the Pioneer Column bypassed Matebeleland on its way up to Mashonaland in 1890.

"Probably because they also wanted to give the Matebele *impi* a wide berth," Carol suggested with a know-it-all-look on her face.

"Probably right!" Angus laughed with her, then continued: "The first problem was, what was Matebele land? Here I think Lobengula did made a mistake, not from his perspective perhaps, and encouraged by the missionaries but certainly a mistake from a legal British perspective.

"We've talked about the maShona living in small tribes which made them easy to raid whenever the Matebele felt they needed more cattle or another lovely wife. We've talked of the missionaries persuading them not to keep raiding and killing. Whatever the reason, and for the first time, the Matebele didn't bother to actually occupy today's Mashonaland.

"I smell a loophole comin' up" said the ever ready Aidan.

Angus continued: "The British Government, whether with intent or not, decided that Mashonaland was <u>not</u> part of Lobengula's territory. Too easy – because if it belonged to nobody except a few disparate tribes, it was up for grabs.

"Later however, when the Portuguese decided they'd like a chunk of land around the Mazoe area, the UK Government changed its mind and said 'Oh no! this is Matebele territory!'"

Aidan threw his arms out wide and shrugged his shoulders. "What have I been tellin' you about the Brits!" he exclaimed triumphantly. "Don't trust them a bloddy inch!"

"Where did the maShona fit into all this?" Prune interjected.

"Well again . . . when the Pioneer Column first arrived, the Shona quickly denied allegiance to the Matebele. But when the Matebele attacked the pioneers, they denied allegiance to the Pioneer Column!"

"Lalan was always very strict about telling the truth. Why did all these people just lie? I don't understand it, especially at such a high level! Why didn't they tell the truth?" Prune was puzzled and insecure.

"It's called 'saving your skin' Prune. If something is unclear, there can be many truths. Believe me, this was only the beginning!

"As the Pioneer column crossed the Limpopo, Lobengula ordered several regiments to 'shadow' it – just to keep an eye on everyone who settled in Mashonaland. For three years, these regiments kept watch at the edges of what they knew they could claim as Matebele territory. But otherwise, there are no indications that the King was at all worried about the pioneers as they moved into Mashonaland.

In fact, he felt secure enough to despatch two of his top regiments north again to clear out the Batoka lands – just in case they were needed.

"The route through Mashonaland was hard going for the Pioneers. Nobody with such a large number of men had done it, but because of his knowledge of the country from hunting, Selous felt confident that although tough, it was possible. He may not have detailed the crossing of huge rivers full of crocs and hippo or the menace of big game as they climbed trackless granite hills, cutting impenetrable bush for roads passable by wagons!

"When we drive to Beit Bridge, do you remember the gap in the *kopjes* after Fort Victoria?" Angus asked Carol. She puzzled - then remembered.

"Providential Pass! Of course. Why haven't I ever wondered why it was called that? Stupid girl!"

"Providential Pass gave the British South Africa Company the ability to confirm it had not at any stage broached known Matebele territory.

"Despite the rights or wrongs of it all the Pioneers were extraordinary How nerve wracking must it have been trying to cut their way through bush with no paths or roads, most of it completely unsuitable for heavily-laden wagons – with lion and leopard watching every move of their cattle . . . and always under the steely gaze of Matebele warriors?"

Nobody spoke as they tried to envisage the scene. Angus went on: "How agonising must it have been for the Matebele to see that mass of foreigners calmly moving through what they regarded as their territory?

"Frustrating . . .

"Infuriating . . .

". . . and worse, they had to watch maShona villagers going about their daily lives protected by the Pioneers – taking every opportunity to taunt the Matebele too. All this, happening on land the Matebele had previously raided and regarded as theirs, but now, they couldn't touch."

"Lobengula must have been a strong man to keep them in check." Aidan could not believe it. "The Irish would have revolted . . ."

Beating Roger Bannister

"By 1893, a priority for the Pioneers in Fort Victoria however, was trying to establish communications with the Cape. They had carefully loaded precious copper wire, stanchions and other necessities onto already over-loaded wagons for the initial long journey. The maShona however, took a fancy to the beautiful shining copper wire – perfect for snares and a hundred other daily needs! For the last three years, every time they had just got communications established, the copper wire was stolen! The Pioneers were infuriated – but nothing they did, stopped it happening.

"What could they do? Carol asked. "They didn't have any money!"

"Exactly right. It was eventually decided that the only thing that might stop them, was to take their cattle as payment."

"Of course . . . Oh no!"

"Oh no is right. To punish the maShona was the King's business - the settlers had taken cattle that rightfully belonged to the King."

"It doesn't take much of a spark to start a bushfire," Prune muttered.

" . . . which was lit when the Matebele inflicted their own punishment by teaching the maShona who had not returned Lobengula's cattle a bloody lesson. But, it didn't stop there. They killed those who had started working for white settlers, including one young boy who was brutally killed in front of his employer. The tender little Englishman had probably never experienced anything like this before and he was outraged."

"Whether the small garrison stationed there was looking for an excuse or was trigger happy anyway being so closely watched by Matebele warriors all the time, we don't know. But for the man in charge, Captain Lendy, this might have been the excuse he was looking for. He ordered the Matebele to get back across the Shashi River, which was about 30 miles away, and to do it in 2 hours. Or he'd drive them off by force.

"Here's a mathematical problem for you Prune. Three years ago, Roger Bannister ran the first under-four-minute mile. Could they have made it?

Prune didn't have to think about it for long. Very gravely, he said, "They'd have had to beat Roger Bannister."

Angus nodded sadly.

"Every report I have read says they wouldn't have made it anyway. But worse, was that Lendy didn't wait two hours – he ordered pursuit after an hour or so and 30 warriors were killed.

"This is generally accepted as the start of the Matebele War of 1893. If it is any consolation, he was criticised in the House of Commons 'for disgracing the name of an Englishman.'"

Angus expected another comment from Aidan. But - not this time.

21

THE DESPERATION OF A KING

"King Lobengula was worried. The one thing he had to avoid was war – if he could be blamed for starting a war, all would be lost in terms of the treaty. He immediately asked a man he trusted, James Dawson, to ride as fast as he could, taking with him as envoys, the King's brother Ingubongubo and two senior Headmen, to see John Moffat the British administrator in Palapye, close to the Bechuanaland border.

Lobengula was asking for Moffat's intervention, by telegraphing an appeal on his behalf to Sir Henry Loch, the High Commissioner in Cape Town, saying he would find those who killed the maShona – and asking a simple question: *'where are the white bodies?'*

"When they arrived in Palapye, Dawson went to fetch some water. Stupidly, he didn't tell anyone who the three well-armed Matebele warriors were. While Dawson was away, the envoys took turns shouting angrily at the white men. The Bechuanaland police disarmed them and the Colonel in charge ordered them back across the Limpopo River.

In the fracas, a member of the police shot one of the envoys and clubbed another with a rifle butt. Dawson got back to find both had died. Ingubongubo escaped having first been tied up and beaten.

"Dawson was in absolute despair.

"He wrote to the High Commissioner, stating that the King did not want to fight. The senior *indunas* did not want to fight. What was going on?"

Carol and Prune sat mute, horrified by what they were hearing.

"Why didn't Moffat or the High Commissioner do something?"

"They were only representatives of the British Government. Therefore, they had no immediate authority. They could only appeal to the Chartered Company at the highest level for help.

"For whatever reason, there was no reaction."

"The King must have been shattered."

"He was."

Jabu took up the story. "The King ordered his two regiments back from the Zambezi and put them on battle alert. These two, the Imbezu and Ingubo regiments, played the major role in the battle of the Bembezi that followed.

"Your reference to the battle of Bembezi and the thousands of Matebele lost there is heart breaking." Angus spoke up. "They were just mown down. You might agree that their mistake was that they stuck to traditional Matebele military tactics. These would win every time against tribes without guns, but they didn't stand up against the guns at Bembezi. Particularly the maxim guns . . ."

"My great-grandfather was at Bembezi" Jabu continued "so I know the details very well. He urged the King to use the Rudd Concession Martini-Henry rifles, which my grandfather had already removed from storage in Dawson's store. I've never known why they didn't . . ."

"They might have had the rifles, but they might not have known how to use them and felt more comfortable with their stabbing spears."

"It was slaughter."

Angus nodded – his expression grim. "It was. Even though the Matebele were vastly superior in numbers, they lost thousands. There are reports of the bravery of the small number of whites and the Matebele were astonished by their courage. But there were many more stories of the bravery of the Matebele, your great-grandfather's regiment, the Imbezu, in particular.

"One British captain, Sir John Willoughby, wrote in his official account back to the military in England:

'the pluck of these two regiments was simply splendid and I doubt whether any European troops would have stood for such a long time as they did under terrific fire.'

Jabu looked at the ground, his voice full of sadness.

"In the next battles, they did use the guns – but it was too late. The stories told by those who were there, say the King was completely disillusioned by the betrayal of the white men he had come to trust – so he ordered the burning of this capital which is where we are now."

He sounded completely defeated by the reliving of it all.

The final betrayal.

Angus let the silence lie for a time between them.

Then very quietly and slowly he said: "Dr Jameson, on his way back from the battle of the Bembezi himself was dismayed to see Bulawayo burning.

The BSAC and the British Government were anxious that no harm should come to the King. The intention was always to treat him with dignity and give him a say as to where he would like to go."

"Jameson sent a messenger off immediately to translate his message: *'To stop this useless slaughter, you must at once come and see me at Bulawayo, when I will guarantee that your life will be saved and that you will be kindly treated.'*

"Lobengula responded, saying as his capital was now burned to the ground, where was he to stay?

"Jameson wrote again.

"This time the King was slower to respond. Because of the killing of the envoys, he felt he would also be killed. He did eventually write, saying he would come. He gave two of his trusted *indunas* some gold and asked them to take the gold and the letter to Jameson.

"Oh no!" Prune and Carol understood.

"Oh yes," Angus nodded sadly.

"They stole the gold." Prune said.

"Well no, <u>they</u> didn't. The *indunas* met two prospectors and gave the message and the gold to them, thinking they would have a better chance of getting the message straight to Jameson.

"*They* stole the gold." Carol said, aghast.

Angus nodded while Jabu held his head in his hands.

"The prospectors had 'discovered' all the gold they needed, and Jameson never got the King's letter.

"This will begin to answer your question Prune, about what happened to King Lobengula."

Angus continued: "the King waited for two more days, then decided Jameson was not going to answer. During that time he consulted Mlimo asking what the future had in store and was told '*your future lies in the gusu*[86].'

So he started to move north, perhaps heading for the Zambezi, with his most faithful *indunas* and wives around him."

"Did he get there?"

"Jabu, do you have any insight on that?"

"There were reports of the King being seen on the other side of the Zambezi and Major Forbes was even shown a photo. Another report said the King did cross the Zambezi but he couldn't move by himself and a party of Nguni people carried him. When the local Chief Mpenzeni came to visit he crawled in on his hands and knees to greet the King. According to this source, Lobengula died shortly afterwards and the big rock on the road from Fort Jameson to Fort Manning split and fell. Nobody knew where he was buried.

"Others say there is a cave at a place they call M'lindi in Chief Pashu's country and yet more people say it was in the Gokwe district near the Wankie border. Some say the King was buried sitting in his chair and there was a saddle and a rifle buried with him. One of his sons, Nyamande, took this rifle and a woman called Shoko took other things. Others say his bones were removed and buried with Mzilikazi at Entumbane – but that grave is all concreted up, so we will probably never know.

"Others say he was too big to still ride a horse, but all the oral stories say he did ride away. Some others that he was sick, others that he and Chief Magwegwe had agreed that they would take poison. Others say smallpox or a bad strain of malaria killed him.

Angus asked Jabu: "What do you feel really happened?"

Jabu thought for a moment. "I do know that only a King is ever buried in a cave and that some of the items found with him have been mentioned as being gifts from the British Government. I do know that the King spoke to the other *indunas* with him, telling them to trust his Chief *Induna* Mtjaan, my great-grandfather, to talk to Jameson on their behalf, as he would make sure they were well looked after."

He couldn't continue.

Angus took it up.

"Although Major Forbes did set out to try and find Lobengula, the Khumalo family did not want it to be known where the cave was. Out of

---

[86] *gusu*: forests

228

respect for the family, it was not released until 1943 that the national heritage department might have found the site. Then a series of interviews took place[87] most of them saying similar things but with all the contradictions you have already told us Jabu."

"You didn't agree with me when I said Lobengula was killed. But he might as well have been." Jabu was staring into the distance.

The silence hung heavily. Angus chose his words carefully.

"Your great-grandfather Mtjaan Khumalo, respected *Induna* of the Imbezu Regiment, did what he had been asked. He reported back to Jameson and spent many weeks negotiating on behalf of the amaNdebele people. He also told Lobengula's friend James Dawson that he stayed with the King until the end.

"He confirmed that he and Busangwane, the chief *svikiro*, buried him in a cave, sitting upright in all his regalia, complete with shields and *assegais*. In accordance with their custom of releasing the spirit, Mtjaan opened his stomach with an *assegai*."

Angus didn't want to break the silence that followed.

After a while, he added quietly: "Clouding the death of Lobengula for the whites was the massacre of the Allan Wilson patrol at the Shangani River. The patrol was following the King's wagon tracks to try and find him, then bring him back to Bulawayo. They crossed the Shangani River in hot pursuit. That was when they realised that they were close to an extremely angry Matebele regiment. They turned back, but there had just been a lot of rain, and they couldn't get back across the river. Three scouts managed to break through Matebele lines, and they galloped away to get reinforcements.

"It was too late.

"Thirty-four men backed up against an ant heap and faced 3,000 Matebele – this time, as you said Jabu, they had guns. As the patrol's horses were killed around them, they used the bodies of the animals as shields to return fire. As their numbers fell, the Matebele reported that the remainder sang. Speculation is that they sang God Save the Queen. The last man left alive stood on top of the ant heap and was speared. Most of

---

[87] See appendix 4: Lobengula's last resting place.

them were officers from the British and Bechuanaland police.

"It was Dawson who led a team to follow up and find out what had happened to the Allan Wilson patrol . . . as well as to try to find the King and if possible talk him into coming back.

"They found the bodies of the Shangani patrol members and buried them under a tree, on which Dawson carved a large cross."

"Again, your great-grandfather played a pivotal role, Jabu. He is reported to have said to Dawson *'These were men of men and their fathers were men before them.'*"

"Yes, my grandfather used that same phrase when telling us the story. They were brave men."

"You would also know Jabu, that Rhodes thought so much of your grandfather and his strength and integrity in the way he looked after the Matebele people that he ordered the Chartered Company to give him a monthly allowance until he died in 1907 at the age of 75. He was a big man in more ways than one – apparently well over six foot tall."

"That's where I get my height from!" Jabu gave a deprecating laugh, as he had grown no more than five foot ten – which was very ordinary.

As the tense atmosphere was broken, Angus leant over to Jabu and handed him a scrap of paper.

"Matebele' Wilson wrote a poignant piece about King Lobengula and the killing of the Shangani Patrol. Jabu, I'd love you to read it."

Jabu took it reluctantly and spent a few long minutes reading it first.

Then he stood up to declaim Wilson's words about King Lobengula.

"I only ask for fair play to a black man who stood by the white men to the end of his life. I must say this that no man could condone all the terrible things that happened in this country, even in my time – superstition, witchcraft, bloodshed, and the massacre of thousands of people within the reach of their spears.

"I shall always have a kindly feeling towards the one man who deserved a better fate. Lobengula died a king. It was better than death in captivity. Had those two rascally troopers on Forbes' patrol only approached the authorities, as Lobengula desired, the Wilson disaster on Shangani might never have happened. It was another instance of Lobengula's thought for the white people."

There was nothing to say. They sat crushed by the stupidity of it all. Jabu broke the silence:

"When you said that the Allan Wilson Patrol was following the wagon tracks trying to find Lobengula – they were misled – just as the King intended.

"My great-grandfather said the King rode a horse but sent his queens and others in the wagons in a different direction to put the white people on the wrong path.

"There is a tradition among my people that because his bones have never been identified, he will one day come back to lead us again. My great-grandfather said he had left a strong message for the amaNdebele people: '*Be patient; be watchful; wait for the right moment . . .*'

"Our King was disappointed and despairing, but he was urging us to be on our guard. The regiments might have lost their cattle after the war, but now, they made sure they safely stored all the guns and ammunition they received from the Rudd Concession."

22

SLAVERY, STEAMSHIPS AND A THEORY

"Dramatic things were happening in the outside world around this time. And all of them affected this country in one way or another.

"Is this where the Berlin Conference comes in?" Carol asked.

"It does – we won't dwell on it but it's important for you two A-levellers in particular to understand all these impacts. First of all, in the early 1800s, many countries in Europe were coping with increasing problems but also massive opportunities, due to . . . what?"

They all looked blank – except Prune could hardly contain himself.

"I've been waiting for it … James Watt, the Industrial Revolution!" he shouted.

Angus had to smile – remembering the scrap of humanity he'd first seen in the clinic 18 years ago. Prune had been worth all the effort put into trying to save his tiny life.

"He found a way to use steam power to drive engines." Prune was rattling on and bursting with excitement. "No more hand power needed to produce food and clothing, fewer cattle, horses and windmills ploughing or grinding corn as steam machines took over."

"How do you know about this Prune?" Carol was fascinated.

"Well I told you about my friend Neil Thain who plays the bagpipes? His dad has a little gold mine in Bushtick and I go there. I love watching the steam engine, which pumps water out to keep the mine dry. Mr Thain told me all about the development of the steam engine."

Angus smiled, then took up the story.

"You're right - the growth in knowledge was enormous. The man in the street found more employment and better health as a result. There was a surge of optimism. The British in particular felt invincible, and tales were told of great heroism and adventure.

"You're paintin' a glowing picture Mr Davidson – working conditions were bloddy terrible!" The Irish in Aidan wasn't going to let him get away with that trite comment.

"Granted. The working conditions were terrible – initially. But even you must agree that after a time, standards of living increased dramatically and created opportunities never available to the likes of you and me - only to the landed gentry."

Aidan grinned and mimicked Angus's response. "Granted! But the workhouses were inhuman, deliberately demeaning places."

"They were – but what an incentive to escape as society changed! A picky boy in a copper mine could aspire to almost anything as he learned new skills – which he did very quickly."

"If things were improving, why didn't they use their skills in their own countries and not come out here to destroy ours?" Jabu wanted to know.

"They needed things they didn't have in their own country to keep all that new industry going." Themba spoke up.

"Coal to run steam engines for instance and copper was drying up in England about then I think – now, look at Northern Rhodesia it's making a fortune mining copper for England."

"Not bad Themba. Combine that with being able to carry goods round the world by ships now powered by steam engines rather than being dependent on wind . . . and Imperialism became the order of the day."

"I've often seen that word, 'Imperialism'. What does it mean?"

"It means, in simple terms, the extension of your own country through collaboration if possible, or colonisation if not."

Jabu gave a dismissive shrug of his shoulders.

Angus ignored it and went on: "Collaboration occurs when there is similarity of understanding, language and capability. Colonisation is an alternative, if that is not the case.

"European countries were looking round the world in the mid 1840's and there were precious few countries with copper or iron who had either the capability or expertise needed to mine it. So they looked for places which might have the what they needed, looking at Africa particularly, because it seemed to be a land where constant tribal fighting was taking place and there were huge tracts of uninhabited land as a result. The Transvaal was a case in point, as there were surprisingly few Africans left to live there after the 'mfecane when King Mzilikazi was nation building and moving the amaNdebele across the Limpopo. Similarly, with the Rosvi Empire in a weakened state after generational fighting, it was relatively easy for the Matebele to defeat the Changamire – so today's Mashonaland was very sparsely populated at that time

"Coming from an overcrowded continent like Europe, Africa seemed ripe for exploration and development, bringing the local inhabitants new skills, education, good healthcare and farsighted colonial administration."

"They wouldn't have been slow to recognise a source of cheap bloddy labour either!"

"Aidan, you put it so succinctly!" Angus laughed.

"You're right in part. Slavery was now a dirty word and countries were slowly abolishing it. But don't forget, slavery was a huge source of wealth for African traders too. In time, Asian traders found their way up the Zambezi to deal with the Makololo and other river tribes.

"But the slavery issue had created awareness that things had to be done properly when dealing with other civilisations.

The Berlin Conference

"In 1884, the German Chancellor, Otto von Bismarck, invited 13 European nations, plus America, to take part in a conference in Berlin to 'work out joint policy on the African continent'."

"What cheek!" It was Themba who was outraged this time!

"They put together a few politically correct statements," Angus continued, reading a document titled "The Berlin Conference".

"Ending slavery, ensuring treaties were properly negotiated with local leaders and stopping international powers from setting up colonies in name only . . . without investment in local development were key points."

"Sounds good in principle"

"Each European power had exclusive rights – but only in the eyes of the other nations present mind you – to pursue legal ownership of land over which they already had some influence – as long as those conditions were met. Belgian ownership of the Congo was agreed, and other countries would be able to trade freely through the Congo Basin as far as today's Lake Nyasa - as long as the other countries present were informed.

"It was OK to 'possess' new sections of the African coast as well, or what was left as those ruddy Portuguese were already there!

"D'you mean they literally said 'I'll have that bit there.'" Themba was a bit shocked.

Angus nodded. "The Europeans walked into central and southern Africa, arrogant in the knowledge that they had every right to be there as long as they observed the protocols. They had to make sure they were not there just to claim the land, by providing evidence that they would spend acceptable and agreed amounts of money as well as the expertise to develop that land or country."

The youngsters sat, silent trying to absorb it.

"Ironically, none of this applied to our little landlocked country.

"We weren't attractive enough!" Jaws dropped, so Angus hurried on. "We were inaccessible; we had no coastline; no navigable rivers; no roads; plenty of tsetse fly; virulent cerebral malaria . . . and as you said a white ago Aidan, we had the savage Matebele with their bloodthirsty regiments."

"So what changed?"

"Just think of all those stories of untold wealth; truths and untruths about gold and diamonds; Rider Haggard's *King Solomon's Mines*; Mauch uncovering the Zimbabwe Ruins and sending off reports of 'reefs of gold'. In the hysterical mix of heroism and adventure, it was time to make your fortune if you were courageous, despite the dangers.

"By the end of the 1880s, our most besieged of kings, Lobengula, was being asked not just for individual permits to hunt, prospect or trade, but for the right to settle – from countries all over Europe."

"By 1902 most of Africa was under European control. Any ideas on what percentage that might have been?"

Nobody was game to guess.

"90% of Africa was under European control. 90%."

They were astonished. They'd had no idea the so-called scramble for Africa had been so blatant. Everyone was dispirited. Trying to put what was happening in Matebeleland, then Southern Rhodesia, into perspective

236

against developments in Europe was all but impossible. Scales were falling from the idealistic eyes of Carol, Prune and Themba in particular.

Having started down the track of these phrases he had given to Prune and Carol initially, Angus was keen to finish them off so he could finally move on to the real story of the Rudd Concession and Rhodes.

"What excuse do you think these nations had found that allowed them to feel entitled to just walk in? Something else that happened around the same time?"

"Greed."

"Power."

"Wanting to better themselves . . ."

"I'm sure all of those came into play, but they were hardly excuses."

Darwin's theory of evolution.

Carol faltered as she looked at her list. There was only one phrase left.

"It wouldn't have been Darwin's theory of evolution, would it?"

Angus nodded – sad resignation showing in his expression.

"1859 Darwin's theory of evolution it was indeed. With the abolition of slavery, it gave an almost perfect set of ingredients to create the excuse they needed to justify almost any expansionist action. I mean, after all it endorsed the need to develop backward people by passing on of superior expertise and excellence."

"I don't quite understand the excuse bit." It was Aidan speaking – losing for the first time his cheeky Irish nature. He was anxious. Puzzled.

"According to a fast-growing but actually inaccurate interpretation of Darwin's theory, more primitive people, by inference non-Europeans, were lower down the evolutionary scale. In fact, for the real hard-liners it was generally agreed, they were only a step removed from chimpanzees.

"By the 1880s, this was widely and unquestioningly accepted," he continued resignedly.

"People forgot . . . and still forget it is only a theory."

"I don't believe it."

"I do."

The full import of what Angus was saying hit Jabu with a clarity he had never had before. His pointed stars, identifying instances of discrimination that he needed to remember for the future, were identifying something much more fundamental in the present. Africans were seen as less evolved than Europeans.

This was the excuse: the excuse for lower wages, for less access to education, for the deliberate stares and sneering looks he'd felt as he dared to encroach on white man's territory.

He got up suddenly and walked away, down the stony path, drawn to what he knew might have been the King's thinking and *indaba* space – the goat kraal. As he reached the ruin of the King's palace, he threw his head back and roared his hurt in all the clicks and alliterations of his language.

"King Lobengula, this is my promise once again. I will avenge your death. I will make the white man crawl till he understands we are all one. I will make him beg us to take our country back."

Angus sat quietly, eyes shut. Understanding. Dismayed by every word.

Carol knew enough - to understand in part.

Themba and Prune were stunned.

Aidan looked at Angus. "May I go to him?" "Of course."

"I don't think like that Prune, Themba . . ." Carol spoke quietly, her voice breaking, horrified by what she felt she had started.

"Hey! We know that! Come on, that was nearly 100 years ago. Things have changed."

"Mmm . . . perhaps." She gulped. "But Jabu doesn't think so."

She couldn't just sit, so she too rushed down the path.

"Jabu, I'm so sorry!" Her voice trailed away as she stopped short, shocked to see this strong young man – yet still so much a boy – with his head in his hands, his chest heaving.

Her voice trailed off. "You know I don't think like that . . . lots of us don't think like that."

There was no response. She looked pleadingly at Aidan.

He looked away. Just silence.

Silence punctuated by the rasp of Jabu's wretched breathing.

When they finally came, his words were pinched, distorted by his emotion. "I know that . . . but lots of you do."

She thought back to the bully girls at junior school and knew he was right. If she was honest, not many of her friends thought like she did . . . not many had ever even met black people, not socially anyway.

"There's trouble coming." He looked directly at her, commanding her attention, his eyes glistening. "Please. Don't get caught up in it."

Carol felt chilled.

She caught Aidan's eye – he looked away.

Concessions, Treaties and Double Dealings

They could hear Angus talking as they walked slowly back.

". . . we know what Lobengula looked like and how intelligent he was, but how did he shape up as a leader?

"I thought he gave too much of our country away. Now I'm not sure, but he did seem weak negotiating with Rhodes." said Themba.

"No he wasn't." Jabu butted in sharply as he sat down. "Lobengula never met Rhodes and wasn't told the truth of the Rudd Concession."

"Prune?"

"I always knew he was the amaNdebele King . . . defeated in the first Matebele war and he died trying to escape. I don't know anything about the Rudd Concession."

"Carol?"

"I agree with Prune. That's pretty much what we were taught."

"Well, you're all a little bit right and a little bit wrong. So let's give you, as far as I can, some of the truths.

"A fact, repeated in almost every written account, is that Lobengula preferred the British to other countries . . . and the Boers hated the increasing good relationship between Lobengula and the British.

"So the Commandant-General of the Transvaal, Piet Joubert sent a message:

'When an Englishman has your property in his hands, he is a baboon with its hands full of pumpkin seeds – if you don't beat him to death, he won't let go.'

President Kruger asked another of his emissaries Piet Grobler to go immediately and renew a 'treaty of friendship' with the King. Grobler gained an audience and didn't have a good word to say about the British, of course, sneered over their recent defeat at Majuba, of course, said they were hopeless fighters and sowed doubts in the King's mind.

"Nonetheless, Lobengula and his unhappy and suspicious *indunas* none of whom ever trusted the Boers, were still 'persuaded' to sign that 'friendship' treaty.

"It simply stated that Lobengula would provide troops and 'any other assistance' to the Boers 'whenever it was needed' and give preference to anyone from the Transvaal wishing to see him and negotiate.

"King Lobengula was not given one single benefit in return."

"I didn't know that one." More interested, Jabu joined in again.

"Phew! That would not have pleased the English!" Themba said. "I studied the Boer War last year. The hatred between them was intense."

"Bush telegraph would have got that back to the British quick smart."

Angus laughed. "Worst of all, the Dutch had not been deemed worthy to be invited to the Berlin Conference, so this was really beyond the pale."

"Oh boy, there would have been an awful lot of indignation around!"

"Even a 'Good grief, old chap!'"

They relaxed, grimacing at the spontaneity of Themba's faked English accent.

It helped a bit to break the tension following Jabu's angry outburst.

"Lobengula soon realised that to the Boers, friendship did not mean anything like he had been persuaded, or thought it meant. To complicate the issue, Piet Grobler was murdered by Khama's men on his way back to Johannesburg. So no signed treaty was found."

"The Cape Government heard about it of course and asked John Moffat, a long-time friend of the King, to leave his work in Bechuanaland.

"Moffat had been helping King Khama with the procedures he needed, to become a protectorate of the United Kingdom. The job was nearly finished so Khama gave his blessing and Moffat went to Bulawayo.

"He was appointed as the British resident and the Government's eyes and ears, primarily to help Lobengula manage concession hunters. His descriptions are interesting . . . 'moral invertebrate' or 'intelligent but utterly demoralised'."

"He obviously didn't think much of them!" Themba chuckled.

"The Grobler 'Treaty' was discredited and Moffat suggested it was time for a 'proper' friendship agreement confirmi g that Britain would always be loyal to the Matebele people and the King should discuss and ask their advice first before he talked to other nations.

"The King wasn't in the mood to trust anyone much, and it took almost a year for it to be finalised . . . eventually promising that

"*peace and amity shall continue for ever between Her Britannic Majesty, Her subjects and the Amandebele people*'.

"Moffat had the grace to say in a report to the British government

"*the Matebele may like us better, but they fear the Boers and Germans more*'."

"That Treaty just tied the British closer to the Matebele, ready for the final thrust of the spear . . ." It was Jabu again.

But now, the emotion was gone, replaced by a flat resignation.

He went on, "Lobengula made an apt comment when he said,

'*The chameleon gets behind the fly, remains motionless for some time, then advances slowly and gently, first putting forward one leg and then another. At last, when he is in reach, he darts his tongue and the fly disappears. England is the chameleon and I am that fly.*'"

"And that," Angus said sadly, "is one of the most poignant statements on record, coming from a man who became the victim of heart-breaking world events."

"But Dad, you never said Lobengula was a weak man or a victim!"

"He himself was never a victim, but he was certainly a victim of circumstance, of everything that was happening around him."

"He was the true Bull Elephant of the Matebele people. Thank you Mr Davidson I have learned much more and it's changed my thoughts on King Lobengula. He actually was a great leader," Jabu spoke up defiantly.

Themba felt for the words he needed to add.

"An intelligent man – a far-sighted King – although he never wanted to be King; he had to adopt to the savagery of his heritage. Matebele Kings led their people absolutely, making decisions own on punishment, reward or designation of the next raid . . . but a good King made those decisions in consensus with his *indunas*."

"Amongst it all, he was trying to find some sort of truth from many individuals maddened by greed." Angus concluded. "All going on while his *impi* grew increasingly angry and impatient at not being allowed to raid."

"The poor bugger." Aidan said morosely.

"Did they ever find who took the gold?" Prune asked Angus again as everyone else seemed stupefied.

"Jameson was upset and angered by Lobengula's death. So he asked Mtjaan why the King hadn't replied to his message and come to talk to him. Mtjaan told him a reply was sent but when he told Jameson the King had included gold as a sign of good faith, he was furious. He knew exactly what had happened and was in despair. Nobody wanted the King dead."

His voice harsh, Angus continued: "The two prospectors were tried and sentenced to jail. Unfortunately, the Matebele rebellion started soon afterwards, and the scoundrels were released to help fight. History doesn't record what happened to them."

Carol and Prune were taken aback by his cold anger as he spoke.

"Those bastards had no idea how their greed and selfishness changed the whole of this country's history.

"If that gold had been given to men of integrity and had the message been delivered, Lobengula would still have been able, as King or head of the amaNdebele, to work with the Chartered Company – in a similar way to what was done in Bechuanaland. How sad. How terribly, terribly sad."

Angus stood up to stretch and dissipate the frustration he felt. He had always been angered by the story. But surrounded by land imbued with the essence of the King's own capital - the telling of it to these earnest young people, brought home the futility of it all. It was a disaster, which should never have happened.

"Dad, this has been a real eye-opener to me. The final tragedy has to be that there were two bull elephants – both extraordinary men. They had to respect each other's strengths or kill each other."

Jabu looked up as he realised what she was saying.

"The other bull elephant was Cecil Rhodes.

"Of course!"

23

RHODES AND THE BSAC

"We've already spent a fair bit of time on Rhodes, the indaba and his funeral . . . but as the subject has been raised what do you think of him?

"He stole South Africa's diamonds at the expense of us Africans. He rode roughshod over Lobengula and the Chiefs. He was even forced to resign as Prime Minister - the worst thing to happen to Africa."

"That's a bit hard Jabu!" Carol exclaimed. "He certainly made lots of money, and if he hadn't put it back into the country, or into things like Rhodes scholarships, I'd agree with you. But he died in a tiny two-roomed house in the Cape. That surely suggests he took very little for himself."

"I agree more with Carol than Jabu at this stage. I'm studying Rhodes at the moment so I'd say 'visionary' . . . buthe was ruthless in his pursuit of what he wanted."

"Absolutely Themba," Prune added. "Brilliant at business – one of the great men of that time. The way he shared his vision to get the right people working with him, has influenced me a lot in my work."

"He was English, for goodness' sake! A hard-hearted bastard - can't you see?" Aidan was astonished any of them could trust an Englishman. "I left my home country to get away from the bastards. At least in Southern Rhodesia you're a step further away. Africa has made you a bit different. You're tolerable at least!"

They all laughed - couldn't help liking this fiery redheaded Irishman. And he certainly added a different perspective to their discussion.

"OK! OK! - a bit of a hornet's nest. So let's try and put things in perspective.

"He was a visionary, but was he also a villain? Ten writers say one thing. Ten say the opposite - no shortage of information about Rhodes.

"Themba. You start us off."

"I've got to know him from what I've had to study for the oral history exam which is only two weeks' away." He pulled out his notebook.

"At 17, he was sent out to a brother in South Africa to improve his health.

"It didn't work, because at 21 he had a heart attack. To get him fitter, the Rhodes brothers trekked north by ox-wagon through Bechuanaland to the Transvaal. Rhodes loved it all, but as soon as he was well enough, he went back to Oxford.

"He was there for only one term - because he heard an English social commentator, John Ruskin, say:

England must either do, or perish; she must found colonies as fast and as far as she is able, formed of her most energetic and worthiest men; seizing every piece of fruitful waste ground she can set her foot on.'

"That was enough for Rhodes. His role in life became:

'to expand the Empire for the good of all peoples over whom the glory of the British Empire and the superiority of the Englishman and British Rule would reign.'

"There you are ... what pomposity!" Aidan's face was a picture.

Themba went on. "There were many of gung-ho Englishmen around at that time. Rhodes would get groups of people together and say things like . . ."

He turned the page:

" *'the object of which I intend to devote my life is the defence and extension of the British Empire. I think that object a worthy one because the British Empire stands for the protection of all the inhabitants of a country in life, liberty, property, fair play and happiness and it is the greatest platform the world has ever seen for these purposes and for human enjoyment.*

" *'I contend that we are the first race in the world, and that the more of the world we inhabit, the better it is for the human race.'"*

"These groups would have simply lapped it up!"

"Didn't he want paint as much of the map of Africa British Red as possible?" Carol asked.

". . . and bloddy arrogant too!" Aidan muttered.

"That might be true, but I wish you'd stop using that word Aidan. Might be fine in Ireland, but it's a bit confronting here, especially in front of a lady!"

Carol pulled a face at her father.

"Dictators, orators and visionaries anywhere, lead because they are original thinkers and motivators. They have a degree of arrogance, yes, but more important, absolute belief in their capability. Often, they possess a gift of powerful oratory. Rhodes had presence, but …?"

Themba grinned.

"He had a thin, reedy voice. It was what he said that made people listen, then they wanted to be part of what he was doing."

Angus nodded. "They were spellbound, despite his uninspiring voice. From bright university students to keen young businessmen, shareholders in his companies, employees, and business partners . . . the Cape Province who voted him as Prime Minister – and even to Queen Victoria herself."

"And don't forget the African Chiefs . . ." said Prune.

"That's true too. Rhodes needed no more from Oxford - he rushed back filled ideals and ideas, only to find Britain didn't have the money or the will to pay for the expansion of any more colonies anyway."

Themba chuckled. "That was no problem to him. He simply raised the money himself."

"He did! No fear, no doubts about his ability!" Angus laughed. "well done Themba. A great overview.

"He did indeed live thriftily, spending little money on himself. From earnings started on his brother's fruit farm, he paid for the British South Africa Company's formation and charter – dipping into his own pockets time and again for the building of the railway and telegraph lines. Then, when costs should have been covered through investment and earnings, there were endless setbacks. Rhodes had to keep finding more money.

"The estimate on the cost to cover the Pioneer Column on its journey up to Mount Hampden was £87,500 – a huge amount of money in the late 1890s. Any idea of its equivalent value today, at the end of 1958?"

"I know," said Prune. "I know – just give me a moment."

Jabu and Themba couldn't believe their eyes as Prune asked to borrow Themba's notebook and pencil. He was soon scribbling away on the back cover, filling the whole page before he announced triumphantly:

"Just under £500,000 – nearly half a million pounds. Phew! A lot!"

He looked up to see his friends' startled faces.

Embarrassed, he protested: "I've always been good at maths, and I'm not a storekeeper for nothing! I convert currencies to pounds and vice versa all the time, and I'm used to inflation calculations. It's not hard."

"Not hard! That sounds horrific," Carol exclaimed. "Don't ever ask me to do something like that!"

Bringing them back on track, Angus said: "Time to get back to more numbers. The Pioneer Column was made up of volunteers and paid men from the Bechuanaland Police. Any idea how many?"

No idea!

Angus went on. "180 volunteers – a carefully chosen mix of butchers, bakers, engineers, builders, doctors, teachers, traders and anything else they felt they might need.

"But – and this was interesting . . . Rhodes insisted the greater percentage had to be the sons of Britain's wealthiest families. In this way, fathers would not only invest in the project, but if their sons were in danger, they'd force Britain to do something to get help quickly. A very clever move."

Themba interrupted, "In fact Mr Davidson, did you know that Rhodes insisted on interviewing many of them himself and chose the most outstanding young men he could find? There were some good people."

"Something I didn't know. Thanks Themba."

Angus took up the story again. "As the sons of Britain's landed gentry, some were what we tough Rhodesians would describe as 'wet behind the ears', but they hardened up. And the best thing was, they didn't need to make a fortune themselves, as they had plenty of money anyway. So they could get on with the important tasks of developing a new country.

"Many of them ended up, like me, in African administration and expanding on what Themba said, we are fortunate to have had many very well-educated and philanthropic people whose interest and fascination, was the development of the country - and particularly, of the black people.

246

"There were also 300 members of the Bechuanaland Border Police, plus varying numbers of Tswana workers – all courtesy of King Khama. The Bechuanaland King had a vested interest in making sure there would be an unchallengeable border created between him and the Matebele. King Khama was happy to support the column in any way he could.

"Very quickly, a large part of the cost was in getting them here, buying oxen and wagons, food and other supplies - establishing infrastructure, roads, telegraph and railway lines, and eventually public buildings.

"There were 62 wagons - each needing 16 oxen to pull it. Almost 1,000 animals being used every day. Then you had to have spares and backups, so there must have been at least a couple of hundred more. In addition to that, most of the volunteers and police were mounted, so add to the list, a couple of hundred horses as well. There's a lot of organisation just in that little lot.

Ever practical, Carol remarked, "Imagine all the food and water they needed for the people – and presumably feed for the animals must have been pretty unpredictable. What time of year did they go?"

"They started out from Macloutsie, in Bechuanaland, at the end of June 1890, and it took them almost three months before they reached today's Salisbury to fly the flag.

"At least they started in the middle of the cold months of the year, but it would have been getting very dry towards the end. Pretty scary!"

"Britain sat back and thought: 'great! someone else doing it for us!' This must have been a key point behind granting Rhodes a charter to establish the BSA Company in the first place – similar to Clive of India – but even more independent.

"By October 1889, Britain was still keen to expand its empire but it didn't have the money or enough expertise to spare. The Colonial Office felt that rather than sending administrators out from Britain, those already there were better equipped to handle it.

"By the way, what was the country called for the first few years after the Pioneer Column arrived?"

Blank faces again.

"I think somewhere along the line it was called Mthwakazi, but I don't think that was formalised. It was more the name we used," Jabu said.

"Well Mthwakazi would have been a far name than South Zambesia!"

"South Zambesia! No wonder they changed it!"

"It became Southern Rhodesia in 1901 shortly before Rhodes died."

Aidan was keen to get back to the story.

"If Rhodes needed half a million pounds just for the Pioneer Column, how did he make all that money? I know he surrounded himself with the brightest and best and all that stuff, and he had important contacts to invest in his adventures, but there's somethin' very fishy here . . ."

"Well I wouldn't exactly call it fishy Aidan! It was actually a pretty small percentage of his whole financial empire. He made things happen by looking for problems."

"What do you mean Dad?"

"He bought out struggling one-man operations and consolidated them into larger companies. When diamond miners lost heart and went off to the latest gold rush, he bought out the old claims which were now worthless because they reckoned they'd found all the Kimberley diamonds they could in the accessible yellow alluvial clay. Rhodes felt digging down deeper into the blue rock underneath would have massive dividends. One of the claims he bought out, belonged to a couple of brothers called De Beer."

This produced nods of recognition.

"Prune, you told us about your friend who had a small gold mine in Bushtick and how you had learned about the steam engine they used to pump out water. What was going to be the biggest problem for Rhodes if he wanted to go deeper?

Prune's face lit up. "Water of course – how could people get rid of it."

"Dead right, bottom line . . . small operators couldn't afford it, so Rhodes bought up all the struggling water pumping contractors until his company was in charge of pumping water out of virtually every mine on the Rand. Economies of scale Prune – economies of scale."

"Of course, it had to be done to keep the mines going – an essential service! Clever!" Prune stated. "The deeper they went, the more water filled the mines – and the better quality the diamonds! He was no fool."

Prune was full of thoughts about how he could make his stores out-perform Mr Bellini.

"What was the cleverest thing he did?"

Themba jumped in: "My textbooks at O-level said his greatest achievement was recognising that hundreds of miners individually scooping diamonds out of the earth and selling privately, would devalue them, to nobody's benefit. There needed to be wide recognition of this beautiful gem's true worth.

'So through his company De Beers Consolidated, he kept records of how many were produced, identified where they came from . . . separated, sorted, quality categorised them, and then the coup de grace, limited the numbers available so everyone would want, and therefore, be prepared to pay a premium for them."

"They taught you well, Themba. Rather impressed by the French too! What did you get for that paper?"

Themba looked sheepish. "A Distinction."

Carol and Prune clapped spontaneously.

"By the time De Beers consolidated was registered in April 1888, Rhodes and his business partner and friend Barney Barnato had built up the largest conglomerate of mines and miners in the world."

Aidan shrugged his shoulders. "Just ready for the granting of the charter a year later. Why don't I spot opportunities like that?"

"Well I'm going to look for them in my business now," Prune stated with renewed enthusiasm. Everyone was quite sure he would. But he hadn't finished yet!

"Rhodes also tried to move the eastern border so we had a gateway to the sea, and at the same time, he was looking further north, at places round the headwaters of the Nile. At one stage he lost heart because of the expense of the Cape to Cairo rail line, and to his death, he was still determined to build it for the betterment of trade between all countries."

"Oh and at the same time . . ." Themba mock yawned " . . . he was Prime Minister of the Cape Colony."

"Did this guy ever sleep?" asked Aidan.

"Nobody can deny he was anything other than a giant. And you can cross the word Colossus off your list, because that is how he is seen."

"You don't mean the Colossus of Rhodes somewhere off Greece either, do you Dad!"

"No I don't, we had our own real live one!"

"Look, he was brilliant, courageous, a builder of Empire, a true believer that everything the British did was the best model for every other country in the world . . . he was also tough, taciturn, ruthless, rode roughshod over people to achieve his ends, made an absolute fortune out of his businesses, but he never spared himself, despite his poor health.

"Perhaps one of his greatest strengths was that he looked ahead - always spotting difficulties well in advance. For example, and this is appropriate, he wrote:

'I have always been afraid of the difficulty of dealing with the Matebele King. He is the only block to central Africa, as, once we have his territory, the rest is easy . . . the rest is simply a village system with separate headmen . . ."

"That sounds pretty callous," Carol said.

"It does! Realistically, it was a business plan – and perhaps in a funny way, it's was a tribute to the King himself, that Rhodes recognised he was a force to be reckoned with!"

Jabu wasn't so sure about that.

24

TEMPERS SHORTEN : TENSIONS GROW

Jabu was becoming uncomfortable with the discussion that was taking place. Yet, he didn't want to let it go. He needed the information. Even as a small child he had respected Mr Davidson for his knowledge and even handedness – never too busy to stop and answer a question. He knew he'd get an objective view of what might really have happened in the quagmire of contradictions around the history of the country. He had to admit, he'd already learned a lot.

He also found, to his surprise, that he really liked grown-up Prune – nothing seemed to get him down. He was going to go places and Jabu decided he would ask him to join the SRANC before they left.

He should ask Themba too, but something held him back. Irritation – contradiction - idealistic viewpoint perhaps? He wasn't sure.

Carol – well she was just the same. She'd always be a friend.

"There were plenty of people queueing up to criticise Rhodes." Angus had taken up the story. "The British government having lots of 'how dare he' moments – the opinionated leaders of the Imperial Forces, miners and hunters wanting concessions from the King but unsuccessful. Essentially, man doesn't change. Make lots of money and everyone is after you. You'll find good and bad, plus a healthy dose of jealousy and backbiting in every culture. For such is the nature of the thwarted human being!"

Prune liked that sentence. He wrote it down to remember it.

"Rhodes' mistake was probably that he thought he had the right mix of people in place to set up the BSAC in such a short time. He hadn't.

He tended to trust, and appoint, his friends to key positions, but

251

ended up with too few people with solid business or administrative knowledge to understand how to manage it all.

"Jameson was a case in point. A brilliant medical doctor. . . but did that equip him to become administrator of a brand new colony in a country with an existing, disciplined and well-organised people . . . who simply did not understand what on earth white people were on about?

"Programmed to fail at worst, or muddle along at best.

"Fortunately, in the Pioneer Column, the military men, army and police were well trained and in peacetime, they were a reliable backbone.

"You think Rhodes was a good bloke, Dad?" Carol suggested.

"I do - on balance . . . but I have reservations. Rhodes had what would seem to be a lot of money available, but realistically it was never enough to develop a country properly. Let's look at another example.

"In 1600, Robert Clive's East India Company was set up as a trading company with private investors and shareholdings – but with British administrative, financial and military support. Its usefulness ran out 274 years later, having established new markets, procedures and worldwide contacts which improved lifestyles all round. It closed in 1874, only 15 years before Rhodes started work on his concept of a Chartered Company.

"From the British perspective, it was an effective way to spread the Imperialist banner, and minimise taxpayers bearing the load. Realistically, Rhodes had less support than almost anyone else – partly his own doing, but partly massive jealousies which would rather not see him succeed!

"In a funny way, do you think the Berlin Conference with its 'take what you want, as long as you give something back' concept helped a bit?"

Themba asked the question – wondering if he was completely off the track. But Mr Davidson's nod indicated otherwise.

"You said he was no fool, Mr Davidson – I think he was a typical bloddy English idiot even to try!"

"He also knew he would not live a long life. So being the person he was, he couldn't just sit and wait for things to happen fast enough to allow him to achieve his vision.

"There was a lasting and positive side to him of course, in that he gave away vast amounts of 'good cause' money to interesting new ventures. There are countless records of his kindness and philanthropy to those he came across who needed it, both black and white. He mollified those who felt hard done by, rewarded anyone who helped advance the cause – and ultimately, he left parks, public spaces and scholarships for posterity.

"Can I add something on the business side?" Themba added: "Something I found interesting when I was doing my research. Those who worked for him mostly idolised him, including black miners. They wanted 'to work for Mr Rhodes'. While other companies battled to find employees, Rhodes always had plenty. By 1898, he was the largest employer of native labour in Southern Africa. So he must have paid and looked after his employees well to keep them wanting to come back."

Angus agreed. "Also, he had a prodigious memory - never forgot a face, name or context of anyone he had ever spoken to, whether it was a driver who had given him a ride in an ox wagon, the head of key departments in the government, or the Matebele King's youngest and least important wife. When he eventually came up to Matebeleland, he spent time asking about domestic problems and trying to understand the views of Chiefs and headmen.

'I could never accept the position that we should disqualify a human being on account of his colour.'"

"Yes, I've got that quote too." Themba chimed in. "Some of his other quotes are also revealing. I'd like to read them out."

"Go ahead."

"First of all, his definition of a civilised man:

'a man, white or black, who has sufficient education to write his name, has some property or works, in fact is not a loafer'."

"Hmmm . . ." Carol said "he obviously had no time for anyone who was lazy, but I see a distinct lack of any reference to the worth of women!"

Themba pulled a face at her. "This bit was about Southern Rhodesia:

'I find that there are certain locations where, without any right or title to the land, they are herded together. The natives there are multiplying to an enormous extent, and these locations are becoming too small. The old diminutions by war and

253

pestilence do not occur . . . We have given them no share in the government and no interest in the local development of their country."

"That was true," growled Jabu.

" What I would like in regard to a native area is that there should be no white men in its midst. I hold that the natives should be apart from white men, and not mixed up with them. We fail utterly when we put natives on an equality with ourselves."

"And that probably started Apartheid down south."

Themba went on: "In the same speech, he said:

"'If we deal with them differently and say, "Yes, these people have their own ideas" and so on, then we are all right; but when once we depart from that position and put them on an equality with ourselves, we may give the matter up . . . As to the question of voting, we say that the natives are in a sense citizens, but not yet altogether citizens – they are still children."

"So what is your opinion, having brought those quotes together?"

"I wonder if he could imagine the African ever having the same future capability as a European, particularly an Englishman! Whether he'd have conceded that after we had matched education and experience, I don't know. In fact, I wonder what he would think of us now if he could sit in on this discussion!"

"He would be fascinated." Angus suggested.

"It was tragic that two such exceptional people as Lobengula and Rhodes eventually came to war. What a team they'd have been – both were intelligent and far sighted enough to make the country really work. Like Khama in Bechuanaland," Carol spoke passionately, frustrated by how badly it all ended, yet now understanding how good it could have been.

"Perhaps as you said earlier, you simply could not have two bull elephants," Jabu smiled at her kindly. "Pretty idealistic, my friend. Rhodes was just typical of his kind."

He turned to Angus.

"Mr Davidson, you said many of the people coming up here in the Pioneer Column were unpaid volunteers. Well he paid them all right – by giving away our land and our gold."

254

"I acknowledge that, but in his original concept, he didn't plan to give away nearly as much as that unpredictable man Jameson did. This was a terrible sadness that haunted him for the rest of his life."

"And by the way, my friend, unless my maths is way out . . . " Aidan interrupted, "King Mzilikazi came up here, I think you said in 1840."

"That's correct."

"And the Pioneers came here in 1890?"

He turned to Jabu. "Well, you guys had only been here just over 50 years since Mbongo—"

"Mbigo."

"—Sorry, Mbigo and his regiment beginning with Z killed all others in the way. To be fair, it wasn't much time to claim ownership . . ."

Jabu said nothing.

This was not going to plan – Aidan was supposed to be supporting him. Angus could feel Jabu's discomfort and turned the conversation back with the question:

"Could you agree Jabu, that Rhodes did an incredible job establishing the country – a benevolent dictator perhaps?"

"Well no, not really. He used our underpaid, hard labour to make the roads and railway line and make the buildings. In time, we'd have learned how to do it ourselves. We've never been given any credit for that."

Themba interrupted. "Perhaps there wasn't enough time for us to learn enough to compete, Jabu. If it hadn't been the English, it might have been the Germans, and Lobengula trusted them less than he did the Boers. That's why the King did what he felt was best for the amaNdebele and settled with the English."

"That's a boring old argument, Themba. The BSAC changed our way of life - destroyed our pride, our Chiefs and tribal structures - broke our families apart. Mr Davidson told of the disciplines and military genius of the amaNdebele people. Why did it have to change? You're a sell-out to our people, Themba!"

"I'm no sell-out. There are many black people today who seriously want what the white man has brought, who enjoy learning, who feel they can help lead people in new directions so we can compete on their terms

255

and become the leaders of this country again."

"In the white man's world!"

"Not necessarily. There's a huge world out there, full of different people and different cultures. We just seem to have been left behind."

"We haven't. We have a distinct culture and a different way of life."

"I don't deny it, and it's vital we don't lose our traditions and culture."

"How are you going to do that when you're off to a white man's law school and doing a white man's job?"

"I won't be doing a white man's job. I'll be doing my job better than any white man, because I am African - I know the anguish and the joy of people I will work with better than any white man.

"You're happy that we don't have enough people in education and we don't have the vote and we're paid a fraction of what white people earn for doing the same job?"

"No, I'm not happy about that. But seriously Jabu, if you don't want what the white man offers, why are you worried about education and the vote? Or even about earning a living?"

Jabu was fuming. He couldn't believe Themba was thinking like this. And the trouble was that he was so rational and clever that he was winning the argument.

Jabu was only just holding his emotion and rage in check because Carol and Mr Davidson were there.

Angus stepped in to defuse the situation. "There are arguments on both sides. You are all the hope for the future of this country. You have the ability to help find answers for a country so young in terms of its adaptation to another culture and trying to manage what is still an immensely difficult situation. The decisions you educated young people make and the paths you take will make it – or break it.

"Jabu, you've already shown exceptional ability working in the prison. Stick with it. Gradual improvements are being made all the time in many spheres of life in Southern Rhodesia. Nothing happens overnight. Have patience. You have the capability and intelligence to be a great leader."

Angus wasn't sure whether he'd made any impression from the sullen folded arms attitudes of the two boys - but he kept this discussion going because the last thing to discuss was the most divisive - the Rudd

Concession. To do that, there had to be some knowledge of Rhodes and the Chartered Company.

"Your mentioned that Rhodes never actually met Lobengula."

Jabu agreed. "We have no oral history about any meeting. The question is, did he care enough to bother?"

"It was inexcusable - he sent his men up but didn't come himself until after Lobengula had died." He shook his head sadly. "Things might have been very different if he'd met the King."

Aidan was aware his earlier comments hadn't helped but he added: "And that might be exactly why he would've put it off. He knew who he was dealing with and didn't want his views changed! Typical!"

Leaving Prune, Jabu and Aidan talking to Angus, Carol and Themba went off to stretch their legs away from the heat of the argument.

They walked up to the main red brick ruins to look round the outside, as there were piles of rubble in the gaps for doors. They were both longing to look inside, but neither felt quite like invading Lobengula's space.

Angus had given Carol a typed sheet with the description a visitor to the house had made many years before. They stopped, stood and looked and imagined as she read what was written:

"A well-built brick house, that was made for the king by an old sailor named Halyott and meant for a royal residence, but the king seldom occupies it and prefers to live in his waggon. Inside this house the walls are decorated with various prints and paintings, including a large sized oil painting of the Queen in a handsome frame, and he always speaks of the Great White Queen with the greatest reverence and respect. The king has a large pack of dogs of various kinds, but as they are fed solely on meat, present rather a mangy appearance; he has also tame ostriches, peacocks, and pigeons."

"Lobengula didn't sleep in his palace, preferring the comfort of his wagon - interesting." Themba was finding it difficult to be enthusiastic about anything.

As they started to walk back to the truck, she said: "I'm so sorry this has become tense . . . unfortunately, it's happening more and more. The divide is widening between those who want to move forward and those who only want to look back, thinking that is the way to move forward.

"I don't know where it is leading. I just know I am fearful."

25

THE RUDD CONCESSION[88]

The leafy, shaded garden at the back of the Eskimo Hut milk bar was a welcome relief after the sparsely vegetated and parched landscapes they'd left behind. Milkshakes and doughnuts sounded about right to them all as they sat quiet but, for the moment, reconciled . . . relaxed by old friendships and the sociable contentment of food and non-contentious chatter. They looked at the Trade Fair site in the distance, discussing where they had been and what part they had played in the Queen Mother's visit for the Rhodes Centenary celebrations four years ago.

Carol described her first evening there with the Eveline School music students, when she was stunned by the glory of the opera *Aida*. Prune and Themba had been impressed by the military tattoo. Jabu was involved in setting up stands in the African village, where he looked after displays of sculptures, music and dance to enthusiastic black and white crowds – including Princess Margaret, who even joined in a bit of the dancing. There were plenty of uncontroversial events to talk about.

Aidan had gone to get a change of clothes for the extra day.

"Good afternoon Jabulani! How did the cattle sale go?" It was Mr Eddington.

"Very well sir. May I introduce my friends . . ."

Carol shook hands with him, even though she didn't want to. She was in a panic that Aidan would come back too soon and while Mr Eddington was still talking to them. *Don't talk too much Jabu*, she willed him.

"My grandfather had an exceptional sale. He specialises in breeding Tuli, and the prices were far better than he'd hoped. So he is enthusiastic

---

[88] See Appendix 1: The Rudd Concession

about the future. There was an amazing atmosphere, a good mingling of farmers and buyers. And with all the shouts of auctioneers and noises of the cattle . . . it was exciting. One of the biggest sales I've ever been to."

"I'd very much like to come out and see one of those sales in the future Jabulani. And to meet your grandfather."

Once Mr Eddington had left, Angus said, "I think if you play your cards right, Jabu, you could swing Mr Eddington towards a more pleasant way of working. It's worth a try. He obviously thinks a lot of you."

It might be worth a try, Jabu thought, but he had a long list of 'to-dos' from Michael Mawema, and he was going to focus on those first.

They headed back to the truck for the short trip to Inyati. When they arrived, Angus walked across to one of the teachers, Tony Browne, who was seeing the last buses off for school holidays. He came back to say they could go and sit under the big old marula tree next to the church, or if it got too hot they could use the church itself.

"Right, team. What's the history behind Inyati Mission?"

"Mzilikazi gave this land to Robert Moffat and the London Missionary Society. And it was started, I think . . . about 1859."

"Good, Prune. The first mission allowed into Mzilikazi's territory. Any other thoughts?"

"This was near the second of Mzilikazi's capitals Emhlangeni. And as tradition demanded, he left it when his main Queen Loziba died."

"You certainly know your history well."

"I should!" Jabu grimaced. "It was drummed into me when I was a very young boy."

"The proximity of Emhlangeni or as it was also called, Inyati . . ." Angus paused, looking round enquiringly.

"Buffalo!" chorused Themba and Jabu.

"Good! I just wanted to check you were still awake! Anyway, the proximity of Emhlangeni to Inyati Mission, and the proximity of the mission at Hope Fountain to Lobengula's first capital at Gibexhegu is interesting. Any thoughts Jabu?"

"The Kings knew they were at a disadvantage because they couldn't read or write," Jabu responded. "They wanted their people to learn and interpret for them so they could understand the plotting of the white man!

Staff at the missions taught the three R's as well as Christianity. Having a mission nearby meant that some, particularly the sons of Chiefs, would learn. It was a case of know-your-enemy!"

"OK! OK! We're getting the picture!" Carol teased, nudging Jabu's arm.

Jabu mock punched her then grew serious.

"The reason I know a bit about this was that great-grandfather Mtjaan could write his name and speak good English. His youngest son, my *baba 'mkulu* Chief Mehluli – you met him yesterday – can speak, read and write English well because he learned at Inyati. That's why he was determined to send my father out of the country for even more education after he left school, and why my father, after all his hard work, knows how important it is for me and for other African children. It is also why he is respected for his great work in education."

"That certainly gives me more understanding Jabu, thank you. Lobengula must have felt that disadvantage acutely and it certainly didn't help with the Rudd Concession. I hear it said, so often, that Helm did not tell the truth about what was written on the document. It's not easy to get to the absolute truth, but let's see how we go – as this is the final piece of the puzzle which is our history.

"As we know, by 1888, everyone wanted a piece of the action. The British overturned Kruger's friendship treaty, saying, among other things, that he wasn't entitled to it - because he was not a signatory to the Berlin Conference!"

"Perfidious Albion living up to its reputation. They truly are a nation of shopkeepers. Can't think of a good word to say about them!" Aidan was off on his Irish hobbyhorse again. His cheeks and hair seemed to get redder and redder with every outburst.

"Aidan! I'm going to be a shopkeeper – an honourable profession!" Prune protested. It looked as though he was close to punching Aidan.

"Probably is, if you're not English!" Aidan agreed.

"Moving on," Angus said, pulling them back to the subject. "Later that year, Rhodes sent three men to talk to Lobengula: a business partner, Charles Rudd, a Zulu speaker, Francis Thompson and a London barrister, James Rochfort Maguire. Their task was to negotiate for mineral rights.

"Now here's an interesting bit of background, highly relevant to what we were talking about this morning. The third man in the party, Maguire, had no knowledge or experience of Africa. He met Rhodes at Oxford where he was studying law and was called to the bar. But he'd never practised law. He went into politics and was a Member of Parliament.

"Now Aidan, you'll be particularly interested to hear, he was no Englishman. He was an Irish Nationalist, following a man called Parnell!"

Aidan's face was a picture. He was speechless, but not for long. "Must have been a bloddy Protestant nonetheless . . ." he muttered. "There are of course, a few, but only a very few, rotten apples in Ireland . . ."

Jabu couldn't resist it. "So the cause of all our problems was a bloody Irishman – not the English after all!"

Everybody laughed – glad there was a reason to do so.

"It should have been called Maguire's folly not the Rudd Concession." Carol added.

Angus enjoyed being part of this group of lively young minds, but keeping them focussed after a long day was hard and time was running away with them.

"OK where are we ... this was what Maguire produced as the Rudd Concession. I've made copies for each of you, in its original, spider-crawl handwriting."

The cause of all the problems

They couldn't wait to get their hands on it. None of them had seen it before, but this particular concession had been the subject of so much controversy and antagonism that they were all dying to read it.

As they started to look at it, Angus said, "It starts off:

'Know all men by these presents that whereas Charles Dunnell Rudd of Kimberley, Rochfort Maguire of London, and Francis Robert Thompson of Kimberley, hereinafter called the grantees, have covenanted and agreed . . .'"

Angus was watching their expressions as they read. He waited until they'd all finished, then said:

"It was signed in the same way as all Lobengula's letters and treaties:

with his X mark and the elephant seal. There was validation by Charles Helm and other co-signatories underneath.

"Just a reminder . . . Lobengula would not put his X on any paper unless there was a missionary there to watch him do it and endorse it. The British Government in turn would accept no document from the King unless there was a missionary's signature on it as verification. This is vital to our talk this evening.

"Impressions first. Themba?"

"Well . . . I have to say it is the most complex document to try and explain to the amaNdebele people. I can hardly understand it, and I'm in my final few weeks of A-levels. Ridiculous!"

Carol was bemused – she'd never seen Themba so worked up before.

"From the little I know about contracts themselves," he continued: "this one does the right things. Sort of. It identifies what the grantor – that's Lobengula – wants out of the deal and the way that would be delivered. Then it identifies what he is giving away, then adds a provision that if the conditions demanded by the grantor are not met by the grantee – Rudd – that the grant conditions would cease." He looked at Angus in amazement. "But it is so lacking in detail."

"Carol?"

"I have for the first time understood why Lobengula wanted things that seem strange at first hearing. People ridicule this Concession, saying things like 'what would an uneducated man like Lobengula want with all that money, all those rifles and ammunition and a steamboat gunship on the Zambezi!' I've never been able to answer before. But now I can. The guns and ammunition were becoming vital, because the Matebele found that more and more of the tribes they raided had guns – and of course there was always the uncertainty of the white man!

"The Martini-Henry was the most suitable weapon for this type of war; the steamboat gunship meant he must have decided that if, or when, the Matebele had to move across the Zambezi to Batoka lands, a steamboat gunship would help them defend that big river border much more effectively."

Angus commented: "An unexpected fallout from that agreed payment of guns was that Sir Sidney Shippard who was Resident Commissioner of Bechuanaland, had to spend many hours reassuring King Khama that the issue of guns to the Matebele would have no impact on Bechuanaland! He was not convinced as you know, King Khama hated the Matebele. The last thing he wanted was to have them armed with Martini-Henry rifles. His only reassurance was that, as Bechuanaland was now a Protectorate of the United Kingdom, the country would be defended by Her Majesty's forces should any cross border raids ever happen."

"Yes, that makes sense – Khama would have been pretty anxious!" Prune was next in the circle.

"From a business point of view, as money became more desirable and necessary to achieve what King Lobengula needed, it was clever of him to say he wanted to be paid on a lunar moon basis, not a calendar month. This way, he got 13 payments a year. And if they couldn't supply the boat, he'd get a once off payment instead."

"Well, I'd like to add my little bit here," said Aidan. "Even though I know precious little about it, this sentence clarifies somethin' for me:

' . . . *assigns, jointly and severally, the complete and exclusive charge over all metals and minerals situated and contained in my kingdoms, principalities, and dominions, together with full power to do all things that they may deem necessary to win and procure the same . . .'*

"Am I goin' completely mad, or did he only give away the right to dig for gold and other minerals?"

"You're not going mad, Aidan. That is exactly what was given away in this Concession. Nothing else."

Jabu couldn't wait to get his word in. "Ah! But it wasn't what was written that mattered! It was what was not written. They agreed verbally that only ten men would come in to manage the mines. But that, for example, wasn't in the Rudd Concession document."

"And that . . . is the problem, Jabu."

"It was what was discussed at great length, by 100 indunas, but it was *not* actually written into the document, and that caused the problem.

"We have only one eyewitness written report the promise that only ten men would come in was made. Ironically - from Helm himself. Are you aware of stories about this in African oral history, Jabu or Themba?"

They acknowledged that they hadn't heard anything more specific –

just that Helm had lied.

Jabu asked, "Knowing it would sometimes take months to see King Lobengula, how did they get the negotiations going in the first place?"

"This was where Helm did come into the picture. His long-standing relationship with the King was central to gaining an audience. But he was cautious about who he offered to introduce to the King. By this time Helm was so distressed by the pressure and untruths that were being told to Lobengula from every possible quarter, that he was one of many who felt that negotiating with one party was preferable.

"Rudd's party arrived with a letter of commendation from the High Commissioner, Sir Hercules Robinson. This would have been enough to persuade Helm to help. Having agreed to try and get them to see the King, Helm went to the capital. The King greeted him in his usual welcoming way but had other business to attend to.

"It was another ten days before he could see him. Ten days later, and as he did with anyone else he felt the King should know about, Helm put an outline of Rudd's proposals to Lobengula. The King listened, then said he would talk to his *indunas* and see him in a week's time.

"Rudd's group was delighted that they would see Lobengula but the man they had employed to interpret for them, was no longer available. They needed a replacement urgently. Helm describes what happened:

"'As they could get no one to interpret they came and asked me to interpret for them. I would rather have had nothing to do with gold concessions and told the Chief so, but not thinking that harm could come from simply interpreting I consented and the Chief said he was glad that I should do so and that he perfectly understood that I had nothing more to do with it.'

"The party of three were still not admitted into Lobengula's presence. So Helm, the King and another twenty or so of his most senior Headmen spent a whole day in discussion. Helm described every possible aspect of what was being asked by telling and repeating; stopping the meeting; going off to seek assurances and clarification from Rudd; going back to answer more questions; telling again and repeating again; seeking more assurances and reporting back to Lobengula.

"Lobengula said he was now ready to meet the other men. They arrived a few days later, with Helm to interpret for them.

"The King offered hospitality but refused to talk business! Helm was asked to come back the following week to talk again. This time, the King wished to call an *indaba* of up to a hundred *indunas*, which lasted . . . well, some reports say half a day, others two days!"

"What a convoluted process!" Aidan protested.

"Jabu, your thoughts on this – why did Lobengula call such a major *indaba* taking as much time as was needed, to discuss this particular concession?"

"I didn't know he had! And Mtjaan is not here to ask! I'll speak to my *baba 'mkulu* next time I see him, in case he knows anything more."

"Putting my novice, about-to-be student lawyer's hat on," Themba said, "if I was Lobengula and I'd had a hard time fending off concession seekers, I'd be really keen to try and get this right. I've never believed Lobengula was naïve enough to be taken in by this Concession. He was a man way beyond his time, and clever enough to know that any concession from Rhodes or the Chartered Company had to be taken seriously. That's why he called an *indaba*."

"Makes sense. And as John Moffat said, he seemed to like the British better than the others.

"Helm stayed with Moffat when he was not at Hope Fountain and would have kept him fully in the picture about what was going on while getting his advice from the British Government's perspective.

"Sir Sidney Shippard arrived on a routine visit in the middle of all this. He spent time with Lobengula discussing the murder of Piet Grobler by some of Khama's men. As he was about to climb into his wagon to return to Bechuanaland, Shippard reported that the King came out of the Goat Kraal, and Shippard saluted him by lifting his helmet. The King then courteously shook his hand. Shippard writes:

'it seemed he was familiar with European ways.'

"Each man seems to have been suitably impressed by the other, and the coincidental visit from this eminent person might also have been a factor in Lobengula agreeing to sign the Concession.

"Helm, Rudd, Maguire and Thompson set off once again to see the King. During this meeting, Lobengula told Helm he refused to allow him to return to Hope Fountain, in case he needed to talk to him.

"As they were about to leave this meeting, a letter arrived from King Khama. Lobengula asked Helm to read it out.

"He was in the middle of doing so, when he was interrupted by the entry of what remained of a large *impi* that had been away for months on a raid beyond the Zambezi. There's an interesting description of what happened, from a man called Cooper Chadwick. Your turn Carol."

" 'Their numbers were greatly diminished from famine, sickness, and fierce contests with other tribes, whom they found a harder nut to crack than maShonas. In fact, the expedition had been a failure, or, as they said, 'The ground opened and swallowed them up.' The captives that were brought back were a wild-looking lot, their bodies tattooed all over and hair curiously arranged into fantastic shapes: many of them showed marks of the ill-usage they suffered along the road as they bowed down trembling before the King, who then distributed them among his people as slaves.' "

"It must have been arresting for Rudd's group to see Lobengula in his role as absolute King of his people. Perhaps he had organised it to demonstrate exactly that!"

"Perhaps he had!" Jabu agreed – and smiled to himself.

"One of the King's most important *indunas*, Lotshe, was very positive about Rudd's offer. He was an old man now and had seen enough of wars and killing. He urged Lobengula to make friends, not enemies of the English, as he said they would look after the Matebele people.

"The night before the final meeting, the King called a small meeting where only *Induna* Lotshe and 'Matebele' Thompson were present. The decision was made to sign the Rudd Concession and Rudd and Maguire were informed.

"At 6'30 the next morning, Rudd, Maguire and Thompson arrived to sign the document. They had to wait first, and then found they were invited to join yet another *indaba* of over a hundred headmen.

"So it's incorrect to say the only people present were Lobengula, the Rudd team and Helm. Lobengula's chief *indunas* were present too.

"It had taken six weeks of debate, and the Matebele recognised it as a critical event. Understandably, Lobengula was anxious. After repetitions to the full *indaba* of everything written in that document, punctuated by Helm seeking more verbal assurances from Rudd before any signatures were made, consensus was eventually reached.

"I've never believed Lobengula was naïve enough to be taken in by this Concession. He was, as we now know, a man way beyond his time, and quite clever enough to know that any concession from Rhodes or the Chartered Company had to be taken seriously. That's why he called an *indaba*."

"The Matebele people, not just King Lobengula, decided that signing a concession with one large British organisation was their best option."

"Perhaps you should have been there, Aidan, to tell them differently!"

"Well, there's still a question hangin' in the air . . . was the British Government in cahoots with the Company? That's the unspoken bit, the unanswered bit," Aidan added. "I'd lay my bets on it!"

Angus laughed. "Aidan, I don't have a full answer. I'd like to hope it was not deliberate . . . approving the Concession would have been convenient for the British government. They had had nothing to do with it up to this point . . . but they were about to get a nasty wake-up call!"

Chaos, confusion - and The Lord speaks.

"Following the signing, Lobengula sent a notice to the *Cape Times* saying all mineral rights had now been negotiated. Concession seekers were now to stop bothering him, as *'their presence was obnoxious to him'*.

"No sooner was that published than all hell broke loose! There is so much conflicting detail that it's almost impossible to sort out exactly what happened next.

"There were at least 30 thwarted concessionaires who'd lost out completely – and you can imagine what happened. These men told the King he had signed his country away and he must repudiate the Concession immediately, so the British Government refuses to accept it. Lobengula became convinced he'd made a mistake and immediately sent a letter of repudiation to the High Commissioner.

"Now a question. Why had the concession hunters lost out completely? That's something none of you picked up!"

Themba was first to read out – almost to himself: "

'. . . I have been much molested of late by divers persons seeking and desiring to obtain grants and concessions of land and mining rights in my territories, I do hereby authorise the said grantees, their heirs, representatives, and assigns, to take all necessary and lawful steps to exclude from my kingdoms, principalities, and dominions all persons seeking land, metals, minerals, or mining rights therein.'

"Wow!" His eyes were like saucers. "They weren't going to be able to approach the King directly for concessions in future!

"The Rudd Concession administrators would now be responsible for the granting of concessions, and more important, the removal of anyone they deemed unsuitable, who wanted to search for minerals in the country.

"The concession-seekers had only one chance of survival – destroy the Rudd Concession. Quite honestly, and from what we have seen, that wouldn't be hard to do."

"Themba, you'll make a good lawyer! Carry on reading the next bit in Helm's report."

" 'After that, they told him he had sold his country, that the Grantees could bring an armed force into the country. Depose him and put another Chief in his place. Dig anywhere, in his kraals, garden and towns. The Chief sent for the copy of the Concession he had asked me to keep and sent for me to read and interpret it to him. I did and gave the same interpretation as at first. I told him the Concession said nothing about land, only about minerals in the land. That no power was given to the Grantees except to get gold out of the land and that necessarily the Grantees in his country had to abide by the laws of the country. It was simply nonsense to say that under the Concession the Grantees could do whatever they liked in the country.' "

"The thwarted concessionaires were not going to let the only opportunity they had to sink the Rudd Concession get away from them. They leapt onto the bandwagon, agreeing the King had given away his kingdom, that Helm had not told the truth about what was written and that the copy did not say the same as the original.

"Too easy! Particularly when the original document wasn't there and was inadequate anyway.

"John Moffat was very disturbed about the pressures on Lobengula.

"As for the British Government – it was simply furious! It was coping with a flood of letters and telegrams from enraged and disconsolate concession seekers. There had been many questions asked about Maguire's inclusion in the Rudd Concession anyway, and now his atrocious work was open for all to see."

Themba added, "So not only was the ultimate demise of the King brought about by the British, it was an Irishman who hammered the final nail into the coffin."

Nobody knew whether to laugh or cry.

Themba went on, "Another problem was that as you mentioned yesterday Mr Davidson, it had been agreed within South Africa that no guns were to be issued or sold to 'natives'. While the British Government was coping with that fall out as well, it was put forward that 'guns were less damaging than *assegais*'."

Angus looked serious. "I think Helm, and another missionary David Carnegie, did make one strange judgement. They wrote:
'the substitution of the long range rifle for the stabbing assegai would tend to diminish the loss of life in the Matebele raids and thus prove a distinct gain to the cause of humanity.'

"The British administrators agreed with what they said and with the amount of guns and ammunition which had been included in the Rudd Concession. Lobengula had actually been receiving guns for years . . . as we found out earlier, as a payment in guns had been a condition of entry the country since 1870 - a few months after his accession to the throne."

When they had pulled themselves together again after all that new information, Prune asked, "Where was the mention about the ten men?"

Angus handed him another of Helm's reports. "This is the only time it was mentioned – in a report to the London Missionary Society."
" *'The Grantees explained to the Chief that what was necessary to get out the gold was to erect dwellings for their overseers, to bring in and erect machinery – to use wood and water. They promised they would not bring more than ten white men to work in his country; they would not dig anywhere near towns etc., and that they and their people would abide by the laws of his country and in fact be as his people. But these were not put in the Concession'."*

"The question is: why wasn't it put into the Concession?

"Some say it was too complicated to include all the assurances made and that an Englishman's word is his bond—" Angus looked at Aidan expecting another expletive "—but there's an equally valid argument that Maguire had never practiced law anyway, and that he had precious little idea of what should be included in a legal document of this nature.

"Conspiracy theorists ever since have suggested there may have been a deliberate cover up. I don't think so.

"Here, Carol and Prune you can cross another item off your list– magnificent naiveté. Helm believed Rudd would keep his promises.

Outright felony and really bad movies.

"My question is, not whether the figure of ten men was mentioned, because it undoubtedly was, but how did the Company justify the settlement of Mashonaland with the Pioneer Column so soon afterwards? Uncomfortable questions. No definitive answers – there had to be more to it, so you dig deeper."

"This is more and more like a bad movie! What happened next?" Prune asked.

"Just to show you how impossible it is to arrive at the absolute truth, I have three versions of the same points found in my discovery process. You lot have been making me work hard!"

"Yes, but you love it Dad!"

Angus had to agree as he handed out the papers.

"Themba, you start."

"A few months after the signing, the faithful Lotshe who had recommended that Lobengula sign the concession, was condemned to death. He and 300 of his family were executed.

"Thompson, who was in that meeting with Lotshe and the King, was terrified that he would be next. So he buried the document in a pumpkin gourd with a little seed corn, so that in the event of his death, the growing corn would reveal its position to his Zulu servant Charlie. He was afraid that someone might get hold of it and tear it up.

"He then wrote a letter back to his family in England:

'After riding for hours in the blazing sun I had to make a hat by tying four knots in my handkerchief, and stuffing it with grass. Towards sundown I found myself in unknown country in the middle of the Kalahari Desert.'

'May I read that Mr Davidson?" Jabu asked.

He found himself acting out the part with exaggerated hand gestures.

" *'I had neither food nor water, and I might be attacked by lions. I tied my horse, climbed into a tree and there spent the night. The next day I rode until the horse knocked up, and then I walked. Walking and running, I covered thirty or forty miles. My tongue became swollen, and towards evening stuck out of my mouth. My eyes were so bloodshot that I could scarcely see and my breath was short.*

" *'I met some Makalaka natives cooking a pot of mealies, and from them, in exchange for my pocketknife, I bought some mealies to eat. Luckily I came upon a trader with a mule waggon. He gave me a lift to Macloutsie. Whereupon I met up with Jameson, who urged me to return to Matebeleland . . . to retrieve the document!'"*

"Apart from perhaps a little literary licence, and dramatics fit for a stage Jabu, the last thing poor old Thompson would have wanted would have been to return to Matebeleland. Carol, your version now."

" *'Rudd left immediately for the south with the Concession in his pocket and a request that he would bring up his 'big brother Rhodes' next time. Rudd apparently had the most terrible journey, for the waterholes across the Bechuana desert were dried up at that time of the year, and rains were later than usual in breaking. Had it not been for the help of some kindly Bechuanas who found him lying unconscious and gave him water from a buried ostrich egg, neither he nor the document would ever have been heard of again.'"*

Themba interrupted. "Well, that's wrong for a start, as they wouldn't have been Bechuanas. It would have been Bushmen who resuscitated him, because they're the ones who survive the desert by burying ostrich eggs filled with water."

"Well spotted."

Carol said, "I haven't quite finished. *'Rudd said he had hidden the precious concession in an ant-bear hole . . .'"*

Prune didn't want to be left out. " *'In that report that we read from Helm, he said he had the copy of the Rudd Concession and produced it for the King when asked to repeat what it said. And he did so again once the original was returned, so that Lobengula could compare them.'"*

Carol chimed in, " But my note says

'one of John Moffat's biographers said it was Moffat who had been given a copy of the document. Oh boy! You don't know which to believe.'"

"No, but the threads are there."

"Somebody or two somebody's were given a copy of the Concession"

"The original document was hidden in a pumpkin gourd by somebody and/or an ant-bear hole by somebody else!"

"And to cap it all," Jabu said scornfully, "two stupid people tried to cross the Bechuanaland desert in October – the hottest month of the year, before the rains come. Crazy!"

They were only now beginning to understand the frustration of trying to arrive at something near the truth.

26

AKUNGITSHIYE! LEAVE ME ALONE!

After a little rummaging around in the Inyati chapel kitchen Carol managed to produce six mugs of tea and some Eet-sum-mor shortbread biscuits. She carried them out to hear her father sounding serious.

"There was mayhem enough surrounding the Rudd Concession, but the next episode shocked me more than anything else.

"I don't know the full details of it all. But what I've found is appalling. It concerns a German concession seeker called Lippert – fiercely anti-British, and even more fiercely, anti-Rhodes. Arthur Keppel Jones in *Memories of Rhodesia* describes what I'm talking about, as:

'a long and complicated story of intrigue, cross-examination, bribery and judicial murder!'

"Lippert[89] read the Rudd Concession and afterwards, he wrote:

'I saw clearly that Rhodes could not show legal title to any land, and further, that in spite of all efforts, King Lobengula, already involved in a dispute with him arising from the previous concession, would refuse to give him an inch of ground. Here I intervened!'

"A reminder that the Rudd Concession had only asked for permission to prospect for minerals.

"Those rather chilling words *'Here I intervened . . .'* are exactly how this man Lippert seemed to work. First of all . . . he gained approval from Paul Kruger President of the Transvaal, to import dynamite. He then sold it to small miners and corporations at an exorbitant profit. There was outrage! A conference was held to demand Kruger to revoke his monopoly.

"It was dramatically disrupted when one of the small miners arrested

---

[89] Lippert Concession: APPENDIX 2

everyone's attention saying, trembling as he did so, that he had heard the voice of God.

God's message was that should Lippert's monopoly be revoked, disaster would befall the whole industry. The miner's belief was so absolute that it changed the tenor of the conference - and Lippert kept his monopoly.

"It was only weeks later when in a moment of careless bar-room talk, Lippert agreed he had indeed heard the voice as he was in the next-door bedroom. He then said, with mock surprise, that he was interested to note that God had a Cape Dutch accent!"

"You mean it was Lippert in the bedroom pretending to be God?" Prune was aghast!

Angus just shrugged his shoulders. "The lengths people will go to, to protect their interests is pretty disgusting Prune."

"As a German, opposed to the British and particularly to Rhodes and his success, he was, of course, hand in glove with the Voortrekkers."

"He had to have some redeeming features!"

"Just listen to this before you make any more judgements Aidan!" Angus was teasing . . . but he wanted them to understand the gravity of what happened next.

A blank sheet of paper

"Lippert apparently couldn't spare the time to see Lobengula, so he asked his agent, Renny-Tailyour to negotiate with the King's *indunas* for a concession, for as long as it took.

"After all the lies and mischief over the Rudd Concession, Lobengula did not want to see anyone, as you can imagine.

"First of all, Renny-Tailyour joined the chorus of hate determined to kill the Rudd Commission even though he had now spent several months in Bulawayo without seeing the King. Behind the scenes, he kept pestering key *indunas* . . . repeatedly telling them that Queen Victoria backed his request, and therefore it was important for him to see the King."

"Wouldn't Moffat have been saying the same thing?" Aidan asked.

"Absolutely! Moffat was right. Lippert's men were wrong! Telling whopping lies didn't seem to bother them at all.

"Lobengula called Moffat in to find out just who these people were.

"Moffat reassured the King that the Queen of England would never do anything in secret, and convinced him that these men were telling lies. But Lippert had plans to put himself in a position of such strength that Rhodes and the BSAC would be forced to negotiate with him.

"How he did it, ranks amongst the most nefarious deeds ever devised.

"Before talking to Moffat, Lobengula, bowing to the enthusiasm of his brainwashed *indunas*, fave Renny-Tailyour an audience, had even sent a letter to the Kaiser saying the British had robbed him of his land and asking for his intervention. He was persuaded that signing a concession with the Germans would weaken the Rudd case.

"Themba put your lawyer's hat on and read this next piece . . . slowly"

" *'One of Mr Lippert's team, Mr Renny-Tailyour, managed to convince Lobengula that he could not draw up the concession properly there, but would make sure it was correctly put together in Johannesburg. He offered two blank sheets of paper. One bore only the date, the elephant stamp, Induna Mshete's mark, and the signatures of Renny-Tailyour and two others, Acutt and Reilly."*

Themba's reading became slower and slower as he realised the implications of what he was reading.

"I don't believe that – I just don't believe it," he said, shaking his head. "Two blank sheets of paper. Who on earth signs a blank sheet of paper? Not Lobengula for a start – he would surely have known better."

"Vested interests," said Jabu in disgust. "You're right only Mshete would not have really understood what was happening. That is terrible.

Angus continued: "There was no missionary signature either and the King's elephant seal was very accessible in the drawer of a desk belonging to a trader called Fairbairn. This whole blank sheet was just mocked up."

Angus could hardly continue, as he felt his own anger rising.

"Those blank sheets of paper were given to a 'supposed' Advocate in Jo'burg who put together what Lobengula had 'apparently' agreed, all into 'the correct form'. What did that piece of paper suggest that the King had eventually given away, Jabu?"

Almost reluctantly, he reached for Mr Davidson's notebook:

" *'The sole and exclusive right and privilege for the full term of one hundred years, to lay out, grant or lease, for such periods as he may think fit, farms, townships, building plots and grazing areas, to impose and levy rents licenses and taxes; to get in, collect and receive the same, to give and grant certificates in my name for the occupation of any farms; to establish and to grant licenses for the establishment of banks; to issue bank-notes; to establish a mint . . . etc. etc. etc."*

Jabu's voice faded in disgust and despair, Angus concluded:

" *'In return, the price ultimately settled was one thousand pounds down and five hundred pounds a year.*

He paused, then read with anger in his voice: "after all this and much later, Lippert wrote:

' *. . . after many efforts my delegate succeeded in sending me a treaty with the king which granted to me all the rights asked for.'* "

There was no response from anyone – just a stunned silence.

"As had to be done with all legal documents, this concession was sent to Sir Henry Loch, British High Commissioner in Cape Town. Fortunately, he was immediately suspicious and sent it back to John Moffat to find out more.

"Moffat showed it to one of the signatories, Acutt, who simply said 'it contains very much more than was specified at that time'.

Moffat tried to find an opportunity to speak to Lobengula and show it to him, making sure he understood what he had given away.

He was not successful. Lobengula had had enough. To him now and despite his long family friendship, Moffat was British. He had had enough of the lies and deceptions of the British, the Germans and everyone else.

"I have copied some excerpts from Arthur Keppel Jones' book, which goes into more detail." He handed them out and gave them a minute to digest what article said.

"The more you read, the more you understand what Lippert intended. He followed up by saying he would appoint a man called Ferreira, described as a 'dubious character and penniless' to be the administrator of his yet unformed new company – if he took this letter to Kruger.

"Unsurprisingly, the Bechuanaland Police at Macloutsie arrested Ferreira, for many known and previous convictions!

They 'happened' to find Lippert's letter on him of course and unsurprisingly, this arrest also 'happened' to occur just as Dr Jameson arrived in Macloutsie, on his first trip up to Matebeleland!

"How convenient that they discovered it just as the new administrator of the British South Africa Company arrived?"

"Sounds like a letter from God!' Prune said with such melancholy in his voice that everybody had to laugh.

". . . or are our conspiracy theories runnin' a bit wild?" Aidan added.

"Sadly – probably not. Jameson would have read the letter in growing disbelief. Lippert had written that he was quite sure the concession would be ratified, that he'd obtain recognition by the Chartered Company and would Ferreira please go ahead . . . to do what Themba?"

". . . and shortly issue titles to 500 farms in Mashonaland. For the first 500 farms I have fixed the price at £5 for 3,000 morgen and £2 per annum. For the next 500 farms the price will of course, be raised . . ."

Themba couldn't go on. His eyes were wide as Angus continued, "Exactly. It is now widely acknowledged that the letter was written deliberately as bait to be 'discovered' by the Chartered Company. More important, did Lobengula ever actually see those blank sheets?

"The letter exactly achieved its objectives. This was when Dr Jameson demanded that Thompson of the swollen tongue, must turn round straight away and return with him to Matebeleland to rescue the original version of the Rudd Concession. The other was to telegraph Rhodes and tell him what he had found out about Lippert.

"Rhodes demanded a meeting, telling Lippert to bring a copy of the concession signed by Lobengula. Lippert told him the document was with the High Commissioner in Cape Town. The High Commissioner had already returned it to John Moffat."

They were gripped – and horrified - by what they were hearing.

Angus went on,

"When Jameson and Thompson got back to Bulawayo, the King called everyone together for days of discussion, accusation and counter-accusation still largely based around the Rudd Concession. Moffat had called Helm to ask him to go to the meeting. Your turn Carol.

" 'He asked me to read the copy of the Concession to his Indunas and the white men present. I did so - a long discussion ensued continuing till sunset. It resumed next morning and ended about 5 p.m. Mr. Thompson was asked what he told the Chief. He said " 'I told the Chief I had no cattle, no sheep; I want no land, I only want to seek for gold. And today I say the same.

"He offered to give them a written statement signed for himself and Messrs. Rudd and Maguire, denying that under the Concession they had any power to settle in the country and renewing promises as given before. But the opposition party (Lippert's group) strongly objected to receiving said statement. The same things were said over and over again for a day and a half."

"By now, the opposition was not only Lippert's lot but all those many thwarted concession seekers. They weren't going to allow Thompson to do anything that might show him in a good light – so they refused to accept or endorse a written statement that the Rudd Concession had no power in the country other than to dig for gold."

"So what's new . . .?" There was exasperation to Aidan's Irish lilt.

"When, at last, the original document was returned and handed to the King, to compare it with the copy held by Helm—"

"Or Moffat," Prune reminded him with a smirk.

"or Moffat," Angus conceded. " the King spent time comparing the two. Then he turned to the concession-seekers. Prune – here's a continuation of Helm's report."

" 'What have you got to say? There is the paper,' Their spokesman answered. 'King, this document is all right. We were wrong in all we said.' With a smile on his face the king looked at them, and rubbing his hand across his mouth, he said, 'Tomoson, has rubbed fat on your mouths. All white men are liars. Tomoson, you have lied the least.' "

"So there we go – those who had been tryin' to wreck the whole thing smiled sweetly and said 'we were wrong'. No bloody apology!"

Jabu shook his head in dismay. "It is no wonder Lobengula is documented as crying out '*Akungitshiye!*' – 'Leave me alone!'"

Prune and Carol slipped out to make up a fire and prepare sausages for the braai as Angus continued. He was becoming concerned by the growing resentment between Jabu and Themba, and wanted to be sure they had a very clear picture of what had taken place.

"I'd love to say this was the end, but it was only the beginning. It went on to involve so many, from the highest echelons of British Government to Queen Victoria herself. Backbiting, misrepresentation, plots and counter plots, duplicity, filibusters, Voortrekkers trying to get rid of Lobengula and support a senior *induna* called Gambo, British Government asking whether Lobengula really did have rights over Mashonaland anyway - then deciding he did – not for the sake of the people, I hasten to add, but because they didn't want the Portuguese stealing the Mazoe area!

"Lippert in the meantime got the ear of the press and said if Rhodes did not negotiate with him, he'd take out a full page advertisement offering land and leases to the Voortrekkers.

He knew, and Rhodes knew, that if he did so there would be such a rush that the Chartered Company would be finished anyway.

"That could not be allowed to happen and for the first time Rhodes and the British Government agreed, the Boers would be allowed no access.

"Using another of Rhodes' quotes, he does show concern, as he wanted:

"*to secure the cautious development of the country with a proper consideration for the feelings and prejudices of the natives.*'

"Alfred Beit, a long-time partner of Rhodes, advised him to negotiate rather than fight Lippert. Rhodes agreed to do so, provided Lippert went back to Lobengula to get the concession properly agreed and ratified. The King still thinking he was dealing with the Germans and that this might weaken the grip of the British, accepted – and signed.

281

"The King didn't know that Lippert was already in discussion with Rhodes. And Lippert was not going to tell him.

"John Moffat, as Resident employed by Her Majesty's Government, was ordered to be present when this re-signing took place. He wrote to the High Commissioner, saying the deceit was utterly detestable, whether viewed in the light of policy or morality.

"'It was very much against my will to be present.'"

"Moffat lost his job and position as a result."

27

IRISH, ENGLISH AND A ROYAL VISIT

After the revelations of the day, Aidan felt drained by the disrespect shown to the Matebele King – particularly by the British.

"I tell you, what's new? Nothin' – absolutely bloomin' nothin'." Aidan shrugged his shoulders helplessly.

"You've obviously had experience, Aidan!" Themba laughed.

"I'm Irish, my friend. Believe me, they're a manky lot. Around the time we're talking – that's the mid-1800s – our tenant farmers couldn't provide for their families, let alone sell anything elsewhere. And they were living at subsistence level. So we became dependent on the most nourishing and easiest crop to grow – potatoes.

"Then this feek – which ironically means 'a beautiful girl' by the way – called Phytophthora blight killed the whole crop for about five years. We were a part of Britain at that time, and the British government did nothin' at all to stop us starvin'. The peasants couldn't pay their rent; the landlords ran out of money; hundreds of thousands of Irish farmers and labourers were evicted.

"We lost nearly two million people. About a million died of starvation or typhus, and the rest went wherever they could to get a job. Believe me, you can't be Irish, especially an Irish Catholic, and trust the British to look after their own people . . . let alone bother about anyone in the colonies."

Themba and Jabu were bemused to hear this side of things.

"And what's more, there's huge trouble brewin' in Ireland, which is why I left. The Protestants don't give the Catholics a chance!"

Angus intervened: "It would be interesting to talk about the Irish problems tonight, Aidan, but let's just finish this off quickly.

"Lobengula, had granted the Rudd Concession, repudiated it, and finally accepted it again, and was gracious enough to work with the BSAC once he was satisfied that it was the best way. He went on to do everything possible to make the entry of the Pioneer Column smooth and uneventful."

"However, there was one more twist to the tale while we're waiting for the braai to cook – a man called Maund. He'd just been sent by Sir Sidney Shippard to tell the King about the formation of the Bechuanaland Protectorate and to reassure the Matebele of the continuing loyalty of the British Crown. Maund suggested the King might also consider asking to become a protectorate of the Queen of England.

"How different we'd have been today if we had done so.

"But don't forget, King Lobengula was no King Khama, and the peaceful Bamangwato people were most certainly not the Matebele!

"King Khama had needed Queen Victoria's protection from both Boers and Matebele. With British troops looking after Bechuanaland's interests, he knew that there'd be a secure border between them."

"Are we supposed to remember all this Dad?" Carol asked nervously.

"Remember what you can. I'm just giving you an idea of the chaos of the time, and I'm not including even half of it!"

Angus grew serious. "Matebeleland was like a sickness. This man Maund, having been sent on government business to inform Lobengula, then joined the concession seekers – and turned out to be one of the most troublesome of all!

". . . and I said I still had one burning question that made me feel uneasy about the Rudd Concession."

Prune, Carol, Aidan and Themba looked mystified, but Jabu said quietly: "Ten white men."

"Ten white men – correct." Angus nodded. "How did the Chartered Company justify the Pioneer Column? It did the right thing by skirting Matebeleland and headed to Mashonaland along a carefully planned route designed not to interfere with any Matebele villages. But there were over 400 men in that Column! How did that happen?

"The British Government was still dealing with angry concession-seekers and the fall-out from the Rudd Concession. They were, at last, about to agree to a Royal Charter based on the East India Company.

"But something was holding it back."

Just pay them out Rhodes . . . just pay them out!

"Now listen! Rhodes was ordered, by Her Majesty's Government 'to make good' the losses of concession-seekers. So, a couple of questions . . .

"Was this an unwritten condition – to take place before, or after, the granting of a Charter? Was this why Rhodes did buy out the smaller concession seekers, none of which would have been of the slightest advantage to the Chartered Company? Most had no concessions anyway, but they were still making a nuisance of themselves."

Angus asked another rhetorical question: "Was this why Rhodes was eventually forced to buy out the bigger players like Maund and Lippert as well? When both concessions were proved to be completely false anyway? Orders from above? Or perhaps, with his history of buying up the competition, did he spot an opportunity?

"Somewhere in all of that, there is Dr Jameson. He was a man whom Lobengula admired to the extent that he made him an *induna* of the Imbezu regiment. He was as driven as Rhodes, but he had a mercurial and unpredictable side to him, and that became a problem.

"He asked Lobengula for 'the road' into Mashonaland, assuring him they would not touch Matebele territory. Anecdotal evidence portrays Jameson as hectoring the King until, sick and tired of it all, Lobengula waved him away."

Angus gave a dismissive wave of his hand.

"Jameson took that to mean he had agreed. He immediately set about organising the Pioneer Column. I can only find that the ten men became 400 on that flimsy pretext as well, of course, as by gaining the settlement conditions detailed in the Lippert concession."

Angus was overcome by the emotion of revisiting these events.

But Themba wasn't finished yet.

"Mr Davidson, you mentioned Maund and said he was important, but we haven't heard about him yet."

"OK, last one. Maund was important. When Sir Sidney Shippard sent Maund up, he wrote to Moffat warning him that, in his eyes, Maund was a 'mendacious adventurer' and a 'dangerous man'."

"So why on earth did he send him? What stupidity!" Carol burst out.

"Administrators were pretty thin on the ground . . . there was probably nobody else available to go."

"Whatever the situation, Maund managed to persuade an influential member of the British aristocracy, Lord Gifford, that he was the man to try for a concession on their behalf, for land in Mazoe.

"Lobengula must have been fed up at Maund's change from advisor from Shippard, to irritating concession-seeker.

"He said he'd consider it – on one condition – that Maund took two senior *indunas* to England to see if there really was a White Queen, because he didn't know whether to believe those who said there was or those who said there wasn't.

"Maund said he'd be delighted. He would organise it and be back in three months to collect the *indunas*. The King said, 'The *indunas* will be waiting for you to take them tomorrow morning.'"

They all laughed, but rumbling tummies and the need to get to Shiloh to make camp were becoming an imperative.

Angus saw Tony Browne approaching and got up to bid him farewell. He returned and said, "Tony suggests we stay here instead of going on to Shiloh. The schoolchildren have all gone home for the holidays, so he's offered us the assembly hall to put our sleeping bags in."

There was relief all round, Tony was invited to join them for the braai.

"Can I tell an Irish joke or two then?"

"You can indeed, but we'll have our braai first, Aidan!"

And so they did.

Soon they were seated, eating sausages squashed between the crusts of a stiff roll prettied up with a leaf of heat-wilted lettuce and the mandatory circle of tomato. After a day of surprisingly raw emotion, it was good to be friends again – eating together, laughing and chatting.

To London, to London to visit the Queen

"I can't wait to hear about the *indunas* going to England," said Aidan, "come on Mr Davidson, what happened?"

Angus finished his roll and took a long drink from his Castle lager. He'd brought enough for all of them - the first taste of European beer for

Prune and Themba. They soon got used to it!

"As promised, the two *indunas* were waiting for him the next day. Do you know their names, Jabu?"

"Babjaan and Mshete."

"Babjaan and Mshete . . . with Maund and Johann Colenbrander, as interpreter, went to England to see the Queen - without an appointment! It was pure luck that on the ship, they found someone from a strategic political position in Britain. This man was able at short notice, to arrange for a special ceremonial dinner at Windsor and he met them in London bearing an invitation from Queen Victoria herself!

"Maund had a rambling letter - purported to be from King Lobengula, decrying Portuguese interests, stating his boundaries and making a pointed reference to 'my country on the Mazoe river'."

"Wasn't that where Maund was trying to negotiate a concession?"

Angus just smiled, raised his eyebrows and nodded, waving another piece of paper in the air. "Unknown to Maund, the *indunas* had their own letter for the Queen." Carol reached over, and read:

" '*Lobengula desires to know that there is a Queen. Some of the people who come into this land tell him there is a Queen some tell him there is not. Lobengula can only find out the truth by sending eyes to see whether there is a Queen. The Indunas are his eyes. 'Lobengula desires to ask her advice to help him, as he is much troubled by white men who come into his country and ask to dig gold.'*

"The Queen would have been as confused as anyone else!" Carol shook her head.

"And Maund must have felt very awkward that he didn't know about their letter!" Themba burst out. "It seems to me that Lobengula was really only interested in one thing – was there a white Queen? Somehow all that stuff about the Portuguese doesn't quite fit into the envoys visit."

"You're right Themba, Maund was a chancer and he was not going to miss an opportunity to mention his particular demand – I suspect his letter was quietly side-lined.

"But, there was one important thing Maund did do, and that was to keep a diary[90] of everything that happened, so we have a very clear picture of what must have been an astonishing event for the *indunas*. And for everybody who met them, too!

---

[90] Maund and the indunas to London: see APPENDIX 3

"So finish your meal, settle down, enjoy this glorious starry evening and we will all share this wonderful description of an extraordinary event.

"To set the scene, the Indunas set off wearing loincloths of skin and carrying shields, small spears and knobkerries. Any other possessions were tied up in a small bundle. Maund's report continues:

" '*I rushed them into a store and clothed them in neat suits of blue serge. On getting into the train at Kimberley a decided look of horror came into their eyes as they began to rush forward. I turned around to Babjaan and said, 'What! a King's soldier and afraid!' On which, to show that he was not, he put his head out of the window and kept it there for half an hour, much to my concern, for I was afraid it might come in contact with something.*'

"Jabu, you'll appreciate this bit once they boarded the ship."

" '*They went into raptures over the incoming waves, likening the rollers dashing in to the shore to the columns of Impis rushing up to the King at a review. They called the steamer, 'the great kraal that pushes through the water' and when we got into rough weather in the Bay, they said, 'the river is full to-day.*'

" '*Off Lisbon, when told it was Portuguese, they sat on deck with their backs turned to the land, and said: 'How is it the White Queen allows Portugal between her and Africa?*'"

Themba couldn't wait, and picked up the reading.

" '*The Indunas travelled to Windsor in royal carriages awaiting them at the station. The Queen had considerately sent four picked men of the 2nd Life Guards, who lined the approaches to St. George's Hall.*

"*The Indunas were astonished at the immobility of the soldiers. They concluded they were stuffed, until one of them saw their eyes moving.*

"*On the conclusion of the interview, Her Majesty said: 'You have come a very long way to see me; I hope the journey has been made pleasant for you, and you did not suffer from the cold.' In acknowledgment, one of them stepped forward, bowing with truly courtier-like gesture, and replied, 'How should we feel cold in the presence of the great White Queen?' adding 'Is it not in the power of great kings and queens to make it hot or cold?'*

"*It was easy they declared . . . to recognise which was the White Queen, from her manner and bearing.*'"

Carol hugged herself with delight at the colourful descriptions and demanded her turn too.

" 'They were taken to see the lions at the Zoological Gardens. Their excitement was intense. When they came to these animals Babjaan could scarcely be restrained from attacking one of the lords of his native forest with his umbrella, nor could he understand why he was prevented.' "

Jabu's face broke into a huge smile.

"What most astonished them was the telephone. They were placed a mile apart, and talked together. Afterwards they declared that they could imagine such a machine might talk English, but how it could be taught to speak Sindebele they could not understand!"

Prune could hardly contain his impatience. "My turn please!"

" 'As the grand finale to the sightseeing, the Indunas were taken to Aldershot, where a sham fight and inspection was held in which about 10,000 men of all arms were engaged. Babjaan and Umshete were almost mad with excitement. Standing on their seats they eagerly watched every movement. 'Such mighty horses – so big, so strong, and such discipline among the men,' exclaimed Babjaan. 'Come and teach us how to drill and fight like that, and we will fear no nation in Africa."

"OK Aidan, we won't leave you out!"

"Finally! Thank you Mr Davidson!

"'. . . the Indunas were taken over the Bank of England. On being allowed to lift bags of gold the Indunas remarked that it made their hearts sick to see so much gold, which they could not put into their pockets. At this point one of the Indunas wished it to be remembered that when their King received any distinguished visitor, he showed him his flocks and herds, selecting the largest beast to present to the stranger. The hint was not taken.' "

"They could have given them just a small bar of gold!" Carol was indignant.

Angus went on:

"The envoys had their final meeting with Lord Knutsford, the Secretary of State for the Colonies, at the Colonial Office on 26th March. He presented each of them with a ram's horn snuffbox mounted in silver and a large portrait of the Queen for King Lobengula. He also gave them a letter to take back to the King. It started off by saying:

"A King gives a stranger an ox, not his whole herd of cattle, otherwise what would other strangers arriving have to eat? The Queen sends LoBengula a picture of herself to remind him of this message, and that he may be assured that the Queen wishes him peace and order in his country. The Queen thanks LoBengula for the kindness which, *following the example of his father, he has shown to many Englishmen visiting and living in Matebeleland.*

Angus looked at the group and laughed, saying: "Now this is the best bit of all!

"Before their departure the next morning, the envoys decided on an early night while Maund went to the theatre. During the interval, he had a call from the hotel, requiring him to return urgently.

"Babjaan had caused great consternation in the hotel lounge:

"'*by searching, stark naked, for his snuffbox, which he had left there! To make matters worse, the Induna couldn't find his snuffbox immediately, as it had fallen beneath a table, from where he proceeded to retrieve it on his hands and knees. The society ladies and gentlemen in the crowded lounge were stunned to silence!*'"

"Begorrah! I'd have given me back teeth to see the looks on those stuck-up English faces. Brilliant!"

They were doubled up with laughter imagining the consternation it would have caused in the cloistered gentility of a five-star London hotel lounge when the very upper-class patrons spied a naked African man crawling under the table. Most of them would have never seen anybody black – let alone naked!

"Chief Babjaan would have had no idea of the consternation he left behind him. It must have been hilarious!"

"And can you imagine what they'd have said had they been able to understand his parting comment. Aidan finish it off"

"*He returned to his room mutterin' that one of the ladies had helped herself to some of his snuff.*"

This prompted another howl of laughter. Aidan turned round to Jabu and said,

"Tell you what Jabu, I'd have shaken that man's hand, naked or not!"

It had been a thoroughly satisfactory conclusion to the evening. As they all went off to bed, Prune had another reason to be happy. He was writing 'snuffbox' in his notebook to remind him of Babjaan and Mshete.

He added three new words to his memory: nefarious, obfuscation and scurrilous.

Kind of summed up the whole day really

28

… AND SO IT ENDS.

Waking up this morning, there was that unmistakable smell of dampened earth as cracked ground slaked its drought parched thirst. It sent out the welcome message 'at last, we've had our first real rains.' How could you ever forget it! Wet, fresh, invigorating. You could almost hear the plants growing after two downpours in as many days.

Tonight, flying ants would start fluttering in follow-my-leader swarms. They'd live out their few hours of existence dancing in lamp light, before wings and little brown bodies piled up against obstacles in their path.

"I'll have to introduce Aidan to those delicious fried flying ants tomorrow – looks as though that rain has produced a good crop."

"No thanks, Jabu. I've done some weird things in Africa, but eating ants is not going to be one of them."

"Just you wait. They're not really ants, they're fat little termites."

"O yuck, that sounds worse!"

"Bacon and egg rolls anyone?"

"As long as they're not a cover for ants . . ."

Angus watched the easy friendship between these young people, and his hopes for the future of the country rose. It had such incredible potential, but it was so precariously balanced.

His head buzzed with the challenges ahead – the burgeoning population, the nightmare of the land question, the education demands. They seemed endless. He felt battered after the dissolution of the African Affairs Board, and now, an extra twinge of anxiety about Nkanyiso's concerns for Jabulani. He looked over at him, wondering what circles of influence he was moving in.

He turned away to see Tony Browne walking towards them.

Angus walked up, only to become even more disheartened when Tony asked if he'd heard about trouble in the Government. The Cabinet was about to resign, because members felt they couldn't trust Garfield Todd's more liberal views.

"It's pretty underhand" Tony said, trying to understand and explain what was going on "particularly as Mr Todd is in England at present."

"I didn't realise he was away. I was hoping to call in at Hokonui Ranch to see him on our way home." Angus in turn, shared his news about the African Affairs Board.

"Oh no – I'm particularly sad about that," Tony sympathised. "You were achieving important changes with that Board. Unfortunately, like Todd, you've come up against a toughening of attitude that I find is happening more and more. Why, and where it's heading, heaven knows."

Angus shook his head in gloomy agreement. "Despite everything we've been through, we've had a steady thirty plus years as a self-governing colony, since the demise of the Chartered Company, and largely with a wonderfully co-operative spirit between the races.

"It's been heartening to see strides being made in education, health, agriculture and African development. We have an opportunity to see this country open up to what it should be – but if Garfield goes . . . we could all, white and black, lose the advances we've made."

They walked back to find Themba holding the floor. He seemed to be the most stirred up of all of them about yesterday's discussions.

With the others sitting on the ground eating their breakfast, Themba was standing gesticulating as he spoke with frustrated determination.

"King Lobengula was a great man, but the tragedy, as you said Carol, is that he came into conflict with another great man. Imagine how different things could have been if only they'd met.

"I never thought he was a weak King. And what we have talked about in the last couple of days has shown he was anything but . . . how on earth he kept his *impi*, particularly those more militant Imbizo, Ingubo and Insuka regiments from completely wiping out the small number of whites in the country before the Matebele rebellion, I just can't imagine."

"If that Captain Lendy had given them half a chance we'd never have lost as many as we did during the Matebele Wars," Prune spoke gloomily.

As he sat down, Angus added, " . . . and realistically, we might have had tens of thousands killed had the fury of the British Empire descended on us seeking revenge for murders particularly, of their sons of aristocracy.

"Don't forget Babjaan and Mshete had had a taste of the military might Britain could and would turn out should the need arise. The King would have listened to them very carefully."

"I suppose there were some white people who cared about the King."

"I think there were an awful lot of people who cared about him, Jabu. There is hardly a report written by missionary, trader or hunter that doesn't talk of Lobengula with respect and even affection. In fact Aidan, this is something that would interest you."

Angus riffled through his papers and pulled one out, thankful that it might just help to recapture the light-hearted mood of last night.

"It's just one of many notes about what happened at the White Man's Camp one year when they were celebrating St. Patrick's Day. A Mr Doyle told King Lobengula all about St Patrick driving the snakes out of Ireland. The King was very interested and said St Patrick must have been a wonderful man. He liked the white man's custom of remembrance. There's a colourful description you might like to read."

"Oh I would," exclaimed Aidan.

"Lobengula then declared his willingness and pleasure to join us in drinking to the memory of St. Patrick. The champagne and glasses were produced, and soon corks were flying round the royal quarters. Three small bottles were then placed before the king, who, seated in his arm-chair in front of us, gravely drank them off one after the other without a wink, graciously bendin' his head and mentionin' St. Patrick's name before each one."

"Well I have to say if I didn't particularly think about the King before, now I love the guy! He's one of us after all!"

The mood was positive again – matching the glorious fresh-after-the-rains morning.

"When was the Charter actually granted Dad? I need that information for my exam."

"15th October 1889." Carol and Themba made notes.

"The B.S.A. Company requested that the Colonial Office arrange for a letter from Lord Knutsford to be specially delivered by hand. "He wrote:

> "'The Queen has made the fullest inquiries into the particular circumstances of Matebeleland, and believes it would be better for you to deal with one approved body of white men, who will consult LoBengula's wishes and arrange where white people are to dig, and who will be responsible to the Chief for any annoyance or trouble caused to himself or his people.
>
> " 'The Queen, therefore, approves of the concessions made by LoBengula to some white men who were represented in his country by Messrs. Rudd, Maguire, and Thompson. The Queen has caused inquiry to be made respecting these persons, and is satisfied that they are men who will fulfil their undertakings, and who may be trusted to carry out the working for gold in the Chief's country without molesting his people, or in any way interfering with their kraals, gardens, or cattle.'

"Two officers had set sail from Southampton for Cape Town and once they reached Kimberley by train, a magnificent four-wheeled coach painted red and yellow with the insignia "VR" and a crown in gold paint was unloaded. By January 1890, it had been drawn up to Tati by four mules, and was then escorted to Bulawayo by a troupe of Horse Guards.

"Queen Victoria sent several presents to the King – a revolver and case, field glasses, sporting knives and blankets. He was intrigued by the breastplates and helmets of the Horse Guards as he hadn't quite believed Babjaan when he told him they wore iron. The breastplates also kept the Matebele Queens intrigued, peeping at their reflections with many giggles.

"One of the Officers, Captain Ferguson, presented Lobengula with his full dress uniform when he left, as the King had admired it so much."

Aidan was shaking his head.

"That's all very interestin' and I don't know if I keep missing the point here," he said, "but didn't this same Lord advise Lobengula to give a visitor an ox, not the whole herd? Here he is saying he should put all his eggs in one basket – the complete opposite."

"You're not missing any points, Aidan. Lobengula must have been very confused – he'd responded to Lord Knutsford's first letter confirming Babjaan and Mshete's message to him understanding that

"'The Queen says I am not to let anyone dig for gold in my country except to dig for me.'" Something else for you to think about . . . but we do need to be moving shortly, as I'd like to see two sites on our way up to the 'nThaba zikaMambo – the Umguza and the Shangani. This is your country Jabu. And it will fill out our picture to hear about your initiation. That should give Carol and Themba information enough to fire their imaginations and give them both the highest of high distinctions!"

Always recap - then move on

"Dad, you've always said it was good to recap before you move on. We did so much yesterday that I'd appreciate getting things straight first."

Angus smiled indulgently.

"You're right my girl, hang fire for a moment Jabu, and let's look at Lobengula first. Right everyone . . .from when we started was Lobengula a weak King over-ridden by Jameson, Rudd and Rhodes or not?

"OK!" Carol said with a bravado she didn't feel. "He was an absolute ruler who used savagery to manage a savage people because that was what they knew. But they were a disciplined and orderly people with sound traditional cultures in cattle management, spiritual life and family structures. They respected courage and his people were absolutely loyal to Lobengula – as he was to them."

"I didn't realise he was so wise and clever," Prune followed. "And his leadership was amazing in difficult times. He was able to control his people and say 'no more raiding' because the missionaries said it should stop. He was able to control his regiments when more and more white people came into the country. I still think that is amazing. Some people said things took too long to happen – well white man's clock is faster than ours! He took things carefully and didn't break promises I don't think."

"I had no idea about his early life either, or that he was trained by Mlimo." Jabu was choosing his words carefully. "We were told he was in the highest rank of *sangoma* – second only to Mlimo himself. But I didn't understand this had happened because he was in hiding or that he was not accepted into the royal enclosures. It's given me a lot to think about.

"I am not really comfortable that the King enjoyed being with white people. He might have been persuaded to give away too much. I don't remember being told about him riding horses or hunting with white men. And certainly not about having a white person as his nanny. I remember being a bit irritated by a quote I saw when I was still at school. In fact, you quoted a bit from the same letter from 'Matebele' Wilson earlier on:

"'*If ever a native deserved to be called the white man's friend, it was Lobengula . . . May his spirit still have a good time fluttering over the country he once ruled.'* "

"All right, let's follow that . . . he might have been the white man's friend, Jabu, but was he the black man's friend? Themba, your thoughts?"

"Oh yes, he was. Definitely. It does sound as though he enjoyed the white man's world, but he didn't know enough about how it operated. He must have been disheartened by broken promises, trickery and devious ways. He did know his own world – the Matebele world – but he also knew it had changed and if they were going to survive, they'd have to change even more whether they liked it or not. The tragedy is that he was besieged by greed on all sides. He had no easy way out."

"You want a comment from me?" Aidan asked in surprise as Angus looked across to him and nodded.

"Look, I really don't know enough about it. But perhaps the biggest surprise to me is that this all happened *less than 70 years ago.*

"Britain had its own tribal savagery of course, very similar to what we've been talking about – particularly those wild Scots. But that was thousands of years ago. I suppose, in their own way, the Danes and Romans brought civilisation and democracy to our woad-painted Celts and we should be thankful for that. But that was so long ago that I feel no connection with them.

"In Southern Rhodesia, your connection to your past history is only a couple of generations away – your grandfathers and great-grandfathers! People you could have known. That's staggerin' . . . really. I know I've gone away from Lobengula a bit, but I agree he was a great African King caught in change that was happening terrifyingly fast."

Everyone fell silent. Aidan's viewpoint had brought a new and rather challenging perspective.

"OK. What about Helm?"

Carol started slowly. "He seemed to have the interests of the Matebele people at heart. Perhaps he was a bit naïve?

Themba added: "I know what you mean now, by another of those headings you gave Carol and Prune - magnificent naiveté. If you live in a

Christian bubble, surrounded by other Christians, you believe, or at least hope for, the best in people. When Rudd said there would only be ten white men, I bet Helm believed that's what he meant.

"Jabu?"

"It's hard because we have always been told Helm was the main problem in all this and it is always useful to have someone to blame. But I have to say that with all that background on Lippert, I am beginning to wonder why we blame the Rudd concession, not the Lippert Concession. I do think that the statement by Helm about guns not assegais was a bit odd though!"

"OK – so where were the worst mistakes made?"

"Treating us like chimpanzees." Jabu was quick off the mark. "Thinking we'd never be as good as them. And the stealing of Lobengula's gold by those two white troopers, just when he was wanting to go back and talk. If they'd only given that message to Jameson, things might have been very different."

Themba was almost as quick to follow.

"Something we haven't covered in detail yet but it has been bothering me . . . you mentioned Jameson demanded that Lobengula 'give them the road' – then the King's dismissive wave of the hand as being a sign that he didn't mind the Pioneer Column going up to Mashonaland. That should surely have been agreed upon, documented, witnessed by a missionary and counter-signed . . . or something like that. What made Jameson think he could just do it?"

Carol added: "Themba, Jameson thought he could 'just do it' in the Jameson Raid as well. He went ahead against the Boers without waiting for confirmation from the Cape Government. He should have stuck to medicine. And Rhodes should never have allowed him to take a powerful administrative role. For my money, Jameson was a big problem.

"But I also think Lobengula's decision to burn his capital and head north was a dreadful mistake. He was a brave man, and even if he was concerned about his own life because the *indunas* he sent down to see the High Commissioner were killed, I think he should have had more negotiations with Jameson first."

"I feel overwhelmingly sad – and angry – that Rhodes never took the time to come and see the King . . . there should never have been any excuse for the war to start." Themba agreed.

"Interestingly though, one of the things we heard as kids about the Matebele Rebellion was that Mkwati promised that there would be rain after a long drought in return for white man's blood, but that the bleeding must not start before the full moon," Jabu reminded him.

"That's right! I'd forgotten that."

"The *impi* were so fired up that they didn't wait for the full moon. They started the killing about a week early. Then it rained all right – after the bleeding of <u>our</u> blood. Our people took it as a sign that they would have won and thrown the white people out if they had waited for the full moon. From the Matebele point of view, that was a bad mistake."

"On the other hand," Themba said, "I wonder whether Lobengula and the British South Africa Company could have co-existed peacefully." Themba's heart was heavy considering these missed opportunities.

"What about Rhodes? Were his decisions right?

Prune wasn't going to be left out of this bit of the discussion.

"Rhodes felt he could do everything Mr Davidson – Prime Minister of the Cape; running huge companies like de Beers; in charge of everything to do with the Chartered Company; working on taking us over and negotiating for countries up as far as Lake Victoria as well as moving the Mozambique border. Building an Empire was just another business to him. He must have ridden roughshod over a lot of people."

Themba agreed. He pulled out a piece of paper at the back of his notebook. "He set up the Chartered Company, but didn't have enough money to do it himself, so he turned it into a business and paid dividends to investors. Investors eventually call the tune. It sounds as though he employed people he trusted, but who were not as good as he was. Listen how fed up Rhodes sounds in this letter to two of his employees:

"*We have settled with Maund at the request of H.M. Government so as to have no opposition in interior they will then I believe support Concession. You must work with him and we leave all details to your mutual brains I think you should read my old letter of instructions to you to him and in case faulty, amend as you all think best.*

"*You will be a Council - for goodness sake pull together or you will bogle all.*"

"For goodness' sake, pull together!" Carol repeated. "He was fed up!

It's ridiculous to think one man could do all that, especially with people he wasn't sure could do what he wanted."

The conversation was flowing fast now. Prune was on a roll.

"I've done more research. Rhodes wrote to Thompson when Jameson was on his way for his first visit to Bulawayo.

"I should have accompanied Jameson but I have to deal with the following:

(1) Sir S. Shippard

(2) the police question to which I am contributing

(3) Home Board of Charter

(4) Extension of railway and relations with Sprigg

(5) Extension of telegraph Mafeking to Tati for which I am paying

(6) Amalgamation with Bechuana Co

(7) Negotiations with Paul Kruger to arrange giving up all claims to the north.

"If I were to isolate myself in the interior at this moment the whole of the base would go wrong. Yours truly, C. J. Rhodes"

"No excuse" growled Jabu. "I agree that he had far too much on his plate. But how can you justify the terrible cost to us?"

Prune didn't seem to hear.

Jabu found himself withdrawing from the conversation. He wasn't sure where anyone's loyalties lay any more – even Aidan's. He felt more and more isolated.

"Mr Davidson," said Prune again. "Rhodes didn't do his feasibility studies – he just barged in. I know he was sick and he felt time was short, but I'm angry with him that he achieved so much but trampled on us and treated us badly, with little consideration. Once he had talked to the Chiefs at the *Indaba*, he changed completely. Why couldn't he have done that sooner?"

Prune sat back, suddenly feeling abashed for having taken up so much time with all these clever people around.

"Having said that Prune, he was honoured and admired, and not only by the whites – he was revered by blacks too. At his funeral, space was made for 500 Matebele to attend at the top of World's View. The man responsible for organising the whole thing was Marshall Hole, and he had to think quickly when over 3,000 came up.

"Africans always revere their Chiefs – and Rhodes had become the Chief to them." The words came as a growl from Jabu.

299

"As the coffin was being lowered into the granite, don't forget it was your grandfather Mtjaan, Jabu, who stood and gave that great cry of '*Bayete*!' This was followed by a tremendous roar from all the Matebele present. That word had not been heard in the Matebele kingdom since Mzilikazi's death. As the ceremony ended, once again a great roar of '*Bayete*' echoed round the Matopos.

"Tony do you have anything to add?"

Tony sat quietly for a moment. "I am fascinated by what you've discovered. And if you two don't get Distinctions in your A-level exams, there is something very wrong with the system. I think our greatest challenges as a nation lie ahead of us. This Federation is not working – it was cobbled together by the British to solve their problems, not ours.

"Ghana will get its independence in a couple of years – but that country has had hundreds of years more exposure to democracy and trading that we have – so our people have so much more to learn. Others countries will follow.

"Are we patient enough to understand how much more needs to be done here or will we want to be the same as them, and push for independence now? You five, I include you in this, Aidan, because your ideas are fresh and new and you see our peculiarities clearly – you five will determine whether we succeed or fail."

Aware it was getting late and wanting to end on a positive note before they left for the Umguza and 'nThaba zikaMambo, Angus said, "Were there any heroes?"

"Lobengula himself."

"Mtjaan!"

"The Missionaries . . . including Charles Helm!" There was a wry smile from Jabu.

"Selous!"

"Robert and John Moffat."

"Babjaan and Mshete."

"Chief Mncumbata and Sarah Liebenberg."

"Len Harvey and his Tuli cattle."

"Jameson was an exceptional doctor – a bit irresponsible perhaps."

"Godwane Ndiweni and Mzilikazi himself of course."

"Garfield Todd."

"I almost hate to say it in this company, and it's really against everything I believe about the British," Aidan spoke up, "but as you've already asked my opinion, Mr Davidson, that whole Pioneer Column was made up of heroes – they must have been extraordinary men who went on to do a lot for the country."

Angus laughed. "You're right, Aidan. They were extraordinary men and have been largely unappreciated since."

Themba said, "And Rhodes . . . he was a hero certainly at the *Indaba* and in paying for lots of things that happened, such as the railway and roads and banks and post offices . . ."

Carol had kept quiet, but now she added, "There was also amazing heroism during the Matebele wars, with white and black equally commending the courage of the other."

Angus brought the discussion to a close. "In an ideal world, all loss of life is unnecessary . . . but let's not forget the heroism of your own grandfathers, Jabu and Themba. Prune, we'll find yours one day, and I'm sure he will prove to have been just as much of a hero."

"Thank you, Mr Davidson! And I have always meant to thank you for all the time you took trying to find out about my mother when I was born. I think you are a hero for the work you do for the African people. You think like us, and you want to do the best for us. So I put your name in as a hero."

Angus smiled his thanks and Tony said, "I quite agree. Carol, you have a remarkable father."

Carol was so pleased.

The final straw and Jabu snaps.

Angus stepped in again. "Jabu your grandfather Mtjaan was a real hero – a man of unmatched courage and leadership. And, after all, he was Lobengula's most senior *induna*. I wish we had more information on that man, because he was certainly as intelligent and far-sighted as Lobengula.

"Themba—" Angus turned to look at him "—your grandfather Motshodi was legendary. Saving those children in the Magaliesberg and

301

taking them to Moffat was a big enough story in itself, but the work he did for Khama and the Chartered Company as Jan Grootboom was a stunning story . . ." He trailed off seeing a stricken look on Themba's face.

He turned and saw the thunder on Jabu's face as he slowly rose to stand menacingly over Themba.

"I knew I'd never liked you Themba," Jabu spat the words out robotically "but I never knew why.

"Your grandfather was Jan Grootboom – a man who pretended to be amaNdebele. A man who went among us spying and listening to what was being said, who betrayed us to Khama, to the Voortrekkers. Then he helped Rhodes.

"The same man who was responsible for the death of two of my uncles and the destruction of my village.

"I never knew, but I should have guessed it was something like that. I was going to ask you to become a member of the SRANC, but thank goodness I didn't! Or you would have whispered everything we were planning to those working against us, just like your sell-out grandfather."

He picked up his bag: "Aidan – we are going – back to Ntabazinduna. I cannot stay here."

Tears of alarm and fear were pouring down Carol's face.

Angus could not allow the horror of what he felt to take over. He knew it could not be undone at that moment but the most critical thing he could do was to say something positive to Jabu.

He put his hand on Jabu's shoulder and said: "Jabu, you have always been a leader, someone I knew would one day be a great model for the younger generation. Have patience, think of the consequences of anything you decide and know that regardless of whatever that may be, we will continue to care for you and be your family."

"I think the time will come when that will be hard to say," Jabu's voice was tight and harsh with emotion. "But thank you Mr Davidson. I have always respected you. Thank you for your time and your friendship."

Jabu went to Carol and took her hand. He looked at her for a long time and his eyes told her that he longed to reassure her. But he didn't.

He walked off, Aidan following close behind.

Tony glanced at Angus and signalled goodbye. He walked briskly after Jabu and Aidan saying: "I have to be in Bulawayo by 10. I'll drop you off."

29

FROM THE NDP TO ZAPU

Jabu walked past Haddon and Sly, pausing to look at the bright red and green Christmas decorations. He particularly liked the little blonde angels dressed in white and gold with sparkling lights in their hair. Christmas and fair hair reminded him of Carol, and he wondered what her history results had been like at A-level. The last time he had seen her was four years ago – just before she wrote her exams in November 1957.

While they were all learning and thinking about the country's history Mr Davidson, Carol's father, had been anxious about some ominous signs on the political horizon. His fears had been realised.

The Cabinet of Prime Minister Garfield Todd had resigned en masse only three months after they had met at Ntabazinduna. The Cabinet felt he was trying to make too many changes, too quickly. Although Mr Todd tried to form another political party, he was not accepted. With his defeat went a stubborn, often impractical but visionary man who'd made many advances for Africans in education and their right to vote.

The new Prime Minister, Sir Edgar Whitehead, was a former diplomat and academic Englishman. Surprisingly, Sir Edgar had achieved something within his first few months of office that Mr Todd had not done. He passed a Parliamentary bill that all hotels would immediately become multi-racial.

Jabu had half an hour to wait for Bongani to finish work. He had vital information to give her, and he knew it would make her very sad. So he decided he'd tell her in the comfort of the lounge at the Grand Hotel. He had always longed to be able to go into the Grand with its arched balconies and the little building on the roof, the cupola. Now he could do so with no fear of being chucked out.

A music student played the piano in the big lounge, and huge bowls of flowers were reflected in wall-wide mirrors at the end. The sofas and chairs were extra comfortable. His friend Josiah was the lounge manager, and Jabu intended to talk to him and ask him to make Bongani feel very special as he had something important to tell her.

Sure enough, Josiah greeted him at the door. Once Jabu told him about Bongani, Josiah took him over to a quiet table in a corner. Jabu ordered a cup of tea to steady his nerves. Josiah brought over a tray with china teacups and a matching teapot along with "compliments of the house" . . . some cucumber sandwiches. Jabu relaxed.

He knew it was right to bring Bongani here. She had not been inside a hotel yet and was apprehensive about meeting him at the Grand. Jabu had reassured her that everything would be fine.

As he drank his tea, he thought back over the last couple of years. With the increasing violence and petrol bombs, the Prime Minister had declared a State of Emergency in February 1959. Fairly soon after that, the SRANC had been banned. In May, the government introduced the Preventive Detention Act. This meant most of the hundreds of people now in gaol had been sentenced without trial.

Fortunately, a few, such as Joshua Nkomo, Michael Mawema and TG Silundika, were out of the country. Jabu was thankful for Michael Mawema's advice to keep out of the limelight, as his work in the prisons was now not only critically important but also extremely demanding.

Ins and Outs - and hearing Robert Mugabe.

Mr Eddington had asked Jabu to take more responsibility. He was to be an Information Officer, acting as a go-between for the "big-name" nationalists in Bulawayo as well as in Salisbury. Jabu was asked to keep an eye on them, to keep his ear close to the ground and to report back any plans they might be "cooking up". He was also to make sure that they were looked after as well as possible from the perspective of the Prisons Department.

Jabu said he would certainly be interested in doing that, but it was difficult work, and he might end up dead. Mr Eddington was alarmed at the thought, but he understood Jabu's reasoning.

Jabu asked Mr Eddington to trust him on certain things, such as attending illegal meetings, as this was a useful source of information and would be important to his understanding of what was going on. He asked Mr Eddington to get him clearance from a new Government Intelligence arm – just in case, he explained, he was detained by mistake.

Mr Eddington urged him to be careful, putting a hand on his shoulder and saying, "My boy, you can do invaluable work for us. We must understand this wave of disturbances, why people are suddenly getting so angry. What we might be able to do to prevent it. We are entrusting you with huge responsibility, I know that. I also know that, with your family's desire for peace and progress, you will be able to do great things for our country."

It was the most emotional speech Mr Eddington had ever made, and Jabu felt a little ill at ease, not knowing how to respond.

Mr Eddington then went on with a smile, "By the way, at the cattle sale last month, your father let slip your birth date. I see you are suddenly no longer 30, because you have grown younger to 21." He laughed and clapped him on the shoulder. "Don't worry, I admire your determination even more now. In fact, I can't believe you joined us when you were only 16. None of us ever guessed!"

Jabu had wondered whether it was a wise thing to ask Mr Eddington to his *baba 'mkulu's* cattle sale two years ago. He worried – then he was convinced it was a good idea because Mr Davidson said so. Now he knew it was even better than he had hoped.

New gaols and detention centres had been built, and Mr Eddington's department had taken responsibility for all of them. Jabu was soon travelling all over the country to look after the welfare of prisoners outside Khami, as well.

He now played a fundamentally important role as a go-between . . . passing slight distortions of the truth to the Department of Prisons, but precise and accurate messages to the external nationalist leadership. Sometimes, he felt uncomfortable with himself, then he thought back to all he had learned from history and realised he was just finding ways to achieve an objective. Then he didn't feel quite so bad.

The NDP was formed on New Year's Day in 1960 with the same aims and objectives as the SRANC. The NDP's new leadership team was promptly detained. James Chikerema, George Nyandoro and Edson Sithole were among them.

One of the first things he wanted to do when he heard this was to get to Salisbury to talk to those three main detainees. He arranged it quickly for a day in July 1960, because he wanted to be there when a protest march against their detention took place.

He drove overnight to Salisbury, having arranged to see Chik and Nyandoro first. This was before the march took place, so that he had an idea of what they hoped would happen. They asked him to be their eyes and ears to the world outside the prison and to keep them in touch with government thinking. Jabu was very certain he could do that.

They specifically asked him to look out for a young white man, Peter Mackay, who had helped organise the planned march now that TG had returned. Jabu was to ask him, and only him, to get in touch with them urgently.

Jabu joined the crowd from the hostel where he was staying. He was astonished at its size . . . at the number of people walking down the streets and gathering around the Town Hall in Harare Township. He saw headlined in the Rhodesia Herald next day that the estimate was 7,000.

He slipped through the crowd until he found a number of other NDP members from Bulawayo to stand with. The crowd grew silent as "TG" stepped out onto the stage. He was not only the organiser of this march, but also the man who had defied the police and bravely led the march to the Town Hall. It was good to see him back in the country again.

The courage of this man had impressed everyone, so when they realised who he was, the crowd began clapping, cheering and shouting, making so much noise that TG had to put his hands up before he could start to speak. He welcomed everyone, saying that people had come from Bulawayo and Umtali and even as far as Kariba and Beit Bridge. The crowd was impressed.

TG then introduced a well-dressed young man as the guest speaker. He was from Rhodesia originally, but had a wife who was from Ghana, and he was living there at the moment. He started talking about how Ghana had obtained its independence by connecting with Marxist countries and how that was the solution for Africa. He talked in English because of his poor Sindebele and Shona. If you shut your eyes, you would think it was a white man talking.

He was a compelling speaker. He talked of the exciting developments in Ghana since 1957 and of the benefits of Marxism and its care for the oppressed povo. He said the word "proletariat" was too long to remember, but both the word "povo" and "proletariat" meant the same thing – the poor people who work, work, work and never make enough money.

His name was Robert Mugabe.

It was an exciting meeting, but there was rioting and shouting outside the Town Hall afterwards, and tear gas was fired. Jabu pushed through the crowd in the opposite direction as everyone else left the hall to see if he could find the young white man and give him the message. But it was impossible in the rush, and he couldn't see him anywhere.

He managed to get to the stage and asked an older man if he could take him to TG. He wasn't prepared to give the message to just anyone.

Eventually, Jabu got through and spoke quietly to TG. He told him who he was and the job he was doing. TG was interested. They went to a quieter corner to talk some more. He told Jabu he was working closely with Joshua Nkomo and that he would be going back to work with him in England. Jabu asked TG to salute Joshua Nkomo. "He will remember me. My name is Bhekisizwe."

TG smiled. "Restorer of your people – it is a good name."

TG asked so many questions that Jabu almost forgot to give him the message. He asked TG if he knew who Peter Mackay was, but he didn't.

Jabu noticed some African police officers standing behind them. As he did not yet have his clearance pass, he apologised for leaving TG to the police and sank back into the small crowd gathering behind them. TG turned away to talk to the police.

Jabu was so impressed with his wisdom and commanding presence that TG instantly became another of his heroes.

Winning friends and playing soccer.

After the big meeting last year, the government introduced the Native Affairs Amendment Act prohibiting any meetings of more than 12 people.

307

This was already making life difficult for Jabu. If he was seen talking to more than 12 people, they could all be detained. His clearance pass helped a little, but not entirely.

When he first started working with the SRANC, Jabu had been asked whether he wanted to work getting memberships in Bulawayo or in the rural areas. He had realised that the greatest problems were in the rural areas because of the Native Land Husbandry Act.

So he had chosen to work in the rural areas. He would always make sure to introduce himself to the local police or the District Officer first and tell them what he was doing. He made sure he stressed the fact that they were a non-violent group trying to raise the standards of living for Africans, to get the vote for everyone, to remove discrimination and increase school numbers. They were very impressed with what he said.

He learned to use the name Bhekisizwe everywhere he went on SRANC business, but he gave nobody any way to contact him. They were happy with that.

Bongani was not happy, because he was away all the time. Jabu said she should come and help. She said she could do that, but only if there was someone she could stay with in the village.

If she did decide to go with him, her father Mandhla would be watching her with strong eyes, which said "Don't you get pregnant with that Jabulani." She knew if she kissed him too much she would be pregnant, so it was better to stay with someone else in the village.

Jabu agreed that was true.

He was getting 50 to 100 people coming to hear what he had to say in every village he visited. Every weekend Jabu and sometimes both Jabu and Bongani went to the rural areas, getting memberships first for the SRANC, then when it was banned, for the NDP.

He now had to think long and hard about how he could overcome the 12-people rule. It was Bongani who told him what to do.

"Sometimes for a clever boy, you are very stupid," she said. "You, my Jabulani, are a good soccer player."

"That is true," Jabu answered, "but I play at Barbourfields stadium, for Highlanders. When I am in the rural areas, I am on business."

Bongani looked at him, her head cocked on one side and her hands on her hips. Now Jabu couldn't think of anything – not soccer, not rural areas – just Bongani and how much he loved this cheeky girl!

"Jabu concentrate!" she laughed at him. "Highlanders need new players all the time. They can give you soccer balls, and you can go out to teach the young boys in the rural areas. Two soccer teams, even small soccer teams, add up to more than 12 people, but because you are training, that will not be contravening the act!"

So Highlanders gave him soccer balls, and Jabu started teaching soccer. He would visit the member in charge or the local DC to pay his respects and let them know that he was now here to teach children to play on behalf of Highlanders. They were very impressed, because everybody loved Highlanders.

For the soccer fields, he had to speak to the *'mdalas* about giving up some of their land so they could make a field. They also needed to cut down two of their mopani trees to make goal posts. Then he taught them the special way to cut the wood for goal posts. In other places, they already had sort-of soccer fields.

When they saw things were going well, Highlanders gave him more balls and he became "the one" to arrange village matches where he did the training, always giving a few tips and lots of political information. The rural membership of SRANC, then NDP, grew very fast. Highlanders gave him shirts for the teams, and he became very popular.

Too popular.

He had to think about what he would tell Mr Eddington if anyone asked a difficult question.

Marching to a sousaphone!

Nearly a year after the march of 7,000, there was another chance to hear TG speak. This time he was in Bulawayo. But Jabu and Bongani found it impossible to get past all the barricades and police with their dogs. They were stopped on the way and their names were taken. Jabu's special pass from the Prisons Department didn't help at all.

They turned away, disheartened, and walked back towards Bongani's home. Jabu was in despair, thinking they'd never be able to get to the meeting. Then Bongani put her finger to her lips: "Listen!"

In the distance, they heard the Sunday morning marching band. They looked at each other and ran off in the opposite direction to join what they knew would be a very different crowd.

The Salvation Army band was playing its way down the streets of M'kokoba. The number of followers grew with every corner it turned!

Young black Africa was enjoying the music and heading off to worship with great excitement. The Major led the march with a flourish, playing his shining new sousaphone, a present from his brother in Ohio. He had only unwrapped it yesterday, and its deep reverberating tone had had a greaat effect - he had never had a crowd like this before! He gave thanks for the opportunity to spread the Word of the Lord - and thrilled to the triumphant resonance of his instrument.

On and on the parade went down the long Main Street of Bulawayo. The spirit of celebration in the brass and beat of the band echoed off the buildings as they headed for Centenary Park, where they were to hold an open-air service.

By joining the group, Jabu and Bongani were able to evade the restraining arms of the police, who now kindly and jovially removed the barricades to let them through. They sang and marched to the music as they made their way into the centre of the city.

But, of course, not all were heading for Centenary Park. Those at the front did a disciplined left wheel into Third Street, followed by a throng of devotees. By far the greater number towards the back of the column, by now a mass of youngsters and just as disciplined, wheeled right.

As they continued marching in time to the music fading into the distance, they started laughing. Many others had had the same idea as Jabu and Bongani, and now all of them headed straight for Stanley Hall, no police barricades anywhere in sight.

TG had just come back from being with Joshua Nkomo in London. The Federation had never worked well, and now it had been decided that it would be broken up again. So TG and Joshua had been asked to become part of the NDP delegation to the Southern Rhodesia constitutional conference in Salisbury that was chaired by a British MP, Duncan Sandys. They had been working for a on it long time and were now negotiating the details of a new constitution put forward by the Prime

Minister, Sir Edgar Whitehead. TG had played an important role in the negotiations, and he'd come to Bulawayo to tell them how it would work.

The meeting had been given permission to proceed, as the government said it was important for the people to know they should vote at the constitutional referendum. But there were extra police everywhere, just in case, with their dogs and with tear gas.

The NDP had recommended that eligible Africans should register to vote in the constitutional referendum to come. However, rumours had got round that something had changed, which was why there were barricades and so many young people marching to see what was going on.

There were hundreds inside Stanley Hall, with loudspeakers broadcasting to thousands outside.

Jabu made sure they were close enough to a loudspeaker to hear what was being said - yet sufficiently far from the main crowd to be able to slip through a back entrance behind the stage if they needed to.

There was thunderous applause as TG took the stage. But it died away as the crowd saw the solemn look on his face. When it was absolutely quiet, he spoke.

"You all know how long we have been working to find a solution to ensure as many people as possible are eligible to vote in the referendum due in a few months' time. This morning, I received a telegram from London where the Southern Rhodesia Constitutional Conference is taking place, confirming that we have won a total of 15 seats for African Members of Parliament, and for the first time about 50,000 Africans will be able to vote. It is approved by your President, Mr Joshua Nkomo."

There was another huge round of cheering and clapping at the name of the beloved President of the NDP.

TG continued, "I am not going to go into any more detail, because we have only 30 minutes. But I have just received another telegram from the NDP Secretary for External Affairs, Leopold Takawira in Cairo. I have not had time to absorb it fully, but I decided it was important enough for us to read to this meeting."

There was a sudden silence full of apprehension.."The telegram says:

"'*We totally reject Southern Rhodesian constitutional agreement as treacherous to three million Africans.*'"

There was a flutter of surprised concern among the people.

"'Agreement diabolical and disastrous. Outside world shocked by NDP docile agreement. We have lost sympathy of friends and supporters. We have undermined Northern Rhodesian constitutional conference."

TG had to shout above the noise, "Takawira told us to

"'denounce, reject and reverse our decision'."

There was a howl of disappointment from the crowd inside and out. The police were on the alert and surrounded the people with dogs, calling up reinforcements with their two-way radios.

TG called for silence. But nothing was going to silence the confusion, anger, dashed hopes, defiant hand punching or dismay for their President. For Joshua Nkomo was everybody's hero. He was their Chief.

African police had mounted the platform either side of TG, and the noise had dropped enough for him to say:

"We will take this to our council meeting tomorrow night, and there will be an article in the newspaper the next day. I ask you to go home quietly—"

A fuse had been lit, but nobody quite knew what for.

Jabu was now sitting with his second cup of tea, remembering the bittersweet nature of that day. He couldn't believe that Takawira would dare discredit the decision made by Nkomo and Silundika. That was not the way Africa worked. After months of negotiations, they had eventually arrived at a consensus. TG and Joshua had been going all over the country, telling people how important it was for them to vote and what they needed to do in order to qualify – then in the middle of it all, this bombshell.

He still felt sick about it sometimes, and this was one of those times. He felt sick because it had been done in a cruel way – not because he didn't believe that it may have been right.

Bongani was late! He hoped she just hadn't taken fright. His mind gradually drifted back to what had happened after that meeting.

Jabu and Bongani had realised it was time to leave. They slipped out to walk nonchalantly down the street with their arms wrapped round each other, every footstep making them a little safer from what Jabu knew would be gathering chaos at Stanley Hall. There would be a general meeting for members as well as a council meeting tomorrow night. That was something he could not afford to miss.

Somehow, as they walked home slowly, Jabu felt the net was tightening round him. He was too well known. Mr Eddington would soon find out. It was time to pull back a bit. But first, there was a meeting to attend.

The breaking of a great man's heart.

It had been held in a private home. Jabu made sure he was there in good time, because there had been a Council meeting earlier, and Joshua Nkomo, having signed the documents in London, had flown back to Bulawayo. He knew if he was there early, the President would notice him.

As he entered the house, he walked in on a group of people having a whispered discussion. They saw him and made a space for him to join them. "There is a big fight going on – they have been meeting for nearly three hours now, and our President is very angry. Just sit quiet and don't disturb them."

Jabu sat as near to the closed double doors as he dared. Nkomo was speaking slowly and heavily.

"Takawira must be suspended. You don't know what is going on. Sithole, Silundika and Chitepo were with me. They know . . . I signed the agreement. Takawira is now telling me to disown my signature. Then he tells Duncan Sandys he was the one who persuaded me to sign . . . he is a snake."

Then other voices. "Nyerere has asked the UK to remove Southern Rhodesia's self-government when the Federation breaks up. He doesn't think we can rule yet . . ."

"He thinks we are bloodthirsty . . ."

"If we order people not to vote in the referendum, the Dominion Party, the DP will get into power. That will mean we just go backwards again."

Nkomo sounded gloomy. "You do realise that every one of the parties debating the constitutional conference eventually agreed and signed the document. Except the DP. With them in power, life will become more and more difficult."

"That's fine – the country will be so obviously racist with the DP in power that we can call on England to step in."

"Perhaps the Constitution could be made to work, but in a different way . . . We still have time to change it . . ."

"Russia says it's time to militarise our youth and remove the Southern Rhodesia government. They will help us . . ."

Nkomo again: "Egypt has already given us arms. Whitehead is repealing some of the discrimination laws. He has promised to remove the Land Apportionment Act . . ."

"But you know why that is – because Sandys has ordered it. And he needs 50,000 Africans on the voters' roll . . ."

"Yes . . . but that is tokenism. And who says Whitehead will win the next election?"

"If we pull out now, Whitehead definitely won't win the next election. But who do we get instead?"

The shouting became so great that Jabu felt uncomfortable and walked out to stand with the growing numbers waiting for members' entry.

They waited another hour before Joshua Nkomo himself came to the door to ask them to come in. The crowd entered quietly, anxious and confused to see their party leaders disturbed.

The Council members walked in slowly to sit at a long table facing the members. Nkomo stood up. But he didn't speak. He walked slowly round the table to face the Council.

"I want you to confirm your vote in front of the membership. Do we reject the proposed Constitution or not? If you wish to reject it, raise your hands."

Chitepo's hand went up first, then TG and gradually the other members of the Council all put their hands up.

Nkomo walked back round the table and stood in his place. He put his hand up, and very slowly, he said, "I too reject the proposed Constitution. We will not encourage Africans to vote for it, because we cannot accept what it offers."

There was a stunned silence. People wanted to clap, but the atmosphere was tense. Nobody knew what to do.

Jabu stood up. "We, the members of the NDP, representing the African people of Southern Rhodesia, will support you, our President, in your decision to reject this Constitution."

Then all the members stood and clapped for the President of the NDP, Mr Joshua Nkomo. The President looked straight at Jabulani, and he in turn stood up and clapped. Only then did everyone on the Council stand and clap.

In their minds, it was no longer Southern Rhodesia, but Zimbabwe, as it was known to all Africans, that had made its first decision.

Another door opens

As Jabu was leaving, he felt a tap on the shoulder.

"Excuse me, Bheki . . ." It was TG. "I will be back in Bulawayo next week. Could we meet after your work day ends on Thursday evening?"

Of course they could. They arranged a time and place.

As he left the Hall, he thought back to the pain of the decision made four years ago, at Inyati. He had disagreed violently with Themba's beliefs, particularly when he found out he was a close relative of Jan Grootboom. But his heart was heavy knowing he was going against Carol and Mr Davidson. One of his sharp-pointed stars that day had said, "Make sure they are all right."

Now, it seemed that the black people were determined to take their future into their own hands. His mind was made up. He, Bhekisizwe, was going to do everything he could to restore his people. His way.

He had made a great impact on the leaders of the NDP because of the enormous youth membership he had gained for SRANC and the NDP. His thoughts as he left the meeting in Stanley Hall were that the NDP would soon be banned as well and another party would be formed.

This was the first time Jabu did not tell Bongani about the meeting he was having with TG. He wanted to make his own decisions this time. Sometimes his beautiful girl was too sensible. Sometimes she was not. But he was not prepared to chance how sensible she might be over this particular meeting.

Jabu was late for the meeting at the pub at lunchtime and he was a bit surprised to see TG sitting at a table with a young white man. TG saw him and stood up.

"Good evening Bhekisizwe. I would like you to meet Peter Mackay."

So this was Peter Mackay.

Jabu looked at him with interest – tall, thin, sun-tanned, he looked like a farmer, spoke like a well-bred Englishman – perhaps a military man. They shook hands.

"I asked you last time we met whether you knew anything about Peter Mackay . . ."

"I remember that."

"Peter was in the British army. Then he decided to come out to Rhodesia. He has just had his third set of call-up papers for our army. He tore up the last two lots and was fined, but this time it means prison, so he is leaving tonight for Johannesburg. He's been working on a tobacco farm and thinks the whites in this country are snobs, money-grabbers and upstarts!"

Jabu had to laugh. "On the whole I would agree, but there are always exceptions, and I happen to know quite a few of them."

Peter looked enquiringly at TG as Jabu hastily went on ". . . but that doesn't mean I am anything less than 100% behind the fight to improve the lives of our African people. Or in fact that I am against the recently suggested militarisation of our youth."

"Bheki has been responsible for almost trebling our membership, particularly of youth in the rural areas," TG said to Peter. "It is extraordinary what he has been able to achieve, and he's done it without anyone picking it up."

"How have you done it?"

"Playing soccer!"

"Playing soccer, of course! Brilliant."

"Bheki is also meticulous in keeping records. Records within his work at the Department of Prisons are of course essential, but he has extended that to give us vital information in assessing the viability of taking up arms."

Jabu had brought along two of his foolscap, wire-bound notebooks – one concerning people in the prisons and the other for "soccer".

He handed TG the one for the prisons and Peter the one for soccer.

Nobody spoke for a while, so Jabu left to buy beers for them all.

When he got back to the table, they were deep in conversation. Peter looked up. "Bheki, this information is absolutely priceless! Would you be able to tell us which villages, or even which schools, would have young boys who would be prepared to join the fight?"

TG said, "We need to keep your name out of the spotlight so you can continue your work in the gaols. You are like a spy, providing information to both sides."

"I don't like doing this very much and it is dangerous work, TG. I have been feeling lately that someone is watching me and that I should stop. But I am a bit happier knowing you support me. I think I should send you regular reports so that you are informed about everything I pick up. We need to find a safe way to do it."

"How have you managed to go undetected until now?"

"Bhekisizwe is not my real name. It is my initiation name."

"You had a traditional initiation?"

"That is correct. My great-grandfather was King Lobengula's chief *induna*, Mtjaan."

TG shook him by the hand. "You are Mtjaan's great-grandson. I should have known. Peter you cannot imagine how important that is to the Matebele people."

Their discussions went on for a couple of hours. Many beers later, TG asked: "Bheki, would you be prepared to join the armed struggle?"

Jabu was a bit taken aback. "When, tonight?"

"No, not tonight . . . Probably in about six months' time."

"What would I have to do?" Jabu's mind was racing in a hundred directions – Mr Eddington, Bongani, his father . . .

Oh no! His father, and his precious mother.

"First of all, you would need training." Peter Mackay was speaking. "My job is to meet you in Bechuanaland and get you to Lusaka."

"How do you do that?"

"You have to find your own way to Francistown. I will meet you there. We then drive along what we have called the Freedom Road to the Caprivi Strip and cross the river on the Kazungula ferry. There will be someone else to meet you on the other side."

"What happens then?"

"You will be taken to Lusaka, and there will be an air ticket waiting for you to fly to Moscow."

Jabu took time to reply. He wasn't at all sure he wanted to go to

317

Russia. He had heard disturbing things about Russians.

"How did we manage to persuade Russia to help?"

TG answered, "I first went to see them early last year, 1960, and we have been keeping in touch ever since. Where do you think we got the money to print all our brochures and pamphlets? Or for supporting you with a vehicle and petrol on your trips to the rural areas?"

Jabu was astonished. "So long ago you were talking to Russia! Did they agree that we should refuse to vote in the 1961 Constitution? I was sometimes not sure about that decision. The DP were bad enough, but now my friends think that the Rhodesian Front will get into power in December and that is very bad."

"You were not alone Bheki. There were many who were unhappy with that decision. I wasn't party to any discussion with Russia at that time, but I expect they would have agreed that we should not support the Constitution."

So many things happened that nobody knew about. Jabu decided he'd like to be the one who knew everything that was happening. All the time.

"I think I am interested, but I need to think about it because it is not what I had ever thought of doing before. If I do decide to go, I would not like my father to know where I have gone or why."

TG had nodded sympathetically.

"Bheki's father is one of our most educated people, and he is respected and esteemed by everyone. In addition, of course, his grandfather is a leading Chief at Ntabazinduna. It's not easy for him."

"I can see that," Peter had said, "but if you left, Bheki, to lead by example - with your background - it would make our job of recruitment so much easier."

Bongani has tea at The Grand.

Now he had to face the hard part. He looked up to see his beautiful Bongani standing at the reception desk. He was just about to go and get her, when he saw Josiah step up and salute her. Josiah then pointed at Jabu and led Bongani over to him.

Jabu stood up. His heart was in his mouth. No wonder she was late – she had gone home and put on her prettiest dress – the one he had bought her for her last birthday. It was lemon yellow with white butterflies all over the skirt. She had put on some beads too, and as he bent to kiss her, he smelt her perfume and knew.

Bongani had come here sure that Jabu was going to ask her to marry him. And he wasn't.

He ordered more tea and asked for some assorted sandwiches to go with it. Bongani looked round the lounge; she was amazed by the height of the ceilings and the intricate carvings along the edge . . . she had never seen such beautiful flowers or such enormous vases. She was glad there was another black family in the room.

Her eyes sparkled, and she chattered on about how her friend had been here for dinner. Now she, Bongani, could say she had also been to the Grand.

Jabu saw her talking, but he didn't hear a single word she said. He was too busy trying to work out how he was going to tell her.

Josiah came back bearing a tray with more delicate china teacups and a matching teapot and milk jug. There were two kinds of sandwiches, cucumber and cheese and tomato, and "compliments of the house", two scones with jam and cream.

Jabu smiled and thanked him – he would tell him later why it was so important for everything to go smoothly.

They chatted on for a bit. Bongani was still keen for them to continue with the soccer games, even if there was no longer any money to help them. Highlanders were getting good recruits out of the country soccer teams, and they would help give them petrol. Bongani said she would go and see them herself as she knew how busy Jabu was.

Jabu was quiet.

"You don't want to talk about soccer, Jabu?"

He shook his head.

"Is your mother all right? Your father?"

"They are all right, my Bongani." Jabu took a deep breath. "I have made an important decision and I need to tell you about it."

Nobody spoke.

In a tiny voice, she said, "You are going away?"

Jabu nodded.

"To Lusaka?"

"To Lusaka, then to Moscow."

Bongani's eyes widened in fear. He could see everything she was thinking. He put out his hand to hold her. "I will be all right, my Bongani. I will come back. And then we will get married."

The fear of what he had told her far outweighed the promise of marriage. Tears filled her eyes, then broke free and raced down her cheeks. Jabu realised this had not been a good choice for a place to tell her. He needed to hug her, but there was a table between them. People were watching them.

Bongani told him she had heard that people who went to Russia didn't come back.

She couldn't stay here. So she pushed her chair back and walked quickly out of the Grand, Jabu close behind her. He glanced at Josiah and mouthed "I will be back to pay." Josiah knew he would.

The net tightens.

Jabu had been told he would have six months to prepare himself from the time the signal was given. This meant everything would be ready for the first group to go. He had always been a good planner, so he tried to work that extra commitment into his life. Somehow, it kept rising in the priority list and distracting him from everything else.

His salary as Information Officer at the Department of Prisons was now much more than he needed, especially as he was sharing a room in a hostel with two other boys from the party. He had been saving every penny he could for the day he knew was coming – the day he would be sent to gaol himself or sent to work outside the country.

It looked as though it was now going to be working outside the country, but it was not quite what he had thought. He had always imagined himself on the organising side of things – in meetings and decision-making. This was not to be. He would come back to the country as a soldier. He had never even thought of that as a possibility, but with Mtjaan's blood in his veins, he would of course make a good soldier. He was determined to be as brave and courageous – and wise – as his great-grandfather. And what better way to honour him than to fight to restore

320

what had once been lost?

He laughed when he received the latest letter from TG, who was now settled permanently out of the country. The letter said the leaders had determined that he should be trained in intelligence gathering as well as in war. Perhaps Jan Grootboom had taught him more than he thought, as he seemed to be able to blend in with almost everyone he met, black or white. And with little difficulty.

He was told he would be leaving the country in September, when the water level in the Zambezi was lower and there was less chance of the ferry being delayed. September was now only six weeks away. How quickly time went when it was short.

As he had thought, the NDP was banned soon after that meeting in Stanley Hall. He had been surprised that it took only ten days for a new party, the Zimbabwe African People's Union (ZAPU), to be formed after the banning of the NDP. It had the same leadership. ZAPU was now banned as well and had based itself in Lusaka, because the restrictions on Joshua Nkomo were too great for him to operate anywhere else.

Jabu was filled with anger as he remembered how his hero Joshua Nkomo had had to escape earlier this year, hiding and travelling through Nyamandhlovu, to set up the Lusaka base. But once he had got out of the country, it had been a busy year. Soon after that, he went to Dar Es Salaam to spend time with Nyerere, then on to Europe to address the United Nations. He extended the trip to include visits to Russia and China. On the way back to Lusaka, he was a guest of Haile Selassie at the inaugural Organisation of African Unity (OAU) meeting in Addis Ababa.

"One day, I will be like Joshua Nkomo," he thought to himself.

TG was no longer on the ZAPU leadership team, but he was invaluable to the President as his eyes and ears. This was just as well, because that snake Takawira was undermining Nkomo again.

Jabu had been so sad when TG phoned him to say that some ZAPU members were playing "silly buggers". Josef Msika had seen a member of the party, Moton Malianga, giving out some papers outside shops. Josef had thanked Moton and taken one away. He had wondered why Malianga looked anxious.

He knew - once he read the piece of paper.

The paper said it was time the majority tribe, the maShona, had a majority party in control. Although the new party would be open to Matebele membership, it was blatantly obvious exactly what they meant and what they intended, from a single sentence: "It is time to get rid of Zimundebere (the old Ndebele man)".

Josef told the leadership about the pamphlets and could not believe what he had seen. When he heard about it, Jabu could not believe it either. Nor could TG. Both of them vowed they would never leave ZAPU.

Just last week, Takawira, Mugabe, Ndabaningi Sithole, Chitepo and Tekere had held a meeting at Enos Nkala's home. They formed another party – the Zimbabwe African National Party (ZANU) – in opposition to ZAPU.

They began to understand how big the division was when Joshua reported to TG that on his return to Lusaka, he had been to call on Herbert and Victoria Chitepo. Victoria had walked out of the room. A guest at their house at that time was Terence Ranger, who had been influential in his work on behalf of the Africans. Terence came up to Nkomo and told him he was no longer welcome.

Jabu was seething at the story. Another interfering white man – what right did he have to treat the President, Joshua Nkomo, like that? It made Jabu all the more determined to stay a ZAPU man.

Fortunately, Joshua had just been confirmed as President at the congress held earlier that week. James Chikerema wanted his Presidency to be for his lifetime, and so it was. The People's Caretaker Council was also formed, supposedly as a social club. But as ZAPU was banned in Rhodesia, members could lawfully join the PCC – socially!

Every day, there seemed to be more reasons to support his President. If the best way to do so was to go to Russia, then Jabu was determined to look forward to going to Russia.

Today, he must give his notice to Mr Eddington. He spent a long time drafting a letter, telling Mr Eddington how much he had appreciated all he had learned in the Prisons Department.

In the afternoon, Mr Eddington took the letter Jabu extended to him and walked over to the window to read it, his back to Jabu. He read quietly, with no reaction. Then, still looking out of the window, he said, "Jabulani, you have done well for the Prisons Department. You have been very useful to us, and I believe we have been able to make life a little easier for the prisoners you have been looking after."

He turned and looked at him. "I wonder how useful you have been to the nationalists as well."

"I had my suspicions a while ago that something was not quite right, so we put police sleepers in each of the prisons you visited regularly. They have seen you exchange government documents. Do you know what I mean by a sleeper?"

Jabu's heart went cold. He knew very well what he meant by a sleeper. Some sneaky African sell-outs had been reporting back to Mr Eddington.

"I have told the police I need more concrete evidence. They will produce everything in 48 hours. So I am giving you 24 hours to get out of the country."

"Thank you, Mr Eddington. I will remember this."

"What do you want me to tell your father and your *baba 'mkulu*?"

"Just tell them . . . tell them I have taken on another job and that I have not left a forwarding address."

Twenty-four hours! He had never thought about how short that time could be.

His first phone call was to Peter Mackay. "There will be a car waiting to be picked up at the Shell station. Just leave it in Francistown when we meet up. Nobody, absolutely nobody can come with you."

Fortunately, Jabu had been given a new passport several months before, so he rushed back to pack the recommended essentials, then forced himself to sit quietly and write a serious letter to his father. ". . . *the spirit of Mtjaan lives within me. I go to restore his name and that of the amaNdebele people.*"

Then another letter to his mother: "*I take with me memories of your sweetness and your encouragement and love. And one day you will be proud of me.*"

He reached over for a fresh piece of paper. It was truly beautiful paper, a clear white with no lines, unlike the pages he had torn from his ring binder for the other letters.

This one was for Bongani's father, Mandhla Moyo. It took a long time and many attempts in his ring binder before he got it right.

Then, he phoned Bongani. "But I am at work, Jabu, I can't . . ."

"Yes you can and you must. I will meet you outside your office. I will be driving a green VW Beetle."

He slung his bag over his shoulder – better not leave a note for the boys – they would know he had gone. But he went to the side table beside his bed and picked up a small square navy-blue box.

The car was there, and Bongani was there. Time was flying, as he had to get across the Plumtree border at least one hour before his 24 hours was up. Fortunately, it was not a busy border post, but it closed at 5 o'clock. If he had to wait overnight, he would go beyond his 24 hours. It was still a long drive, and the VW was old and cranky.

They drove in silence down to their favourite place, a little pool with trickles of dropping water from the Matsheumhlope River. He parked in the shade. Bongani didn't speak. Jabu didn't speak. Jabu had bought chicken sandwiches and a Coca Cola each. They walked down to the water – here they were safe and private.

"The time has come?" Bongani asked - but she already knew the answer. "Oh Jabu, how can I stay here without you while you are . . . I don't know where!"

She didn't know she could cry so much. Nor did Jabu. He held her tight to try and calm the sobs shaking her tiny frame. At last she tired. He kept her close, stroking her cheek to wipe away the tears. He stroked her neck and wiped away the wetness that had moved like a new river after drought, filling up the lowest places first.

He followed the little river down its caramel curve and kissed her again and again. When she was quiet, they lay together for a precious five minutes of shared peace and deep happiness. Jabu knew what happened with too much kissing, because Bongani had told him many, many times. But his body did not want to obey.

"Jabu, how can I come to fight with you if you make me pregnant? No more kissing now – no more kissing." She spoke firmly, then took his face in her hands and kissed him once more.

He sat up, so reluctantly. The precious moments had gone, and they didn't know when, or if, they would come again.

"Shut your eyes, my beautiful Bongani."

She did. Jabu pulled out the little box. She couldn't possibly keep her eyes shut – so she took the box and opened the lid to reveal the tiniest little ring – a sapphire and two little diamonds. The tears came spilling again as he put the ring on her finger.

"I love you my beautiful Bongani. Wait for me, I will come back. And I will talk to you whenever I can. And I will write to you every day."

Then there was more kissing until Bongani pulled away and stood up abruptly.

"I will wait only until I can join you in the fight, my Bhekisizwe. When we get married, you can make me pregnant. Now you must go."

30

BLOWING IN THE WIND

After Jabu and Aidan had left, none of the others felt like going on to 'nThaba zikaMambo. Angus Davidson was shattered enough by the demise of the African Affairs Board and Tony Browne's news of what was happening in the Southern Rhodesia government while Garfield Todd was away, let alone the resignation of his whole cabinet shortly afterwards.

He couldn't stop blaming himself for the fact that he'd mentioned Jan Grootboom without anticipating the impact it might have on Jabu. Calls to Nkanyiso and Jabu had gone unanswered since.

All his good intentions seemed to have gone desperately wrong.

Themba and Carol agreed about 'nThaba zikaMambo, and both found that all of a sudden, they really needed to get back to prepare for their exams. And Prune, well . . . Prune had a wedding to organise.

After picking up Mum and dropping Lalan and Prune off at Balla Balla, their sombre little party made its way to Goromonzi School to drop Themba, then returned home to Ruwa. Mum understood something had "gone on" and was content to sit tight while the others tried to make sense of what they had learned.

At least Carol and Themba got their high distinctions.

A few months after the nightmare of Inyati, the Davidsons gave Themba a lift to Balla Balla for Prune's wedding. It had suited him well, because his father Kuda had just retired, and Themba had decided to take a year off before going to university, just in case the law faculty opened and was able to admit him in 1959.

They were all disappointed that Jabu had chosen not to join them at the wedding – but nobody had heard from him for a while.

Prune's store had been so well received in its first few weeks of operation that when they heard that he had bought another store in Shabani, they wished him well, but thought he had gone completely mad!

Discussing it on the way down to the wedding, Angus and Themba expressed great concern at Prune's foolhardiness. But the more they talked about it, the more they had to acknowledge that he had a knack for providing very happily for African and European tastes. And customers loved both Prune and Maura.

"Why do you think he is so good at his storekeeping?" Carol had asked Themba.

"He's so easy with people, black and white – speaks both languages fluently and is miraculous with figures! I've never seen anyone add up or work out complex mathematical problems so quickly in my life!"

"It sounds as though he has got the community well involved in the store from the start too." Angus volunteered. "I spoke to him when I confirmed we'd be coming down for the wedding, and he has been talking to black and white families about selling things through the store. For example, one woman who has a most beautiful garden will be selling roses through the store! Another man makes boats . ."

"What on earth would you do with boats in Balla Balla?"

Angus laughed. "Well I suppose the Ncema dam is not far away and they have plans to make that much bigger in the next ten years or so.

"But I was interested to hear that there is an old man who carves animal sculptures in stone and different types of beautiful wood. For years he has been standing all his sculptures along the Beit Bridge road, sitting beside them for hours on end and trying to sell them. He had little success, because cars travel too fast to stop. Or if they do, they're more inclined to drive in and park outside Prune's store just to buy drinks. So Prune now has these sculptures in the garden he has made round the store – he's sold a couple already. He doesn't miss a trick, that kid!"

Themba added, "There's also that new school there – St Stephens – the boarders are allowed to walk into town and go climbing Baldy rock at the back. So they probably provide a ready market for buns and cokes."

On the day before the wedding, Prune and Maura had finally signed the deeds for their store in Balla Balla and they couldn't wait to be able to do the same in Shabani. Life was full of excitement and enthusiasm.

What a joyful occasion it was! Maura looked luminously happy, and Carol was quite sure Prune's face would never lose its constant huge grin. They were married in the little Anglican church of St Mary in Essexvale. Everyone who had attended Lalan's 70th was there. Even Mr Bellini had made the effort to come. He solemnly shook the bride and groom by the hand, then gave them a generous voucher to spend in his store before he made a slightly embarrassed exit.

Needless to say, the Davidsons couldn't resist buying an oiled wood sculpture of two impala – one alert and one grazing. It was a beautiful piece. They were delighted to meet the talented old carver, and his work brought them great joy. Prune was very pleased!

Themba takes off

Themba's year off had proved to be very useful as he helped build a new home in Bulawayo for his parents. Having always lived in government housing, his father Kuda, needed something of his own now.

Fortunately, he had been as scrupulous with his money as he had been in the management of his work and family life. There was enough in the bank to allow him to build a three-bedroom home under deep thatch, on a wooded half-acre near Hillside Dams. Having always lived in the country, he couldn't quite bring himself to live in the city. Just close enough was quite fine!

Themba built the house to his father's exacting standards – every bit of carpentry or metal work was inspected minutely. He would have been a credit to his grandfather Motshodi, who had learned these skills at Kuruman Mission with Robert Moffat . . . then passed them on to Kuda.

After 25 years working in African Administration in the rural areas, where he was always the nominated handyman as well, Kuda had become an absolute expert in making something useful and beautiful out of nothing.

He invited family and friends round to "christen" the new house, which he called "Shoshong" after the family home in Bechuanaland. Themba's great joy as he left that day was to see his dear old face creased with laughter as various grandchildren took him off by the hand, pestering him to help them climb a small *kopje* close by.

Themba enrolled in the School of Social Studies for the first year, having been told that a careful choice of subjects would act as the first year of a law degree. The year after that, he was one of the first students enrolled at the new Law School at the University College of Rhodesia.

It was a vibrant, exciting time to be at this university – the first two years were times of community building, particularly with the other white law students. For many of them, it was the first time they were meeting socially or forming friendships across the cultures. Black and white enjoyed the process far more than either had expected.

In his last year however, there had been a subtle change. Nobody quite knew why, but the easy camaraderie between students almost imperceptibly gave way to a more pervasive and reproving dialogue of blame between the races.

Themba privately thought the influences came from a couple of idealistic tutors from other countries. They'd been brought in as experts in their field, but some of their ideas were radically out of step – yet they seemed determined to stir thing up. He was sad, because there were always plenty of "itchy ears" to hear what they were suggesting.

What Themba had found more frightening was how quickly it spread. With the breakup of the Federation in particular, everyone seemed to get more radical overnight. If you were a white who stuck up for the blacks, you were in trouble with your own people. Similarly, if you were black and wanted to work with whites, you were labelled a sell-out.

Even Britain seemed to be sticking its nose into things it knew very little about.

"I wonder what their agenda really is?" He asked Carol.

Themba had become much closer to Carol since that dreadful day at Inyati. They found they were able to discuss in depth, subjects few others would touch – particularly those on the political front. Themba had found her to be a reliable and empathetic sounding-board, always ready to listen to what was bothering him at the university.

"Themba – listen to your inner voice. Don't be influenced by every new thought. You need your own Themba thoughts. You know what is right and what is wrong – you have experience many of these city dwellers will never have. Think about what is being said and have your own interpretation on what is happening."

It was sound advice.

Predictably enough, Themba finished with an honours degree, specialising in Agriculture and Natural Resources. Everyone who knew him was delighted. He was such an enthusiast, so positive, so determined to make a difference to the country. Nobody was more excited than his father.

"The blood of Motshodi runs deep within you, my son."

He left university to complete his two years of articles with Dodds and Brown. He loved his time with them and couldn't wait to get in to work every morning.

He'd have been happy to stay on with the company, but Neil Brown came to him one day with a long face!

"Themba, I have just had the head of the Natural Resources Board in to see me. They are concerned about destruction of native forests and uncontrolled hunting in many of the Tribal Trust Lands along the Zambezi border in particular, as well as up in the Centenary and Mount Darwin areas. Your reputation has preceded you – Chief Chiweshe gave you a good rap when one of the Natural Resources Board's officers visited last week."

Themba inclined his head at this news. "Well I am surprised at that, Neil! You remember you asked me to go up and take the Chief to task last month?" He couldn't resist a smile. "He's a crusty old bugger, but I swear I saw a glint of amusement in his eye when he realised he was going to have to give in gracefully over the deforestation of that area near the dam! Especially when he had just told us categorically he had no wood anywhere in the Chiweshe reserve.

He chuckled. "He was a certainly a bit anxious when I suggested we should drive the long route home - and of course, we found stacks and stacks of indigenous wood cut into neat piles, all ready to sell to the tobacco farmers, at a tidy profit. The reserves are entitled to sell what they grow of course, but not what nature provides, unless it is with carefully obtained permission.

"When I asked him where he had planted all the gum tree seedlings he had been given, he said it was too much work to plant seedlings and look after them. Yet in the next valley, you could see several acres of young gums that had been planted by local farmers, especially for the Reserve and for that purpose. The trees were already way over my head in just eighteen months."

Neil Brown shared his laughter and his chagrin at how difficult it was to bring about change to traditional ways. His face grew more serious.

"I have been asked to release you as soon as possible, to the NRB as a Senior Development Officer."

Themba was startled. "What do they want me to do, Neil?"

"It's important work – they have to establish a network of Tribal Trust Land Committees, which will link to the planned Community Development initiatives coming out of Domboshawa.

"I have to say we will be very sorry to see you go, and there is a position here for you at any time, should you want it in the future."

Themba was excited at the thought of the job as Neil described it, largely because it would be based mostly in rural areas, and he could get away from the radicalisation of his contemporaries in the city. But he left Dodds and Brown reluctantly, thanking them for their trust in him and the experience he gained with them. They all knew there were sound working relationships established between them, which would be useful in the future.

He had only a week to finish off, or pass on, the cases he was dealing with, as well as to get across to the Natural Resources Board and discuss his position and salary. They seemed to be very keen for him to join them, and his salary was far more than he expected.

On his last afternoon at the firm, he was about to start going round the offices to say goodbye when Neil Brown called him in to the Board Room. As he entered, he was startled to find, not only all his work mates from Dodd and Brown, but also three of his key clients – all with champagne in their hands.

There was one man he didn't know. But on a second look, he recognised him as the new Prime Minister of Southern Rhodesia, Winston Field. They were introduced to each other, and he spent some time giving Mr Field an idea of what he had been doing so far and his hopes for his position at the NRB. Mr Field was most interested and said he would like to keep in touch.

Themba got quite emotional to see them all there and realised he had some useful champions for the future among them.

Neil called for silence and said, "Themba, I'm not going to make a long speech, but I do want you to know how much we have not only enjoyed having you in our firm for the last two years, but how much we have learned from you. Not only have you fully justified our faith in you since we heard of your progress at Goromonzi, but you have given us a positive indication that the future of this country will be in safe hands. We will be watching your progress with great interest."

There was a chorus of "Hear! Hear!" right round the room. It was the first time he felt slightly regretful that he didn't have a wife or girlfriend at home to share his joy with. He had always been so busy that he had never had time for wives, or even friends, very much.

Carol goes to London . . .

After Prune's wedding, Carol's parents suggested it would be a good idea if she spent a year in England. She didn't think so, still unable to stop yearning about not being in Cape Town with her school friends - but she went anyway. Reluctantly.

She went – and she loved and lived every moment of it to the full, spending a second year there doing her music as well as a business course, learning not just shorthand and typing, but office management and basic bookkeeping as well. She hated admitting it, but thoughts of doing medicine were quickly swamped by the excitements of London in 1958, when rock 'n' roll was taking centre stage.

Carol was one of five girls sharing a large room on Eton Avenue in Earl's Court – all of them music students, all from the colonies and each as broke as the other. For some extraordinary reason, they seemed to survive on cheese and black coffee, saving every spare penny they had for concerts and travel.

They had a favourite café called The Loft in Belsize Park, where you could hear great singers on a Sunday night. Two of their favourites were Harry Webb and the Drifters, and a young composer called Anthony Newley. Harry was a cousin of one of the girls in Carol's room. Anthony had just had a single in the top 40. A few months after they first started going there regularly, Harry came in one night to tell them he was changing his name to Cliff Richard.

He would have to stop singing at The Loft . . . but he promised he'd be back on the odd Sunday afternoon. Sadly for the girls, he became too busy after that to come back, but Carol and her friends were always first in the queue for tickets to hear Harry Webb and the Drifters, who were now the latest big thing in pop music - billed as Cliff Richard and the Shadows.

While she was in England, Themba had tried to keep her up to date with the fast-moving political scene at home, particularly since the resignation of Todd's Cabinet. She welcomed his letters, always filled with so much descriptive detail that she felt she had been on a trip back home every time she read them.

. . . and meets her match.

Carol had managed to get a job with a stockbroker in the City and tried to get her obstinately un-mathematical brain around the vagaries of stocks and shares, all too aware that the slightest mistake in typing share certificates would incur extreme punishment!

In the evenings, she took shifts working behind the mail desk at the Overseas Visitors Club. One evening, she looked up to see a familiar face. She couldn't place him but asked his name so she could give him his mail.

He smiled, realising she had forgotten.

"Hi Carol! It's Simon Watson."

"Simon! I'm so sorry!" she blustered, "I didn't recognise you. Out of context . . ."

Once Simon had moved away, concentration on handing out letters at the mail desk went out of the window! She was lost in the memory of those magical square-dance evenings. She had so hoped they might get to know each other a bit better once she left school, but it was not to be. She'd look out expectantly every time they had a party or a square dance, but he was never there. In fact, he didn't come back to Ruwa in the few months she stayed at home before heading overseas.

And now she had forgotten him! Oh boy! Life was cruel!

She put up the "MAIL DESK CLOSED" notice at 6'15 as always, but found herself loitering with great intent – trying to find little extra jobs to do – in the hope that Simon might come back. There was no sign of him at 6'45, so she started to pull down the big shutter.

"Can I help you?" *Oh yes you can Simon Watson!*

They had a drink at the Blue Grotto, the hub of Club nightlife, and shared their experiences, their conversation peppered with questions. Simon had been called up for National Service almost as soon as he left school, and of course Carol had left for England a few months later, so they'd simply not met again. All this time, Carol had carried close to her heart memories of those brief but tender interludes in her last year at school, those nights when the whole community had got together for a regular night of square dancing. And so, apparently, had Simon! He had decided to do his varsity education at the Agricultural College in Cirencester. Whenever he came up to London from Gloucestershire, he would stay at the Overseas Visitors Club.

Simon saw her home that first evening, and they agreed to go to one of the Proms at the Royal Albert Hall next time he was in London.

He really was as gorgeous as she remembered. She loved the way they walked home through gentle rain, neither of them the slightest bit bothered about getting wet, loving the warmth of being together again.

His visits became more frequent, as did her trips to Cirencester.

The mail desk was a hive of information on how to travel where and when as inexpensively as possible, so as they were both due to go back to Rhodesia early next year, they agreed to spend Christmas together in Austria. Eleven of them from the OVC teamed up and spent happy days sourcing equipment and hotels as cheaply as possible, eventually splashing out a little and settling on a little village called Galtur in the Tyrol. They stayed at the Hotel Ballunspitze.

It was picture-postcard perfect.

The girls' room overlooked a sparkly, trickling river iced up at the edges but reflecting sharp-topped, snow-covered mountains in the clarity of its smooth dark pools. It was a large room, with balconies and four single beds with the lightest and plumpest duvets anyone had ever seen. The boys didn't seem to mind too much that their rooms looked out over the delivery area. They'd been cheap!

Hard days of skiing were followed by mandatory hot chocolate, flirtations with beautiful Bruno, their ski instructor and raucous evenings of singing, dancing and ribaldry ending only when they were just too tired to carry on.

For Carol and Simon, the repeated misery of having to part loomed up as each evening drew to a close. They would share precious moments together before they slipped back into their separate rooms. Carol tried not to disturb the others, snuggling noiselessly into the all-enveloping warmth of her duvet - wishing she could just be with him.

Christmas Day was as traditional as it could possibly be, complete with sleighs and horse-drawn sleds, church bells ringing and a scarlet-clad St Nicholas popping up unpredictably in the most unlikely places. For two little colonials from Africa, this was magical. They had been used to receiving Santa-in-the-snow Christmas cards, while they carved traditional turkey and ham with all the trimmings in baking hot temperatures or slashing semi-tropical rain. Even in the heat, they'd always include Mum's favourite bread sauce, with ridiculously alcoholic brandy butter to go with the Christmas pudding.

Neither of them had ever spent a northern hemisphere Christmas before. Roast turkey and ham, bread sauce and brandy butter tasted so good over here! It was all deliciously different, more authentic and exciting when they walked down little lamp-lit streets on crisp, crunching snow to hear real sleigh bells ringing, as beautifully bedecked horses trotted past.

They sailed home via Cape Town on the *Warwick Castle*, enjoying thirteen days of deck games; being plastered with goo and dunked in the pool during the obligatory "crossing the line" ceremony as the ship full of people sailed unaware of the second it actually crossed the dividing line, between northern and southern hemispheres; and of course, dressing up for the traditional fancy-dress ball.

Carol was lucky that her four-berth cabin was filled with fresh sea air through two large portholes, but Simon's cabin was a deck lower and seemed to be right over the engine room. Practically every morning, he would emerge looking pallid and seasick. This gave them a great excuse to spend a couple of nights sleeping in deckchairs as they moved further south and the air grew warmer. They'd sit watching the luminescent blue fireworks of disturbed plankton as the ship's bow ploughed a shining moonlit wave through the sea.

Memorable.

After three months at home, with Carol working in Salisbury for an advertising agency and Simon out on his parent's farm near Horseshoe, they agreed this separation couldn't go on any longer. They were incomplete living apart when they had been sharing everything together, most of the time during the last year.

Carol went out to the farm at weekends and whenever Simon had a sale in town, they'd have breakfast together at the tobacco floors. They shared a wonderful Easter weekend – lots of family, friends, braais and a hilarious play at the Ayrshire Club in Raffingora.

On the way back to drop Carol off in Salisbury after the Easter celebration, Simon detoured down Rotten Row, asking, "Have you ever been up the *Kopje*?" She shook her head.

"Great views" Simon continued. "Especially at this time of the night." They parked at the top, then sat on a little bench overlooking the lights of the city.

Simon put his arms round her, saying, "I've got a little something for you in my left hand, but you're going to have to fight me for it!'

Carol tried to find out what he was talking about, but he wasn't going to give in. She struggled to get free and a half-hearted mock fight turned into a loving and very satisfying kiss. They sat watching the lights below – extending the moment. After a while Simon stood behind her with his arms wrapped round her. He opened his hand, and in the glow of a street lamp Carol saw the sparkle. She picked it up to look more closely.

"Will you marry me as soon as you possibly can, my darling girl?" What a question! Simon had managed to find a Sandawana emerald, which was surrounded by small seed diamonds. It fitted perfectly – of course!

They were engaged for six months. Then, when all the jacarandas were in full bloom, they were married in the Umvukwes Church by a dear friend of the family, Basil French. Carol's four bridesmaids – great friends Jenny and Jane and little cousins, Mary and little Jane – were all dressed in jacaranda-lilac cotton lawn with an overlay of slightly darker lilac net. Very fashionable, very 1960's!

Loving family and friends surrounded them. Prune and Maura, with Lalan, drove up from Balla Balla. Unfortunately, Themba had just started his job with Dodds and Brown and couldn't get away.

To Carol's sadness, they had no response to the invitation from Jabu.

31

FARMING ON THE EDGE

It was only three months after they were married in August 1961 that Simon came in bursting with excitement to say he'd heard that one of the Centenary farms had been passed in, and the government was considering applications from younger farmers who would not have qualified in the first round of applications.

Centenary was an interesting area in the northeast of the country. It had been opened up as part of the Rhodes Centenary Year in 1953. It was open initially, only to those who had served in World War II.

Carol had an uncle Don, Dad's brother, farming there. They'd often been up to see them in what his wife Rebecca pointedly called "Squalor Villa". The house was pretty awful! As always when establishing farms, barns and sheds were built and money spent on farm equipment long before suitable housing was even discussed. Squalor Villa lived up to its name in looks and temperament, but it seemed nothing could dampen the irrepressible spirits of Don and Rebecca.

Last year, and ten hard years after they had signed the deed on their piece of land, they had at last cleared their massive start-up debts and made a small profit, so plans to build a proper house were under way. It was to have a "'crinkle crankle" wall through which Rebecca could twine her dream of a gloriously English herbaceous border.

Carol and Simon had longed for a farm up there but their chances of getting one were very remote because of the World War II clause and the huge demand for agricultural land. Don had been on the lookout for them. When this one was turned in, he suggested they come up and look at it but with many warnings about difficulties and its remote location.

They pored over a couple of maps, but were still keen to see it. so they drove northeast from the little township of Gatu in the middle of the Centenary block to the edge of the Great Rift Valley, where the land plunged over the edge and down to Mzarabani.

"I must warn you that the chap who took up this land was never able to make it work. He'd been badly injured during the war, and his knowledge of farming was based on his family's farm in England. Not the greatest credentials for growing tobacco in a climate like this.

"The farm is 3,800 acres in total, but you'll be lucky to find 350 arable. So, it is marginal. It's generally pretty stony too. But I did come up here once before and the previous owner had grown a small amount of beautiful, open-grained, typical Centenary spot leaf. So it can be done."

As they turned left off the main road, the track dropped alarmingly. It was little more than a track, following the wheel marks of the odd car and tractor before them. A broken-down old gate signalled an ill-defined entrance to the farm proper.

Squalor Villa was luxurious by comparison. Carol looked in growing dismay as they approached.

When they got out of the car, they found that the entrance to the house was through a tin shed pretending to be a kitchen. It was black with soot from a bad-tempered AGA and as hot as Hades. Broken shelves hung listlessly, and the only tiny window had broken off completely, to lie smashed and splintered outside.

The house had a small sitting and dining area with a tiny bedroom to the left and a rather larger bedroom to the right. From that small central area, there was a door into the bathroom, which was quite simply disgusting. The view from the sitting room was straight into the wall of the grading shed, and the whole house was made of green corrugated iron with an almost flat roof. Carol could see no sign of a garden anywhere.

It reeked of dereliction.

Her heart sank.

There were two barns and a very small grading shed. Strangely, the two barns had been built singly instead of in the usual bank of three or four. They looked like two rather flimsy towers, surprised to still be erect.

Simon came back looking grim. "There is a huge crack running the whole length of one of the barns. They obviously didn't burn the bricks long enough. That would have to come down . . . and the other barn is completely out of alignment, so the thought of people climbing up with *mateppes*[91] of tobacco scares me stiff.

"Frankly, the placement of the buildings right in the middle of the best bit of arable land just doesn't make sense either," Don added.

They were all feeling downhearted. Don asked the price they had been quoted to take over the farm. Simon had thought it was pretty reasonable until he actually saw the place. No wonder they had waived the World War II condition and recognised his service as a Major in the Territorial Army.

Even so, they were going to have to borrow most of the money from family and friends – but should it look suitable, they were confident it would be worthwhile with Simon's training at Cirencester.

"It is remote. Your transport costs will be huge . . ."

"The soil is stony, but I could filter most of that out over time. Having done that, it is good Centenary sand with a bit of guts to it."

"Have you thought about breeding game perhaps?" Don asked.

"Funnily enough, as we drove here I thought it might be magnificent for game, but I haven't seen much evidence of natural wild life around except for hordes of baboons. And that's probably not a good sign. I'm not sure of the viability of game at the moment either."

"It's improving," Don said.

"What about workers, Don? There don't seem to be many Africans around. I'm used to seeing roads streaming with people."

"That's always been a problem up here. The Makorekore are not keen farm workers, so most of us get our workers direct from Nyasaland. There are no jobs up there, and we have plenty here. So by agreement with Northern Rhodesia and Nyasaland, they issue *situpas* for their people to come over and we repatriate their taxes. So they come on a government-sponsored schems providing free transport, accommodation and food to get here. How long that will last of course, I don't know."

Simon and Don walked up to the base of a line of *kopjes* to discuss the feasibility of moving the buildings in order to reclaim some of the arable land.

As they were talking, a well-dressed young African approached them.

---

[91] *mateppes*: thin wooden poles from which 'hands' of tobacco hang to dry.

"Good morning sirs. I am Tinashe, and you need me to be your no. 1 Boss Boy."

Simon smiled. "We do, do we? And why is that?"

Tinashe said, "The boss who was here stuffed up."

Simon and Don tried not to laugh at this very pertinent description.

"His legs were buggered, and he was too cross all the time. I worked for many years for Mr Phillips on the other farm close to Mount Darwin, and I know what to do. But this one – eee – he was not going to listen. Did you see the barns?"

They nodded.

"They're buggered. You will have to pull them."

"OK Tinashe. We agree. We've been thinking we should move all the buildings to the edge of the *kopje*. What do you think?"

"It's good . . . but not this *kopje*. You know where you come in at the gate?"

They nodded again.

"That *kopje* there is good – the land is gentle. If the shed is near the gate, the lorry can get in more quickly to fetch the bales. Here is very far."

Simon looked at Don and nodded.

"OK - I think we should go with Tinashe and have a look."

On the way over, Tinashe kept up a monologue.

"Up here you can grow tobacco one year, then mealies next year, then some silage in year three, then you must rest. That boss, he grew tobacco for four years. Then he just got *mampara*[92]. But he didn't want to listen.

"*Aiyee*. He said he was going to pay us big wages, because it was not right to give us rations. At first we were happy with more money, but we have no store here. So where do we get our mealie meal and relish? Then he paid only sometimes, so the boys did not want to stay. And we have no school for the children except that big *mfuti* tree when it is not raining. And the *meddem*, she did not do clinic, and it is too far to Kingston farm."

The litany of woes was extensive, but both Don and Simon were interested in only one thing – Tinashe knew what he was talking about!

"Tinashe, how do mealies grow here? And pumpkins and beans?"

"I don't know, baas. We didn't grow them because the old baas gave us no rations. But baas John over there—" Tinashe pointed back towards

---

[92] *mampara*: bad, poor quality, thick, low priced

the main road, "—he grows good mealies.

"When you come, you must bring your gun because there are too many *bobbejaans*[93]. No mealies will live because of these *bobbejaan*.

"So there are no leopards to kill the baboons?"

"*Aiyee* no. Lions yes. They kill the buck, not *bobbejaan*."

They had arrived at the spot Tinashe had suggested would be best for the farm buildings. The idea made absolute sense – it was a good flat bit of ground backing into the *kopje*.

They walked through the area, talking as they went. "Don, you reckon there's about 350 arable acres here, and we can squeeze another acre or two by shifting the buildings. But on a four-year cycle, I'm going to need all that and more to grow even 30 acres of tobacco. I had hoped to get to 50 and maybe 70 in that time."

"That farm next door has plenty. You can lease," suggested Tinashe.

"Can we prepare land in time to grow the first 30 acres?"

"Start with 15 or 20 acres. With prices like this . . ."

"We wouldn't make enough to even eat on that . . . "

"I think you could, there are a lot of help schemes around and there's no reason why you can't think laterally.

"Tinashe, have you got friends who would like work?" Simon asked.

"I know many Nyanja boys. And their wives can learn to do grading. We can get more from Nyasaland. Twenty acres is good, and 15 acres of mealies. And 4 for ground nuts – very good for the soil. You need . . . I think me and you, and 20 boys . . ."

"We also need a good builder to make bricks."

Ever the practical one, Simon added: "Before we get all carried away, the real problem is tractors and equipment. I just don't have any money left over. Tinashe, do you have a good driver for oxen? Can we buy oxen to plough?"

Tinashe looked at him with disappointment.

"No tractor?"

"Not for the first two or three years."

Tinashe thought about that and was about to write him off as another boss not worth working for, but something persuaded him.

"Is or'right we can get *mombies* from the valley. From Mzarabani –

---

[93] *bobbejaan*: baboon

they still use oxen to plough. And they have drivers and leader-boys."

They went on planning the positioning of the buildings, the workers' village and the house.

"Please boss, you are putting the village on the edge of the *kopje*. It is not good – the *bobejaan* will come and steal our dogs and our children. If you put barns there" Tinashe pointed to a spot right at the edge of the kopje, "the fires will keep us safe, then the village can come this side."

"Of course, of course. Much more sensible and easier to load *mateppes* of tobacco into the barns and then bales out to the lorries." He grinned and slapped Tinashe on the back. "Thanks Tinashe - you've made up my mind and you are now my first employee!"

A place to call home

And so it was! By the time they had done the figures and taken free advice on agronomy and the latest information from Kutsaga Research Station on preferred varieties and planting ratios, the venture almost looked positive.

They managed to beat down the government and persuade them to sell it as virgin land. The government representative told them the old boss had actually buggered off back to his family fortune in the Cotswolds and really wasn't that interested in what would only have been a marginal payment after costs. They were in no particular hurry to get it to him.

They laughed ruefully to hear he was now living off his fortune in England and had become an instant expert, giving talks and writing books about his much-touted adventure in Africa.

Tinashe, his wife Miriam, and their growing family became an essential part of the Watson farm in helping to grow this new enterprise.

Carol had in turn, done her own bit of scouting. Simon agreed that the existing corrugated iron shack was not an option – and they would build some roomy thatched huts first. Knowing she would be living in a very basic home to start with, Carol suggested any extension of the tin house might be useful designed as a future section of the grading shed. In this way, as soon as the grading shed proved to be too small for all the tobacco and needed to move into a bigger space, she might have a house.

They moved to the farm in March 1963, with just enough time to make bricks, clear 20 acres of land and build barns, then train up the oxen to plough. Don lent them a ridger. Once the stones were removed, the rich sandy soil was indeed good traditional tobacco land. It actually looked quite promising. The seedbed germination was about 80% that first year, which would have given them enough for 100 acres!

Everything was ready for the first rains, which arrived bang on schedule. After the laborious marking out of the ridges with a one-meter long stick, the planting began.

They lived in the huts very happily. They were airy, thatched pole-and-dagga[94] huts plastered with mud and with huge window spaces. Net curtains hung from a wire across the top, which could be looped back and held behind a hook in the wall. As the nights got colder, and after much persuasion, glass was put into the bedroom window spaces first. Blissful!

They had built two huts – one for the sitting and dining room, one for a bedroom with basin and shower, a long drop toilet out at the back and a lean-to shed for the kitchen.

Carol had a disconcerting feeling that she was constantly living with other occupants – beetles, bats, scorpions, spiders, snakes. They all took their turn and were dispatched with varying levels of fear and, eventually, dogged acceptance. As Carol was now pregnant, there was an element of urgency about building a slightly more impervious room for the baby.

The farm did have single phase electricity, sufficient to power the existing borehole, a light in the grading shed and a couple of farm tools, but certainly not enough for the house.

Carol had loved going down to the quarry to watch Lovemore, the builder, with his flock of *piccanins* around, all making bricks, slopping the prepared wet clay into three-brick moulds with leakage space below so they would dry out.

It was so rhythmic – scoop the clay, slap into the mould, smooth it off, and carry it away . . . scoop the clay, slap into the mould, smooth it off - carry it away.

Within days, they had enough to make the first kiln with fire tunnels in the middle and dried clay bricks piled up meticulously all round. The whole kiln was then plastered over with mud, and within a week, the first batch of bricks was cured. The bricks were a perfect orangey-red on the

---

[94] *Pole and dagga; pug and pine; or wattle and daub*

outside of the kiln, and mottled purple by greater heat in the middle – perfect, in turn, to become the protective heat bricks for the planned new barn furnaces.

Within a month, they had enough bricks to build the first four barns.

In three months, they had a new grading shed, and a small brick house extension with running water and electricity, due to be completed after the first crop sales and – hopefully – before the baby was born.

Singing and dancing, the families arrive

The first 20 workers, wives and children, arrived on government-funded trucks driven all the way from Zomba in Nyasaland. Carol and Simon were both fluent enough in Chinyanja to be able to welcome them all with delight. They watched the singing and dancing, learned all the names and allocated new homes to a chorus of *zikomo wambiri's* (thank you's) and traditional clapping of hands in thanks at having arrived safely after a long and hazardous journey.

Then everyone helped everyone else move into their new homes having identified what they needed for their particular family, from the pile of beds, chairs and tables, brought in from Salisbury. It was wonderfully disorganised, happy chaos!

Their huts were traditional pole and dagga but the village had been carefully laid out and built to make sure everyone had a patch of garden to grow vegetables and a big centre space for grinding mealies, cooking and socialising. Carol couldn't wait to hear once again, the rhythmic drumming she had grown up with every night in Tjolotjo. It was beginning to feel a lot like home.

Carol went over to Rebecca to ask about the importance of setting up a clinic - particularly as she had no medical training. Becky advised going to Salisbury to do at least two Red Cross and First Aid courses. This she thoroughly enjoyed of course, with medicine having once been top of her list of what she wanted to do. She returned armed with disinfectants, mixtures for coughs, colds, worms and strong antibiotics to be administered in urgent cases. She also brought a range of dressings, surgical scissors, and basic instruments to sew up small injuries. And that most vital item – a Fitzsimons snake bite kit.

Heart in mouth, she opened her first day of clinic. Many of the children had arrived from Nyasaland malnourished. She doled out cod liver oil and malt (which they loved) and liquid paraffin (which they hated) as needed.

A brick room for the new baby had been designed to be extra-large as the extension to the grading shed - of course! They'd installed a washbasin in one corner, and the whole of one wall was ceiling high cupboards. At last they could think of opening their wedding presents!

They had been truly spoilt with 23 casserole dishes and 12 sets of beautiful cut-glass tumblers and glasses, but no knife-and-fork sets, no ladles or wooden spoons! On their farm on the edge, she wondered if they would ever be able to afford to entertain, let alone use all these lovely but impractical gifts.

Carol's parents had bought them a bed, and Simon's parents, a round dining table with 6 chairs. For everything else, they had made do. Every time a packing case arrived on the farm, it was commandeered and turned into bedside tables, wardrobes, coffee tables, kitchen cupboards and shelves. She had bought some navy blue and turquoise fine cotton off-cuts and soon had curtains hung on threaded wire with hooks over nails in the top corners, covering the windows, the gap across the makeshift shower and even the bedside tables. It looked pretty good.

Both sets of parents came down to stay as soon as they could, with Carol and Simon moving out to sleep on stretchers in the grading shed while they were there.

She was very grateful they were there when, one evening, there was a commotion at the back door. Dick, their cook, came rushing through to call Carol, saying there had been an accident.

She got to the back door to find a deeply intoxicated young man with an axe buried deep in his head! He was giggling drunkenly, pointing to the axe and shouting: "Accident, meddem. Accident!"

It was a hideous wound. Blood coursed down his face and chest. She cleaned up the edges of the wound and staunched the blood as best she could, but nobody was game to try to remove the axe. Angus and Simon carried him carefully to the truck to take him to hospital to be stitched up. En route, he became unconscious, whether from excess of alcohol or other hidden nightmares, nobody was quite sure. But he was delivered safely to the hospital with Angus having held the axe as still as possible the 50 miles of rutted gravel road to Umvukwes.

Carol was quite sure he wouldn't survive, as it looked as though the axe had gone right through the bone of his skull. But there he was, battered and bruised, working in the span reaping tobacco three days later – resplendent, and the centre of attention, in a turban of bandages.

She asked Dick how the axe had come to be stuck in his head. He chortled, "Young man who sleep with old man's wife, gets axe in head!"

It was a great time of building, a great time of creating.

With other tax free incentives from government, they were soon able to build a school of three classrooms for all the new children in the workers' village and cover the cost of a teacher, who was fortunately also from Nyasaland.

Carol started to run a well-baby clinic for new mums. While working with them, she became fascinated by their intricate bead and basketwork. She spent time learning to do it herself and started developing their skills to widen the range of product they could make. Once they'd made a good quantity of necklaces and bangles, baskets and ornaments, she took them to a friend who ran a homewares shop in Salisbury to see if they would sell.

Did they sell! They were so popular that she immediately had orders to fill - plus a better idea of what other products might be in demand. It also gave her a chance to go and buy a bigger and better range of beads. This was greeted with enthusiastic clapping, singing and dancing plus a frenzy of unpacking when she got home again.

When Fiona was born, Carol had to cut back a bit, but she still ran the clinic and watched over the school while keeping in touch with her beads and basket workers.

In one of her regular chats with Prune, who'd just opened up his third store near Marandellas, she told him there was no store between them and Gatu village. He was most interested! Shortly after Stuart was born, Prune rang to say he would like to build a store nearby and asked if Carol would manage it for him. Of course she would - in fact she'd be delighted.

32

THE 'SWORD OF DAMOCLES'

Since their ill-fated trip to Bulawayo many years ago now, Carol had relished deeper conversations with her father about the state of the world and their little corner of the world in particular. She had once asked him what was really behind the resignation of Todd's Cabinet.

As always, Angus was measured in his response. "Well, you know Garfield is a close and respected friend – it's difficult to be objective. He is a striking man and a natural leader - with a generous and compassionate heart . . . but if I'm truly objective, I'd have to say he was a little unrealistic about how he could achieve the things he wanted to – in his timeframe.

"His successes at Dadaya Mission, as well as in those promising early years in government, plus his drive and enthusiasm and a broad worldview was exciting. But as head of a government drifting further and further to the right, it was almost impossible to take them with him.

"I shared his vision for advancement of the African – but mine was tempered, not only by my ability to communicate, but also because I lived and grew up with Africans . . . I knew them, understood and respected them - and never treated them like charity cases. We were part of a whole.

"For me, it comes down to practicalities - top of the list, the terrifying population growth. Unless this is curbed - dramatically - it means targets have to be moderated firstly by how fast change can be tolerated by the rural population particularly; and second, by deciding how to change the 'new Rhodesians' mind-set.

"The country was working together pretty well until about the mid-fifties. We'd struggled through the horrors of the depression and rinderpest, and the decimation of African cattle. But far too many young men, black and white, were lost in the first and second world wars, and in

Malaya. Replacing them with immigrants from Britain albeit with the artisan skills we needed to build the country, seemed a great idea.

It was . . . until these same immigrants became increasingly anti-black, as Africans became increasingly skilled - and, of course, they realised they had to worker harder and better to preserve their jobs.

"That attitude was largely responsible for the change of government and things have become increasingly acrimonious since."

By the end of 1964, the four seemed to be getting on with their lives well – the unknown quantity was Jabu. Carol longed to know how he was getting on, but nobody seemed able to contact him.

After Themba had been in the Natural Resources job for a few months, he wrote to Carol to say:

"I find it completely satisfying. It is exactly what is needed to be done, and exactly what I want to do. We draw up the parameters for each rural community Committee, and I frame a legal structure according to the resources available in their area. Carol, you can't believe some of the wonderful places I have been to or how diverse they are. Have you been down to Gonarezhou?"

She hadn't, but promised to take the family down sometime.

"It is, seriously, the job of a lifetime."

Usually enthusiastic, even Themba had now begun to talk of his uneasiness at the restlessness and increase in almost rudeness he was experience - particularly from schoolkids in the rural areas.

"The kids in these areas are being brainwashed and I just can't put my finger on where it is coming from," he said. "It is so hard, because their attitude affects the older people. In some areas, they seem to want to undo, almost deliberately, everything I'm trying to establish.

"For instance, take really impoverished areas like Binga and Gokwe, where there is still plentiful wildlife. They benefit enormously from hunting licence fees which are now returned by law, to their community. It's helped communities put in schools and community halls, reticulated water and cattle dips . . . generally making life easier and better for them.

"I've been involved in drawing up the legal side of things and how it can all be managed effectively. It all starts wonderfully positively, then for some reason, they go all sullen and won't talk."

Themba had kept in touch with Winston Field, but in the political roundabouts of the moment, he was suddenly ousted by Ian Smith. Suspicion between the races had grown like a contagious disease and open discussion had become almost impossible. So Themba put his head down to concentrate on the job in hand - but his reputation had reached usefully relevant places and people in government.

In August 1965, he was bubbling again, as he wrote to say he and two representatives from the Ministry of Agriculture had been invited as guests to a conference at the Sheraton Park in Washington in November. The conference was about establishing international resources management and co-operation guidelines, to operate across a wide range of disciplines. The Ministry recommended him to workshop the legal issues associated with the preservation of natural resources in a country like Rhodesia.

He'd written to Carol at the time, saying:

"Now that it is recognised that the culture of the indigenous people is a great natural resource, it is a really exciting time to be involved."

Carol was delighted by Themba's news and enthusiasm, but more and more apprehensive about what her father, Angus, had talked about, and now another edge of uncertainty from Themba. After that initial warning from Jabu in 1957, and the various disasters that had happened since, it was hard to stay positive.

UDI – and reality begins to bite.

Simon came rushing home from the farm saying the Prime Minister, Ian Smith, was going to make a broadcast to the nation at 11 o'clock. A terrible fear gripped her heart - surely this didn't mean he was going to declare Independence from Britain. Surely not.

They'd had a film night at the Centenary Club yesterday, and even there as the old projectors clicked and groaned, everyone stood up to sing God Save the Queen with fervour.

Now, they switched on their old radio to hear through the crackle and hiss of distance, the flat Rhodesian-accented voice of Ian Smith:

"Whereas in the course of human affairs, history has shown that it may become necessary for a people to resolve the political affiliations which have connected them with

another people . . ."[95]

Simon drew Carol closer to him and they sat, feeling almost breathless - frozen by its implications - as the whole of that declaration was spoken.

The wording, had been written with the precise opening words of the American Declaration of Independence; the timing, was exactly the 11th hour of the 11th day of the 11th month - the time, date and month of the signing of the Armistice that ended World War I. A sharp reminder to Britain that for the size of its white population, Rhodesia had contributed the greatest percentage of fighting men, of all its colonies to both World Wars.

They sat frozen thinking about the rumours and threats circulating in the local and international media . . . as well as through the differing opinions of friends . . . Britain would bomb Rhodesia's key installations; sanctions would apply immediately across a terrifying range of capabilities . . . each could spell complete disaster.

They sat, waiting . . .

The phone went mad - as friends and family rang with every possible variation in opinion from excitement and exhilaration, to utter disbelief.

They sat, waiting . . . waiting for the drone of approaching bomber aircraft engines.

Nothing happened.

Gradually, as Christmas approached, things got back to normal. But the country soon realised it was no longer the same normal.

Immediately, nobody with a Rhodesian passport was allowed to travel outside the country and this applied equally to those holding English passports with Rhodesian residency.

"It will only last three weeks" British Prime Minister Harold Wilson trumpeted "they will never survive the sanctions that have been imposed."

The incredulity that Britain had immediately involved the United Nations heightened the sense of utter betrayal and made everything terrifyingly much worse. Effectively, the whole world had been persuaded to impose total sanctions on a little land-locked country like Rhodesia because we were now deemed to be *'a threat to world peace!'*

It seemed way out of proportion.

Only South Africa and Mozambique openly flaunted sanctions with

---

[95] see Appendix 5: Text of the Unilateral Declaration of Independence:

relish and plenty of "Up Yours" symbolism.

Underneath it all, the country was stunned.

During her parents visit a few months later, and to give Carol a break, her mum said she'd be very happy to put three-year-old Fiona and their new addition, eighteen-month-old Stuart to bed. Simon had pre-sale figures to work on, so after supper Angus put his arm round her and they walked down the garden to sit under another huge indigenous fig tree.

"OK Dad – what's happening?"

"It's huge! To sum up …1959: Todd, far sighted, achieved some good things, chucked out; 1961: Constitution giving Africans access to the legislative assembly, accepted by whites, rejected by blacks; 1962: Sir Edgar, a great brains of our time, voted out; 1963: breakup of Federation – with chaos in the unravelling of ownerships and infrastructure; 1964: Winston Field, absolute gentleman, but not tough enough with the British, refused to declare independence, removed - another sad loss.

"So here we are at the end of 1965, after intense negotiations most of the year and growing intransigence from Britain - and Ian Smith declares UDI. No wonder we're all a bit shell shocked."

She felt weighed down by it all, particularly now. They'd battled to get the farm to a point where they might start to earn a living, with plans to move into their new house soon.

She commented: "There's been a big change in thinking since Federation broke up Dad. Many friends sound more like South Africans in their cynicism and think UDI was a good idea. Simon and I just shut up!"

They talked on for hours . . . neither of them realising they had talked for so long. Simon reached out sleepily for a hug, as she crept back into her stretcher in the barn.

Carol's panic returns

Carol was running, wracking sobs tearing through her chest as though her heart would break. In her desperation to run faster, her legs moved slower and slower while her panic grew more frantic, as she knew she couldn't escape.

She felt arms tighten round her and used her last remaining strength in the struggle to get free.

"Shhh my darling . . . It's OK. You're at home and safe . . ."

Oh no! Not again.

"Sorry love, so sorry."

She battled back to consciousness and reality, burying her head in Simon's chest. She was ashamed to be so affected by something from her childhood. It was ridiculous. Why? When she was so completely content, at last?

The children, sleeping in the corner of their room, woke up at the noise. Simon went over to tuck them up again so they would go back to sleep while he and Carol pulled a rug off the bed and went to snuggle up on the sofa in the sitting room.

The dream had begun haunting her again in the last few months. She just couldn't understand it.

"I'm turning into a wimp, Si! It's never bothered me until recently. I hadn't honestly thought about it at all until that trip back to Bulawayo . . . it refreshed everything I suppose."

"You're not a wimp, darling. It was a frightening time for you at boarding school – quite out or your experience

"The death of innocence."

"The death of innocence, exactly. And that's very hard. It makes you re-think everything you once took to be the norm."

"You faced similar things when you had to do National Service . . . with all those difficult times on the officer's training course at Gwelo. Some of what you told me leaves my experience in the shade."

"No . . . different scenario. Mine was resolved, and at the end of it I was commissioned. Since then, I've been able to build a good team of guys round me, although, thankfully, we haven't been called up for a while."

"I wouldn't speak too soon," Carol said wistfully. "Jabu warned me when were at Inyati that there was trouble coming. And with the latest developments you can see it everywhere now."

"I know, and we do need to talk about what it might mean for us and the kids. Most of the reason for your dreams is that everything seems so uncertain. We had our world shattered when Ian Smith went ahead and declared Independence from Britain. It feels almost as though time has stopped and nobody knows where we are heading. It's hardly surprising that you feel you have quicksand under your feet.

"Unfortunately, darling, I have to get this next load of tobacco off to the floors, so I must get up. Don't forget we have a sale tomorrow. We can catch up on things then. I'd better get cracking and check the barns." Simon looked at his watch then glanced back at Carol "It is a bit early . . ?"

She laughed. "OK my love, I'll bring you a cup of tea!"

She sent him on his way with a mug of tea and a rusk, then listened to the now-familiar whine of the truck's heat-up button before the diesel engine rumbled into reluctant life and grumbled its way down to the barns.

She walked out to the long front verandah of the house.

She used to bring the dogs here, then as they grew older, the children. They'd climb a short distance up the *kopje* to a place where she'd found a large, stony, but flat piece of land with a magnificent view north over the escarpment.

They'd sit there for hours, not allowing the children to take food up there and keeping an eye open for baboons. They soon didn't see them as much of an attraction – and the dogs were left in peace – although some of the African dogs were taken by baboon if they strayed too far. There was always a warning bark as they arrived, but in time, they seemed unperturbed as the family walked round planning for the new house they would build on that wonderful spot – one day.

After five years on the farm, which they had called Tafara meaning "we are happy", the Watson family had moved at last into the first half of their new house, built in brick and with electricity throughout – and an indoor toilet. Luxury!

They had a large lounge with a little bar built into the corner. It led into the dining room, and from there, into the kitchen. Their bedroom and bathroom had just been finished, but the kids' rooms hadn't. So, at the moment, they were all in one room together.

The house was thatched, and the verandah ran along its entire length. The view was simply stunning. The baboons still had to be watched, but they displayed no aggression towards them - although they did, to visitors.

Simon had finished building the last of the houses for his workers as well – all brick with inside wash and toilet facilities and – much excitement – electricity! The singing and drumming from their village doubled in sound and vivacity with a suitably ceremonial switching on of the lights!

The latest employees were two game guards to keep an eye on the 20 young eland he had managed to fence in, with enough natural veld and food to keep them happy. He was delighted with his latest crops of maize and tobacco – particularly the tobacco which he had managed to push up to his initial hope of 50 acres. The yield this year was enormous and it was beautiful no. 1 spot, so it would surely fetch good prices.

33

BURNING IN THE HEARTS OF AFRICA

Carol had to concede that today was a bit earlier than usual but what luxury it was to be able to make that short walk simply out onto the verandah instead of climbing the *kopje*. These early morning hours, once Simon had left for the day's work and the children were still snuggled up in bed, were Carol's special think-and-pray time.

It was still pitch dark, with a hint of light in the sky on her right. Daylight would creep down the steep escarpment 500 feet deep as it dropped away down to Mzarabani. On the clearest of days, with binoculars, you could see across to the waters of the Cabora Bassa dam in Mozambique and almost imagine the escarpment on the other side of the Great Rift Valley. Extraordinary to think of this massive flat-bottomed trench, cutting through the heart of Africa - traceable most of the way from the Red Sea - and see it below, flattening out in the plains of the northern Zambezi valley.

She'd maintained a lifelong habit of having some quiet time in the morning. It was a time of peace. She'd read a passage of scripture, strengthening her faith and giving her the keys to better manage her life. Today's reading: *"Go to the ant you sluggard, consider his ways and be wise"*.

Perfect! Stop feeling sorry for yourself, just get on with it! She seemed to have been rather over-anxious and uncertain most of her life, and she loved the earthy, practical commands of Proverbs. It was meaty stuff sometimes, and after that dream, this was a distinct message for today!

She allowed herself a bit more time this morning – precious time, where she felt at one with nature, waiting as always for the first tentative chirrups that would rapidly become a symphony to the sun, played by an early dawn orchestra. Oh Lord! What a beautiful, troubled country!

She waited, anticipating the moment the sun would pop up . . . as always mesmerised by the speed that happened in this part of the world. Her two years in England, living with the milky haze of a northern hemisphere sunrise had made her see the beauty and strength of the landscape in her home country through new eyes.

The Rhodesian sun was fiery, energetic, ready to deal with whatever the day might bring. She watched the knife-edged black shadows move rapidly back until that spectacular view lay stretched out beneath her. It was the best time of day to see it, before the shimmering heat of the valley distorted and merged with the rising dust of increasing human activity.

As he left this morning, Simon had shouted, "There's a letter from Themba for you on the dining room table." She went through and picked up a fat envelope with Themba's distinctive writing on the front, his name and yet another new address on the back.

The dawn chorus was in full swing – a glorious cacophony! She settled back into a favourite chair, her ankles resting on an impala-skin pouffe, and ripped open the envelope, looking forward to hearing about his latest trip to America. Soon Carol found herself laughing out loud at Themba's descriptions.

The work he was doing fitted him like a glove. That first conference had been such a success that now he was off to America again with the "guys from the Ministry" to do a study tour in some of the southern states with similar climate and conditions as Rhodesia.

"*There's one major difference,*" he wrote, "*as we drive around, I keep looking for lions, or elephant, or even a zebra. Or impala! There is nothing! I saw some fat black pigs scrabbling in a rubbish bin. The Americans got all excited, shouting and pointing at the 'wild boar!' They looked more like disgruntled overweight domestic porkers to me!*"

He was obviously enormously boosted by this important adventure and seemed to be representing the government internationally more and more. He would come home full of ideas that he couldn't wait to start putting into practice.

"*Of course, I missed UDI . . . and now I may not be able to travel overseas so much anymore because of sanctions.*"

358

Carol hadn't thought of that aspect. Surely they would find a way round these blasted sanctions. She'd write back to reassure him on that point, telling him he hadn't missed much, because the country had been a little subdued by the unfolding implications of it all.

She looked back at the letter.

"Well, it was sure interesting to be in the States, because once Americans knew we were from Rhodesia, everyone cheered us on, saying they had also declared independence from Britain and hadn't looked back!"

He had added a PS: *"By the way, I am going over to Geneva in a few months' time representing the Rhodesian Department of Agriculture at international tariff and trade talks (GATT). I will be going with the head of department, but it won't be long before I do it myself and take on the world!"*

A broken man

On their next visit to Salisbury following a tobacco sale, Carol told her parents about the recurrence of those dreams. She said Simon felt the initial warning from Jabu in 1957 and the continuous disasters and revolts that had happened since, had prompted it. Themba's earlier letters sharing his concern at what he was finding in the rural areas, endorsed this wary feeling and it was hard to stay positive.

"I see huge cynicism in Smith now as pressures mount, particularly with Britain being so punitive – unwilling to consider options other than immediate one-man one-vote. It would be chaos in rural areas, where the vote will still be dictated one way or another, by what the Chief declares."

Angus had to smile. "But the Brits must be scurrying around like demented stoats, trying to find answers, particularly since Harold Wilson said he would have us under 'within a matter of weeks rather than months' following the imposition of total sanctions. Ridiculous comment.

"We are going to have to do things differently – not just to keep our heads above water following sanctions, but in persuading everyone to start working more closely together for the betterment of the country. Stupidly, today's white kids are not taught about the growing capability of the black man. So whites tend to measure everyone against workers on the farms or in domesticity, who go about their lives seemingly content as long as the farmer, or their employer, sorts out their domestic squabbles and takes them to hospital when needed."

"And provides schools," Carol added.

"And provides schools and clinics and farm stores . . . and while they are able to maintain a fairly traditional lifestyle."

"We work very closely with our farm workers and every farmer has a trusted Boss Boy who is incredibly capable. Simon would never manage without Tinashe."

"Of course. Tinashe is invaluable and very bright, but he couldn't step straight into a government ministerial position. All too often, that's what has happened in countries to the north of us, so there is a fair amount of justifiable scepticism.

"Themba on the other hand, is a great example of someone who will, with a bit of experience, be quite able to take up a ministerial position. He is part of the new breed. University qualified, he could earn a place in any society.

"But there are not enough of Thembas to make an impact and convince the white population. And too many have been taught about rights, responsibilities."

"Could we have avoided UDI?"

"We nearly did! But we threw away the chance. The support for Sir Edgar Whitehead and his 1961 Constitution had been blown apart by the time of the 1962 election."

"67% of the European vote endorsed changes that would have speeded up African advancement enormously - increasing the number of African voters by 50,000 and bringing Africans directly into government.

"It incorporated a declaration of rights entrenching fundamental freedoms with no distinction in race, colour or creed. Whitehead knew we'd have a black PM by about 1984. Understood - and accepted.

"The absolute tragedy was the sudden NDP decision to order Africans not to vote . . .

"Do you remember while we were in Bulawayo, I asked which were the most tragic mistakes made in the context of everything that took place here historically?"

Carol smiled. "I used them to introduce my history thesis.

Angus nodded. "I think history will agree the NDP's decision on the 1961 Constitution was the most tragic mistake of all for the nation as a whole. The next most tragic was the white population's decision to vote Whitehead out of power."

"Why did the NDP reject it? They must have known it was a step in the right direction."

"Joshua Nkomo certainly did - but vested interests moved into place – the Northern Rhodesian leaders, and a couple of ours, were deep in discussion with Russia and China. Both were determined to gain access to our mineral resources. Both promising the earth. They became the instant new 'good guys' to listen to.

"Southern Rhodesia was held up as a model of how colonies should be run, but when it came to the crunch, nothing mattered, because the times were changing - independence was rolling down Africa. despite that, even Julius Nyerere expressed doubt as to whether Southern Rhodesian Africans were capable of running the country.

"But all of that was negated by a flaming desire to decolonise that burnt in the heart of black Africa.

"Most of the countries gaining independence to the north of us had had hundreds of years of exposure to democracy. Since settlement in 1890, with widespread initial resistance to education and the white man's ways, Rhodesian whites have had only 20 to 30 years to pass on the skills necessary for good governance of a modern society – substantially less than the time Mzilikazi and Lobengula spent as rulers here, changing the lives of the locals to accept their Matebele Kingdom!"

"Did any Africans vote?"

"Oh yes, they did – mostly businessmen and traders – and the greater percentage were in agreement with Whitehead's policies. We've just had figures, suggesting that only another thousand black votes would have kept the UFP in power. An absolute bloody tragedy."

Carol looked at him reprovingly. "Dad, you're sounding like Aidan!"

"I know." He grinned ruefully. "Sometimes that's the only word that sums it up.

"I feel it particularly, because almost everything embodied in the proposals for the 1961 Constitution came about because of the hard work Nkanyiso and I put in on the African Affairs Board. A double heartbreak."

"We need one more educated generation. The tendency is to still to look to the Chief for guidance. And where there is no Chief, they look to the person with the loudest voice. Fine if that person is a benevolent ruler, but if he becomes a malevolent dictator . . . God help us all."

She had watched him leave . . . the slump of his shoulders reflected the death of his dreams. As a District Commissioner, he knew the moment something was wrong. The temperature was going up again, directly affecting the DC's office.

It was the first time she'd really looked at her father in a long while. He'd spent his life trying to find answers for Southern Rhodesia's Africans. He was a good man . . . because of his dedication, they had, as a family, seen him at home so seldom.

All she saw now was a broken man.

The new normal

Carol had felt the sword of Damocles hung over their heads after Angus left that day. She looked down into the valley floor, wondering whether their children would ever inherit the farm that they'd worked so hard to develop over the last five years.

They loved the simple life they led. The establishment cost had been horrendous, and they were only able to operate thanks to the benevolence of the Land Bank. But things were improving. They were now responsible for the jobs and lives of 228 people – the farm workers and their families.

One of the greatest problems was that the farm was so remote. They felt far away from anyone and anything, but they'd discipline themselves to go down to Centenary Club at least twice a week. Carol and Simon started playing golf, while Dick's wife Miriam loved meeting with all the other nannies looking after an assorted bunch of kids.

The kids would have fun in their safely fenced-off area planted with grass and trees. Their nannies' boisterous chats and shrieks of laughter at the latest bit of scandal or news mingled with childish squeals of delight as they played on swings and slides or made castles and moats with buckets and water in the sand pit. It was when they were quiet that you knew something was wrong. But so far, they were just a bunch of good friends, enjoying a day out and wonderful with the children.

Carol and Simon had started to make friends in the district too. Jan and Jono Johnson were close to them in thinking, humour, interest and intrigue in world affairs - and almost the same political inclination. It was a delight to share lives and families at regular braais and pool days. Best thing of all, they were only 20 minutes down the road at Glen Rosa farm. Jono had come over to them in their very first season, as he had had problems with his seedbeds that year. Simon had grown far too many for our needs and was happy to give him what he needed. Their friendship grew from there.

There had been intense speculation at the Club about the effects of UDI. Most were pretty gung-ho, with comments ranging from the bombastic to the concerned to the informed.

"We'll show those poncey Brits . . ."

"Just got to make a plan man."

"Bloody Afs, after all we've done for them!"

"Shit man, I'm a bit blinking scared you know . . ."

"We've just received a big shipment of crude from South Africa, and it's on the way to the refinery in Umtali as we speak."

It was real bar talk, and there was great cheering as these small triumphs were shared. Almost imperceptibly, the spirit of the country was changing.

"We're not going to let the bastards bring us down."

The subject of the latest round of guffaws on their next visit to the Club was that the British Navy had just sent a carrier and two frigates to patrol the Mozambique Channel with a third on its way. In addition, three Shackletons were flying non-stop air patrols. The object of all this attention was quite simple – to prevent any tankers offloading petrol in Beira for the rebel regime of Rhodesia.

On 5th April 1966, the Greek tanker *Ioanna V* somehow slipped into Beira harbour, unchecked by the British Navy and in fact, escorted by a frustrated frigate, the *HMS Plymouth*. The British ship had attempted to persuade the *Ioanna V* to go to another port, but Greece refused permission to divert it, and the *Plymouth* could not use force on an ally! The hoots of laughter and cheering at this announcement boosted everyone's confidence. The *Ioanna V* was the toast of the country.

"Bloody Brits can't even manage their own navy!" became the saying of the day – with "Thank You Ioanna V" tee shirts and bumper stickers to be seen everywhere!

The anger against Britain was tangible. Most white Rhodesians were British one or two generations ago, and all were incredulous at the change in British attitude towards them.

But the reality of what it was going to mean was beginning to sink in. Everyone was talking of cutting back on managers and crop sizes, and the Rhodesia Tobacco Association (RTA) had issued a warning to say that substantially reduced quotas would be introduced for next year's crop.

The member-in-charge called a meeting of all farmers, saying that from now on, there would be weekly situation reports or SITREPS.

Yesterday's SITREP was introduced by saying, "However exciting it is that the *Ioanna V* sneaked past the British naval blockade and docked, the reality is that we are going to be very short of petrol."

The policeman on duty presented a clear picture of the security situation, saying that the government was issuing a system of petrol coupons so everyone was going to have to conserve petrol and that it would probably result in long queues in the cities. Farmers would be assessed on their current diesel and petrol usage and would receive 75% of what was estimated at the beginning of a crop-growing season, with an adjustment occurring towards the end of each season.

Carol left the meeting wondering just what it was they weren't being told.

Today they were heading into Salisbury for the last tobacco sale of the season. It had been a short selling season for them, as their acreage was still relatively small. But the prices had been outstanding. Simon knew the quality of the bales he had submitted this time were amongst the best yet.

Those tobacco sales were always thrilling, with the buzz and excitement of entering the huge auction rooms, with the warm biscuit smell of mature tobacco leaf. The distinctive calls of larger-than-life auctioneers were preceded by the shout of a starter giving a suggested price point. From there the lines snaked between the tobacco bales as international buyers used their own secret language to let the auctioneer know they'd buy. The marker would write the agreed price on a ticket and throw it onto the bale. Once the main party had passed, farm owners

364

could 'tear the ticket' in half if they weren't satisfied with the price. Then the bales were towed away by a small golf cart to be sent off to wherever they had been purchased – or back for re-sale. It was an clean and efficient process and gave buyers and farmers a chance to talk about everything of mutual interest.

Today, the talk was almost entirely about the courage of the *Ioanna V* and the ineffectiveness of the British blockade. Nobody seemed to have been particularly hit by sanctions yet. There were some products you could no longer buy, and the quality of toilet paper had slipped a little, but already alternative products were on quickly manufactured assembly lines. More and more people were producing their own finished product from the raw material the country had once, so obligingly, sent back to Britain to be manufactured. They would then add their own value and sell it back to Rhodesia at vastly inflated prices!

Simon and Carol left after their best sale yet and headed off to treat themselves to lunch at Barbours. They made plans to take the children down to the Cape for their first family holiday ever. Regardless of what else was happening, life was looking up.

Prune buys another store.

A few months ago, Prune confirmed that he had bought the corner plot of land on the turnoff to the Alpha trail. He "borrowed" Lovemore to make bricks for him to build his store. Carol and Simon had of course said yes, he could certainly have Lovemore, but it delayed the building of their own house by another frustrating few weeks.

Prune then asked Carol if she would confirm that she was able to go in a couple of days a week, keep an eye on the place and do the book keeping. She was very happy to do so, and Jan offered to have the children to play with her two littles, Tommy and JoJo on "store" days.

Carol loved working in the store, and Prune was due up in a few days to see how things were going in this, his fourth and latest store. She had marked it on her calendar: 14th May 1966.

By the time they got home from the sale, Prune had arrived.

Prune and Maura now had two little boys – one of four, the other of two and a half. They were Vusimuzi and Mtokozisi. When little Vusimuzi was born, his mother said he was such a gift that the name stuck. Gift – Carol had written to say it was a great name. But she wrote again to say she didn't approve of Mtokozisi being called Skellum! Maura wrote back to say it was a Scottish word "which Lalan used when she said, 'Oh but he is such a skellum', meaning a naughty boy!" The latest news was that Maura was pregnant again.

Now that Lalan had retired, Prune told Carol he had built her a house next door to them. She loved looking after the children when Maura had to work in the store. That was if she wasn't too busy still dropping in to help the little clinic in Balla Balla.

Carol had made up one of their stretchers in the grading shed – sorry the house was not yet finished. Next day, they drove down to the store, loving the cacophony of blaring smanje-manje from the little radio in the corner, barely audible above the shouts of women arguing and bargaining, with the men recounting the latest disaster midst howls of laughter and slapping of backs.

Carol loved it. So did Prune, and that wonderful grin was back again. Prune proudly brought out photos of his two boys, who were only 11 months apart. He explained that "Gift" and "Skellum" didn't seem right as they grew up, so their English names were "Naison" and "Macloud" in honour of each of his adoptive parents. Maura was 7 months pregnant now, and they had decided that if the baby was a girl, her name would be Rosie.

The tills jangled constantly in cheerful counterpoint to the hubbub as scruffy old notes changed hands or women brought in homegrown vegetables to sell. The store was already trading well above budget. Prune had come up just to see if there were any little opportunities they could take advantage of or perhaps better processes they might use.

When Carol had told him a couple of years ago that there was no store in the area, he had made what appeared at the time, to have been another crazy business decision, setting up a store in such a remote location. But it was right on the corner of the main road with the left-hand turn-off twisting and dropping its way down the escarpment to Mzarabani.

He now looked with satisfaction at the many well-worn walking paths coming from every direction and knew his decision had been right. He hoped it would serve not only the commercial farms in that northern area of Centenary and the mission at St Alberts, as well as supplying fertilizers and other farming needs to small-scale farmers in the valley.

Keeper Tendai was a gloriously rotund bundle of good humour and honesty. His face lit up with conspiratorial joy at every breath of scandal, perfect for ongoing discussion and dissection, enhancing each with every retelling. His wife Tsitsi, complete with an equally chubby little Tendai strapped to her back, was busy taking money, negotiating on purchases and giving back change.

Prune was hard to impress. He'd become a tough taskmaster, not allowing himself or any of the Store Keepers any latitude, except Carol, who could almost do whatever she wanted.

He had to admit he was impressed with Tendai's salesmanship and his wise recommendations on buying for the specific local wants of the area, particularly now, in light of the sanctions following UDI.

Despite everything, the year ahead looked promising. It was Tendai who handed out seeds to regular customers, urging them to grow cabbages, carrots, potatoes and beans and assuring them that the store would buy them back at a good price and sell them to its other customers. Even fishermen were bringing in fresh bream from the Zambesi – so there were a lot of happy customers. Carol took the chance to bring in the bead and basketwork from the farm, and sales boomed.

They had just been granted a licence to sell petrol and diesel, because there was no garage up at this end of the Centenary block. The British navy ships might to be unable to prevent oil tankers from unloading in Beira at this stage, but that would change. The truth was that they were beginning to feel the pinch with the emergency application of petrol coupons and rationing, so Prune wasn't sure whether he had been wise to take it on.

They spent the bulk of the morning in the office just off the main store, planning for the extension of a small eating area providing café style buns and tea. The figures looked promising. It was certainly worth a try – Carol and Tendai both agreed to the details, taking up Prune's offer to invest a little themselves into the new business.

Tendai went back into the store to help Tsitsi while Carol and Prune finished a basic contract for them all to sign.

Then the store went quiet.

Deafeningly quiet.

No chatter. No laughter.

No ribald stories or women buying. Only the endless smanje-manje crackling of static from a remote and badly tuned radio.

Prune put his finger to his lips.

They lifted their chairs as they stood noiselessly, moving to a crack in the woodwork that looked straight along the front counter. The customers were standing frozen or trying as nonchalantly as possible to find an excuse to leave.

There were five men at the counter, dressed in distinctive pale khaki long trousers tucked into heavy hiking boots, their long-sleeved shirts buttoned up to a band collar. They wore military style Cuban caps with a flap down the back.

Tendai was serving them.

But gone was the jovial master storyteller. This Tendai was grey and taut. He was responding instantly to their requests for drinks, chocolates and cigarettes.

Carol signalled to Prune that she would go out as if there was nothing amiss pretending to ask Tendai a question. He urged her not to, but Tendai had a problem on his hands and she could help.

She walked out with her eyes fixed to the contract they had been signing.

"Tendai, would you have a look at this . . ." she began and trailed off.

The leader of the group had abruptly turned away, but not before a shaft of recognition hit Carol, almost physically.

It was Jabu.

The men left and walked quickly down the path towards the escarpment.

"Tendai, who were those men?"

"*Tsotsis* . . . *'mgandanga*," Tendai said under his breath.

"What do you mean? What is *'mgandanga*?"

Tendai looked at her for a long time before he said: "They mean to kill us . . ."

Prune had walked out and caught the last words. "What do you mean, Tendai?"

The store was filling up again as customers dared to move back. The atmosphere was frozen, faces blank, expressionless.

"I have heard stories of people that they call *'mgandanga*. They have been threatening to kill some of us in Mzarabani. They've been saying they are freedom fighters."

Tendai's alarm was almost tangible. Prune looked at Carol, and they walked back into the office. "I saw them," she said.

Prune nodded, and she knew he had seen them too.

He had also seen Jabu.

"What do we do Prune?"

He shook his head dumbly.

"We must do something. If they can be stopped now, perhaps we can prevent Jabu being killed," Carol pleaded.

"Or he could go to gaol."

Time froze.

The noise in the store started to swell back to something like its normal levels, but nobody looked anybody else in the eye. They were scared, uncertain, a bit excited, but a lot apprehensive.

Prune picked up the phone and put it down again.

Carol said, "No Prune, let me cope with the fallout. You must stay uninvolved."

"No!" Prune cried. "Jabu saw you! He will know you are here."

"He's my twin, Prune. We bled fingers."

"That's the one reason you cannot be the one to ring."

Carol reluctantly handed him the phone.

Prune dialled.

It clicked over-loudly as the call was answered.

"Centenary police, good afternoon."

END OF BOOK ONE

ABOUT THE AUTHOR

Jill Baker spent her childhood years in Matebeleland before moving to Mashonaland at the age of 14.

From school she studied music at the Guildhall School of Music in London, while doing a business administration course. Marriage to a tobacco farmer meant their lives on the farm ended shortly after UDI and Jill and the family moved to Salisbury to work for the next 15 years as a journalist, news and documentary presenter and producer in radio and television.

On moving to Australia in 1983, Jill managed a radio station before opening her own business in consultancy to the tourism industry.

Her first book, Beloved African told the story of her father's life as a headmaster in African Education from 1936 to 1966 and went to three editions. Sadly very few reached Zimbabwe. To correct that wrong, Jill has producing an e-book and will record an audiobook of Beloved African, which will be published at the same time as the audiobook for The Horns.

Jill was awarded the Order of Australia Medal in 2005 for her work in settling Zimbabwean families into Australia.

THE HORNS: WHO'S WHO

PRUNE (Vusimuzi) MSIPA
    Adopted by: Sister McLeod (Lalan)
    Guardian: Naison Msipa
    Married: Maura
    Children: Vusimuzi (Gift) / Naison
             Mtokozisi (Skellum) / Macloud

JABULANI (Jabu: Bhekisizwe) NCUBE
    Father: Nkanyiso Ncube
    Girlfriend: Bongani Moyo (father Mandhla Moyo)
    Grandfather: Mehluli Khumalo
    Great grandfather   Mtjaan Khumalo

CAROL DAVIDSON
    Father: Angus Davidson
    Brother: Tim
    Married: Simon Watson
    Children: Fiona and Stuart

THEMBA MOTLANE
    Father: Kuda
    Great grandfather: Motshodi / Jan Grootboom

AMANDEBELE KINGS AND CHIEFS

MZILIKAZI, KING	1790 - 1868:	reigned 1823 - 1868
LOBENGULA, KING	1836 – 1894;	reigned 1870 – 1894
NKULUMANE	missing heir to the amaNdebele throne	
MTJAAN KHUMALO	Lobengula's Chief Induna	
BABJAAN,	Envoy to England	
MSHETE	Envoy to England	
MBIGO	Chief Induna of the Zwangendaba Regiment	
MNCUMBATA	Regent critical to Lobengula's accession	
MAGWEGWE	Ordered to burn Lobengula's first capital; died with Lobengula	

EARLY MISSIONARIES

MOFFAT, Robert	Kuruman, Bechuanaland
THOMAS, Thomas Morgan	Inyati and Shiloh
HELM, Charles	Hope Fountain
CARNEGIE, David	Hope Fountain

HUNTERS, CONCESSION SEEKERS

SELOUS, Frederick Courtney
PHILLIPS, Sam (Induna Sam)
DAWSON, James
COLENBRANDER, Johann
WILSON, Michael 'Matebele'

RUDD CONCESSION

RUDD, Charles Dunnell
THOMPSON, Francis
MAGUIRE, James Rochfort

LIPPERT TREATY

LIPPERT, Eduard
RENNY-TAILYOUR, Henry

BRITISH GOVERNMENT OFFICIALS

KNUTSFORD, Lord	Colonial Secretary
LOCH, Sir Henry	High Commissioner for Southern Africa
MOFFAT, John Smith	Administrator: Bechuanaland
	Advisor and Queen's representative: Matebeleland
SHIPPARD, Sir Sidney	Resident Commissioner of Bechuanaland

BRITISH SOUTH AFRICA COMPANY

RHODES, Cecil John	Founder and Managing Director
BEIT, Alfred	
JAMESON, Dr Leander Starr	

THE EXPLORING COMPANY

GIFFORD, Lord
CAWSTON, George
MAUND, Edward

THE HORNS: HISTORICAL TIME LINE

1790 (est.) Mzilikazi born

1821   Robert Moffat is appointed to Kuruman Mission

1823   Mzilikazi breaks away from Shaka

1829 / 1835   Moffat meets Mzilikazi.

1836 (est.) Lobengula Born

1838   Mzilikazi crosses Limpopo River and heads north with 2 regiments:
            Godwane Ndiweni leads remainder of population to Matebeleland

1840   Mzilikazi returns: son Nkulumane to be inaugurated; throws all
            collaborators, sons, relatives off Nthaba zi'Nduna. (Ntabazinduna)
            Lobengula hidden in the Matopos
            Capitals: Mahlokohloko; Inyathi; Mhlanhlandhlela

1853   Early Boer 'friendship' treaty signed with Mzilikazi

1859   Moffat meets Mzilikazi for the last time and Inyati Mission is
            established close to King Mzilikazi's capital, Inyathi – built by John and
            Robert Moffat; first missionary William Sykes

1868   Death of Mzilikazi

1870   Accession and inauguration of Lobengula
            Capitals: Gibexhegu/KoBulawayo; Umhlabathini

1881   Destruction of KoBulawayo by fire

1887   'Renewal of friendship' Grobler treaty

1888   Moffat treaty – peace and amity for ever …'
            Rudd Concession (30th October)

1889   20th December: Charter granted to the British South Africa Company

1890   Lippert's Treaty/Concession
            Pioneer Column 28th June – 13th September

1893   Matebele war

1894   Lobengula's death

1896   Matebele rebellion and indaba

1922   Referendum: Union with South Africa or Responsible Government

1923   BSAC Charter revoked
            Southern Rhodesia became a self-governing colony

1953   Federation of Rhodesia and Nyasaland

1957   Southern Rhodesia African National Congress (SRANC) formed

1958   Garfield Todd's cabinet resigns:
            Sir Edgar Whitehead becomes Prime Minister

1959   SRANC outlawed: National Democratic Party (NDP) formed

1961   NDP outlawed: ZAPU formed
            Referendum: 1961 constitutional changes

1962   Rhodesian Front wins the election : Winston Field Prime Minister

1963   Dissolution of the Federation
            ZANU breaks away from ZAPU

1964   Ian Smith becomes Prime Minister

1965   Unilateral Declaration of Independence

October 30th, 1888.

"Know all men by these presents that whereas Charles Dunnell Rudd of Kimberley, Rochfort Maguire of London, and Francis Robert Thompson of Kimberley, hereinafter called the grantees, have covenanted and agreed, and do hereby covenant and agree, to pay to me, my heirs and successors, the sum of one hundred pounds sterling British currency, on the first day of every lunar month, and further to deliver at my Royal Kraal, one thousand Martini-Henry breech loading rifles, together with one hundred thousand rounds of suitable ball cartridge, five hundred of the said rifles, and fifty thousand of the said cartridges to be ordered from England forthwith, and delivered with reasonable despatch, and the re-mainder of the said rifles and cartridges to be delivered so soon as the said grantees shall have commenced to work mining machinery within my territory, and further to deliver on the Zambesi River a steamboat with guns suitable for defensive purposes upon the said river, or in lieu of the said steamboat, should I so elect, to pay to me the sum of five hundred pounds sterling British currency, on the execution of these presents, I, LoBengula, King of Matebeleland, Mashonaland, and other adjoining territories, in the exercise of my sovereign powers, and in the presence and with the consent of my Council of Indunas, do hereby grant and assign unto the said grantees, their heirs, representatives, and assigns, jointly and severally, the complete and exclusive charge over all metals and minerals situated and contained in my kingdoms, principalities, and dominions, together with full power to do all things that they may deem necessary to win and procure the same, and to hold, collect, and enjoy the profits and revenues, if any, derivable from the said metals and minerals subject to the aforesaid payment, and whereas I have been much molested of late by divers persons seeking and desiring to obtain grants and concessions of land and mining rights in my territories, I do hereby authorise the said grantees, their heirs, representatives, and assigns, to take all necessary and lawful steps to exclude from my kingdoms, principalities, and dominions all persons seeking land, metals, minerals, or mining rights therein, and I do hereby undertake to render them such needful assistance as they may from time to time require for the exclusion of such persons and to grant no concessions of land or mining rights from and after this date without their con-sent and concurrence, provided that if at any time the said monthly payment of one hundred pounds shall be in arrear for a period of three months then this grant shall cease and determine from the date of the last made payment, and further provided that nothing contained in these presents shall extend to or affect a grant made by me of certain mining rights in a portion of my territory south of the Ramakoban River, which grant is commonly known as the Tati Concession.

This given under my hand this thirtieth day of October in the year of our Lord eighteen hundred and eighty-eight at my Royal Kraal.

APPENDIX 2: THE LIPPERT CONCESSION

FROM RHODES AND RHODESIA: The White Conquest of Zimbabwe 1884-1902
Arthur Keppel-Jones

We have seen Lippert's agents – chiefly Renny-Tailyour, Boyle and Reilly, but Colenbrander had originally been one of them – at work in Bulawayo from an early date. In July 1889 it had been reported that they were 'coquetting' with Rhodes on the Rand, but were careful not to change sides at Bulawayo too obviously.

The course of this coquetting did not, however, run smooth. By the time the Pioneers were on the march, the Lippert party was doing all it could to frustrate their enterprise. Thus on 17th July, it was Boyle and Reilly who "had the King's stamp over at their place for nearly two hours".

Reilly . . . read to the king an extract from the Diamond Fields Advertiser which assured nervous settlers that Lobengula was doing all he could to help the Company in Mashonaland. This was true, but to publish it in Bulawayo was a neat way of shattering the king's careful diplomacy. The news of these doings reached Loch in a telegram from Moffat while the interviews with the delegation were in progress. The high commissioner accordingly warned Renny-Tailyour and Boyle that if they continued to stir up trouble they would not be allowed to enter Matebeleland. When they did return in September, Moffat reported that they were "all going to be good boys in future."

Only up to a point. On 22 April 1891 the "good boys" got something which they claimed was the concession they were after and of which a copy afterwards reached Loch. The story of this concession, can be pieced together from subsequent statements by Acutt and Lippert. Renny-Tailyour "represented to the King that, while the Charter Company had merely obtained a gold concession, they were taking the land also. Mr Tailyour undertook to go and contest the matter with the Company, and the Chief said that on his return from doing so he would give him a concession.

Mr. Tailyour wanted a sort of general power of attorney, and said he could not draw it up properly here, but would put it into proper form when he got to Johannesburg." He therefore equipped himself with two pieces of paper. One remained a blank sheet, except that it bore the date, elephant stamp, Mshete's mark and the signatures of Renny-Tailyour, Acutt and Reilly. The other was supposed to contain, in layman's language, the details that were to be transferred to the first " in proper form."

Either the contents of the second paper were written by Renny-Tailyour and not shown to his colleagues or to the king, or what was transposed to the signed and sealed paper in Johannesburg was very different from what the second paper had contained when it left Bulawayo. Lippert, who professed a kind of childlike innocence in such legal matters, consulted Advocate J W Leonard (a well-known figure in Uitlander history), who "then put the concession into the form it now bears. When a copy of it reached Moffat from Loch, the former showed it to Acutt, who said "it contains a great deal more than what was specified on that occasion."

Lobengula's – or should we say J W Leonard's – concession to Renny-Tailyour gave:

the sole and exclusive right and privilege for the full term of one hundred years, to lay out, grant, or lease, for such periods as he may think fit, farms, townships, building plots and grazing areas, to impose and levy rents, licenses and taxes; to get in, cllect and receive the same, to give and grant certificates in my name for the occupation of any farms (etc); to establish and to grant licenses for the establishment of banks; to issue bank-notes; to establish a mint . . .

The concession, in the form it assumed in Johannesburg therefore, gave Renny-Tailyour, who transferred it to Lippert, the sole right to grant land titles in Lobengula's dominions. Whether or not Lippert had misgivings about the strength of his precious document, his policy was to assume a confident and aggressive air. In playing against Rhodes one had to have good cards, or a good poker face. The Company had a weakness in its inability to grant land. If Lippert could acquire the right to do this, he could hold the Company to ransom.

Small as it was, Lippert intended to make use of it. On 15 May he had written t the Company's secretary in Cape Town, suggesting a meeting. Negotiations had dragged on unsuccessfully. The Company could not afford at that time to pay Lippert's price, and Rhodes affected to regard the concession as worthless. Lippert therefore turned on the heat. F J Dormer, editor of the Johannesburg Star, informed Rhodes that Lippert would not sell for less than £250,000. If Rhodes did not give a favourable answer within ten days Lippert would publish his concession in full page advertisements "in all leading papers"; the rush to get farms under the scheme might then all but sweep the Company away.

However dubious the Renny-Tailyour concession of 22 April may have been (Lobengula in his customary way now denied to Moffat that he had granted it, but the full story of the "blank cheque" was not yet known). Alfred Beit had persuaded his cousin, Lippert, to delay the threatened publication, but had warned Rhodes that he must either negotiate or fight. Accordingly, Rhodes told Loch that he had given Rudd the authority to negotiate with Lippert.

On 12 September 1891, Lippert and Rudd signed a contract, by which the latter agreed to take over the concession on condition that Lippert went to Bulawayo, had it confirmed in really 'proper form' by Lobengula and gave proof that the king had actually accepted the down payment.

Lippert had to conceal from the king all evidence of collusion with Rhodes. Lobengula's sole reason for giving or confirming so dangerous a concession was to thwart the Company, to throw the affairs of the white invaders into a disarray which would slow down their operations and win precious time for him. Moffat knew the truth, but to his intense disgust was under instructions from Loch to join in the game and keep his knowledge to himself.

Published McGill Queens University Press 1987

Lobengula presented the Indunas, Babyaan and Mtshete to Maund and Colenbrander as his Ambassadors to England. The *Indunas* set off on their visit wearing loincloths of skin and carrying their shields, small spears and knobkerries.

E.P.Mathers, in his book *Zambesia, England's El Dorado in Africa* gives an account of the *Indunas'* travels: *"The two men were willing to go - they had no option. The party started, one of the Ambassadors being at first very sulky. The King provided some cattle for the road and agreed to pay all expenses.*

Babyaan, Maund, Mtshete, Colenbrander

On asking how much the travelling expenses would be he was informed that their amount would be about £600. His Majesty thereupon got into his wagon and took down a handkerchief full of English sovereigns, some of which had been obtained by the Rudd concession.

"Babjaan was . . . a charming and dear old man, always ready to do anything he was bid, pleased with everything, and one of the most unselfish of men I have ever met. He gave up all his presents. I never had the least difficulty all the time with him.

"The other man was about 65 years of age. It was impossible to please him, do what one would, for he was ever trying to see how much difficulty he could put in the way. On the way down he stood up for being the first of the two. He sometimes sulked for three days at a time under a tree and would not speak to any of us because we gave him the same food as the other. I treated him exactly like the other, though he considered he was of a better caste.

I halted the wagon several miles out of Pretoria, rode on, and rushed them into a store and clothed them in neat suits of blue serge. The inside of the Johannesburg and Kimberley coach was taken at a cost of £110. I had previously interviewed Oom Paul [Kruger] and [General Piet] Joubert, and found out they knew nothing about the Indunas, whom I thought would be stopped.

At Johannesburg men who had booked their seats for the inside were furious at (Babayane and Mshete) being inside, but I stuck to my point, offering anybody, should it be rainy, to come inside and rest themselves if they liked. Two gentlemen accepted and got into conversation with the Indunas. The health of the old men was very bad from the hard travelling, their legs and feet being swollen to an enormous size through sitting still. We got them down to Kimberley.

On getting into the train for the first time at Kimberley a decided look of horror came into their eyes as they began to rush forward. I turned around to Babjaan and said, 'What, a King's soldier and afraid! on which, to show that he was not, he put his head out of the window and kept it there for half an hour, much to my concern, for I was afraid it might come in contact with something.

When I accepted the mission there was no accredited Government agent with LoBengula, he being an independent king beyond English jurisdiction. He had chosen to send the men on his own account, specially instructing me not to halt by "the gates by the sea", but at once to go over the water where the white men came from, and that his Indunas must see with their own eyes before they return whether the White Queen was alive."

"I have had long interviews with the two Matebele who are described as headmen in letter received from LoBengula; they say LoBengula has been so often deceived by Europeans of different nations telling him there is no such person as the Queen, others saying that they come from the Queen, that they want to know whether England and the Queen exist; they have no other message. This, as far as they are concerned, is the sole object of their mission. They are to see with their own eyes and go back and report to King; they say they will be killed on their return if they do not cross the sea. I advise that they may be allowed to proceed. They have funds for such purpose. Mission is most anxious to proceed by next mail".

Maund's description of the voyage follows:

At last a start was made for England on board the "Moor", and the Matebeles had further experience of the ocean which had interested them so much at Cape Town. They went into raptures over the incoming waves, likening the rollers dashing in to the shore to the columns of their impis rushing up to the King at a review. On board the steamer, which they called "the great kraal that pushes through the water", the Indunas were neither sick nor sorry. The officers and passengers were extremely kind to them, and Lady Frederick Cavendish, who was voyaging to England by the steamer, took a special interest in them. So much impression did this lady make on the natives that when they returned Babjaan desired specially to be remembered to the "Queen's woman Induna." We shall allow Lady Frederick to speak now as to the next experiences of the Matebele envoys

"I had an interview with them, and took pains to convince them that there was a White Queen, assuring them that I had had the honour of serving Her Majesty and had kissed her hand. One of them thereupon touched his eyes and replied, "We believe it, as you say so, but we are taking our own eyes to see." When we got into rough weather in the Bay, they said, " The river is full to-day." Off Lisbon, when told it was Portuguese, they sat on deck with their backs turned to it, and said, -" How is it the White Queen allows Portugal between her and Africa?"

During the voyage I considered very much how I could advance the cause. I became very anxious indeed that it should be successful, and that we should contrive an interview, but I believe we should never have managed it if we had not fortunately touched at Madeira, and taken on board Lord Lothian. I knew very well that, even if Lord Knutsford approved of this deputation, there might still be some difficulty in obtaining Her Majesty's consent to an interview, as she is not in the habit of receiving stray black men, especially with no accredited person in attendance on them. However, when I saw Lord Lothian, I thought at once that he was the best person to interest in the matter, as a member of the Government, though not in the Cabinet.

We had not much time, for we took him on board on Friday, and we landed at Southampton on Tuesday, but I at once introduced him to Lieut. Maund and to Mr. Selous (who was also with us, and who knew Matebeleland well, as he spends most of his time hunting there), and by the time we landed, Lord Lothian, after an interview with the two Chiefs, and after hearing the whole history, was quite as keenly interested as I was, and assured me he would do his utmost.

On the Tuesday when we arrived at Southampton a brother of Lieut. Maund came on board, and he caused us some dismay by saying that Her Majesty was going to Biarritz the very following Monday. So we had very little time to spare. Lieut. Maund gave up all for lost, but I assured him that the hurry was all for the best, as there would be so little time for pros and cons. On the Thursday afternoon I received a happy letter from him, saying that consent had been given, and that the Chiefs were to be taken to Windsor Castle on Saturday, at 3 o'clock.

I hoped all was now in good train, but on the following day – Friday afternoon – a terrible hitch occurred. Lieut. Maund wrote me word that, though the Chiefs were to be welcomed, he was not to be allowed to accompany them - the fact being, as Sir Hercules had foreseen, that it is not usual for a private gentleman to be received on such a mission at Court. He wrote to me therefore to say he was in a great difficulty; he was not at all anxious to intrude on Her Majesty, but the Chiefs would not stir without him. They said, "The King told us that Maundy was to be our Father. We were not to be afraid of the great White Queen; we don't understand this at all, and if Maundy does not go with us, we shall go straight home to Matebeleland."

I immediately tried to find Lord Knutsford, and put the case before him, but I could not succeed in seeing him; I could merely send a note up to his room. However, late in the evening I ascertained that Lord Lothian had set to work afresh, and had overcome the difficulty and that all was settled for the interview on the following day. It is amusing to notice how these two blacks had brought all the authorities round!

The scene on the arrival of the Indunas at Waterloo may be described. The night was a bitterly cold one, and the Matebeles needed the shelter of heavy overcoats to protect them from the "cauld blasts" which swept London.

They had arrived during the day at Southampton, and little time was lost in conveying them to the capital. They left the port by the 5.15 train, and got to Waterloo Station "on time" at 7.40. As the train drew up to the platform one or two pressmen soon scented their presence. They had travelled in a first-class compartment, and were in custody - it almost seemed so - of a white gentleman whom ultimately I recognised as an old friend. A little natural eagerness was shown on the part of the small knot of Fourth Estate Scribes to come near the door of the compartment.

Orders were quickly given by the gentleman in charge of the royal spokesmen to allow no one to approach the door. "Aye, aye, sir," was the ready response of two porters, who did not say they had any eye to the main chance in the shape of a possible lump of gold from one of the Matebele concessions. They were quickly joined by a stalwart commissionaire - not concessionaire, whose row of medals, hanging proudly on his manly bosom, glanced fitfully in the dismal lamplight.

It was possible, just possible, to get a " keek" at the distinguished arrivals by watching a chance when the persons of the three conscientious guards unbent a very little.

They - the distinguished arrivals - did not look happy, well, not so happy as they would have looked had they had no overcoats and no anything on, and had been dancing in a blazing sun a war fandango, preparatory to a look in on Khama or the Mashonas. They were huddled up in their respective corners, and from beneath their unaccustomed "wideawakes" there was to be seen no trace either of amusement or surprise at the bustling scene being enacted outside. Quite the reverse; they bore themselves, as far as the low temperature would allow them, with that impassive dignity familiar to all South Africans as a characteristic of the superior native. If they had voiced their emotions they would probably have asked for a fire. They were taken to Berner's Hotel, where they remained *during their stay in London.*

On the Saturday following, the Indunas travelled to Windsor by a train conveying the Cabinet Ministers, and royal carriages awaited them at the station. The Queen had considerately sent for picked men of the 2nd Life Guards, who lined the approaches to St. George's Hall, through which the party marched. The Indunas were so astonished at the immobility of the soldiers, that they concluded they were stuffed, until one of them saw their eyes moving. This speaks well for the steadiness of the troopers.

On the conclusion of the business part of the interview, Her Majesty said to the Indunas, "You have come a very long way to see me; I hope the journey has been made pleasant for you, and that you did not suffer from the cold." In acknowledgment, one of them stepped forward, bowing with truly courtier-like gesture, and replied, " How should we feel cold in the presence of the great White Queen?" adding, with a shrug of his shoulders, "Is it not in the power of great kings and queens to make it either hot or cold?"

They were greatly delighted at their reception by the Queen, keeping on speaking about it. They said that their eyes had seen and their ears had heard her voice. "It was easy," they declared, "to see among the assembly at Windsor which was the White Queen, from her manner and bearing"

Needless to say, the Envoys did a great deal of sightseeing when in England, and some of their quaint impressions may be recorded. They consider (as of course they should) the Queen the greatest woman they ever saw, and Lady Randolph Churchill the most beautiful.

The Envoys were taken to "see the lions" – among them the literal lions at the Zoological Gardens, which naturally attracted a good deal of their attention. Their excitement was intense. When they came to these animals Babjaan could scarcely be restrained from attacking one of the lords of his native forest with his umbrella, nor could he understand why he was prevented.

It would interest LoBengula to learn that his representatives went to the Alhambra, and that they were undisguisedly satisfied with the ballet. For that occasion their eyes became twice their natural size. London, they said, was like the ocean; a man might walk, and walk, and walk, and yet never get to the end of the houses. If Englishmen were killed, they reported, for every drop of blood another would spring up to take their places; what most astonished them was the telephone.

They were placed a mile apart, and talked together. Afterwards they declared that they could imagine such a machine might talk English, but how it could be taught to speak the Kafir language they could not understand.

They visited Portsmouth and were shown over the fort by the commander. A steam launch was placed at the disposal of the Envoys, and in this they steamed about, the places of interest being pointed out and described to them by one of the Flag-Captains. To these, however, they seemed to pay but lukewarm attention, and requested that a rocket, which produced such an effect in Zululand, might be sent up and two were fired off for their benefit. The Nordenfelt guns were described to them, after which they were shown rifle practice at movable dummies. "Oh," said they, "is that the way you teach your men to shoot? Capital practice too."

As the grand finale to the sightseeing, the Indunas were taken to Aldershot, where a sham fight and inspection was held. It was the first big field day of the year, and it was whispered that the troops were turned out earlier than they otherwise would have been, in order to give the Envoys an idea of the capabilities of the English soldiers. The elements were rather unkind, and the review was opened under lowering skies and a drizzling rain.

The programme consisted of an inspection of cavalry and artillery, in the forenoon, in the Long Valley, and subsequently a sham fight upon the Fox Hills, to the west of the North Camp, in which about 10,000 men of all arms were engaged, under the direction of the new commander of the station, Lieut.-General Sir Evelyn Wood.

The Envoys, who were escorted by an aide-de-camp of the General, arrived from Aldershot, where they slept overnight, in an open barouche, and from this they witnessed the manoeuvre. The artillery and cavalry moved with precision and dash, which the British army have so long been famed.

After the charge of the cavalry upon the artillery, the troops sweeping past like a tornado, the Lancers spread out as if in pursuit of a discomfited force. Babjaan and Umshete, who had never seen such a display before, were almost mad with excitement. They fairly jumped with astonishment, and, standing on their seats eagerly watched every movement of the troops. Babjaan was the first to speak. " Such mighty horses - so big, so strong, and such discipline among the men,"

"Come and teach us how to drill and fight like that, and we will fear no nation in Africa," remarked both.   After the review, General Wood earnestly hoped that the troops they had seen maneouvering that day would never be required to fight against the Matebele people.

The Matebeles replied that they had now seen the real strength of England, and when it was explained to them that it was not a fair idea of what England really could turn out in case of necessity, they were greatly astonished, and remarked, "How can there be more? this must surely be all!" It was explained to them that General Wood was the General who turned Cetewayo out of his stronghold, and brought the assegai to Queen Victoria. Prince Albert Victor, who was with the General's staff, was introduced to the two Chiefs, and they remarked, " We can see why the Queen puts him with the big warrior - to teach him how to manage the Army himself."

The Indunas were taken over the Bank of England. They were first of all shown the room in which a machine automatically weighs the sovereigns fresh from the Mint. On being allowed to lift some bags of gold the Indunas remarked that it made their hearts sick to see so much gold which they could not put into their pockets. The Indunas were next conducted to the bullion room containing many piles of ingots, some of which they tried to lift, Babjaan being scarcely able to raise one of the ingots. At this point one of the Indunas wished it to be remembered that when any distinguished visitor was received by their King he showed him his flocks and herds, generally selecting the largest beast to present to the stranger. The hint was not taken, I am sorry to say."

On the evening of the envoys return from Aldershot, they retired to their room for the night, or so Colenbrander thought. The story goes that Colenbrander took the opportunity to go to the theatre with a friend, Captain Dainty. In the interval, Colenbrander had a call from the hotel requiring him to return urgently. It turned out that Babyaan had caused great consternation in the hotel lounge, by searching, stark naked, for his snuffbox, which he had left there! To make matter worse, the Induna couldn't find his snuffbox immediately, as it had fallen beneath a table, from where he proceeded to retrieve it on his hands and knees. The society ladies and gentlemen in the crowded lounge were stunned to silence! He returned to his room muttering that one of the ladies had helped herself to some of his snuff.

Bulawayo Books of Rhodesia
Libraries Australia

APPENDIX 4: LOBENGULA'S BURIAL PLACE

Excerpts from: HIS FINAL RESTING PLACE AND TREASURE
by C. K. Cooke (Archaeologist; Historical Monuments Commission)

ACCOUNTS SUGGESTING LOBENGULA CROSSED THE ZAMBEZI RIVER:

17th September, 1940, written by a European (name not disclosed):

"I cannot say for certain whether it was '94 or '95 when I met Lobengula, but I am quite sure he was introduced to me by Mpeseni. I do not believe the diamonds story, as I think Lobengula would have told me.

"On my return to Blantyre I told the story that I had seen and met Lobengula. He was supposed to have died, but I contradicted the fact. Major Forbes, the head of the B.S.A. Company in Blantyre, came to see me . . . I showed Major Forbes a photo of Lobengula taken by me at Mpeseni." *(Upengula,* p. 113.)

Mr. Gordon Lancaster, who has made extensive enquiry regarding the "Angoni" in Northern Rhodesia, published the following account in the *Proceedings of the Royal Anthropological Institute* (v. 67, 1937):

"Lobengula crossed the Zambesi at Manyere Drift and arrived at Mtenguli Uka Sosera village on the Lietembwe River in January, 1894. He was carried by an Ngoni who had been sent for that purpose. He was a very heavily built man with a large protruding belly, and breasts like those of a woman heavy in milk. So cumbersome was he that he had to be helped to move about from one place to another. He had a great pipe in which he smoked Hemp. If he passed the pipe he would talk, but if not it was a sign that he wished to be alone.

"When chief Mpenzeni visited him he used to crawl on his hands and knees to greet him. It is not known where Lobengula was buried; he was a fugitive from Justice. The secret was closely kept.

"It is said he died shortly after his arrival from the Zambezi in 1894. This information was given by an aged Ngoni councillor, named Ropu, who resided near Fort Jameson and died in 1927. This story is little known and usually all knowledge is denied."

ACCOUNTS SUGGESTING HE DID NOT DO SO

"An account of a discovery of Lobengula's Grave: related by Mrs Nortjie to A. C. Adams"

"In 1912 George Horton of Kalomo wanted to send some cattle across the Zambesi into Southern Rhodesia for the good grazing there, and my father arranged to take them for him. The cattle were loaded onto railway trucks at Kalomo, carried across the Zambesi, unloaded at a siding near Wankie, then trekked east to a place called the Ngamo Flats on the Gwaai River where they were put out to graze.

"A little while later, two Bushmen who worked with the herds approached and said they had heard that he and my father wanted to see Lobengula's grave. They said they knew where it was but they would only take them there if Piet Bree would shoot them an elephant. My father and Bree thought about this for a while and then decided to agree to the Bushmen's terms, so Bree went to Bulawayo the following day where he obtained a licence to shoot the elephant.

383

"The elephant was finally shot on the edge of a large water pan on the Ngamo Flats. Only when it actually lay dead on the ground did the Bushmen consent to lead the way to Lobengula's grave . . . the Bushmen told my father and Bree that they had seen Lobengula when he first came to the area, accompanied by twelve Matebele men and a coloured man, but they had kept out of sight as they were afraid of the Matebele who killed all the Bushmen they found.

"They camped in the plain near to a cave they had found, and after a little while the coloured man left and did not return. Then Lobengula had nearly all of the possessions he had brought with him moved into the cave, and one night after, this had been done he and two of the Matebele, who appeared to be Indunas, killed the other ten men with spears as they lay sleeping.

"The following day the two remaining Matebele took the remainder of Lobengula's possessions into the cave and then came out into the open alone leaving Lobengula inside. After a short while he too came out carrying a rifle and shot the two remaining men and dragged their bodies into the bush. He then went back into the cave and did not come out again. The Bushmen then pointed out where the ten Matebele had been killed and scuffled the sand with their toes to show where bones were still lying scattered around.

"They then went on a little further and at last stopped by a large thorn bush which they pulled aside revealing a cave, the entrance of which was below the level of the sand and cut into bedrock.

"My father and Bree climbed into the cave and went 29 paces along a passage which then opened out into a chamber, but they could see nothing as they did not have a light. They returned to the surface and sent for a lamp, lighted it, and then went along the passage and entered the grave chamber.

"Lobengula was sitting alone, with his head thrown back on a large wooden chair in the middle of the cave, his legs and shoulders covered by skin karosses. On the ground around him were skins, clay pots which appeared to have contained food and water, wooden utensils and a few weapons. On a spur of rock protruding from the side of the cave was a saddle and bridle which my father later thought to be the one presented to Lobengula by Queen Victoria. By the side of the chair were a Martini rifle and bandolier, and a walking stick. The body was completely dry, being only skin and bones, and the chair was riddled with borers. The skins were rotten and fell apart at a touch as did also the saddle when my father tried to lift it.

"My father and Piet Bree searched the cave thoroughly but could find no trace of the money which Lobengula was thought to have carried with him when he fled from Bulawayo. The cave contained no valuables whatsoever except for the silver fittings on the saddle and bridle. Piet Bree took the Martini rifle and walking stick as souvenirs, and my father the silver saddle fittings and the bandolier, which was still in good condition.

During the latter half of 1943 information was received at the Native Commissioner's Office, Bulawayo that the grave of Lobengula had been discovered and was about to be entered by treasure seekers. The following statements and letters give the story of the events leading up to the declaration of the site as National Monument No. 48 by Government Notice 547 of 12th November, 1943:

I, The Provincial Native Commissioner, Bulawayo.

Office of the Native Commissioner, Bulawayo. 29th October, 1943.

GRAVE LOBENGULA'S

I met members of the Kumalo family in this office on the night of the 22nd instant, and they are satisfied the King was buried in this cave. They ask that the articles removed by Shoko from the grave should be returned and that this should be done by me.

In the event of the Government recognising that the cave is the burial place of the King, some steps will have to be taken to protect and preserve the site. The entrances should be sealed up with stone and cement and the area fenced. The *ruwari* containing the cave and a suitable surrounding area should be declared a National Monument in terms of the Act.

On the other hand if the Government desires further evidence it will be necessary to take Siayatsha, Twalimbiza, and possibly the late Chief Pashu's son, to the site and undertake further investigations.

Before any final steps are taken in the matter, members of the Kumalo family residing elsewhere should be consulted as a matter of courtesy. I mention some:

Ntola Kumalo, Essexvale.

Albert Lobengula, Inyati (Grandson of the late King).

Sidojiwe Kumalo, Que Que (Son of the late King).

Ndanisa Kumalo, Matopos.

Lothse Kumalo, Filabusi.

Onondo, Inyati.

Sibongosibi Kumalo, Nyamandhlovu (Grandson of the late King).

Nyanda Kumalo, Gwanda.

Bavumi, H. M., Inyati (son of Mtjana).

(signed) A. J. Huxtable Native Commissioner

A few interviews conducted subsequently at the Native Commisioner's office.

Siayatsha states:

I live in the Bubi district. I am a headman. I married Sedambe, a daughter of the late King Lobengula. I married her after the King's death.

When the battle of Shangani took place I was a young man of about 16 years of age. I was a member of the King's party before the arrival of the European force at Pupu (Shangani). Before the battle the King left on horseback accompanied by Sipolo, Twalimbiza, Njube (Albert Lobengula's father) and Magwegwe. They moved down the Shangani River and turned northwards to Pashu's country.

My party, which consisted of all the Queens, other members and servants of the Royal household, followed a different course as we had been warned not to follow the King as our spoor would indicate his whereabouts. We travelled north not following the river as the King had done. We came to Nkoka's country in the Sebungwe District. After a time a message came that the King was at Pashu's and we swung round in that direction to join him. We found the King, Magwegwe, Sihuluhulu, Mtofu, Ndonza, Makubazi, Mtjana, Twalimbiza, Bozongwana (father of Gula Kumalo) and others. All these people are now dead with the exception of Twalimbiza, who resides in Queens Kraal, Bubi.

We joined the King and his people in Pashu's country at a place now called Mlindi. The King was camped with his Counsellors and we camped some little distance away. After a few days there came word by one Baza that the King's impis had surrendered. I overheard the King speak to Magwegwe.

I overheard the King speak to Magwegwe. He said "Do you remember your words?" Magwegwe replied "Yes, King." The King said again to him "What were those words?" The reply came "When you die so shall I." As soon as these words had been said the King took a small bottle and drank some of the contents. Magwegwe picked the bottle up and did likewise. After three or four hours the King and Magwegwe, *Ilunda le Nkosi* (meaning the mouthpiece of the King), died.

The same day Mtjana drove some oxen to the camp, including a black one. This was killed and skinned and the King was wrapped up in it. Magwegwe was buried in the ground close to the camp near a *ruwari*. The camp was close to the river. I actually saw Magwegwe being buried.

The King was carried on a stretcher by Mtjana, Sihuluhulu, Ndonza, Mlonyeni, Ntuta and others. He was carried to a cave quite a distance away, which had been pointed out by Pashu and his people. Mtjana had sent word to Pashu to find a cave and Pashu was present at the burial of the King.

The younger people were not allowed to see the King buried so I do not know what actually occurred. I have never seen the cave. I did not actually see the King drink out of the bottle, or Magwegwe. I was told this took place in the King's camp. I was camped with the Queens 500 yards away. Magwegwe was my uncle.

I did see the King's body being placed in the black skin and later being carried away on the stretcher; the body was in a sitting position and next to him was placed his chair. There were some rifles but how many I cannot say. These were carried by the elders. There was the King's stick which looked as if it had been made of brass, and also a saddle. All these things were put in the grave with the body. There were other articles but I was not near enough to identify them. There were no safes and I cannot say if there were any valuables.

After the burial of our King we remained at the camp for some days. Mpando and Mlonyani died there from illness. Many people died at this camp, amongst them some of the Queens, from, I think, malaria fever. There were no signs of smallpox.

Later we moved away from the camp at Kana. Quite a number of people died on the way. At Kana we found others with cattle. I cannot remember if Manja Kumalo was there. We all then, with the cattle, travelled to Pupu, thence to the Shangani River. After crossing the river we proceeded to Gwampa where we met a wagon laden with food sent to us by the Europeans. The war was over, and we all then returned to our homes with the exception of the Queens. They accompanied the wagon and were settled in the area now called Queens Kraal, Inyati.

A King is always buried in a cave, but not a commoner. Twalimbiza was personal servant to the King. He was in the King's camp at the time he (the King) died. He would know what things were put in the cave

18th October, 1943.   (signed) Siayatsha his X mark

Twalimbiza states:

I am an old man. I live beyond the Queens Kraal on the Bembezi River, Inyati.

I am of the Mlimbi (or Mbimbi) tribe and was born beyond the Zambesi River

(N. Rhodesia). As a young child (indicated about 6 years of age) I was captured by one of the King's *impis* and brought to Bulawayo. Thereafter I was a servant of the King.

I remember when the King left his camp on the Pupu river. I was a young boy (15 years of age indicated). The King left before the battle of Shangani. He rode on horseback accompanied by Ndonza, Ngaiya, Sipolo, Sihuluhulu, Gwati and others. Later the party was joined by Mtjana and others beyond the Kana River. I and other servants travelled with the King.

I remember a messenger being despatched to the Queens telling them we were at Pashu's and that they were to meet us there. After about six days they arrived and camped close to us. I know the word Mlindi. This was the name given to that place by Ndonza and Ngaiya. These two men were great hunters and used to bring ivory to their King.

Later still I remember Basa arriving at our *Isihonqo* with the news that the King's soldiers had surrendered. The King became depressed as his people no longer followed him. I did not actually live in the same *Isihonqo* as that of the King, but occupied one close by. I did not see the King die. I did not hear conversation between him and Magwegwe. I heard that the King and Magwegwe had died, but I did not see them buried.

Mtjana ordered me to go with the other young boys to join the cattle at Masola. Njube (father of Albert Lobengula) was also a young man but was too sick and remained behind. Siayatsha and the Queens also stayed.

I do not know the exact place where the King and Magwegwe were buried. The King had rifles with him, his chair and a stick. I cannot say if there was money and other valuables. I have seen the rifle and other things in the Native Department, Bulawayo, but I am unable to identify them. I know the King and Magwegwe were buried in Pashu's country near the Mlindi. At Masola we were joined by Siayatsha and the Queens. We found the cattle there and drove them to the river Kana. We stayed until Jimsoro (European) and Makakamela (European) instructed us to move to the Bembesi River where we would stay.

At Gwampa we met a wagon with food sent to us by the Europeans. We then travelled to Queens Kraal where I worked for Queen Lozikeyi until her death. The King's wagons were left at Pupu. I am unable to say if they contained valuables. I did not come close to such things.

Nyamande joined us at Pashu's, but was driven away by Mtjana before the King's death.

27th October, 1943. (signed): Twalimbiza his X mark.

Gundwani states:

I live in my own kraal, Shangani Reserve.

My father, Nsibazenungu, told me he was present when the King was buried. He did not give me any particulars about the burial, or what had been placed in the grave with the body.

One day many years ago, when I was still a young boy, my father pointed out to me the cave in which the body of the King had been placed to rest. This cave was near the Manyanda or Mubobo River and not far from Mwanapenzi. I know the word *Mlindi.. Mlindi* means a haunted place where there are spirits.

When my father pointed out the cave to me he told me that the King had been buried there and that I was never to disclose this fact to anyone. We were passing through this place one day on a visit to some of Pashu's people. The cave is on the border of Wankie and Gokwe districts.

Last month (September, 1943) Ginyilitshe and Shoko came to my village on the Shangani. Masitulela (Wessells) came later after I had visited the grave with Ginyilitshe. Shoko, when she arrived, told me she had come for the purpose of visiting the "Amalinda" to *Tetela* to the grave.

I asked Masitulela (Wessells) what he wanted and he replied that he had been called by Shoko to look for Solomon's Mine. Masitulela and Shoko and several others left for Mwanapenzi. Wekeni, my younger brother, guided the party to the village where I knew Siansokobale would take them to the grave. Shoko . . . referred to the King as her grandfather. He was not her grandfather. I did not accompany them. I refused to go. I was afraid. Wekeni was offered money to guide the others.

Masitulela and Shoko camped outside my kraal in different places for about a week. I did not hear any conversations between them. Masitulela (Wessells) took his donkeys with him to carry food and blankets. The scotch cart remained at my kraal.

After Shoko and the rest had left a Police Messenger arrived from the *Inkosi* in Bulawayo with orders that Shoko and myself were to report to Bulawayo.

Wessells had left one of his natives, Sangondoma, at my village. I sent him after Shoko. He returned after two days riding one of Masitulela's donkeys. The donkey did not carry anything else. I am sure of this. Shoko sent a message that she would follow. I later heard that Shoko had returned and was at Lubimbi. She did not return to my kraal as she had swollen feet. Masitulela (Wessells) had passed through my village with his cart and donkeys on his way back to Gwamajula (Lonely Mine). I spoke to him. The Police Messenger was present and inspected his cart. He found nothing in it.

The next thing I knew was that Chitemamuru and his party had arrived and moved on to the grave with Wekeni again as a guide.

I am sure the cave I pointed out to Ginyilitshe is the grave of the King. My father pointed it out to me. A King is only buried in a cave.

Shoko is the only one I know of that has entered the grave. She returned with a rifle, iron tool (bullet mould), saddle frame, bottle and pieces of leather. I fear the grave. My father also told me not to disclose its whereabouts. I showed it to Ginyilitshe because Shoko said that Nyamande, before his death, had told her to come to me. Shoko also related that she knew where it was. I have never heard it said that Nyamande had rifled the grave.

11th October, 1943.   (signed): Gundwani his X mark.

Manja Kumalo states:

My father was Somhlolo. We are related to the Royal House. My father and Lobengula were cousins.

I was a young boy when the battle was fought at Shangani. I was herding cattle and goats not far from the battle ground. I could hear the thunder of the guns. I heard after the battle was over that the King and others had left and moved northwest. The King was on horseback. His wagons remained near the battlefield and were afterwards taken to the Kana River (about 14 miles north east of Lubimbi Valley) where they were captured by the Europeans.

My father Somhlolo followed the King and his party. I later went to the Kana River with the cattle and camped there. Later I was told to take the cattle to the Shangani River. Before we arrived there my father rejoined us. He had been absent for about three weeks. He reported to us that *Ilanga Litshonile Ko Pashu* meaning "The Sun had set at Pashu". That was all he said. My father died that night and was buried near the Shangani River the following day.

I am an old man. All these years I have remained silent though I was aware the King had been buried in Pashu's country. It was our wish that the grave should never be found. I have talked now because I and others have seen the grave and there is no longer any necessity for secrecy.

Recently I went with Chitemamuru, Cronje Ndondo and others to Pashu's country. There near Mwanapenzi's village we came to a cave on the Mubobo River. The main entrance had at one time been stoned up but when we arrived it was open. I entered the cave with Chitemamuru. I could see it had been disturbed. The ground had been dug up and rocks inside had been removed. I saw the top of a skull, a shin bone, three pots, seven bottles and some poles. I think these same poles had been used as a stretcher to place the body on. I am sure the cave had been rifled because the poles were under the stones in the cave.

In my opinion I am sure it is the King's grave. For one thing there is the locality and the things that were found inside the cave. I refer to the rifle and pieces of leather, and there is the fact that only a King is buried in a cave.

Our custom is that the burial ground of a King must not be disclosed. It should only be known to those who accompany him on his last journey. I cannot say if any treasures were buried with the King.

Cronje Ndondo states:
I am head native clerk, Bulawayo Native Department office. I have had 21 years service. I have been stationed at Gwaai and Inyati.

During 1927 when I was at Gwaai I heard that Nyamande, the son of Lobengula, had gone to Pashu's country, and taken out some rifles from the cave Mlindi, which it was alleged was Lobengula's grave. Madhloli, who is now head, told me. He was a first cousin to the King and he was annoyed at what Nyamande had done. This is all I heard in the Gwaai.

Nyamande died during 1929 or 1930. He was a wealthy man. He spent considerable sums on buying horses. He paid £80 for a black gelding in Bulawayo. For the last year or two I have been stationed in Bulawayo.

Recently Shoko came to Bulawayo from Victoria and asked for a *sikonsi* to help her count her cattle at Lupani. I think she wanted a *sikonsi* to show the people that she had the support of the Government in searching for the grave. She had no cattle at Lupani.

The *sikonsi* returned later and reported to Mbizo (Mr. Johnstone) that Shoko had no cattle. He also reported that Ginyilitshe, who had accompanied them to Lupane, was following. The latter duly arrived and told Mbizo that he had been at the King's grave with Gundwanzi at Shoko's orders. It was on account of this information that I, with Chitemamuru and others, left for Pashu's.

On the 1st October, 1943, our party left by car for Lupane. There about 7 miles north of the road and at a village we found Monki. This man guided us to the Lubimbi valley. From the Lubimbi I and others went to a kraal about 3 miles distant where we heard Shoko was resting. We found her there with Wekeni, the younger brother of Gundwani, and others. She was suffering from swollen feet. She admitted she had been to the King's grave and produced an iron saddle frame, pieces of leather and a bucket handle. She mentioned that she had sent a rifle to Bulawayo. All these articles she stated had come from the grave. She did not say she found anything else.

Shoko said she had found the grave two years ago and had left it alone. She did not mention that anyone had guided her to it. Later, the spirits were worrying her and compelled her to return and see what was inside. On the second occasion Wekeni was her guide.

On Saturday, 2nd October, 1943, we continued to Pashu's country guided by Wekeni. We travelled via Mwanapenzi's village and thence north to the Mlindi. Near the Manyanda River we saw a cave the entrance of which had been stoned up. When we arrived the stones had been pulled down and it was open. Chitemamuru and Manga Kumalo entered and what happened had already been described by Ginyilitshe and Manja Kumalo. Mlindi is not the name of the country there but of that particular rock where we found the cave.

In my own mind I am satisfied we found the King's grave. Only a King is placed to rest in a cave. A commoner is buried in the ground. There were the pieces of leather. We know the King left the Shangani on horseback and there was also the rifle.
8th October, 1943.   (signed) C. Ndondo

Arthur John Huxtable States:
I am Native Commissioner, Bulawayo. My native name is "Chitemamuru".

Some two months ago Shoko returned to Bulawayo and called on me. She asked for a *sikonzi* to go with her to Lupani to help her count her cattle. I gave her a *sikonzi*.

Later the *sikonzi* returned and reported to Mr. Johnstone (Mbizo), the Pronvicial Native Commissioner, Bulawayo, that Shoko had no cattle and that Ginyilitshe, who had also accompanied Shoko, was on his way in. Ginyilitshe duly arrived and on the information he supplied, Mr. Johnstone was of the opinion that Shoko and Masitulela (Wessells) had either found or were looking for Lobengula's grave.

On the 30th September, 1943, at about 2 p.m. after further information had come in, the Provincial Native Commissioner asked me if I would leave as soon as possible and endeavour to reach the grave before Shoko and Wessells. I left by car at daybreak the following day (1st October, 1943) with Cronje Ndondo, Ginyilitshe, Manja Kumalo, Dagamela and others.

Our object was to prevent anyone entering and violating the grave. There have been many rumours current in the past that money and precious stones were buried with the Chief. We also were well aware that the Ndebele people would resent most bitterly anyone tampering with the grave.

We arrived at Lupani and here it was necessary to find a guide who knew the road to the Lubimbi valley. Ginyilitshe, when he first visited the grave with Gundwani, had travelled by a different route.

Here we ascertained that Shoko was at Gundwani's kraal lower down the Shangani River and that Wessels had parted company with her. We also learnt that the cave had been entered and that certain things had been removed.

We then proceeded to where the Gwaai River crosses the Shangani River and eventually came to the Lubimbi Valley. At the valley certain of my party were detached and instructed to proceed to Gundwani's kraal three to four miles away, to find Shoko and Gundwani and bring them to me. They returned later in the evening with Wekeni, the brother of Gundwani. Shoko was unable to walk on account of the condition of her feet and Gundwani was away from his kraal. I was told a rifle had been removed from the cave and taken by Samagula to Bulawayo.

On the 2nd October, 1943, we left on foot at about 4 a.m. guided by Wekeni, and arrived at Mwanapenzi's village in Pashu's country after walking some fifteen to sixteen miles. Here our party was strengthened by two of Mwanapenzi's sons and we left for the grave three miles away.

On the extreme west is the King's grave, in the Gokwe District near the Wankie Border. The King was called *Ndhlovu* (elephant). I feel he is not lonely at nights. There are elephant signs everywhere in this locality.

The main entrance to the cave is approximately 14 feet by 10 feet at the highest point. It had been sealed up with stones which had been removed. It was obvious that the cave had been entered recently. After obtaining permission from the Kumalo, I entered the cave with Manga, who is related to the blood.

There are three smaller entrances. Two at the back (northern end) and one on the south eastern side. The stones had been removed or fallen down from one of the entrances at the back. It would be possible for jackals or even hyaenas to enter here. I mention this as wild animals must have removed most of the bones of the skeleton.

Of the body there was the top of the skull of what was obviously the body of a big man, and a shin bone. There were no other remains.

There were three pots, seven bottles and a few pieces of leather, but nothing else. On the floor of the cave were stones which looked as if at one time they formed a platform, and on the ground near them some poles. The stones and the poles had been disturbed and there is no doubt the cave had been searched by others.

Before leaving I gave instructions for the entrance to be sealed up once more.

In the afternoon we left the cave and travelled again through Mwanapenzi's village to Lubimbi, arriving in camp at 9.30 p.m.

The rifle and other articles taken by Shoko and her party have been recovered and are now in the office here. They must be returned to the cave. I am of the opinion that the cave was used as a burial ground for Chief Lobengula for the following reasons:

(1) There is evidence that the Chief died in Pashu's country and I would lay particular stress on the information supplied by Siayatsha, Twalimbiza, Shoko and

(2) Gundwani, apart from other circumstantial and hearsay evidence.

(2) The fact that a cave was used to bury the body.

(3) The fact that a rifle was found in the cave and the iron frame of a saddle and pieces of leather. There is ample proof available that the Chief rode from Shangani on a horse.

(4) The fact that all other evidence, however circumstantial and hearsay, dovetails.

I am convinced that if any valuables were placed in the cave they were looted on occasions prior to Shoko's visit. Ample opportunity has been afforded to others to rifle the grave. Pashu's people, Nsibazunungu's people and others must have known of the whereabouts of the cave however silent they may have been in the past. A. J. Huxtable Native Commissioner

BRIEF SUMMARY: MR C COOKE.

Because of respect for the Amandebele people and especially the Kumalo section of them the whereabouts of the cave was kept a secret. It was, however, visited from time to time by the Monuments Commission's inspectors.

The grave was not disturbed, as far as we know, until 1967 when Dr. Oliver Ransford was taken there by the District Commissioner, Binga. During September 1967, accompanied by Mr. B. J. M. Foggin, Under- Secretary of the Department of Internal Affairs, and Mr. I. Findlay, District Commissioner, Binga, I visited the grave.

There was no doubt that the cave had been visited after Dr. Ransford had entered it. A modern African earthenware pot had been placed in the centre of the cave. The pot contained modern glass beads and a piece of paper. The paper proved to be part of a Customs Department "Declaration Form".

To facilitate entrance much of the rough stone walling was removed. The cave floor was covered with the dung of rock rabbits *(Heterohyrax* or *Dendrohyrax)*.

Who but the King would have had a number of guns and rifles? Who would have had a silver-mounted pipe holder and exotic medicines? There is no record of any European dying at that period near Lupani and no other African than a chief would have had so many possessions. Everything points to the cave being in some way associated with Lobengula. There are three possibilities: (1) It was his grave; (2) It was the cave in which his possessions were buried; (3) The items were hidden as a ruse to mislead the pursuit whilst he (Lobengula) escaped across the Zambezi.

The evidence for Lobengula having crossed the Zambezi is slight and unconfirmed. Posselt in his book *Upengula* (p. 112) says "Many natives definitely state that it [i.e. the grave at Malindi] is not [his] and that the fugitive king fled north, as was his apparent intention, and expressed as such by him, and crossed the Zambezi, evidently with the object of reaching the Anguni under Chief Mpezeni, his kindred people. They point to the fact that he still had some wagons and a horse at his disposal, and was accompanied by many of his household guards, the *Imbovane,* none of whom, it is said, ever came back. Though many of his cattle may have been struck by 'tsetse fly' such cattle may well survive for a period of months. Once across the Zambezi, the king, who was a heavy man, could as a final resort be carried on a litter."

There are many conflicting reports about the state of the trek oxen, one account saying that there were insufficient beasts to supply the skins for the King's burial. But the fact remains that the Queens returned to their kraal outside Bulawayo by wagon. Would the King have left all his wives to return to Bulawayo and take none with him? This does not seem to have been a likely action even on the part of a fugitive.

The statements taken by Mr. Huxtable only mention a small party with the King, being followed on a different route by the Queens. There is no mention anywhere of the *Imbovane.* They may well have been part of the fighting force left to engage the forces at Shangani.

How sad it is to think that the despoiled grave, far from the haunts of his ancestral spirits, is all that remains of Lobengula, second and last king of the Amandebele. His warriors are scattered; his grave is fittingly inhabited by rock-rabbits because this animal is the totem of the Kumalo clan of the Amandebele people.

The grave will be sealed with stones and cement and as this is done we should quietly and reverently murmur the Royal Salute "Bayete" in the hope that his spirit is disturbed no more.

POSTSCRIPT

Mr. Cooke adds: Since writing this article the following information was given me by a Matebele man who for obvious reasons does not want his name disclosed.

"Lobengula was buried in the cave described by you but his bones are no longer there. They were removed by the Matebele after peace was restored and were secretly taken across to Entumbani and put into the same cleft of rock which contains Mziligazi's remains."

Enquiries have not confirmed this but as this information was given me voluntarily without any question I think it may well be true. However, no European who knew Mziligazi's grave prior to it being closed in with masonry and cement remembers how many skulls were in the grave.

APPENDIX 5: UNILATERAL DECLARATION OF INDEPENDENCE:
November 11, 1965

PUBLIC DOMAIN

Whereas in the course of human affairs history has shown that it may become necessary for a people to resolve the political affiliations which have connected them with another people and to assume amongst other nations the separate and equal status to which they are entitled:

And Whereas in such event a respect for the opinions of mankind requires them to declare to other nations the causes which impel them to assume full responsibility for their own affairs:

Now Therefore, We, The Government of Rhodesia, Do Hereby Declare:
That it is an indisputable and accepted historic fact that since 1923 the Government of Rhodesia have exercised the powers of self-government and have been responsible for the progress, development and welfare of their people;

That the people of Rhodesia having demonstrated their loyalty to the Crown and to their kith and kin in the United Kingdom and elsewhere through two world wars, and having been prepared to shed their blood and give of their substance in what they believed to be the mutual interests of freedom-loving people, now see all that they have cherished about to be shattered on the rocks of expediency;

That the people of Rhodesia have witnessed a process which is destructive of those very precepts upon which civilization in a primitive country has been built, they have seen the principles of Western democracy, responsible government and moral standards crumble elsewhere, nevertheless they have remained steadfast;

That the people of Rhodesia fully support the requests of their government for sovereign independence but have witnessed the consistent refusal of the Government of the United Kingdom to accede to their entreaties;

That the Government of the United Kingdom have thus demonstrated that they are not prepared to grant sovereign independence to Rhodesia on terms acceptable to the people of Rhodesia, thereby persisting in maintaining an unwarrantable jurisdiction over Rhodesia, obstructing laws and treaties with other states and the conduct of affairs with other nations and refusing assent to laws necessary for the public good, all this to the detriment of the future peace, prosperity and good government of Rhodesia;
That the Government of Rhodesia has for a long period patiently and in good faith negotiated with the Government of the United Kingdom for the removal of the remaining limitations placed upon them and for the grant of sovereign independence;

That in the belief that procrastination and delay strike at and injure the very life of the nation, the Government of Rhodesia consider it essential that Rhodesia should attain, without delay, sovereign independence, the justice of which is beyond question;

Now Therefore, We The Government of Rhodesia,
in humble submission to Almighty God who controls the destinies of nations, conscious that the people of Rhodesia have always shown unswerving loyalty and devotion to Her Majesty the Queen and earnestly praying that we and the people of Rhodesia will not be hindered in our determination to continue exercising our undoubted right to demonstrate the same loyalty and devotion, and seeking to promote the common good so that the dignity and freedom of all men may be assured,

Do, By This Proclamation, adopt, enact and give to the people of Rhodesia the Constitution annexed hereto;

God Save The Queen

Given under Our Hand at Salisbury, this *eleventh* day of November in the Year of Our Lord one thousand nine hundred and sixty-five.

Prime Minister *(signed by Ian Smith)*
Deputy Prime Minister *(signed by Clifford Dupont)*

Ministers *(signed by John Wrathall; Desmond Lardner-Burke; Jack Howman; James Graham, 7th Duke of Montrose; George Rudland; William Harper; A. P. Smith; Ian McLean; Jack Mussett; and Phillip van Heerden)*

REFERENCES

Baines, Thomas	Baines' Goldfields Diaries
Balfour, Alice	Twelve Hundred Miles in a Wagon
Barber, James	The Constitutional Conflict
Boggie, Jeannie M	First Steps in Civilising Rhodesia
Bulpin, T. V	Scouting on two continents
Carnegie, David	Among the Matebele
Cary, Robert	The Pioneer Corps/ African Nationalist Leaders in Rhodesia
Child, Harold	The History of the amaNdebele / Mzilikazi / Robert Moffat
Chigwedere, A	From Mutapa to Rhodes
Cooke, C	Lobengula's last resting place (Rhodesiana #23)
Cooper-Chadwick	Three years with Lobengula
Cornwallis Harris W	Mzilikazi
Gale, W D	Heritage of Rhodes
Garlake, Peter	Early Zimbabwe: from the Matopos to Nyanga
Gelfand, Michael	Witch Doctor/ GuBulawayo and Beyond
Glass S	The Matebele War
Hancock, Ian	White liberals, moderates and radicals in Rhodesia
Hiller V W	The Concession Journey of Charles Dunnell Rudd
Hole, H Marshall	Old Rhodesian Days
Jones, Neville	My Friend Kumalo / Rhodesian Genesis
Keppel Jones, Arthur	RHODES AND RHODESIA: The White Conquest of Africa
Knight-Bruce G W	Church and Settler in Zimbabwe
Lovemore, Jessie	Missionary Life under Lobengula
Mashingaidze E K	The role of liberation movements in the struggle for Southern Africa, The impact of the Mfecane on the Cape Colony
McDonald J G	Rhodes – A Life
Marston, Roger	Own Goals
Mathers E P	Zambesia
Moffat, Robert	Missionary Labours and Scenes in Southern Africa
Newton, Gwenda	The Helms of Hope Fountain (Bulawayo memories) / The Go-between – John Grootboom. (Rhodesiana #29)
Nyathi, Pathisa	Various historical articles
Nkomo, Joshua	The Story of my Life
Olsson	Crucial watershed in SA politics
O'Reilly, John	Pursuit of the King
Ranger, Terence O	Voices from the Rocks / Revolt in Southern Rhodesia
Ransford, O N	White mans Camp (Rhodesiana #18) / Historical Battleground of Rhodesia
Selous, F C	Sunshine and Storm / African Nature Notes and Reminiscences / A Hunter's Wanderings in Africa
Smith, R C	The Rennie Tailyour Concession (Rhodesiana #38)

Thomas, Thomas Morgan   Eleven Years in Central Africa
Samkange, Stanlake   On Trial for my Country / African Saga
Shubin, Vladimir   The Hot Cold War
Vambe, Lawrence   An Ill-Fated people
Wood, J. T   So far and no further: Rhodesia's bid for independence
Wills W A and Collingridge L T   The Downfall of Lobengula
Zvobgo, E J   African education:

Made in the USA
Las Vegas, NV
15 December 2023

82926104R00227